UNEXPECTED BEAUTY

by

Tara Sosa

Copyright

Dedication

For my mom, who knew I would achieve my dream before I did. You believed in me and loved me unconditionally, and with your encouragement and support I made my dream become a reality. I dreamed. I believed. I never gave up … I love you.

For my husband … quite simply, you're my 'always and forever.'

CONTENTS

__Prologue__

"Where am I?"

Silence.

"What happened?"

More Silence.

"Who are you?"

A look of confusion.

"Who *are* you?"

A look of horror.

I started out asking the questions quietly, but found myself getting louder and louder when the man standing next to me stayed silent. A man who was overwhelmingly gorgeous despite the bruises, the cuts, and the ripped and bloody clothing.

What the hell happened to him? And who the hell is he? And why is he not answering my questions? Why is he staring at me like that?

"Don't you remember?" he asked me. "Anything?" he pleaded.

I stared at him trying to remember, but I remembered nothing. What were those emotions running through his eyes? Why was he emotional? Who the hell is he, and why don't I remember anything? Why doesn't he just give me the answers I'm looking for?

After my own prolonged silence and my lack of response he slowly says, "I'm Liam," as if that's supposed to be the key that unlocks all the answers I am seeking. As if that one revelation is supposed to be important to me.

It doesn't, and it's not.

'Liam' means nothing. This man means nothing. His emotions mean nothing.

He then added, "I'm pretty sure I'm your boyfriend."

Okay.

What? What does that even mean? How does he not know if he is my boyfriend or not?

That doesn't help me. It doesn't unlock anything. It doesn't reveal anything.

It … *he* … still means *nothing*.

Chapter 1

Oh good Lord, who is that? As I look across the room I see the most unbelievably good looking man I've ever seen, and my thoughts completely ran away from me. *I envision him and me all tangled up in my sheets. Him professing his undying love and devotion to me, and only me. Him saying he loves me, and he wants to marry me. Me walking down the aisle towards him in my wedding dress. Him playing football with our son in the backyard, while I watch them through the kitchen window as I'm rocking our daughter to sleep.*

Holy. Shit.

Where did those thoughts come from? I don't even know him, but that doesn't even matter. That's not the point. I am way too young for thoughts like that. Right? *Happily-ever-after?* I have no relationship experience – *because I do not want any* – and even if I wanted the experience it wouldn't be with someone like him.

Especially like him.

I don't want to be tied down with a husband and kids, or even a boyfriend, no matter how gorgeous this man is with his short black hair, ice-blue eyes, and tattoos covering both of his well-muscled arms. *Tattoos?* When did I mentally start drooling over tattoos, huge muscles, men with black hair and ice-blue eyes? *When* did I mentally start drooling over a man, period? This isn't me. I've come too far to let thoughts like that into my head. Been there, done that. Moved on.

Get it together already!

Oh, no. No, no, no.

Why is he heading straight for me?

I put a smile on my face as he approached, and waited to see what would happen next.

Before I knew it he was in front of me.

"Hi," he said with a smirk, as if he knew exactly what I was thinking, revealing dimples and a set of straight white teeth in the process.

Of course he would have dimples.

Apparently, I'm also a person who now mentally drools over dimples too.

"Hi," I replied in a voice that sounded strangled and small.

Holy shit!

When did I get knocked off the confident, self-assured, I am an adult woman and can handle anything, pedestal? When did a smirk, dimples, and all that awesome beauty turn me into a bumbling girl who is finally talking to her varsity football captain, completely out of her league, smoking hot teenage crush?

Awesome beauty?

Who even thinks that shit? Holy. Fuck. Where the *hell* did my goddamn confidence go? *Who is this girl?*

Just have a normal conversation with him. You do it with men all the time.

Before I could manage to get myself together and say anything else he asked, "Do I know you? Have we met before? You were staring at me pretty hard, so I figured I had to have met you."

Of course after he said all of that he plastered his smirk back on his face.

I felt a blush heat up my cheeks at having been caught staring at him. I instantly become pissed at him for not remembering an encounter that never even happened, and also for being able to embarrass me and piss me off all at the same time.

It's good to know that I *wouldn't* be someone he would remember. *Why would I be? Look at him.*

Where in the hell is this coming from? *Jesus Christ.*

He looked at me waiting for a reply while I was having a complete mental breakdown in my head. Perfect. What should I say? Definitely something that gets him the hell away from me before I completely lose it.

"I must have been lost in thought and staring into space. Sorry about that. I definitely wasn't looking at you."

Yeah, take that, you condescending, arrogant, smirking, *beautiful* jerk. I saw the smirk leave his face. *Finally.*

"Ouch. Okay then. Well I'm Liam by the way. Now you've met me. Feel free to stare at me all you want."

Did he just say that? With a straight face?

Are you kidding me? Stare all I want?

Did I not just tell him I wasn't staring at him even if I was a big fat liar? Who did this guy think he is?

"And you are?" he asked. When I stared at him without answering, he just continued on. "Okay, well you don't have to tell me your name then. I'm definitely going to stare all I want even if I have no idea who you are. I'll just make up a name for you." He looked me up and down, *slowly*, and I felt my blush deepen even more. My body also started to feel like it was tingling in places that should not be tingly.

"How about I call you … Red?"

"Red?" My hair is dark brown like my eyes. Where the hell did he get 'Red' from?

"Yeah, because right now your face looks as red as a fire engine."

Oh. My. God. I guess I got my answer.

Did I seriously think he was gorgeous before? No. No I did not. Definitely not. No way in hell. Time to move along, and get the hell away from this guy.

"No my name is not 'Red' and you're seriously a jerk," I told him with narrowed eyes and a snotty voice.

Jesus, am I really going to act like a teenager now too? I couldn't come up with anything better than that? I'm surprised my dumbass didn't add a foot stomp to complete the trifecta.

"Sorry, Princess. Oh wait, is it Princess?" he asked me in a deadpan tone, but I knew he was mocking me, and he knew that I knew. It made me upset that he called me Princess. Only one person called me Princess, and it definitely wasn't Liam. And it would not *ever* be Liam.

I couldn't answer him. I really needed to get myself together after he said that.

My silence didn't seem to bother him in the least. After staring at me for a bit, he just continued on by saying, "I'll take that as a no. So no 'Red,' and no 'Princess.' How about 'Sweetie,' or 'Baby?'"

Seriously, where the hell did he come up with this stuff? Did this actually work with other girls? *Please tell me it didn't.* That would just be too fucking sad. I looked at him, *really* looked at him one last time because I *knew* this would be the last time I was seeing him – and for as much as I was bothered by him, he really *was* pretty to look at, so I just had to. All I said was "nope," before moving around him.

Just as I thought I was in the clear, is when I heard it. It was sudden, loud, and completely direct.

"Samantha."

I whipped around to look at him, but it wasn't Liam who said my name from behind me. It was a different tall, muscular, heavily-tattooed, dark-haired, blue-eyed man. This one just happened to be my brother.

Liam didn't know that though from the way he was looking between me and my brother. The smirk that seemed to be glued to his face the whole time he was talking to me was no longer present. His face now resembled stone. His eyes were hard, no longer the glittering blue of a few moments ago – the exceptionally glittering blue that I knew I could get lost in if I gave myself the chance. His arms were also now crossed over his extremely broad chest, making his muscles stand out and his tattoos look even more incredible in the tight black t-shirt he was wearing. Also, if I wasn't mistaken, it looked like he was clenching his jaw. Now *that* was interesting.

There was no way I was letting Liam find out that this other guy was actually my brother. Let him think this was my boyfriend. Let him think that I already *have* a tattooed, muscled guy who might actually look better than him – even if it is my brother – and *gross … I can't believe I just thought that.*

Let him think that there was no way that offending blush that graced my face before was for him, because I had something already that was just like him. Let him think that there was no way that I was drooling and fantasizing things – dirty and confusing things – about him. If his rigid body is any indicator of what he is thinking, *please* let him just continue to think whatever that is. Let him just continue on thinking whatever it is he is hopefully thinking, while I figure out a way to get Connor to not say anything bad, and the hell away from this guy.

I only had one option to go with.

With a blinding smile I said, "Hey, Connor. I was just going to find you."

Of course my asshole brother had to ruin *everything*.

"Why the hell are you smiling like that? You're creeping me the fuck out. And yeah, Mom wants to see you in the back. Have fun with that shit. She's being really bitchy today." He smirked at that last part. He *fucking* smirked before walking off. Of course he did. He gave me a smirk that reminded me all too much of Liam in that moment. Liam, who I knew was listening to our conversation, even though I didn't look over at him once the whole time Connor was talking.

As a final parting shot before he went out of the door, my brother said way too loudly, "Yeah, whoever this guy is that you were drooling over before, don't let Mom or Dad see him." He said *that* while pointing straight at Liam.

"That shit will not end well."

He was still standing at the door, not freaking leaving. Why was he not leaving? What could he possibly add to make this any worse or inappropriate considering he was saying all of it in front of not only Liam, but all the rest of our customers?

"He seems marginally better than the last few douchebags that showed up here looking for you though. Or that one prick from school, remember?" Once again he was pointing towards Liam as if I had no clue who he was talking about. Connor just had to add what I already knew. "That shit *definitely* didn't end well. That little prick still hasn't learned yet … but he will."

And with that, he finally left. He left me with Liam, and all the now amused customers who were conveniently staring at me. At least they seemed amused and not upset. *Jesus.*

Holy. Fucking. Shit.

Connor just went to the very top of my shit list.

****

After I took a few moments and got done killing Connor in my head, I finally looked at Liam.

He sure didn't look like stone anymore. He sure wasn't clenching his jaw, flexing his muscles, looking confused, or like he was going to beat the shit out of someone. Nope, not him. I'm pretty sure that's how I looked now though, thanks to my dickhead brother.

Liam looked like he couldn't wait to say a whole bunch of new things to me.

Perfect.

Smirking again, he walked over to me. "Samantha, huh?"

I didn't say anything. I just waited for something.

What exactly, I didn't know, but I *knew* there was something.

"Nice to meet you Samantha ... but I still prefer 'Red.' It suits you. You sure as shit are as red as an apple right now," he said before laughing, turning around, and heading towards the door.

Jesus Christ, I should not appreciate a laugh like his, especially when I am the reason that I'm hearing it. I do though. His deep laugh makes my stomach flutter in a way that I know it shouldn't.

My gaze stayed on him. I know I should've looked away, but it was impossible. He stopped at the door, and he turned to look back at me.

Great. He caught me staring at him, *again*. He grinned at me, and then he winked.

Holy – "I'll see you around, *Samantha*," he said. Then he opened the door and left.

Jesus.

Why did I feel like when he left all of the air went out of the room with him? He was a jerk. He was an arrogant, obnoxious, condescending jerk. Also, why did I feel like when he said he would 'see me around' it sounded like a warning? Like nothing good for me was going to come from seeing him again?

Seriously.

What just happened?

Why do I feel like whatever it was, it was something significant? Did I want it to be something significant? No. Yes? Definitely, not. *No way*.

Jesus Christ, what is wrong with me?

I need to forget this ever happened.

I needed to forget all about Liam, I needed to forget all of the memories that were coming back to me that I thought I had buried long ago that were now running through my head thanks to him, but most importantly I needed to get rid of all of these fantasies that I had no business having of some cocky guy I didn't know and had talked to for only a few minutes.

Best way to do that that I could think of, at least for now anyway … I needed to go deal with my Mom who was apparently in bitch-mode.

Chapter 2

"Who was that?" were the first words I heard when I went into the back room. I didn't know if I should pretend I didn't know what she was talking about, or if I should just tell her who it was.

Which was worse?

I didn't know anything about Liam. It's not like I was hiding anything from her.

Not like I hid things about Aiden.

Aiden.

Aiden was a different story.

There were still things she didn't know about Aiden. Things she would hopefully never know, since he was out of my life thanks to Connor.

Sure, I could see the physical similarities between him and Liam, so I could understand why she would be upset. I knew Liam and Aiden were different though. I don't know *how* I knew exactly, but I could tell from that brief encounter that Liam has a playfulness about him that Aiden never had towards me in the months we were together … at least not a playfulness in *that* way.

Aiden was always intense, mysterious, and protective. I didn't get that from Liam.

Aiden was also someone in my past. It was time to bury all of these thoughts about him once again, and Liam too, and move on. The past was best left exactly there … and my present and future would be best without any thoughts of Liam.

Is that true?

Jesus, maybe I could lie to myself but not my mom.

I needed to just go with the truth. "That was Liam. I just met him."

"Well he looked like trouble. What did he want?" she asked in both an accusatory and weary way. Her tone sounded an awful lot like it was my fault he was talking to me. Like I did something wrong.

What should I tell her? I honestly have no idea why he stopped in. He came in the door, stood there for a few moments, and then came towards me. He didn't look at any of our products. He didn't ask for anything other than to find out who I was. Why was he in the shop? Why did he want to know who I was?

Why did he say the things he did?

I shook my head and once again went with the truth. "I don't know what he wanted."

"Well, I didn't like him. If I see him again, I'll ask him what he wanted and why he was here."

I should have made up an excuse.

I should have lied and said I knew him from school or something.

Something tells me lying to my mom would have been better and saved me even more embarrassment, because I know if Liam comes into the shop again and my mom catches him, there will be no amount of charm that Liam has that will dampen my mom's worry about me and some guy that looks like him. She won't get past the looks. She won't want to get to know him.

The more important question I found myself entertaining against my better judgment is, will I? Wait … why am I even thinking things like this?

Because I need to be realistic, that's why.

Something tells me I will be seeing more of Liam.

Whether I want to or not.

Liam's statement of seeing me around was not only a warning, but a promise. I knew that. It should probably make me a bit scared or worried, especially with all of the emotions that he stirred up in me, but for some reason right now it doesn't. Thoughts of seeing him again actually has butterflies dancing around in my stomach. How does that happen in one conversation? A conversation that for the most part was obnoxious, confusing, and one-sided.

I don't know where all of these questions and feelings are coming from. Why am I questioning everything?

Maybe I will never see Liam again. I mean where did he come from all of a sudden anyway?

Shit, maybe I should feel worried after all.

I should be worried over why he is affecting me like this, and why I am confusing myself with all of these different questions that are floating around in my head all of a sudden. What is *wrong* with me?

Then it hits me.

Jesus Christ.

Maybe Aiden fucked me up more than I realized.

****

Going home was the best thing for me, because I needed the chance to clear my head. I needed to clear out all of my mom's comments that she made the rest of the afternoon, I needed to clear out the encounter with Liam, but most importantly, I needed to clear my head once and for all of all things Aiden.

Most people wouldn't understand my relationship with Aiden.

Actually, nobody did.

Not my parents. Not Connor. Not even me most days.

Aiden was my friend. He was my best friend. We met senior year of high school when his parents shipped him off to go live with his aunt and uncle. I don't know why he chose me to be his friend, but he did. Even in high school he had tattoos on his arms, he had a man's muscular body, he had piercings, and every girl's attention. They absolutely loved him and wanted him.

Aiden wasn't popular in a way jocks are popular. He was popular for all the *wrong* reasons. I never mentioned him to my parents, and I never mentioned him to Connor. I knew what Connor would say, think …what he'd *do*. Thank God he was at college and never had a chance to meet him.

At least until that night that changed everything for me, and for Aiden.

I literally ran into Aiden when I was trying to get to my class. I was late, and he just didn't care. He started a conversation much the same way that Liam did – completely out of the blue. One minute I had no idea who he was, and the next he was talking to me and asking me questions. I didn't know what he was doing, especially not with someone like me, but there he was. In my face. That was also where he stayed.

We became friends. I don't know how, or especially why we became friends, but we did.

The kids at our high school didn't understand. How could I blame them though? I didn't understand.

I was the awkward girl. I knew I wasn't ugly. Nobody could tease me because of that. I wasn't drop dead gorgeous either like all of the girls vying for Aiden's attention, so that couldn't be why he wanted to hang out with me either.

We weren't *like* that.

After a time, it was more big brother, little sister. We started out by just saying 'hi' here and there, and then having some general conversations. Then he would walk me home from school where we gradually began to learn more and more about each other.

Or where I began to learn about only the things he wanted me to know about him.

However, he knew *everything* about me, even things I didn't want him to know.

Though I will say there was one thing he didn't know. He never knew about my crush on him. *I don't think.* If he did he never mentioned it, and he never gave me a clue that he knew. It was a stupid teenage crush anyway. It didn't mean anything. Not really. I didn't – or *we* didn't – let it mean anything.

For the most part he kept his flock of girls away from me, along with his drinking, his tattooed muscled friends, and the trouble he sometimes got into.

His family.

His *past*.

We could talk about anything except his family and his past before he ended up living with his aunt and uncle. We could talk for hours, but not about that. We would go to the movies sometimes, go out to dinner, or we would end up driving around and just be us, and everything was always okay.

But nobody understood us.

We never kissed. We sometimes hugged, but rarely. Sure we held hands, but it wasn't *like* that. Sometimes it was hard for people to believe that there was nothing there, especially after Aiden beat the shit out of Kyle Ross at a party we were both at because he heard Kyle Ross tell his friends something about me that Aiden refused to repeat … but once again it *wasn't* like that. He was just protective of me.

For other people that night solidified the thought that 'Aiden and Samantha' had something going on. That there was more to Samantha that people obviously didn't see if badass Aiden wanted to be with her. We would laugh at all the rumors, and questions, and stares. In the beginning I secretly wished all of the rumors were true, but after a while of being his friend, the crush slowly melted away. I mean, I was a teenage girl, and he was hot, so I didn't completely stop feeling a certain way about him, but I knew what we had was so much more.

It was indescribable to a teenaged me. If I were being honest it is indescribable to an adult me too.

It was what people wrote books about where the bad boy and good girl meet in high school, where they start out as friends, and then they become so much more. However it wasn't the book where he falls for her and they live happily-ever-after with a bunch of words, and scenes, and drama, and ups and downs, and sex, and all the angst thrown in the middle. It was where the mysterious bad boy falls for the nerdy good girl and takes her under his wing and makes her his best friend and vice versa.

It was a story in which he would do anything to get to know her, and protect her, and keep her safe from scumbag losers because he knew those losers only came around to mess with him or her. It was like I was his mission.

But why?

I have no clue.

Over the years I have tried to figure out what exactly we were. I've tried to understand what made me special to him, and him to me. Even after all this time and all my doubts and questions, I know he found me special in *some* way. He *had* to. Otherwise, a girl like me would have never received a hello from him, not to mention anything else.

The story of 'Samantha and Aiden' does follow one key thing that one seems to find in all books lately, or at least my favorite types of books that I always seem to end up reading. We did have a big fuck-up in our relationship that ruined everything.

There was a huge misunderstanding.

There was walking away.

There was hurt, anger, sadness, confusion, and heartbreak.

However, unlike in all those goddamn books, we didn't fix anything. We weren't put back together. He broke my heart and left, and he never looked back, taking pieces of me with him that were never returned.

Pieces that I still feared I would *never* get back.

I can still remember everything about that night. I remember what I was wearing. I remember what he was wearing. I remember the time. I remember the way he looked at me when he came through the door. I remember the way he smelled. I remember every word that he said to me, and the way he said it. I remember the way he touched me.

Mostly, I remember Connor's words and his face, and the look in Aiden's eyes as he walked out of the door never to come back.

****

I can still remember it all perfectly.

I was closing up late that night at the shop, but unlike other times I wasn't alone – Connor was with me. When I was closing alone, no matter what, Aiden showed up and walked me home. It was that protective thing of his again.

Up until that awful night Connor and Aiden never met.

Just like all the other times Aiden did come to pick me up that night, but unlike all of the times before, Aiden had been drinking. I never saw drunk Aiden before, I never had to *deal* with drunk Aiden before, and I didn't know what to do. He was mean, and ugly, and demanding, and he tried kissing me.

He never tried kissing me. For the millionth time we just weren't like that.

I didn't know what to do. The only thing I was sure of was that I knew he didn't really want me, that there was more to what was happening, and that I needed to find out what was wrong because something obviously was.

I knew I was not going to let anything like that ruin months of friendship. Months of something that was beautiful and needed for both of us.

We needed each other's friendship.

We may have never said that exactly, but we both knew it.

He needed me, and I needed him.

Why, I am not sure, I just knew it.

Just because he was drunk and didn't know what he was doing or saying shouldn't matter. It shouldn't ruin anything. I couldn't let it ruin anything. I just knew I needed to get him out of the shop before Connor came out of the back room and saw him.

It just didn't happen that way.

What Connor saw when he came out of the back room was someone trying to "attack" his little sister's mouth, someone groping and "attacking" his little sister's body, someone who his sister was trying to push away to save herself.

Connor didn't see things right.

What Connor didn't see was a hurt friend who was drunk for an obviously painful reason, or a friendship that I was trying desperately to save by pushing Aiden away to get him to leave before Connor saw him. Connor didn't give any thought to my screams for him to not get involved, or to leave Aiden alone. He didn't care that I told him that Aiden was my friend, and that he'd been drinking and didn't know what he was doing.

Connor didn't care that I begged him to stop while he beat Aiden up to the point where there was blood everywhere, and I was a crying mess on the floor begging for him to leave Aiden alone. Connor didn't care as I was sobbing to Aiden to not leave when he eventually picked himself up off of the floor when Connor was finished pummeling him, and he didn't care when Aiden looked at me with a heart-shattering look before he went out of the door.

Eventually Connor cared though.

Connor cared for days and weeks after, when I wouldn't talk to him or *anyone* else when I found out that Aiden dropped out of school and moved away, and that he was never coming back. He cared when I came home crying my eyes out, when I locked myself in my room for three days straight after I went and visited Aiden's aunt and uncle and they wouldn't tell me anything. He cared when I told him I would never forgive him and that he was dead to me when he told my parents everything that had happened that night, and I had to endure the grilling and the lecturing about an Aiden they didn't even know. They only knew Connor's version of Aiden, and his version was fucked up and untrue. I had to endure a grilling and a lecture that didn't truly matter because Aiden wasn't even there anymore, and he wouldn't be again.

It took me a long, long time, to forgive Connor. I didn't forgive him until I started placing blame on Aiden and myself, and not so much on him.

Why didn't I text Aiden when I found out Connor would be with me until closing? More importantly, why didn't I explain my relationship with Aiden to anyone in my family in the first place?

Why?

Sure, realistically I knew how Connor would act and the things he would say, but maybe that night would have been different if Connor knew *something*. Maybe he wouldn't have beaten Aiden so bad. Maybe Aiden wouldn't have disappeared. Maybe, maybe, maybe.

I knew Connor was only trying to protect me, and after I cleared things up about Aiden and what happened, and what had been happening, I knew he finally understood some things.

He just didn't know what was going on that night.

Hell … on that night I didn't even know what was going on.

I did know *one* thing for certain though.

Aiden broke my heart.

He took his friendship away from me.

He took the *specialness* of my world away from me. He took my other half. He also took a lot of unanswered questions with him. Questions that ran through my head for years.

Why did he show up drunk like that? Why was he so mean and demanding? Why did he kiss me? Did he, after all that time, *want* to kiss me? Was I a substitute for something, or *someone* else? Did he actually have feelings for me and I never knew? Was I really special to him? Why did he leave me? Was he ever coming back? What the hell *happened*?

The most important question though that came from Aiden leaving wasn't a question I could ask him, or a question that anyone else could answer other than myself. The most important question was:

Could I ever trust anyone to get close to me again?

Chapter 3

After all of my thoughts of Aiden came crashing back, and all of the rehashing of my past that had consumed me all night, having to wake up to go into the shop was not something I was looking forward to. I'd rather it not be my summer vacation. I'd actually rather have classes and deal with 'the douchebag' my brother mentioned last night than have to go into work this morning, so that's saying something. Meeting Liam yesterday brought back a lot of old memories and feelings I thought I was over.

Or at least memories that I had bottled up so tight I forgot about them. That made me dislike Liam even more.

As I got dressed every thought I had was of Liam and why thinking any thoughts of him was a bad idea. Liam brings up too much fucked up shit for me. Last night I realized I normally stay far away from guys that might remind me of Aiden, which is why I was probably able to bury all of my emotions and thoughts for years. I wanted to stay away from Liam too, he just didn't let me. More so than yesterday, I really hope I never see him again. If I do, I have every intention of staying away.

****

"May I help you?" I automatically asked the next customer in line, before I looked up to see who was standing in front of me.

"Sure. You can give me your phone number, Red."

I looked up and stared into the ice-blue eyes I thought about all morning, even after I said I wasn't going to think about him anymore.

How did I not know he was in the shop? Why didn't I pay better attention?

Why didn't I take a break sooner?

Why the hell is he asking for my number when we only met yesterday?

Screw that ... didn't he pay attention to my not interested signals? He has to know that I am not interested.

Liar.

Of course, because I am having thoughts and a full-blown conversation in my head about all the thoughts I had of him all night and morning, I do the one thing I never wanted to do in front of him again – I blush.

"There it is," he said.

I tried really hard not to look at his mouth, but of course I did. Sure enough, he had that smirk that always seems to be plastered on his face while he is in my presence out in full force. Dimples pretty much taunting me.

"There what is?" I said, trying to sound unaffected by the sight of his dimples. I had too much other shit going on in my head to be affected by something like that.

Of course my mind was off wandering through the land of beautiful dimples, so I didn't put it together quick enough, and I *had* to ask something I should have just let go.

"Your blush. I was waiting for it. *And there it is*." He said it so matter-of-factly and with a devilish smile. I should have known. Of course I should have.

I decided it was best not to say anything about his comment and just move it along.

Shaking my head I said, "Look, I'm not giving you my number so is there anything else I can help you with?"

I didn't know how it was possible but his smile got even bigger and his eyes definitely darkened. I could only imagine what he would like me to help him with. I had a list of things that *he* could help *me* with, but I am now telling myself for the thousandth time this morning that that is *not* going to happen.

Ever.

"There are many, many, things that I think you could help me with. I'm almost positive you're the perfect person who could help me with a bunch of things I'd like," he said with way too much innuendo in his tone. I wish I could say 'there it is' to what he said because I *knew* he would have something to say like that, but there was no way I was going there. Regardless, my thoughts had to obviously display themselves all over my face.

I could just feel my blush deepen. I am completely out of my league with this one. We aren't even in the same galaxy. I have held my own when it comes to flirting and innuendo, mostly because I knew all the guys I flirted with were harmless and nothing would come of it except maybe a few kisses and nothing more.

But I knew without a doubt that Liam is dangerous territory.

I don't think he insinuates anything that he isn't prepared to back up, or says things he doesn't mean. He truly thinks that I can help him with *some things*, but he doesn't know me. I won't be helping him with *any* of what he thinks I should be *helping* him with.

"Yeah, you can definitely help me. I'll take a large coffee, black, no sugar."

Well damn.

He threw me off again.

Did I completely mistake what I thought he was implying? Like I said, I am out of his league. Maybe I just assume too much when he speaks a certain way. Hell, maybe it's wishful thinking, though there should be absolutely no thinking anything when it comes to him. Especially nothing wishful.

"Sure, coming right up," I responded to him as I turned around to get him his coffee.

I could have sworn I heard him quietly say "you sure will be coming alright," but there was no way he would have said that to me, and *definitely* not here with other people around. I quickly turned around to see if I could see any signs that he actually said what I thought I heard, but when I turned around he was digging in his pockets not looking at me.

I finished getting him his coffee. As I handed him his coffee he handed me the money he pulled out of his pocket. He told me to keep the change and I responded how I always respond to our customers when they are leaving.

"Thanks for coming, come again." Never have I thought about how that sounded or how that could be taken by certain people, until it was out of my mouth and directed at him. The blush that finally disappeared while grabbing his coffee was back completely and more heatedly, and I knew just by looking into his eyes that what I thought I heard before and dismissed, was actually said by him. He told me that I would be coming. He told me I would be coming as if it was a foregone conclusion. And now I just told him 'thank you for coming.'

And to actually come again. Holy fuck.

Is he just going to ignore it?

Please, please let him ignore these last twenty seconds and what I said, and how I reacted.

"Oh I plan to, Samantha. I'm going to come especially for you. Over, and over again."

In those few seconds I learned that there is no ignoring anything when it comes to Liam apparently. I also learned in that space of time that you can definitely have full blown sexual fantasies with spectacular orgasms in your head based upon a few words that were full of double meanings and some hot stares.

With that, Liam turned around and headed towards the door while I followed him with my eyes the whole way.

Before he left, he turned around and winked at me.

Winked. At. Me.

Holy hell.

I knew I was so fucking screwed.

And not in a good way.

****

"You're lucky Mom's not here. What the fuck was that?" Connor demanded from behind me.

Where the hell did he come from, and why was he always around when I didn't want him to be?

"What are you doing here Connor? You aren't supposed to be working today." I learned the best way to not have to answer something was to ask something else instead. Too bad it didn't work with Connor.

"Stop trying to distract me. It's not gonna happen. That's the same guy from yesterday. What did he want, besides the obvious of getting in your pants? That shit's not gonna happen. You know that right? Does he fucking know that? You need me to tell him that? I'll fucking tell him that."

"Watch your mouth. Stay out of my business too while you're at it."

Connor gave me a look that I knew all too well. He was not going to stay out of my business. He would be in my business forever. Connor thinks it's his God given right. He did thankfully leave me alone and head into the back. He also left me with thoughts of my conversation with Liam.

Was it even possible that he looked better today than yesterday? The way that baby blue shirt made his eyes stand out even more than they already did, and the way it fit his chest – *Good God*. Why did he even ask for my number? He has to realize he isn't my type. Maybe he doesn't though with all my blushes, and staring, and fumbling around I do when he talks to me. I really need to get myself together and stop acting the way I do when I see him next time.

I know now that there will definitely be a next time.

Maybe even tomorrow.

I had to either be on the lookout so I could get away from him as fast as I could, or I needed to completely shut him down when he talked to me and make it more than obvious that I am in no way interested in giving him my number.

Or anything else.

Maybe if I was different, I would give in to him. Maybe if I wasn't so badly hurt by Aiden I could give Liam a chance. If he even wanted a chance. Guys who look and act like him don't normally date. I know it's unfair of me to lump Liam in the same category with Aiden, or other guys. I know it's unfair to not give him a shot based on my past experiences. I know that just because he looks like someone who has hurt me, it doesn't mean he *is* him. Liam could be perfect inside like he is on the outside.

That's the thing though.

What happens if I do get to know him and he *is* perfect? Aiden was pretty much perfect too.

Perfect for me anyway.

Until he wasn't and he crushed me.

It is what it is though. Liam brings up too much stuff. I can't do it.

Tomorrow I will either evade, ignore, or shut down.

Chapter 4

After a few hours I realized the error I made. I underestimated Liam. I fully expected him to not give up and come by the next day, leaving me enough time to come up with a game-plan. What I didn't prepare for was seeing him again, now. Right now, in front of me, only a few hours later. So much for evading and ignoring.

"Hey there, Red. I told you that I would be coming for you. Again and again." I could see the smirk of his develop as he said the words to me slowly, and that just made me equal parts flustered and pissed.

"To the store. Coming back to the store." That was my lame comeback. *Way to have something good to say, Sam.* Way to let him know his words don't affect you. *Jesus.*

I needed to be clearer and get rid of him once and for all, so then maybe my mind can get some peace and I can go back to my nice little "normal" where I am unaffected by gorgeous, drool-worthy, frustratingly flirty men.

"What do you want, Liam?"

"That's the first time I heard you say my name. I like you saying my name, Red. I especially like you saying my name when I am coming for you." Those words left his mouth at the same exact time that his eyes heated, and almost at the same time that his grin started to expand on his face and my skin started to tingle.

So much for holding my own and being strong and forceful. I just wanted him to stop talking to me like that. The way he was talking to me was doing something serious to my insides. Things I didn't know whether or not I should like.

"Look there's other people behind you. You need to either order or get lost." Maybe if I was rude he'd finally get it.

"I'll have what I had before. I know you remember. It's the same thing I will order again later when I come back to see you, if you don't answer a few things for me now."

What the –

"First, what makes you think I even remember what you ordered before? Second, why would you have any questions for me, and third, why the hell do you think I would answer them?"

Why is he doing this to me? Though I will admit as much as he is frustrating me to no end right now, I am curious what his questions are. I am also pissed that I do remember his drink order and that I specifically remembered it because it was him and his order.

I really needed him gone, not back again.

"You remember, Red. I know you do. Since you want to pretend that you don't, I don't mind telling you again. I want a coffee, black, with no sugar." Seeing as how I was staring at him the whole time I could see something change in him. I could see the playfulness in his eyes turn to something else. What exactly, I wasn't sure. Hopefully it was finally the understanding that I wasn't going to play his game – whatever the game was that he was playing.

"Okay then. Black, no sugar. I'll get that for you right now."

"I'm not done yet, Samantha," Liam said as I began to turn to get him his coffee. What more could he possibly want? Do I want to know? Am I *ready* to know?

"I told you I had questions. Questions that I really would like you to answer, and then I will leave you alone today. I promise."

His 'I promise' sounded so damn sexy, and *damn it*, I wanted to know what he wanted to ask me that it was so important for him to come back and see me today. I just didn't know if I was mentally prepared for what he wanted to ask or what he wanted to know. All I knew was that I just wanted him to hurry up and go, more than I wanted to know his questions. Especially before Connor sees him again. Connor seems to always fucking see me at my worst, or when it's the worst fucking time. Like now. I needed to shut this down. I didn't like what I was going to say, but I really did need him to be gone.

"You know Liam, you are starting to seem like a stalker or a douchebag. I've had enough douchebags in here to last me a lifetime. So why don't you ask what you want to ask, maybe I'll answer or maybe I won't, then you take your coffee and leave."

Now laughing at my statement, Liam says "Wow, *Princess*, you sure are in a wonderful mood today, huh?"

Even though I wasn't angry with him before, only frustrated, anxious, and curious, *and* maybe a bit turned on and even excited, his calling me 'Princess' made me turn ice cold. It made me not only cold, but upset, mad, and hurt. Yesterday when he said it, it stunned me, but after all my thoughts last night and today, when he said *that* word it didn't stun – *no* – it flipped a fucking switch.

There was nothing I could do to change the feelings running through me. He said the one thing that changed *everything* for me. I couldn't help my emotions and where they were leading me. I especially couldn't help what was coming out of my mouth.

"Do not call me that. *Ever*. Here let me get your coffee, forget about the questions, and then just go. Okay?"

He must have noticed the change in me. Not only was my voice harsh, my words were very quick and direct. There was no more playing around. No more games. No more light and warmth.

For me, there was only dark and cold.

I had to turn around and busy myself with his coffee. That was the only way I could get through this encounter with him without falling apart even more than I already had.

"Samantha? Samantha, look at me." I couldn't look at him.

"Look. At. Me. What just happened?"

I couldn't turn and look at him yet, so I took a little longer getting his coffee than I should've. I just needed a few more moments.

When I turned back around I saw the concern in Liam's eyes, and for the first time I also saw something that scared me. I saw the understanding that he made a mistake by calling me 'Princess.' He doesn't know why, but he knows that I meant every word of what I said when I told him not to call me that. He also doesn't know why, but I can see that he understands that he hurt me.

"Samantha … Red. I …" he is trying to say something but I don't want to hear it. I just needed him to go.

"Just take the coffee. I don't want your money. Just go." I looked at him and I knew by the look on his face, that he was going to argue. I could feel the tears forming behind my eyes, and I knew if he didn't get out of the shop I was going to lose it completely. That was something I haven't done in a very, very, long time. It was something I didn't want to happen in front of Liam.

So with a very quiet voice I said something to him I know he wasn't expecting.

"Please, Liam. Please, just go. *Please.*"

He didn't know what to do. I could tell he didn't know what to do, but then neither did I. I begged him to go. I actually begged Liam to leave. I could tell he was shocked, and even a bit hurt that he had inadvertently hurt me with a stupid nickname, and I could tell he still didn't really know how, or why. I also knew he had no idea how to fix it, and it bothered him. It bothered me too, because I don't think he *can* fix it and a huge part of me wishes that he could.

I wish that he actually did ask those questions that I was having fun thinking about not even five minutes before. I wish that I didn't give him so much attitude and then maybe he wouldn't have called me Princess.

I wished for a lot of things.

I especially wished that I didn't turn to ice and that I didn't hurt when he said one stupid little word. One stupid word that still has the power to make my mismatched, patched-up heart, crumble back into pieces.

Liam looked at me for a few more seconds before he said something that I thought would never come out of *his* mouth.

"I'm sorry, Sam." The look he gave me while apologizing was absolutely sincere. He was sorry. So was I.

With that, he turned and walked away, and for the second time in as many days when he walked out of the door I felt like all the air in the world was sucked out with him.

It was also the second time, but with quite a few years in between, that when a boy I had a connection to went out of the door I cried right after they left.

I knew without a doubt why I cried the first time. I had to ask myself the hard question of why exactly I was crying *this* time.

Was I crying for me?

For Aiden?

For the past?

Or was I crying for what I secretly wanted to start with Liam but was too afraid to?

****

I had a few more hours to go on my shift at the shop, but there was no way I was staying when I was a mess. There were enough people in the store today to cover me when I left. I didn't need to be here. I just needed to get my stuff, and get away from this place that seems to always be the center of everything fucked up in my life. I just had to avoid my brother on the way out. There was no way he wouldn't be asking me questions about why I was leaving, and why I looked like I did.

I went into the back, but I didn't get very far before I heard my brother's voice.

"What happened out there just now Samantha? The guy was back. I saw him talking to you. I also saw him before he left and he looked like you either kicked him in the nuts or told him you're actually into girls."

I can tell that Connor is trying to get me to crack a smile by the look on his face. He knows something's wrong, and I know he isn't going to leave me alone until I tell him what it is. That's why I wanted to avoid him.

My avoidance of everyone today just didn't work.

Awesome.

"Liam and I were just talking. He came back for more coffee, and he wanted to ask me a few things, but then he called me 'Princess' when I tried to shut him down. I maybe flipped out a little bit."

Connor knew what that meant to me. I told him how Aiden used to call me that after Connor went and made the same mistake Liam just did one night. Connor knew that Liam calling me 'Princess' crushed me a little, because he knew without me having to say anything that Liam reminded me all too much of Aiden, and he knew *exactly* what that word did to me – what it brought back to me.

Connor being Connor though, said the things that only came most natural to him, even in a situation such as this. I should have known he would find a silver-lining in my messed up situation that worked in his favor.

"I'm sorry he called you that Samantha. You know I am. But at least now I don't have to talk to him about you not being interested, and him never getting into your pants. You basically did that all on your own."

At my look I guess Connor realized that maybe he shouldn't have said exactly what he did because he quickly added once more, "But I really am sorry Samantha that he brought all that shit back up for you. I know you're not happy right now and you're upset. Why don't you get out of here and go home?"

"Yeah, I'm going to do that," I said before walking out of the back room, back into the coffee-shop and out the front door. I am going to go home *to* nothing, and to *do* nothing. Being alone normally is a peaceful thing for me.

Today, unlike yesterday when I needed to go home so I can sort out all of my thoughts in private, I don't want to go home because I know all I will do is think. I don't want to think about anything anymore today. I just want to go back a few days and be the girl who is fine and content. I worked hard at being fine and content. How could one person, and one encounter, take my life and turn it upside down?

I already had an encounter and a person do that to me already.

Why is this happening to me again?
How could this shit happen twice?

Chapter 5

Last night all I thought about was Aiden and Liam. I knew it was going to happen again as soon as I got home. It started even before I entered my apartment. The thoughts hadn't stopped since I was in the coffee shop.

How funny is it that I wanted to not think about them anymore ever again, especially after yesterday when all my miserable memories came flooding back, and now I can't help but to do anything other than that. I know it was stupid to get that emotional over Liam's saying Aiden's nickname for me. Truth is, it's not like Aiden called me that all of the time. I don't even know why he chose to call me that, unlike how I know exactly why Liam calls me 'Red,' even though I don't appreciate his reasoning.

It *means* something.

After replaying the scene between Liam and I in the shop over and over again with different words and different outcomes, I gave up and started to think about other things.

I had to.

In the early morning hours I was consumed with all the possible questions he could've asked me. I was also consumed by everything that I would've asked him if I had just given myself the chance to get to know him, and if I had just given him the chance to get to know me. Maybe getting to know him wouldn't have been such a bad thing.

Being friends with him *might* be good. Maybe it could help me.

I haven't had a true male friend since Aiden left. I didn't want to take a chance and get to know one, and have the same thing happen all over again.

How quickly things change when one has time to seriously think alone in the dark when they let themselves.

I decided sometime during the early morning get-my-shit-together-reflection-session that if I do happen to see Liam again, which I know might not be a possibility anymore since my complete meltdown yesterday, I can – *I will* – tell him that I'm sorry and would like to be his friend. Maybe he'll be okay with *just* being my friend.

That way, I can selfishly ask him everything my curious mind wants to know and maybe my brain will give me some freaking peace.

I have to admit that even though I got a few issues sorted out, I am still disturbed by a few thoughts I'm having.

What happens if I do get the chance to talk to him and apologize? What happens if he accepts my apology and he does want to be my friend? What happens if I end up actually liking him? Liking him as *more* than just as a friend. I can't go there with him. I just can't.

That's my biggest issue and worry.

I think that is the exact reason why I wanted to avoid him like the plague, and why I wanted him to leave me alone and never return to the store – to my *life*.

The notion of me ending up liking him is terrifying, and it's why I wanted to dismiss him and all thoughts of him, at all costs.

Something that absolutely didn't work.

The last few days sleepless nights and daydream-filled days can attest to that fact.

I know without a doubt I can end up falling for him if I actually take steps to want to be his friend. I know I need to guard myself.

I *must* guard myself.

From that first conversation with him, I knew he was different. From the feelings he gives me I know he has the potential to make *me* different.

Is something like that even worth it for me?

Look what happened last time.

Something deep down tells me that even though Aiden broke my heart by walking away from me, if I get too attached to Liam even after knowing him for such a short period of time, if he were to do the same thing Aiden did, it would *ruin* me. I think I would be destroyed. I know this because the attraction I feel for Liam in the span of a few days without truly knowing him – the attraction and the *want* for him that I tried to stomp out and deny – is so much more powerful than the initial teenage feelings I had for Aiden.

These feelings *feel* different; they feel like *more*.

****

"Well aren't you a ray of sunshine," Connor said as I walked into the café. Why was he even here again?

"Why are you here Connor? Don't you have work at the Firehouse this morning?" I still can't believe that my foul-mouthed, hotheaded, obnoxious brother is actually a firefighter. He went to college, he got his degree in business, and yet all he ever wanted to do was be a firefighter. And now he is.

At least he knows what he's doing in life apparently.

"Nope. I'm not going on shift until tonight. Mom called asking me to help out because Allie called out sick. Besides, I wanted to see what's going to happen between you and Prince Charming today. I was thinking about him and how he looked yesterday when he left. That kid is definitely going to come back." Connor was looking at me as if he was trying to figure out how I felt about all of that.

Truth is, I came into work prepared to apologize to Liam. I am going to ask to be his friend. I am not going to avoid him anymore. I am willing to see where it goes as long as it doesn't go too far.

At least I was completely prepared when I didn't have to worry about Connor's words and his interfering into anything. Instead of him trying to figure me out, I needed to figure out where this was going for *him*.

Why did he care if Liam came back or not?

"So you were thinking about Liam? Is there anything you need to tell me Connor?" I smirked at him, and decided to go with being a smartass because I didn't want Connor to know how much I cared about what he thought when it came to Liam. How was he sure that Liam would come back?

I also didn't realize until Connor mentioned being sure that Liam would come back that it truly was a possibility he might not. I knew it was an *option*. I mean I thought about him not coming back myself, but I just figured that it was my brain working overtime playing out different scenarios. If Connor thought about it too, but then dismissed it, it means that there could have been some truth and potential to that possibility. Now I am stressed that Liam really won't come in anymore and that Connor's wrong. I don't need this shit. I was completely done with thinking about this. I had a game-plan.

Fucking Connor.

"Ha, ha … you're so fucking hilarious Samantha. Yeah, I need to tell you I still don't want you anywhere near Prince Charming. I also wasn't wrong yesterday either. The guy did look like you kicked him in the nuts, but I also saw the way he was looking at you before all that. He isn't giving up." He continued to stare at me, and it looked like he was trying to decide what to say next which had me mentally preparing myself. My brother didn't normally wait before speaking his mind.

Connor wasn't one who bothered to take the time to choose his words wisely.

"You need to be prepared for what you want to happen with him. You need to be clear. Guys like him … you need to be fucking clear. Like crystal. You hear me?"

Wow.

The way Connor said that, I knew he meant every word he said, and it made me realize that I definitely needed to be firm in my boundaries when I got the chance to talk to Liam.

"That guy, he isn't like some of those guys that come in here and try to flirt with you. He isn't like some of those assholes I had to get rid of because they were bothering you. Samantha … he's not … he's not Aiden either. This guy … he'll be coming back. I've watched him look at you each time he was in the store, and I watched you look at him. I don't like this shit. It's fucking different … I don't *like* it. I have absolutely no problem telling this guy to take a fucking hike if you want me to. No problem at all. You just say the word and when he does come in here … *because he will fucking come in here again*, I have zero problem telling him to never come back."

Whoa. As if I felt no pressure before.

Jesus Christ!

Why did Mom have to call Connor today to come in and cover Allie's shift in the shop? Why did Allie have to call out today? Why was Connor all of a sudden giving out this big brotherly advice that sounds an awful lot like it's laced with freaking warnings?

Seriously.

Fucking Connor!

I didn't know what to say to him. What do I say to my brother after he says something like that?

After what he said I realized that I equally loved him for having my back and for trying to look out for me, as much as I hated him in this moment for freaking me out and for getting in my business again.

I had to say something especially with him staring at me like he was.

I go with the only thing I can think of that will maybe get him to not say anything for a few moments, so I am able to gain control of myself and this situation, and so I can turn around and flee to avoid him and any more talk of this for the rest of the day.

"I love you, Connor. Thanks for looking out for me, I really appreciate it. I can handle Liam though. I *will* handle this whole situation."

As I fled from the front of the shop I wondered if anything besides the 'I love you part' was true. I also wondered if Connor believed anything besides the 'I love you part.' Probably not. Which means he is definitely going to be sticking his nose into all of my business with Liam regardless of what I said.

Perfect.

****

After over two hours of stalking the door and waiting for Liam to come in, I decided to busy myself with getting some reading done for next semester's classes in between filling orders for customers. I should be outside enjoying the summer sun, living the life of a newly turned twenty-three year old, and yet here I am. The exciting life of Samantha Brennan.

I don't mind though.

There is nothing else for me to be doing. It's not like I have friends who want to go hang out at the Harbor all day, or summer vacations to go on, or drunken nights of debauchery ahead of me. Just reading, and working ... and waiting for Liam to come through the door so I can apologize and he can finally put me out of my misery.

He doesn't put me out of my misery though.

It's time for me to leave the shop and head home and he didn't show up all day while I was working. So much for Connor being right. Connor, who kept staring at me all day and who watched the front door almost as much as I did. Connor, who gave me a strange look as I was heading home that had looked all too much like worry or fucking pity. I didn't need those looks from him.

What I had needed was for Liam to walk through the door.

I put on my big girl panties for him and decided to apologize and be his friend. I decided that I needed to get over my shit with Aiden so I can be receptive to what's going on with Liam. I needed Liam to come into the store because I had to move on from all of the circus-like chaos of memories from the day before in my head, and the only way I think I can do that is if we set everything right.

He didn't show up though.

****

He didn't show up the next day either, or the day after that, or the day after that. I had prayed that he would show up the day after Connor stuck his nose into my business and gave me his lecture, not only because I wanted to see him, but because Connor was at the Firehouse which would have made talking to Liam a lot easier than if Connor was there. No such luck though. I watched the door like a creeper, stalking it like the day before, and nothing. Absolutely nothing.

So, of course over the next few days I let my guard down. I wasn't constantly checking the door. I didn't look up every time I heard the door open. I didn't search every face of every customer. I had given up thinking that every time the door opened it would be him. Which is why I wasn't prepared for when I saw him.

I felt sucker punched.

He wasn't supposed to look like he did.

I thought he was absolutely gorgeous before, with his tattoos and muscles on display each time I had seen him when he was wearing a plain old shirt and well-worn jeans. I didn't know how much better he could look in a fancy suit and tie. How he could look so much better all buttoned up with only his hair, eyes, smile and dimples on display is something I can't understand. Why was he dressed like that? It didn't match the Liam that had been running through my mind for days now. He wasn't supposed to seem unapproachable as he did now in that suit that just *screamed* wealth.

He also wasn't supposed to be with someone else.

He especially wasn't supposed to be with some equally gorgeous blonde-haired, blue-eyed amazon, who was laughing at something he said showing off her own equally impressive set of dimples. How could he come in here like that with someone like her? How could he flirt with me one day, and now have her laughing like he is some comedic genius a few days later?

More importantly, how come I am acting and feeling like this when I only want to be his friend, and even that took a lot of convincing? How could I feel anything like I am feeling now when I practically chased him out of the shop the other day, and basically told him I wanted absolutely nothing to do with him? I flipped out on him and was completely rude. Of course he wants nothing to do with me. What was I *thinking*?

I have no right to feel upset.

He must have felt me staring daggers at him and the blonde bimbo because he stopped mid-laugh and turned his head, and locked his eyes right on mine. I saw his eyes widen, his face change into something I couldn't figure out, and he immediately turned and started walking my way leaving the blonde bombshell behind. I could only imagine what I looked like to him. If his face and stride are any indication, I must look like a complete mess.

What the hell just happened?

I waited days for this moment and now all I wanted was to disappear. I wanted him to not be in my store. I wanted whoever she was to not be in my store. I wanted to not be in my store.

One person I am thankful that is actually in the store today is Connor. Connor, who was currently coming my way having apparently seen everything that just went on in the past few minutes. Connor, who literally pushed me away from the counter and who now looked like he was going into battle. He was just waiting for Liam to get to where we were, but I couldn't stand there another moment.

I turned around and headed towards the back but I could hear Liam's deep voice calling out to me.

"Samantha, where are you going? Red. Don't go. It's not what you think." I couldn't turn around. I felt like a fool. It shouldn't matter what it was, or what it wasn't. He owed me absolutely no explanations. I shouldn't *want* any explanations. How could I be foolish enough to think that I could just want to be his friend?

I went into the back room but it was completely quiet so I was able to hear everything that went on out front. I knew I should have stayed out there so Connor wouldn't get involved, but I just couldn't do it. So much for Connor's insight on Liam.

I knew Connor was pissed. His words reflected how pissed off he actually was.

"You need to leave asshole, nobody wants you here."

I wanted him here, but without her, without me acting like this, and with him looking like himself.

"Look man it's not what she thinks. I saw the way she was looking at me. I just need to explain. I know I hurt her last time when I was in here. I don't know how I did it, but I know I did. I don't want her hurting again because of me, and because of what she thinks she saw." Listening to Liam say those things it almost makes me wish that I didn't turn around and walk away from him. I should have heard him out, but I couldn't with her there, and with him like that. Connor was right, I should have been more prepared for him to come back into the store.

"Yeah, you did hurt her motherfucker. The other day *and* today. So why don't you explain this shit to me." Connor just *had* to go and tell Liam that he hurt me.

What. The. Fuck.

If my emotions were more in check I would run back into the front right now, get rid of Connor, and deal with this shit myself. My emotions aren't in check though, and I know they need to be when dealing with Liam especially after having another meltdown in front of him. Plus, I wanted to hear what he had to say to Connor.

"That's Karen. She works at my father's company with me. I just started working for him a few weeks ago. We just came in to grab some coffee. I've been back here since that day a few times. Each time Samantha's not here. I've asked." He sounded so sincere when he explained who she was, and about trying to see me. Nobody told me he came around looking for me when I wasn't on shift.

"I wanted to make things right with her. I would have called to make sure she was okay, but she never gave me her number."

It's true. He did ask that day when he came in, but I blew him off ... and then I had a meltdown.

He definitely didn't get my number.

"Man seriously, I am sorry for hurting your sister."

Connor didn't say anything back though. Why wasn't Connor saying anything?

"Look I have to get back to work. I know you think I'm an asshole. I *feel* like an asshole. You need to know though, I am not giving up on talking to her. I will be back every day if I have to. You both have to deal with that."

Connor still didn't say anything.

I fully expected Connor to say something to Liam, especially after Liam blatantly told him that he's going to have to deal with him coming back to the store regardless of what either of us thought about that. He didn't say anything though. I don't know if that is a good thing or a bad thing, but enough time had passed since Liam said he needed to get back to work, so it was time for me to go find out.

****

I peeked into the coffee shop just to make sure Liam wasn't still inside with *Karen*. I didn't see either of them but I did see Adam at the register and Connor heading towards me. I guess I didn't need to go find out what was going on with Connor, because Connor was coming to find me.

"What the fuck was that Samantha?" He wasted no time getting right into it once he stepped through the door.

"What was what?" I asked. Playing dumb is definitely not my strongest ability, and from the look Connor gave me he knew what I was trying to do. I had to hurry up and change my approach before he exploded on me.

"I clearly remember you pushing me aside so you could go head-to-head with Liam. I was just giving you room to do your thing, so I got out of your way."

That didn't go over well at all.

"I *told* you that you needed to be prepared to see him again. I *told* you that he would be coming back. I pushed you aside because you looked about one second away from losing your shit again, and I couldn't stand around and watch that fucking happen. What the fuck is wrong with you? You can pretend with yourself all you want. You don't want him to get lost. You don't *only* want to just be his *friend*. You were looking at him like some jealous girlfriend. I don't even want to get into the way you were looking at that girl he was with.

Holy shit, Sam! I don't know what else to say to you." Connor had finally stopped talking and just shook his head as if he was disgusted.

That's alright Connor, you've said enough.

What is it with Connor lately? What is up with all these long talks and making me feel like a pathetic teenage loser? Where is the dumbass, immature Connor and all his inappropriate one-liners? I don't need this Connor who is making entirely too much sense and who sees all too much.

I guess I didn't say anything quick enough, which must have set him off again, because he started talking some more even after he said he didn't know what else to say.

Apparently he had a lot more to say than he thought.

"I *knew* he would be back. You had days to figure out what to say to him. As much as I would like to throw his ass out if I ever see him again, *because I still don't fucking like him*, he really did nothing wrong either time. Both times, that was you Sam. He's a cocky prick that doesn't listen and he will put up a fight if he has to. I can see that, and I can take care of it, but he's not a creepy douche and that's a different situation.

"He will be back *again* Samantha. I won't be dealing with him next time unless shit gets out of control. You *need* to handle this like you said you were going to, because I can't. I don't want to. Like I said before, I saw the way he's been looking at you. I saw the way he looked at you today when he realized what you were thinking. I don't fucking like him, because I don't like the way he looks at you ... he looks at you like he shouldn't – *it's too much for me to be seeing*. I learned my lesson once though with Aiden and not letting you handle things your own way. So from now on, this is on you."

With that parting remark Connor headed back out to the front of the shop. I never got a chance to say anything to him. I never got a chance to ask what happened to him wanting to see what happens between me and "Prince Charming." I'm pretty sure that's a good thing though, because if I would have said something as stupid and flippant as that, I'm sure it would have set off another Connor explosion.

Even though he *is* the one who said he wanted to see what would be happening between us, I don't think what happened today was what he meant when he envisioned mine and Liam's next go around. He had higher expectations of how I would react.

Yeah well … so did I.

****

I wasn't scheduled to work the next day, so I knew I wouldn't be seeing Liam. I wondered all day whether or not he would be going back into the shop like he said he would, to see if I was there. Unlike the other times when I wasn't there, this time I knew Connor was on shift all day. I wondered what he would say to Liam if he saw him. No matter what Connor said last night about staying out of it, I knew there was no way in hell Connor would keep his mouth shut if he was there and Liam showed up. Those two seemed too much alike. I could only imagine what those two would say to one another.

Again.

God help me, but I can't be worried about that right now. Instead of only apologizing for one freak out, now I have two freak-outs to apologize for and try to muddle through when I see Liam again. How is it that he's pretty much only seen the worst of me so far, and yet he still wants to talk to me? What's up with that?

Maybe I should actually be worried. There could be something wrong with him.

Who am I kidding?

I haven't seen anything wrong with Liam so far, but it's not like I know anything about him.

Yet.

I planned on getting to know him more, *if* he accepted my apology.

I already knew what I wanted to say to him. Despite what Connor thought before, I had planned everything out. I *knew* that I could handle it when I saw him again. What I hadn't factored in was the girl, and the suit. I knew I had to be on top of my game when dealing with Liam. I had already come to that conclusion during my endless hours of no sleep during those first two nights. How could I let myself not factor in all the unpredictable things? I knew from our first encounter that he was different. I should've figured that shit would go sideways and have a game-plan for every scenario. I shouldn't have just assumed that I would see him like I did the first few times, and that he would come up to the register and I would be able to say I was sorry for the meltdown, that I wanted to move past it if he wanted to, and that I'd like to be his friend if he was game.

I knew better than to assume with him.

Next time no assuming.

I needed to be prepared for anything.

****

I wasn't prepared.

I wasn't prepared at all.

I knew that Liam came into the shop yesterday because I called Connor when I couldn't take it anymore, and asked him if Liam had shown up to see me. Connor told me that Liam showed up, but he wouldn't tell me what each of them had said to one another. I could only imagine what was said. Talking to Connor didn't take away the nerves that I had, it only increased them, but I knew what needed to be done and I was going to do it.

I waited for him, and waited. I was back to stalking the door like a creeper because I wanted to get this over with … but somehow I missed him.

Not Liam.

I didn't miss Liam.

I missed the sleazy asshole that Connor was talking about the first day that I met Liam. The one that Connor had asked to leave a few times, and yet he still manages to come back like nothing ever happened. I met him in one of my classes last semester and was nice to him and helped him out on a project, but apparently some people you cannot be nice to.

He took my niceness and in his twisted mind turned it into interest, and he hasn't left me alone since.

He seemed harmless enough at first, he just asked for my phone number, asked if I wanted to go out, and asked if I was dating, but when I kept saying no to his advances he became pushy and insistent. He just didn't know when to give up.

He made me uncomfortable.

I told Connor about it, and when he showed up at the store a few times not looking for drinks or something to eat, but to ask me the same questions over and over again Connor dealt with it.

Or so I thought.

He came back again. And again. I thought once last semester was over I would never see him again. Apparently I was wrong. Connor wasn't here and I didn't feel like dealing with him today.

Not today when I should be concentrating on seeing Liam.

Liam, who I also fucking missed coming through the door thanks to the asshole who is now standing in front of me.

When I looked up to see who else I could get to help me out of the situation that I knew was brewing, I saw the unmistakable icy-blue eyes, dark hair, tattoos and muscles.

Liam was not wearing his suit and tie like the last time I saw him, but a white shirt and dark jeans that fit his body perfectly.

For a moment I zoned out and didn't remember what any of my problems were, because he really was that amazing to look at and because he was really here.

When I heard the unmistakable clearing of a throat in front of me and I knew who it belonged to, it all came crashing back. I needed to deal with one problem before tackling the other.

I really wasn't prepared for this shit today.

I needed to get him out of the store fast. I didn't want him tainting any time that I had with Liam, now that he was finally here and I had the opportunity to fix everything.

I had to tear my eyes away from Liam, which was exceptionally hard to do, but I needed to deal with this.

"Hello, Aaron, what can I get for you?" I said in the most dismissive and rushed voice I think I have ever used with a customer.

"Hello, Samantha. You look lovely as always. I haven't seen you in a while. How have you been?" he said in return.

Are you kidding me? I look lovely. *Gross.* He actually wants to pretend we are friends, and he thinks I want to have a conversation with him? I need to keep this simple and not give him any reason to think I am interested. Not that it matters. I gave him no reason to think so before and look where that got me.

"I'm fine Aaron. I am really busy though, so can you please tell me what you would like?" I waited for his response but he said nothing.

Talk about uncomfortable and awkward.

I looked behind him at Liam who I knew was hearing everything we were saying. I could tell from the look in his eyes, and his arms-crossed-over-his-chest posture that he was trying to piece together who exactly this guy was that I was talking to.

If he only knew.

I was seriously losing whatever patience I had left. I didn't like the way Liam was looking at Aaron and me, and I definitely didn't like Aaron eating up all of the time that I could've been talking to Liam.

"What do you want Aaron?" I said in such a way, we all knew I wasn't talking about what he wanted from the store anymore.

"You," Aaron had said in such a tone that I actually felt chills run up and down my spine.

What the fuck?

I actually took a step back.

I don't know if I looked at Liam with a panicked expression, or if he just didn't like what he heard – probably both – but he made his presence known to Aaron very quickly after Aaron said he 'wanted me.'

"Hey dude, you need to leave."

Aaron was taken aback by Liam coming up alongside of him and telling him he needed to go. Aaron should know better than to say things like that to me in here. He's lucky Connor isn't here, because

Connor would have already thrown him out of the door. Or kicked his ass. Connor *definitely* wouldn't have liked what Aaron had just said.

Aaron got over his shock kind of quick though because he turned to Liam and asked, "Who the hell are you?"

"Buddy, I am someone you really don't want to fuck with right now, so you need to get the fuck out of here." The way in which Liam said it, Aaron must have known not to fuck with him.

Aaron looked at me, gave me a really crude stare and then he turned around and headed out the door. I was trying to process everything that had just happened, including how turned on I had become all because of the words that had just poured out of Liam's mouth, but I had to stop processing everything quickly because I knew that there were other things to be done. Like talking to Liam. I needed to talk to Liam.

And Liam was right there in front of me.

Something that I wanted to have happen for days.

I knew what I wanted to say. I knew what I wanted to happen between us.

I had it all planned out. Everything I needed to say was on the tip of my tongue.

Then he placed his hands on the counter, he leaned towards me a little, he smiled wide revealing those amazing dimples that I secretly wanted to dip my fingers into, all while staring directly into my eyes, and I completely forgot everything I wanted to say.

After a few moments of complete silence he said, "Hello, Red. I've missed you."

Yeah.

Okay.

In that moment I really, really, *really knew*, I wasn't prepared for him. *At. All.*

Chapter 6

I am not prepared. I am not prepared. I am not prepared.

I am not at all prepared for the way Liam is looking at me, and I'm definitely not prepared for what he just said.

Did he really just say he *missed* me?

For the second time in a handful of minutes I can feel chills all up and down my spine. These chills are for an entirely different reason. These chills might even be more worrisome to me than the ones I had before.

What do I say to him?

Do I admit that I've secretly missed him too? That I've waited days for him to come back so I could apologize? Admit that I've waited for days so that I could ask to be his friend and get to know him? Admit that I think I've been fooling myself, because what I have been feeling for him is *definitely* not friendly, but so much more? Admit that I've actually missed the butterflies dancing around in my belly whenever I got the chance to see his face?

And what a beautiful face it is.

I can't say any of that.

I also can't get any of the acceptable words that are rolling around in my head to come out of my mouth with the way he is looking at me. It's like he has rendered me speechless.

Did I just say that? He made me speechless?

I can't help but stare at him the same way he is staring at me. The way we are staring at each other should be awkward, especially because we are in a crowded café and there is a line waiting behind him, but it's not awkward.

Looking into his now darkened blue eyes, I couldn't help but to think that everything we wanted to say and have been trying to say to each other for days, was now being said with our eyes alone.

Whatever it was that was happening, it is unlike anything I have ever felt before. I felt like I was lost and yet exactly where I should be, all at the same time.

The only thing I knew with any certainty was that *this*, whatever this was between Liam and I, it was going to be complicated. It already was.

Why wouldn't it be complicated though, right? When has anything ever been normal for me?

With the sight of him and what just happened between him and Aaron, and with all the various thoughts of him and me running through my head, I guess I couldn't help what I should have figured would happen.

It was *inevitable*.

I felt the blush that he apparently loved so much practically radiate my skin, and I knew he saw it because his smile turned into a grin and he finally looked away from my eyes and down.

He started to laugh, and then he said "There it is … Jesus Red, how much of your skin does that blush of yours cover?"

I remembered the last time he said 'there it is' and I immediately thought back to that day and what I had to do now. I completely let the part about the blush slide, and didn't dare go anywhere near how much of my skin this stupid blush of mine covers.

I knew I had to get my apology over with, but before I could he said, "Who the hell was that guy by the way?"

Once again, Liam threw me completely off axis. I was just getting ready to start my apology, finally, and now he wants to talk about some guy I had hoped to never see again? Perfect.

Might as well go back to the beginning, right? I guess since I wanted to rehash old things with Liam anyway, I might as well start where he and I had first started.

"Remember the first day you met me, and Connor mentioned having to get rid of some guy a few times because the guy couldn't take a hint, and he kept coming back?"

"I remember everything about that day, Red. So ... that's the guy Connor was talking about? The prick who hasn't learned yet? He keeps throwing him out, but he still comes back? I can't imagine anyone wanting to come back after Connor throws them out. So what's the story with all of that?"

Of course there is a story. There is always a story. It's just this story doesn't make that much sense, because there is no reason that Aaron keeps coming back into the store other than to bother me. I don't think Liam is going to like hearing that any more than Connor did.

I decided to go with the truth though. I don't need any more misunderstandings or half-truths between us.

"I met Aaron a few months ago in one of my classes. He needed help with a project our class was working on, and I offered to help. I met up with him a few times before and after class and I helped him out. That was it. At least on my part it was. Somehow he didn't see it as only help but something more and he started asking for my number, asking me out, and when I kept saying no he started to show up here. He kept asking me the same things over and over. I don't know *why*, but he doesn't seem to understand that I'm not interested even after I had to plainly make it obvious that I will *never* be interested. He still didn't get it even after Connor actually had to ask him to leave, or even when Conner literally pushed him out of the door."

I kept rambling on because Liam didn't say anything. His listening and not speaking was making me nervous for some reason.

"I thought it would get better once the semester ended. I wouldn't be seeing him in classes anymore a few times a week, and I assumed he would be going home for summer vacation. Apparently he decided to take summer courses so he's going to be around here the next few months, and he just can't seem to stay away from this coffee shop … or me."

I looked at Liam and I could tell he wasn't pleased. His jaw was clenched, his arms were crossed, and the heat in his eyes was definitely different than the heat I saw in them before.

I needed to defuse the situation fast.

"He's harmless though. I mean you *saw* him. You told him to leave and he left. I just think he really believes we made a connection when we were working on his project together. Eventually he'll get it. I've given him no reason to think I'm ever going to change my mind."

Before I could say anything more Liam finally stopped me.

"I don't like it. He doesn't seem like he understands you're not interested. Plus, he keeps coming back, even after the whole Connor situation? Where is your brother by the way? I expected him to come out of nowhere and toss the guy through the window. I don't like how he said he *wanted* you. You heard how he said that, right? I don't fucking like it. He needs to understand that you want nothing to fucking do with him now … not eventually. Now."

I don't know what it is about him using bad words, but when they come out of his mouth it really does something to me.

The playful Liam I met the first time didn't strike me as someone who had a dirty mouth, even with all the tattoos, muscles, and cockiness, he didn't seem the type. The Liam I met the second time, the one who flirted shamelessly with me didn't strike me as someone who would get me all hot and bothered by his choice of foul words either.

The suit and tie Liam *definitely* didn't strike me as someone who would carelessly use the word fuck, or prick, or asshole in anything other than a bantering, 'I'm just bullshitting with the guys' kind of way.

I guess I was wrong about Liam … *again*.

He wasn't so playful, or as polished as I made him out to be. Sure he was both, but he was also *more*. I also thought he wasn't protective, mysterious, or intense. I guess I was wrong with thinking that too.

He meant what he said when he said he didn't 'fucking like' the situation with Aaron. He meant it when he told Aaron that he wasn't someone he wanted to 'fuck around with,' and he definitely meant it when he told Aaron that he needed to 'fucking leave.' He used those words and the tone he had because he knew he could back up what he was saying if something were to happen. He was ready for it. It seemed like he would be ready *for anything*.

Apparently not only did I meet playful Liam, and polished Liam … I've also now met Alpha Liam.

I thought I was in a world of confusion, chaos, butterflies, and uncertainty before.

I seriously had no idea.

****

I needed to think of something to say, and I needed to think of what to say fast.

I needed to change the course of our conversation away from Aaron and that whole situation, otherwise I would never get the chance to say what I wanted to say to him. The people behind him were getting overly restless, and even though nobody said anything yet, I knew it was only a matter of time before something was said and we'd no longer be able to have this conversation today.

"Look, I can see that you don't like it. I don't like how he keeps coming in here either, but I truly feel that he's harmless even if he also seems a little creepy. I just don't want to talk about him anymore if that's okay. I have something else I want to talk about."

I could tell by the way he looked at me that he didn't want to stop talking about it, and that he didn't agree with me over Aaron's being harmless, but he put his hands down on the counter and leaned towards me again like he did before.

I honestly don't know which pose was worse.

"Alright, Red, what would you like to talk about? I know what I want to talk about if we can't talk about that asshole, but it's alright … you can go first."

Ever the gentleman, this one.

I just needed to jump right in.

"I just wanted to say that I'm sorry for the way I freaked out on you the other day. Both days actually. You caught me off guard with what you said and I wasn't prepared for it … and the suit and tie … and the girl … I wasn't prepared for *any* of it. Can we just start over and be friends? Friends sounds good right? Right? Yeah, so … I'm sorry about the other day … the other days …"

Holy shit my face felt like it was going to explode it was so fucking hot.

Did I just *fucking do that*?

Did I seriously just piece together random thoughts, even though I rehearsed exactly what I was going to say to him in my mind over and over again, and it sure as shit wasn't that?

Did I really just say that I wasn't prepared for his wearing a suit and him being with a girl?

Oh my God, please kill me now.

Seriously ... please let my head actually explode.

Please.

I couldn't make eye contact with him. I had no idea what had just happened to me there. I had to do something.

I had to say something more, because he sure wasn't saying anything, and I couldn't stay silent and let it get any more awkward.

"So, friend's right?"

That's what I chose to say. Lord help me, please. Like that wasn't awkward.

I finally had to make eye contact with him, so I raised my eyes to meet his.

Okay ... I probably shouldn't have made eye contact at that exact moment though, because I caught the laughter dancing in his eyes. I also caught the shaking of his head.

I knew whatever he was going to say, I wasn't going to like.

"Friends? You think we can just be friends, Red?"

"Yes." I answered so quick and so loud that his eyes widened a little bit.

So much for not telling half-truths.

Liar.

He leaned a little bit closer to me than he was before, and he looked directly into my eyes as if he was searching for something.

After a few seconds I had my answer, and I knew exactly what his thoughts were about us being friends.

"I don't think we can be *just* friends. You should know by now that I don't only want to be your friend. I like you. You're interesting. I'll take whatever I can get with you though. So, friends. For now."

Okay … that wasn't so bad. I already knew he'd probably want more with me than only friendship, but he just said he was willing to take whatever he could get, and all he'd be getting from me is the chance to be my friend.

Again he leaned towards me even more, bringing his face alongside mine. I was just about to start freaking out because of how close he was, and because of how good he smelled when he started talking again.

He whispered directly into my ear, "Fair warning though, Samantha. I fully intend on being more than just your friend."

I heard myself gasp from the combination of his voice in my ear, his words, his smell, his proximity.

Did I seriously think I could handle all the things he was bound to throw at me?

I honestly didn't know, but even though I knew I should be worried, that it was going against everything I told myself and prepared myself for, I wanted to find out.

I heard a throat clear and a man ask Liam if he was ever going to order.

I guess the whispering in the ear thing was too much for the customers to wait through. This whispering was too much for me too.

Liam turned around and looked at the guy, and said he just needed another minute. I guess whatever look Liam gave him, it made the man nod his head and Liam turned back around.

He continued to talk to me.

"I wanted to apologize too, Red. I know I hurt you that day but I'm not exactly sure why. I didn't mean to, that's for sure. Can you tell me why you were so upset?"

I could, but I didn't want to.

"I don't want to talk about it. Not yet. Maybe at some point, okay? Just know that I forgive you, but it really wasn't your fault it was mine ... and if you have any intentions on saying anything about the other day with the girl ... that was me too. I don't need any explanations for that."

He seemed to be okay with what I said for now, but I guess he still wanted to clear a few things up.

"Just so you know, she's just a co-worker. She's not even a friend. You know who is my friend though? You. As my friend Red, you really should give me your number ... and also a large coffee, black, no sugar, before all of your customers decide to kill me and I'll never get the chance to get past this whole friends part of our relationship."

I felt a smile start up on my face, not only because of what he said about Karen, but because of the way he nonchalantly added the part about my number and the coffee in there as if giving him both was an everyday occurrence.

I decided to ignore him about the number, because I had an idea.

I needed to turn the tables on him a little bit, so I said "I'll get your coffee right now," before I turned around to busy myself getting his coffee.

I heard him start to laugh, so I looked over my shoulder and saw him reaching in his pocket for his money.

With him looking away getting his money, it gave me the opportunity to do what I decided to do, to give him a *little* taste of his own medicine.

When I was done, I turned around and handed him his coffee, brushing aside the money he tried to give me.

"I don't want your money. Your coffee is on the house today. Think of it as a payment for getting rid of my problem before."

"Okay. Seriously, that's it though? Thanks for the coffee, Red, but you really aren't going to give me your number? Really?"

"Liam, there's a line behind you of customers that have been rather generous in waiting patiently."

He seemed to realize that it really was time for him to go. He stared at me some more in a way that suggested he couldn't believe after everything that had just happened, I still refused to give him my number.

I tried, but I couldn't keep the smile from my face any longer.

My smile might have been the biggest it had ever been before, and it was all because of Liam.

I think the smile that blossomed on my face both startled and pleased him, because he responded by showing off a very impressive grin of his own.

The heat and intensity that exploded into his eyes was as equally startling and pleasing for me, as my smile must have been for him.

Just like I couldn't keep the smile from my face, I couldn't keep the laugh that I felt bubbling up inside of me contained.

My laugh seemed to please him even more than my smile.

When I finally stopped laughing and returned to just a smile, he leaned forward again, but this time it didn't bother me.

"What?" he asked me quietly.

My smile turned into a grin that I'm sure could give his a run for its money, especially when I tapped his cup right where my number was written.

He looked to what I was pointing at and he started to laugh before saying, "I can't believe I missed that."

Yeah, well, join the club Liam because I have been missing a lot of things since you walked through the doors and into my life.

I smiled at him once again before saying, "Good-bye, Liam."

I don't know how it was possible, but he gave me the best smile I think I have ever seen, and I've seen some pretty spectacular smiles from him already.

"Good-bye, Samantha."

With that, he turned and walked past all of the customers he had held up in line not caring at all that he had made them wait. Neither did I. I still had no problem making them wait … I had better things to do. I watched Liam walk the whole way to the door. Like another time that I had watched him walk to the door, I saw him turn around and look back at me, and wink.

This time I was prepared for the wink.

This time I *wanted* it.

His wink let me know that everything was okay between us, regardless of all the meltdowns and misunderstandings. We were going to be okay.

The wink was his way of saying he accepted my apology.

The wink was his way of saying that we were on track to becoming the friends we both said we were going to be to one another.

Okay, so maybe the wink didn't exactly mean the last part.

Even I'm mentally rolling my eyeballs at the word "friends."

Chapter 7

After Liam left, the remainder of work seemed to fly by. I had to deal with a few customers who weren't at all pleased being held up in line, but I also had a few who looked at me with amusement and curiosity, so it wasn't that bad. Once my line was gone the rest of work seemed to be occupied by everything that had happened with Liam, and also the situation with Aaron. Aaron really was becoming a major problem. I was going to have to tell Connor about it, and hope that the next time Aaron decided to drop in, Connor or my parents were there and they could deal with him once and for all.

I didn't like the way Aaron looked at me before he left, after Liam told him to leave. I know I said he was harmless, but the more time I had to think about that look and how what he said made me feel, I think it's best if he really is dealt with. I don't care who got through to him, even if I had to tell my parents of the situation – something needed to get done.

I really didn't need any more awkward in my life.

****

When I went into the shop the next day Allie couldn't wait to ask me questions about what went on with the "hot guy with the tattoos and blue eyes." Apparently Joanna couldn't wait to fill Allie in on what happened yesterday. Joanna should've been working in the back, but it seems she had plenty of time to see what went on between Liam and me which was just fucking perfect.

I told Allie that Liam was just my friend and we were talking, but she didn't buy it for a second. She talked about how he and I were talking for a long time, how the line was practically to the door and I didn't push him along like I would have anyone else, how he whispered in my ear, and I gave him my number.

Jesus.

Joanna definitely wasn't working too hard if she was able to see all of that.

Obviously, I am not a huge fan of Joanna since she hooked up with my brother a few months ago and decided that because she hooked up with him a few times it gave her a right to be a catty bitch to me. Connor kicked her to the curb kind of quick, but she still worked here, and she's as bitchy as ever. That whole situation makes scheduling her and Connor on different days a bitch … just like her. Thank God Connor isn't here that much because of his firefighting job. I would hate to witness any more of them together than I have to. I wish she would just quit already. I also wish that she would mind her own damn business, and not say shit to anyone about anything that goes on with me. What the hell was she doing even talking to Allie? Allie hates Joanna as much as I do, and Joanna hates her.

"Joanna doesn't know what she's talking about. You know she loves to start shit. He wasn't whispering in my ear, and the line wasn't that long. I was just clearing up a few things with him. He's just a friend."

Allie didn't buy that either.

"Yeah, right. Joanna might be a bitch who exaggerates the truth, and I normally wouldn't pay attention to a word she says, but I didn't only hear about the tattooed, blue-eyed hunk of man from her. My friend Brenna was waiting in that line yesterday. You know, that line that really *did* go to the door Sam? She said that Mr. Blue Eyes and Big Muscles got rid of a guy that looked like he was bothering you. I am guessing it was Aaron again by the way she described the guy? She said after that, you and Mr. Dreamy were talking, and smiling, and laughing, and that he did in *fact* whisper in your ear and that you did in *fact* give him your number. She said she wouldn't have known about the number, but you pointed at his cup and you both started laughing, so when he was walking by she made a point of looking at him as well as his cup and she saw numbers. She also said he was drop-dead gorgeous by the way. So seriously … *who is he, bitch?*"

Shit.

"He really is just a friend … if I can even call him that yet. I met him here last week. We seemed to hit it off, but we did have a few misunderstandings here and there so we really were clearing a few things up. You were right, Aaron was here and he got rid of him for me. He also *maybe* whispered in my ear, but it wasn't anything to look too much into like you were. I also don't know much about him because we really haven't gotten that far yet, but I do plan on getting to know him better. As a friend *only*. I only want to be his friend, Allie. I don't need anything else in my life right now."

She kept staring at me as if she needed some more information. What the hell else did she want to know?

Shit. This is Allie we were talking about.

"Your friend Brenna was right … he *is* drop-dead gorgeous."

Allie actually squealed like a little girl. There may have also been clapping of hands too.

"Ha! I knew it! I knew Brenna was telling me the truth, and I knew Joanna was too … I could just see and hear the jealousy pouring out of that stupid whore."

Yeah … Definitely no love lost between those two.

"So what's his name?" Allie continued asking questions while we were getting people their drinks.

"His name is Liam."

"Liam … I like it."

"Did he call?" She just wouldn't take a break from her inquisition.

"Nope, he didn't call."

Allie looked disappointed at finding out that bit of information. She couldn't possibly be as disappointed as I was. After making a big production of getting my number, I thought there was no way he would miss the chance to call me last night. I was wrong. It was not the first time I was wrong about something when it comes to him, and I am a hundred percent sure it won't be the last time. It still sucked though.

"Well that sucks," she said after handing over her customer's vanilla latte and their change. It was like she was reading my mind.

"It's not a big deal. Like I said, we're just going to be friends."

"Well, if you're only going to be his friend, and since he apparently *is* as drop-dead gorgeous as Brenna says he is, do you mind if I take a shot at him when he comes back in here?"

What the fuck did she just say?

She wants a shot at him? At Liam?

Liam and Allie?

Then I heard her laughter.

"Jesus, Samantha. I was just kidding. You should have seen the look on your face. *Sure*, you only want to be his friend. Girlfriend, you're not kidding me! You may be kidding yourself, but you're not kidding me. I wrote the book on that shit. You have got it bad for him already. You hear me? B ... A ... D! I can't *wait* to meet this guy. This guy must be something special for you to act like a normal twenty-three year old woman! Holy shit, Hallelujah for Liam!"

Good God.

Holy shit is right!

****

Allie pretty much left me alone after that. It helped that her shift ended an hour after mine started, so I didn't have to put up with her endless teasing. I loved her and all, but I couldn't take much more of her questions, her teasing, or her all-too-knowing looks.

I was especially happy that she left when my phone started vibrating, signaling that I had a new text message. I wasn't sure who it was at first because it said 'Unknown,' but after reading the contents of the message, I quickly discovered it was Liam. Thank God Allie really wasn't here, because I could feel my face heat up just because of how happy it made me to see his text, and I knew she would never, ever, let me live it down.

I don't think I'll let *myself* live it down. It's only a text message, and I'm acting like a freshman girl getting asked to senior prom. Jesus Christ! How does Liam keep doing this to me?

Friends. Friends. Friends.

I need to start repeating that shit to myself over and over again, because the way I'm feeling and acting, it's anything but friendly. Or adult. I'm a freaking adult. I needed to start behaving like one.

It's only a text message. Nothing more.

I'm not supposed to want it to be anything more.

I needed to just respond already and stop going over every little thing.

Unknown: Hey, Red. How's your day going? You have a minute?

I quickly added Liam's number into my phone, that way he wouldn't be popping up as an 'unknown' anymore. I didn't like thinking of him that way.

Me: Today's going good. Yeah, I have a minute … I'm at the café, only a few more hours to go. How's your day?

Liam: It would be going a lot better if I could see you. What time do you get out?

Me: Six.

Liam: Can I come see you at work?

Me: You know, you don't need permission to come grab some coffee. You've done it a few times now.

Liam: Ha. Ha. I just figured I would ask. Maybe we could actually talk this time. Alone. You know, without a line of people waiting and uncomprehending stalkers taking up my time. You know, maybe grab a table or something …

I could feel my heartbeat pick up speed. What the hell?

Me: What time do you get out of work?

Liam: Six … same as you. I don't work that far from the café, so I can meet you there after work. Is that okay?

Me: It's okay.

Liam: Okay then.

Okay then? Okay then? That was it?

He didn't say anything after that.

What did I just end up doing? I'm going to be meeting him here to talk? When big-mouthed Joanna is supposed to be here to cover for the rest of the night? Perfect. This won't be weird with her lurking about just waiting to get all up in my business or anything like that.

I can't even deal with all of that right now.

I have more important matters to think about. Like what are we supposed to talk about? Is this meeting to talk alone considered a date or something? If he thinks it's a date or something I needed to shut down that thought really quick. Friends don't date. *Shit.* I guess friends could go out, have coffee, go to dinner and the movies, get some drinks. I did most of those things with Aiden when we were friends.

Aiden.

I don't even know why I thought about him just now. I've tried to not think about him the past few days, and I really don't plan on starting to think more about him now when I should be thinking about what's going to happen later with Liam.

You know what? I needed to just forget all of it.

I can't think about Liam and what's going to happen anymore. I just needed to focus on my customers for the next few hours and not make myself crazy before Liam actually gets here.

He's seen enough of my crazy already.

Chapter 8

It's only five minutes after six o'clock and I'm already at a table waiting for Liam to show up. I told myself over and over not to think about all the possibilities of what could happen when Liam finally showed up, but I should've known that was never going to happen. I just needed him to get here already so he could make all of this craziness in my head stop.

Then he was there, walking through the door. Once again, he wasn't looking how I had expected him to look. Liam said he worked until 6:00, and he was coming right from there, so naturally I assumed he'd be wearing a suit and tie. He wasn't in his suit and tie though – I had prepared myself for seeing him like that.

He saw me sitting at a table near the front window and he immediately came over and sat down across from me. He didn't say anything right away, he just stared at me.

Finally he said, "You look beautiful, Red. This is the first time I'm seeing you in anything other than your black *Brew* shirt, and black pants … and you look beautiful."

He was completely right. I've seen him in a few different shirts and jeans, and that amazing suit, but normally he always sees me in my black *The Brew* t-shirt and black skinny jeans.

When I see him, I think the word beautiful. I don't think at any time, in whatever outfit I have on, that *I'm* beautiful … but he said it though. I know for a fact that I've never been called beautiful by any man other than my father … and now Liam. I'm really not sure how to feel about that, especially because Liam is the one who said it.

He can't find me beautiful right?

I mean, I'm wearing a white tank top and dark blue jeans with flip-flops, and my brown hair is pulled up in a seriously messy bun. How could anyone find that beautiful? Besides, friends like us shouldn't say that … right? I don't know what to say, so I just ignore it.

"So, no suit and tie? I thought you were coming from work?"

"I finished up with a project at work early, so I went home to change before coming here. It seems some people find my suit and tie intimidating." After he said that, his trademark grin with the dimples appeared on his face.

I wouldn't call his suit and tie *intimidating*. Mouth-watering, distracting, fantasy-inducing, or rational-thought-preventing, would be more accurate terms. Those terms could also be applied to the dark jeans he has on now, with another baby blue shirt that matches his eyes perfectly. I wonder if guys like him, who have eyes like that, buy those color shirts on purpose.

They must.

They *have* to know what they do to women.

Before I got the chance to say anything, I heard a voice next to me that I really didn't want to hear.

"Can I get you two anything?"

Joanna was at our table. Sometimes if there isn't a line waiting for coffee or the pastries and sandwiches we sell, we go around to the tables and ask our customers if they need anything. Of course there would be no line right at this moment, and she would pop on over here with all her perkiness asking if we want anything. She could care less about what I wanted. If I said I wanted anything she'd probably spit in it. She would just *love* to give anything to Liam that he asked for – and I do mean *anything*. She made me sick.

"Do you want anything, Red?" Liam asked me after only giving Joanna a brief glance.

"Who's 'Red?'" Joanna asked in her sickeningly sweet voice.

"Samantha. She's my Red."

I don't know who was taken aback more by his comment, Joanna or me. Did he just call me *his* Red? She was probably thinking the same thing.

"Okay. Well, whatever that means. Do you want anything Samantha?" she asked me all huffy. Bitch.

Yes, Joanna I would like something. I would like you to stop looking at Liam like that. I would like you to get away from our table and leave us alone. I would like you to wear a bigger shirt to work and looser pants, so that way you don't pop out of either article of clothing. I would like if I never saw you again.

I didn't say any of those things.

"No thank you, Joanna. I don't want anything. How about you Liam?"

"I think you know exactly what I want, Red" Liam said, in a deep voice that was unmistakably laced with amusement and an all too obvious deeper meaning. I set him up perfectly for that one.

To my absolute frustration and horror, I felt the tingling warmth of my blush creeping up into my skin. I can't believe I would have this type of reaction in front of such a hateful witch. Liam must have sensed my discomfort because he looked away from me and turned his attention to Joanna, quickly ordering his usual black coffee. I did know exactly what he wanted in terms of coffee, but we both knew he meant something else before. Joanna fucking knew it too.

She didn't say anything after he gave her his order, she just turned around and left. I guess she realized she wouldn't be getting anywhere with him. If my face didn't feel like it did, and if I wasn't a little embarrassed by the situation, I probably would've done a happy dance that he wasn't interested and that she was probably mortified that he didn't pay any attention to her because he was totally focused on me.

I *was* a little embarrassed though, that *she* of all people witnessed me at a moment like that. Why couldn't it have been someone like Allie who heard and saw everything that just happened? For as much as she loved to tease me – and she would have teased me in private for days afterwards if she saw my blush and heard his words – she would have at least rose to my defense and said something witty that would have had *him* embarrassed instead of me. Hell, I would have even taken Connor in that situation because then I know that Liam would have never made the innuendo that he did.

Seriously though, why couldn't I be an adult for once and have shit like that bounce off of me? Or why couldn't I be knowledgeable and witty enough to say something back that would make *him* react like me. When was I going to stop turning beet red at everything Liam said that made me feel even remotely giddy, and tingly, and heated?

Seriously, why couldn't I have something witty to say in return, especially with Joanna standing there? *Fucking Joanna.*

I knew he sensed my discomfort before, and it was confirmed when he said, "I'm sorry for that, Red. I didn't mean to embarrass you in front of your co-worker. I just can't seem to help myself when it comes to you. I love seeing you blush. It amazes me that women still do that. I knew that you would probably turn red if I said what I did and I wanted to see it, so I said what I did without really thinking it through. I didn't think about how it would make you feel or how it would seem if others saw it too. *Fuck.* All I keep doing is apologizing to you, Red. I keep fucking everything up."

He loved seeing me blush? I kind of knew that before, but the way he explained it now, it didn't seem like such a bad thing anymore. I still hated it, and I still didn't like that because of the stupid blush he could pretty much tell what I was thinking and feeling, but hearing him say how much he loved it, and that it amazes him, and that he purposefully *wants* to see it – it makes me hate it a little less.

"It's okay Liam. I mean … it's not okay that I end up embarrassing myself by blushing all the time when you're around, but I know it's not always your fault. *This time* it was definitely your fault, but you're forgiven. Can you just not say anything more like that in front of her? She sucks as a person, and I really don't need her to see me like that again."

He started to laugh at my comment about Joanna. When he was done, he said, "I won't let her see you like that again, Red. I promise."

Before I could say anything else to him, his phone started vibrating on the table. I saw a picture of a really beautiful woman pop up on his screen and I felt like either my heart was going to stop, or I was going to throw up all over the place.

Why was I acting like this? Of course he had gorgeous women calling him all of the time. Remember, I am just his friend, and will only ever be *just* his friend? No big deal.

No big deal that I just wanted to grab his phone and smash it into a billion itty bitty pieces by stomping on it. No big deal at all.

What *was* a big fucking deal is his response to the phone call.

"Red, I'm sorry, but I really need to answer this."

"Um … okay." No. Not okay. What the fuck?

He didn't get up and leave to answer the phone. He just sat there where I could hear every damn thing he was saying. He answered the phone with a smile on his face, so he was obviously pleased to be hearing from whoever it was. I heard him asking how she was, and what she was doing. I heard him asking when she was going to be in town next. I heard him asking her to let him know the moment she got back because they had a lot of catching up to do, and he couldn't wait to see her. I heard him say that they should definitely go out and grab dinner, maybe some drinks. *Definitely*, they should go to *Molly's* and play some pool. I also heard him say he loved her. That he couldn't wait to see her. That he missed her.

Wait what? He said he loves her, he misses her, and he can't wait to fucking see her?

I tried not to pay too much attention to him as he was talking so I could give him some semblance of privacy, but at the mention of his loving someone outrageously beautiful I couldn't help but whip my face away from what I was supposedly looking at out the window and look directly at him.

When I looked at him I noticed that he was looking at me strangely, and that he was also done with his conversation. I was happy he was finally done talking, but I didn't appreciate the weird look on his face. Shouldn't I be the one looking at him, how he's looking at me? I wasn't the one who just answered a call from some hot guy, and who made plans for when they're in town next. I wasn't the one who said I love you, and that I can't wait to see you. I wasn't the one who said I *fucking* miss you. I was ready to get the hell out of here. Fuck being friends.

"Samantha … You should know after you saw me in here with Karen, that not every girl I talk to is who you think they are. I am not involved with *anyone*. I am too interested in some girl who says she only wants to be my friend to even *think* about another woman in that way. I am too interested in an unbelievably *confusing*, interesting, *beautiful* girl who is too busy thinking the worst of me all the time. You know, you really need to stop thinking and assuming the worst of me all the time, right?"

I didn't know what to say to him, so I said nothing. I felt awful for assuming the worst, but what else was I to think? He just told some random girl that he loves her and misses her. He was saying all this, and making plans with her when he was the one who insisted on hanging out with me tonight. What's up with that? Who is she? Maybe I'm being super foolish. He seems too smart to answer the phone and say all of those things to someone else when he is trying to start something with me and I'm sitting right across from him. However, I did tell him that I didn't want anything more than friendship, so maybe he didn't care one way or another what I heard him say to some other girl on the phone. He did care though, otherwise why would he say the things to me he just did? Why would he say he's interested?

As if he knew what I was thinking and how my brain was coming up with all these different ideas, he answered my unspoken questions. What he said made me feel even worse than I did before.

"That was my little sister Riley on the phone. She's away at college taking some summer courses. I haven't seen her in a few weeks and I can't wait until she gets home – she comes home for the weekend next week. I just wanted to let her know that she's mine as soon as she gets home. She has some friends still here, and I know she probably has a ton of plans, but I wanted to catch up with her before she goes off and does her own thing."

Wow can I feel any more pathetic? His sister? A man who loves and misses his sister, and who actually wants to spend time with her – and he actually tells her all these things? How the *hell* am I not supposed to fall for him when he does and says things like that?

"Wow … I guess it's my turn to say I'm sorry. I don't know what's been going on with me lately. I really am sorry. I promise, I don't mean to jump to conclusions like that. I think it's awesome that you want to spend time with your sister, and that you miss her and all that. It's sweet that you tell her you love her and can't wait to catch up with her. I mean, I know Connor loves me and I love him, but I could probably count on my fingers the number of times he's actually said he loves me when he's not just saying it to get something he wants or because he's forced into it."

"So, you're not going to deny that you were jealous?" he asked, completely bypassing my apology. Seeing as how he said it with a grin on his face and a glimmer in his eyes I knew he was playing with me. He knew that I knew that *he* knew, I was a little bit jealous of what I assumed was a girl he was hooking up with.

"You also said that I was awesome, and though I don't particularly like the word sweet, I'll take it. I mean I prefer charming, smooth, spectacular …"

"Stop it. I said that *it* was awesome that you want to do things with your sister and that you miss her, and that's *it is* sweet that you tell her all the things you feel … not that you're awesome and sweet."

"Ouch. So, you don't think I'm awesome or sweet? You weren't jealous either? Don't think I forgot that you didn't answer my question, Red. You're seriously wounding me here."

For once in my life I was happy to see Joanna walking towards me. She had Liam's drink on her tray. It took her long enough to put it together and bring it over here. It was a plain coffee for Christ's sake. At least if she had to take forever, she was now actually interrupting something that I didn't mind being interrupted.

As she reached the table, she gave me a nasty glare before turning to Liam and putting his coffee down in front of him. She asked him with her megawatt smile if that was all he'd be wanting. Thankfully, he learned his lesson from before because he said the drink was fine, and that was it. Joanna quickly left and then it was just the two of us again.

I wasn't sure what to say, but I didn't have to think of anything because Liam decided to take control of the conversation once again.

"So Red, are you working tomorrow?" he asked. I didn't think he would go in a completely different direction with the conversation than that of what we were discussing before, but I would definitely take the change in topic.

"Yes, I do. I work from 9-3," I told him.

"What's up with the weird hours? Some days you're here, some days you're not, and when you are here, it never seems to be at the same times."

"My parent's own the place, so I make my own schedule. I make sure I have enough hours to pay the bills, but since I normally have nothing to do I come in anyway to help out when my parents need it. They try not to ask me to come in too much because it's my last summer vacation before I graduate college, but it's not like I have anything better to do on my days and nights off, so …" *Oh. My. God.* No, no, no, *no!*

Did I just say all those things to him?

That I basically have no life, and that I'm a lonely, loser, weirdo? Yes. Yes, I did.

"Well maybe we need to get you out more. It would be a waste to do nothing on all of those days you have off, or when you have nights free. What about today? You want to go out tonight, Red?"

"No. I have things to do tonight," I quickly said. I was proud of myself for not hesitating, or for not blushing at my obvious lie.

"Liar." He knew me too well already. I had absolutely nothing planned except going home and reading a book, maybe making myself something to eat, and taking a long hot bath. Most women would kill to be asked out by Liam. I would rather say no and read, and take a bubble bath. Well I wouldn't say I would *rather* do that, but it is what I was going to do.

"It's okay, Red. Maybe next time. Is it okay if I stop by tomorrow though around noon? I have an hour lunch and I'd like to see you again. I'm becoming partial to your black shirt and jeans … and the coffee. The coffee's pretty good too. Maybe we could grab a sandwich though, if that's okay with you?"

I thought about it for a minute, while he looked at me with a smile on his face.

"You know, Liam … I think I would like that. I can take about a half hour break. Fair warning though. Connor is here tomorrow. Something tells me he won't be as pleasant or as willing to accommodate all of your *needs* as Joanna was."

"I think I can handle Connor, if it means I get to hang out with you, Red." He stared at me like he wanted to say something else but he didn't. I really wanted to know what he was going to say.

"I really wish I could sit here and talk with you some more Red, but I have to get going. I'm meeting up with some of my friends tonight to watch the ball game, though I *definitely* would have canceled on them if you decided that you did want to go out with me tonight … *but* unfortunately you're being difficult. I'll see you tomorrow though, so it's okay. Hopefully we can talk about actual things tomorrow. It seems that once again all we really did was clear up some misunderstandings and trade apologies. Don't get me wrong, I could probably sit and stare at you in complete silence and be completely and utterly content, but I want to get to know you. Actually, I think I *need* to get to know you. So tomorrow, be prepared. I fully intend on getting to know you better, Red."

With that he got up and got ready to leave. I sat there and tried to process what he said. He said that he would be content to just stare at me in silence. He also said that he needed to get to know me, and I felt the same exact way, for both things.

As I continued to sit there I guess he got worried because I wasn't moving to go with him towards the door, nor was I getting my things together to leave.

"Are you not leaving too? Do you need a ride home or something?" When I didn't respond he asked, "Is something wrong?" I thought about everything that was said during the conversation and all the things that weren't said. I thought about all the words, looks, actions, and I found myself speaking before really thinking things completely through.

"Yes." I said yes. I said yes, and I blamed it on me feeling all mushy because of his comments about silence and being utterly content to just stare at me; I said yes because of how he talked about his sister; I said yes because he said he wanted and needed to get to know me; I said yes because of the way he makes me feel; I said yes because even though he gave me a pass, I actually did want him to know how I actually felt in that one particular moment of time. I said yes because I felt like I had to give him a little something, the same way he's been giving me all of these little wonderful something's tonight, and over the past few days.

"Yes, something's wrong? What is it?" he asked, and I could see the concern line his face and cloud his eyes.

"No! No … Nothing is wrong. I meant "*yes*" to the question you asked me before. I don't know why I'm answering it *now*, but I just feel like I have to. Like I owe it to you because I made it awkward once again when you were doing something that I truly find amazing and sweet … something most guys your age wouldn't be doing or saying … So, my answer to you is yes … *Yes*, I was jealous. I was jealous before when you were talking to your sister because I didn't know she was your sister … Just like I didn't know Karen was your co-worker and I immediately thought something else and I didn't like it …"

When he didn't say anything I felt a little stupid, and I wished that I had kept my mouth shut, but I had to go with it now.

"I was jealous because I thought she was some girl you were with. Just like I was jealous when I thought you were with Karen. I don't like feeling like this. I meant it when I said I only want to be your friend. I *still* mean it. I just felt jealous, and I don't know why. I didn't – *I don't* – have any right to be. I was though. It completely sucks! *Shit* … I don't know what I'm saying, or doing … so just please forget it. *Jesus* …"

I stopped myself from speaking anymore. God, why do I ramble?

He came closer to me, and started to speak as if I didn't make a complete fool of myself.

"Yeah, it does suck, Sam. If it makes you feel any better I knew you were jealous, and I really was going to let it go. I was only teasing you about it because I found it so damn cute. Since you manned up, I guess I should let you know that I was jealous too. The first time I saw Connor I was jealous, and then when I saw you talking to Aaron and I

96

thought it was something more, I was ready to rip his head off. When I heard him say he wanted you ... *I was ready to fucking kill him.* So, yeah, Sam, jealousy is a bitch. I've never done jealous before. As awful as it sounds, I thought it was only a girl thing. I can tell you I was definitely one hundred percent wrong about that shit."

Wow. Okay then. So I guess I didn't have to feel stupid about everything I just let slip to him then.

"So what are we going to do about it? Friends, remember? I don't think friends are supposed to get jealous of things like that," I partially mentioned, partially asked him.

"Seriously, Red? After all of this? You think we can still be 'friends,' and be okay staying like that?"

"Yes. We have to be. Or at least ... I have to. There is so much you don't know ..." I started to say to him before he cut me off.

"Well then *tell* me. I told you I want to know *everything*. It seems like something is holding you back from wanting anything more than friends. I don't get it. I really feel like you are interested in something more, like you are interested in *me*, but you're not letting yourself open up to the possibility or the potential ... *why?*"

I still can't go there with him.

"Liam ... you have to stop. Please. I can't get into it yet, okay?" I said.

"Yet? So you may eventually tell me?"

I thought about it, and I could picture myself telling him. I could picture myself doing a lot of things with him.

This was one of those moments.

Whatever I said now could change the course of my life forever. I didn't used to believe in that shit but certain things in my past taught me that there are certain moments in everyone's life where they make decisions that change their outcomes. Regardless of my eventual outcome, I needed Liam with me here … in the now.

"Yes … eventually I may tell you."

"Then that's good enough for me. That you're thinking about telling me what's holding you back … it means that you're actually thinking about telling me because you're thinking about me as being more than just your friend. If you really wanted to be friends and stay friends forever, you would never even consider thinking about telling me something that is so bothersome or worrisome to you, something that has you acting like you are. You wouldn't be considering telling me something that's made you hurt, something that's made you weary, something that's made you … *you*. You wouldn't tell me because you know how I feel about you. A normal friend you would tell, *sure*, but not me. You wouldn't tell me those things unless you wanted something more too. You know I want to know you, Samantha, and you know that I want more. I seriously cannot tell you how happy it makes me that you are exploring options, Sam. I am all up for exploring."

Sweet baby Jesus!

After a few moments, as his words were still sinking in, and when I continued to say nothing, he started to talk again.

"Okay Red … I think that is more than enough for tonight. I promise I won't push you for anything. Not intentionally, anyway. I meant everything that I said."

When I still didn't say anything, and when I still hadn't moved from my spot at the table, he asked me about leaving again and if I was okay.

"Are you sure you are fine to get home, though? I really have to get going now."

He really was sweet, making sure I was safe to get home. I couldn't resist saying what I was about to say, because I knew he would get a complete kick out of it. After everything that was said in the last few minutes, I knew that I needed to lighten the mood instead of leaving things as they were now.

I stood up, and walked next to him, preparing myself.

"I really am fine. You see that *red* car right over there?" I pointed to the car right in front of the side entrance door that only my parents, Connor, or I used.

He looked to where I pointed and I could see the smile start to form on his face. I saw it fully engulf his face when I said, "That's my car."

He started laughing.

It was a full deep-throated, full-bodied laugh that made me go all gooey inside. I knew it would be worth it to tell him and endure all the teasing I knew would come of it.

"Samantha … Red … Oh … My … *God*. That is *fucking perfect!*"

"I knew you would get a kick out of it. Go on, get out of here. Go enjoy your game. As you can see I will be perfectly fine. It was good to see you Liam. I'll see you tomorrow."

"Yes you will, Red. Yes, you will. Have a good night."

With that he turned and went towards the door. Before he left he turned around and winked. Then he left.

His wink was better than any hug I had ever received from any guy. His wink was better than any kiss I've ever had too.

His wink was the perfect way for me to end my night.

I really couldn't wait until tomorrow.

God … I really was in deep with him, wasn't I?

Chapter 9

Waiting for noon to arrive was going to be the death of me. I was busy dealing with the endless line of customers, questions from Allie, and the disapproving stares being thrown my way from Connor, and because of it my happy mood was starting to disappear. Not only did I have to mention to Connor the whole debacle with Aaron and what he said and how it made me feel, I also had to tell Connor that Liam was coming into the shop to grab some lunch – *with me*. None of that went over well with Connor. I told him that he had better be on his best behavior, but saying that to someone like Connor isn't asking for much. I would just have to hope for the best.

After hours of stares from Connor, and whining and questioning from Allie, I actually forgot about keeping track of the time. It wasn't until Liam was right in front of me that I actually noticed that it was already after noon.

"I'm guessing you're having a really crazy day so far, huh, Red?" I heard his deep voice say.

I had been looking down writing some things on our inventory paper that needed to be refilled, so I didn't see that he'd come in or that he was right in front of me, but as soon as I heard his voice I whipped my head up so I could look at him.

And what a sight he was.

"Hi ... Hi. Wow, is it already time for lunch? W-What do you want? Um ... I mean, what would you like? You look really good. I-I-I ... Um, I didn't mean that. *No*, I didn't mean *that* like that either. Jesus, you *do* look good, but I didn't mean to say that. Oh, God ... *Holy shit*, just kill me now. Look ... I'll place your order and then meet you at a table, but I need to know what to get you first ... So what would you like for lunch, Liam?"

I was a stuttering, stupid mess. A stuttering, stupid mess who just blurted out that he looked good, took it back, and then actually said it again. *Crap!* Of course he looked good. *I just can't believe I said it.* He just came from work so he was dressed in another amazing suit and tie. I thought the first time I saw him in a suit he was breathtaking. Seeing him in *this* suit and tie though, I can't even describe how it's making me feel. Actually, I guess I can – it's making me feel like a freaking stuttering idiot. A stuttering idiot who didn't know when to shut up.

The black suit he was wearing today made him look very powerful, and the pale blue dress shirt that matched his eyes – *now I really do think he buys that specific color on purpose* – made him look like he just walked off the set of a photo-shoot, not out from behind a desk at his father's company. His tie, combined with his whole look, is what did it for me though. His loosened tie and few undone buttons, made him look not only very powerful, but also very, very *bad* ... but in a really, *really good* way. No wonder why I was a stuttering, mumbling, mess. I've never seen anything like him.

He must have been having a field day with my reaction. If his laugh is any indication, my reaction to him is on par with winning the lottery.

"See, I *knew* it. I *knew* the suit and tie intimidated you. You like me in a suit and tie, you all but just admitted it, and I *fucking love that!* It's only right that something gets to you ... because I have to be honest here, Red ... *everything* about you gets to me. You could be in your *Brew* shirt and your black pants, you could be in the jeans and shirt you were wearing yesterday, you could have your hair up in that messy bun, in a ponytail, or half way down your back ... you could be stuttering over your words, you could be blushing as red as your car, you could be as witty, funny, sarcastic, awkward, silent, or as *beautiful* as you want – as you *are* ... it's just *you* ... so it doesn't matter ... *you get to me.*"

Did he just say that to me? Liam? *To me?*

What he said was absolutely amazing, so completely unexpected, and it was also a lot to take in. It was also something that I couldn't dwell on for long because before either Liam or I could say anything more we both heard two very distinct voices speaking to us, or rather *at* as.

One said, "Oh. My. God," while the other said "Dude, you need to give her your fucking order already and get out of line. There are other customers behind you and I'm tired of hearing your fucking Prince Charming bullshit, especially when it's directed towards my sister."

How could I forget about Allie and Connor? It was obvious they both heard everything we said, but when I looked at Liam he could've cared less that they heard everything. Lucky him.

He turned his head towards Connor and Allie.

"Hey Connor, it's good to see you again."

Connor didn't return that sentiment.

Liam then held out his hand toward Allie so he could introduce himself. By holding out his hand for her to shake, I knew his estimation in her eyes went up about a thousand.

"Hi, I'm Liam."

"Hi, Liam. I'm Allie. It's nice to finally meet you. I have heard *a lot* of things about you," my best friend said to him, while stealing a glance towards me. I could tell from the little twinkle in her eyes that she just couldn't wait to share the news that she and I had been talking about him.

"Good things I hope," Liam countered.

Allie just smirked at Liam with far too much coyness in her smile and gaze. Then she said a little too breathily for my liking, "Wouldn't you like to know, handsome?" Allie then turned around, grabbed Connor's arm, and I could hear her laughing while she led him away. I would definitely have to thank Allie later, right before I killed her for telling Liam that I talked about him with her.

I needed to get his order so we could sit down and have lunch. I only had a half hour break I could take, and his hour allotment was rapidly coming to an end.

"So, Liam … let's try this again. What could I get you for lunch?" I asked without stuttering this time. I felt like patting myself on the back.

"I think I will have the turkey club, and I'll take an iced-tea instead of coffee today."

"Alright, I'll put the order in and then meet you at the table that is open by the front window if that's okay? One of the other workers will bring the food over when everything's ready."

"Okay. Perfect." He went to go sit down by the window, hanging his suit jacket that he had taken off on the back of his chair. Seeing him with his loosened tie and in his dress shirt that was practically molded to his broad chest, and knowing that I would have to stare at all of that while eating and talking to him … *Jesus*, it really didn't look good for me.

I am beginning to realize more and more, that I really don't stand a chance against all of the things that Liam wants.

I'm not even sure I want to be against all of those things anymore.

I think I may want exactly what he wants too.

Those are some scary things to be considering.

****

Liam watched me the whole time as I was walking towards him carrying our drinks. He stood up as I approached him, and grabbed his iced tea before pulling out my seat and helping me sit down. I've hung out with a few guys before, and never once has one pulled out a chair for me so I could sit down. It felt a little strange that this was the first time that it was happening … in a coffee shop of all places, where my brother was staring daggers at what was going on, but I honestly didn't care in the least.

I didn't get a chance to thank him for pulling out my chair, because before I knew it he was already sitting across from me and talking. He obviously didn't know how big of a deal it was that he just pulled out my chair. Maybe he did stuff like that all of the time, so for him it probably wasn't a big deal, but for me it definitely was.

"Thanks for bringing me my tea. Now I have to ask you … were you embarrassed by what I said about you in front of your brother, and your friend?" Liam sure knew how to get to the point of things. No beating around the bush for him.

I just sat there and thought about it for a while. Was I truly embarrassed?

I liked what he said about me. Did I like that he said that to me though, when we were only supposed to be friends? I wanted to be completely honest with him, because I felt like the answer to the question was a part of another one of those moments, where the absolute truth is what will keep us on the path that we are currently on. I liked the path, and the possibilities of where we were heading.

I guess I didn't think of a response quickly enough however because he started to speak again.

"Maybe I shouldn't have said what I did. I meant absolutely every word of what I said, but I promised you yesterday that I wouldn't push you right now for anything more, and I don't want you to feel pressured by anything that I end up saying that seems kind of forward or too much. I also wasn't thinking clearly saying it in front of your brother and Allie, but when you reacted like you did to seeing me ... I had to let you know that I understood what you were feeling – *completely*. You make me feel the same way too, Samantha."

God, what is wrong with me?

How could I have ever thought we could be platonic friends? Didn't people say that men and women can't be *just* friends ... they must have especially meant it when the men look, act, and speak like Liam.

"I was embarrassed, but I also *wasn't* embarrassed. I can't believe that Connor and Allie heard me make a fool of myself ... I can't believe *you* heard me make a fool of myself ... *that* was embarrassing. *You* didn't embarrass me though. I'm not exactly sure what you made me feel ... but it wasn't embarrassment." I had to let him know the truth. The truth is the only way I think I could hold my own with him. I know most people wouldn't say that. Most people think that keeping a few of their secrets is the best thing when trying to figure out the balance of relationships, especially new ones. I've had secrets once before though, and it didn't turn out well for anybody, and I didn't want to go that route again. I didn't need something like whether or not Liam embarrassed me in front of my brother, or how I felt about what he said, to be something that I needed to keep hidden. After all of the things I have experienced so far with *this* particular man, what happened before was just a tiny blip.

"Okay. That's really good then. Truthfully, I wasn't sure if you were embarrassed by what I said or not because you blushed ... but I mean, that's just a given with you." I heard his words and saw his smirk, so I knew that we were past everything that had just happened. I couldn't even be mad at what he just said. I was just too damn happy that everything was okay. He was okay with what I said, he was okay knowing that I was fine with what he said, and now it was time to move on.

But then I saw his smirk disappear. It wasn't replaced by a normal smile, or even his very appealing grin. He just sat there with a straight face. I didn't know if I wanted to know what he was going to say next. He seemed too serious all of a sudden. I'm not sure I liked that particular look on Liam's face. I had become used to his more easygoing attitude.

Before I could ask him what was wrong, he answered my unspoken question.

"Your blush, Red ... I seriously hope you never lose it. I know it's crazy, but I want to be the only one who gets to experience it from now on. I want to be the only one who gets to be the cause of it."

Whoa.

I knew without a doubt that my face was doing that thing he was just talking about. I could feel it. From the way his eyes were now blazing like little blue flames, I knew that he could see it.

I don't think there is any doubt Liam that I will ever lose my blush around you, just like there is no doubt that you are the only one who can, and most likely will, be the cause of it.

I wasn't sure how I would begin to respond to what he had said, but it really didn't matter.

We were rudely interrupted.

"Here's your shit. Are you two done making asses out of yourselves yet?" Connor asked as he put the tray carrying our food down right in between us.

"What's your problem Connor?" I was really annoyed with Connor for disrupting what was going on with me and Liam. I knew that the food would be coming but it couldn't have come at a worse time, or have been delivered by a worse person. Even Joanna would have been better than Connor right now.

"Yeah, Connor, I don't think I was an ass. Your sister definitely wasn't one either. I'm perfectly fine with everything I've said so far today, and she should be too. *Why*, should we have a problem with what was said? Do *you* have one?" Leave it to Liam to say those things to Connor. What is it with men like these two? Why do they always feel like they should get the last word, and that something always needs to be said? I knew if they both kept this up, this whole lunch get together would be going nowhere good, fast. I had to stop Liam and Conner before they went any further.

"Connor you need to leave. I told you not to start. The only one who looks like an ass around here right now is you." He better not say anything to me. He better not say anything more to Liam either. He was making everything uncomfortable. The look I must have given him when I just told him to leave must have penetrated his thick skull, because he actually listened to me for once.

108

"Alright Sam. But I'm right over there, you got that?" He pointed behind him towards the front counter.

"Don't think I can't freaking see you." I don't know which one of us he said that to. Probably both of us.

I didn't care about what Connor said, and I didn't worry about the fact that he was probably going to ignore every customer just so he could stare at every little thing that Liam and I did. I'm sure if he could get close enough without me saying anything, just close enough so he could overhear our conversation, he would. I knew when I asked him to be good I wouldn't be getting anything remotely close to a normal person's idea of what good is. But still … holy shit.

Liam started taking our lunch off the tray. He took his sandwich and handed me mine. When he saw what my sandwich was, he started to smile.

"Peanut butter and jelly, Red?"

I guess neither of us were going to say anything about what just went on with Connor, and I was perfectly fine with that.

"Yeah. It's only one of the best things to have for lunch, *ever*."

He started to laugh.

"I can't even tell you the last time I had peanut butter and jelly. I'm kind of enjoying the fact that you think that peanut butter and jelly is one of the best things to have for lunch … *ever*."

"Honestly, I'm not a big lunch person. Or a breakfast person either. If I'm really hungry during the day I normally just grab a bagel or a doughnut, and I fill up on coffee. I don't really like feeling full during the day."

"So you don't like breakfast at all? I love breakfast." He kept the conversation going, in between eating his sandwich.

"No, I actually enjoy breakfast, but only if I'm eating it later in the day. I love having breakfast for dinner. I'll eat it in the morning if there's a special reason to be eating, like brunch or something, or if I'm visiting my parents and they insist on having breakfast together, but I don't get up in the morning and think 'I *must* have breakfast' so I eat."

"Really? That's just sad. You don't know what you're missing."

He looked at me then. He seemed to be considering his words.

"So, you're not a fan of breakfast in bed then?" he asked.

"What? No. Who wants to eat breakfast in bed? Wouldn't that require actually getting up out of bed early, to then deal with the hassle of making breakfast, only to then jump back *into bed* to eat and *not* try to make a mess? Why would anyone want to do all that?" I asked him, in all seriousness, not comprehending for a few moments that Liam had just asked me a very loaded question. When I did realize what I had walked in to, and what I had inadvertently revealed about myself, I felt the tingling in my cheeks start.

"You truly do amaze me, Red. You know the *messes* of that whole breakfast in bed thing, is the best part right?" When he said *those* words in that voice of his, I could feel other areas of my body start to tingle like my cheeks were.

I knew I had to be blushing a brilliant shade of scarlet.

No, I didn't know about the mess that was created in any regard when it comes to breakfast in bed.

Or the various ideas of 'mess' that I am sure he was speaking of, and very well versed in.

I couldn't do anything other than shake my head. I was so over the topic. Even though what he said made me feel all tingly in rather interesting ways, I didn't want to continue with it any longer.

I didn't want to think about him having breakfast in bed with other women. I didn't want to think about him creating messes that led up to women spending the night, and then them eating together in the morning. And then the possible messes after that.

I can't believe I didn't clue into what he meant sooner. If I had, I *never* would have said what I did.

He must be loving how naïve I am when it comes to stuff like this.

How did something as simple and childish as peanut butter and jelly turn into breakfast the morning after?

Childish.

Peanut butter and jelly.

And me, obviously.

I felt the blush actually leave my cheeks, and I could feel the frown forming on my face. I didn't know what to say to express my displeasure of the conversation. If I said one thing I would be perceived as too naïve or jealous. If I said something else it could be taken as me being frigid or abrupt. I was in a no-win situation.

"Okay, so that conversation really escalated kind of quick. I didn't mean for it to go there, the question just sort of came out. It was meant as a joke, but I think that part was missed a little too late. *Completely my fault.* How about we backtrack about a thousand steps?" Liam glossed over my discomfort, and my naivety in flirty dialogue, and gave me an out. An out, which I was actually grateful for, even though a part of me wanted to kill him for putting the images in my head of him and other women eating breakfast all cozy in bed after doing God knows what.

I just nodded my head because I wasn't sure what to say to him. Nor, was I sure how my voice would sound right at the moment.

"Okay, since we are supposed to be doing this whole *friends* thing – even though I think we are both past that already if I do say so myself …

but absolutely no pressure or badgering or anything I promise – let's start with the basics. I mean we really should know the basics, right? So, Red, what's your favorite color?"

My favorite, what now?

Liam's been known to throw me for a loop, but really? My favorite color? After the whole breakfast in bed thing? Talk about a complete turnaround.

He does have a point though. We never really talked about the most basic of things – likes and dislikes. As he said, we're supposed to be friends. Friends would know these things.

Though I'm not over the previous topic, I decided to let it go for now and not completely ruin what was left of the time I had with him. I would answer his hopefully simple questions, without stepping in it again.

"Pink," I told him.

"Pink? Really? I didn't peg you as a pink person. Pink seems so girly."

I gave him a bland stare, so he continued on by saying, "Don't get me wrong Red, I can definitely tell you are all girl … all *woman* … but I just don't see the pink in you. I want to though. *Trust me*."

Okay, so not touching that one with a ten foot pole …

"So, Liam. Sticking with this topic, what is *your* favorite color?"

"It's a toss-up between blue and black. I like both colors but for different things. I guess if I had to pick just one though, I would say blue."

You also look really phenomenal in both colors, especially blue … but I don't say it.

"Okay, my turn again. What do you like to do when you aren't working here or when you aren't at school? Where do you go to school by the way, and what are you studying? What do you plan on doing when you graduate? And, I guess I should also ask, how old are you? I mean, I guess I should know if you are old enough to drink so that way when I ask you out for drinks, I don't seem like a complete asshole when you can't *actually* drink."

All I could think while he was asking away was: *Thank God.* I could actually handle these questions.

"Wow. That's a lot of questions all rolled up into 'your turn.' Okay, let's see. I love to read. I know most people would find reading boring, but I don't. I could read for hours and hours, and think I've had an insanely productive day when I'm done. I like to write as well. Let's see, what else ... I go out with Allie sometimes – and yes, I can actually go out and have a few drinks with her because I just turned twenty-three – so I can in fact drink legally. I love going down to the Harbor and spending a lot of time there sitting by the water and watching the tourists, and just soaking all of that energy in, especially this time of year. Also, I will admit that I am a television junkie. Seriously, I am embarrassed by how much television I watch. It's sad, I know. Um, what else? Sometimes Connor and I go to ball games. We both love baseball. He and I used to go with my dad all of the time when we were younger. Now, he and I go to a game every few weeks – it's kind of a tradition with us. But, anyway ... I go to the University of Maryland, and I'm an English major. Obviously with me telling you about my love of books, I'm guessing you don't need to ask why I decided to be an English major, right."

I took a few breaths before continuing on answering Liam's questions.

"What you did ask that is a really good question though, is what do I plan to do when I graduate? Truth is ... I don't know. I could always be a teacher, that's an option ... but I just can't picture myself in a classroom every day. I always wanted to be surrounded by books all day, so I thought I might pursue being a librarian, but I'm not sure about that either. A writer? An editor? *I'm really not sure.* I know I should probably be worried about being done with school in less than a year and having no future plan, but for some reason, at least for right now anyway, I'm not worried. I'll figure it out. I have options, I just haven't decided. I definitely know that having many options is better than no options. Besides, look at my brother. He went to college, got his degree in business, and he ended up being a firefighter. So, see … there are always options. Nothing is ever set in stone."

"Your brother's a firefighter? Here in Baltimore? He works for the BCFD? What company?"

Out of everything I had just told him about my life, he asks about the one thing I mentioned about my brother? Are you freaking kidding me?

"Yes he is, and yes he does. He works for Engine 2, Battalion 2."

"No fucking way. Seriously?"

I looked at him skeptically. Why was he making such a big deal out of this? I mean I know my brother likes to talk trash, he's hot-headed, and he's obnoxious and rude at times, but you would think Liam would be more incredulous that Connor graduated college with a business degree, not that he's a Baltimore County Firefighter. I mean, the Liam underneath the suit didn't look like he would be someone you would see in a boardroom working at a major company, so why was he acting like what I said about Connor was something so completely foreign? What's the deal?

"Yes. Seriously? What's wrong with that? He loves being a firefighter, and he's an awesome one by the way. He may act crazy sometimes, but he is passionate about his job. It's his life …"

"Whoa, whoa, whoa, Red. I'm not saying anything bad about Connor. Easy there tiger. I'm just surprised because not only is he a firefighter but he works for Engine 2. My best friend Ryan works for the same Company. Talk about a small world. That was it. Nothing bad."

Small world indeed. I've heard a few things about Ryan from Connor. I wasn't going to mention it to Liam though. Some of the things that Connor said about him I wouldn't feel comfortable talking to Liam about. From what I've heard, Ryan takes the term manwhore and raises it to another level. And Ryan is supposedly Liam's best friend? What does that say about Liam?

Before I could start questioning myself even more about Liam's friends, he started talking about college and what he liked to do in his own spare time. Thankfully he liked to read as well, and he also liked to go to the Harbor, but he isn't as fond of television as I am unless hockey, football, or baseball's on. He also mentioned putting in quite a bit of time at the gym in his apartment building, which didn't surprise me in the least from the looks of him. He also was very understanding about college and said he knew exactly what I meant. Apparently, he went to school and obtained his master's degree in marketing because that is what his dad had expected, so he figured he would just do it. He always knew that was going to be his field of study because of the open position that was waiting for him at his father's company after graduation, but he wasn't really sure that marketing is what he was meant to be doing for the rest of his life.

"So what do you think you should be doing other than working at your father's marketing company?" I asked, fully interested in learning what else his desires might be.

"You know, when I was younger I loved to draw. I always wanted to build things. Bridges, buildings, houses … even just drawing people's faces, or bodies, or general objects ... I loved it. I would draw a building or a house on paper and I would always think ... one day I'm going to make what I draw. I always wanted to do something like that, but like I said, I knew it would never happen because I always knew that I would take over my father's company one day. Don't get me wrong, I love doing what I'm doing now ... it's just ... I feel differently about it. When I had a vision in my head of what I wanted to draw and then I drew it ... that feeling was *unbelievable*."

"Wow, Liam. I know you said you like doing what you're doing now, but the sound of your voice when you talk about drawing ... Do you still draw?"

"Not as much as I used to. Just a few things here and there. I actually have something I'm working on now though. I've also designed most of the tattoos that I have. I'm working on a new one of those too." After he said that he became silent for a while.

I looked at him, and it looked as if he was lost in thought. Maybe he was thinking about what he was working on. Or maybe he was just thinking about how much he told me and how much he revealed about himself. Whether he realized it or not Liam was very passionate about drawing – more than marketing, I think.

I have many things I want to ask him about his drawings and his career now, but I don't. I couldn't bring myself to say anything and ruin what I was seeing.

Enjoying his face and the silence, I found myself thinking about his drawings some more, wishing he didn't have his suit on so I could study his tattoos in even greater depth than I already had. To know that he designed most of his tattoos, it makes me believe that each tattoo must have a very deep meaning for him. He's not someone who inked his skin for the hell of it, or because it would make him look cool or something like that. I wanted to know the reasons behind all of them. I wanted to see each and every single one, especially the ones that were hidden underneath his shirt. I wondered how many he actually had, and where they all were. I just didn't know how to go about saying I wanted to see them all, without it turning into something else.

When he came back from whatever place he was visiting in his mind, he had a few more questions for me. He asked about my favorite movie, favorite television show, favorite book, favorite flower, favorite type of food, favorite type of music, and such things as: do I prefer cats or dogs, hot or cold, summer or winter, and so on. He asked me things you would probably ask someone on a first date.

It actually *was* starting to feel like a date.

Then Connor came back to the table, and I quickly realized that there is no way a date would *ever* include Connor.

"Your break is up Sam. It's probably almost time for Prince Charming to get back too."

"Hey Connor, Samantha was telling me that you work out of Engine 2. So does my best friend, Ryan Flannery. You know him?"

"No shit. Are you kidding me right now? You're friends with Ryan?" Connor seemed a little disturbed by finding out this news. It was probably because of everything he had mentioned in passing about 'that guy Ryan who works at the Firehouse.'

"Yeah ... he's been my best-friend since middle-school." Liam hesitated a little with his response. I guess he could sense that maybe telling Connor that Ryan was his best friend wasn't as good of a thing as he thought it would be.

"No shit. Your *best-friend*? Since middle-school? *And you want to fucking date my sister?* No fucking way."

"Connor! Are you kidding me?" I was completely mortified.

117

"What? I'm just saying. He keeps coming in here, practically panting after you, and let's not pretend I didn't hear him before or when he came in the other day … or *shit*, I heard a few things he said before when you were alone too. My God. And now he's best-friends with Ryan *fucking* Flannery? There is no way this shit is happening." If I thought I was mortified a few seconds ago, it was nothing like I was now.

"*What is that supposed to mean?* What's wrong with Ryan? And seriously, I don't think you get a say in whether or not Samantha goes out with me. She's a big fucking girl who can make up her own mind."

I didn't know what to say to being put in the spot I was put in. I didn't like how either one of them was talking to the other, or how they were talking about me. I needed to stand up for myself and say something.

I ended up making a strangled sound in my throat. When the fuck did I become a woman who couldn't speak up for herself? Shit.

"Let me ask you a question Liam. Do you have a sister?"

"Yes." Liam responded slowly to that question, not sure where the change in topic was going. Neither was I.

"Does she have a boyfriend, Liam?"

"*No*, she doesn't have a boyfriend, Connor."

"Okay then. How old is she?"

What the fuck?

"She's twenty-one. Why?" Yes, seriously, why are you asking these things Connor?

"Perfect. Why don't you bring your sister out on this magic date that you want my sister to go on with you … *you know*, the date that she can go on because she's such a big girl and all – because she doesn't need anyone looking out for her or anything like that – *yeah*, you bring your sister and Sam will bring me, and you can then know what this shit I'm seeing and hearing feels like."

Connor really must be going off the rails.

Liam was quick to respond, though I don't know how he was, because I was still trying to wrap my head around what Connor had just said.

Did any of that even make sense?

What did he just say exactly?

"Yeah, that's not gonna happen."

"*Why not?* I want to make sure you're nothing like Ryan Flannery, and I can't have my baby sister going out with you until I know that you are *nothing* like him."

"What is your deal with Ryan, dude? I think you have Ryan pegged totally wrong, man. I've known him since middle school. Like I said, he's my best-friend."

"Yeah, he is also someone I wouldn't trust anywhere near my sister."

Liam seemed to think about it. He started to shake his head, but then he stopped. I was surprised when I heard him say, "Fair enough."

"I still plan on taking out your sister though." Liam was adamant about that, and he was no nonsense when he said it to Connor.

"Yeah … and I was fucking serious about taking out yours. So it seems like we have a fucking problem here." Connor had crossed his arms, and he was not backing down one inch. Even though what he was insisting on was completely stupid. He didn't know Liam's sister. He would never be able to get her to go out with him.

"You've got to be fucking joking. She's not even in town. Even if she was, I would never agree to someone like you taking her out on a date."

As soon as the words were out of his mouth, he knew exactly what he had said.

"See! I fucking knew it! You wouldn't trust your sister with someone like me, but I'm supposed to trust someone like *you* with mine? Get the fuck out of here." If Connor knew he wouldn't look like a tool punching his fist up in the air in victory, I'm sure that he would've done it.

It looked like for the first time, Liam was actually uncomfortable. He played right into Connor's hand.

He didn't say anything for a bit. Surprisingly neither did Connor. It looked like Liam was thinking something over. He actually closed his eyes and looked down for a few seconds and when I heard him inhale kind of deeply, I knew I wasn't going to like what he had to say before he even started talking again.

"I cannot believe I am going to say this … but maybe you're right. Maybe all of us going out wouldn't be such a bad thing. That way you could see I'm a good guy – *not that anything you think should fucking matter* – but I seriously don't need you as a goddamn problem in my relationship with Samantha. Something tells me that you can, and *will*, be a problem for me if you don't get your goddamn way. I wouldn't normally care about you and what you have to say, but I can tell that all of this is affecting Sam … and I don't fucking like that. Maybe it's best if we all do go out. I just don't know if Riley would be onboard with this. Not to mention, your sister, who looks like she is ready to nut punch both of us, doesn't seem to be onboard with your idea either. She hasn't even agreed to go on a date with me yet, and now you want the four of us to all go out together? Holy fuck, this whole thing isn't good."

Liam couldn't be more right. This whole situation was completely and totally fucked up. What the fuck did Connor just create? What the fuck had Liam agreed to? Why the fuck do I feel like I am being strung along? And what the fuck am I even about to say to all of this shit?

Nobody said anything for a while.

Then I said, "Okay."

Connor and Liam both looked at me. It was the first time I had spoken in a really long time, and even though they were both talking *about* me, it was almost as if they forgot that I was even here.

Liam was the first to respond to what I had said.

"What?"

"I said okay. If Riley agrees, and if it actually gets Connor off of our backs and out of our business ... as messed up as all of this is, if she agrees to go ... I'm in. I'll go out with you."

"Seriously, Red? Like that? You'll go out on a date with me like *that*? With your brother, *and* my sister?" He sounded baffled, and a little confused.

Why was he baffled and confused?

Did he not just agree with Connor that his stupid date thing wasn't such a bad idea? Why am I the one who gets looked at like I shouldn't have said what I did?

"Yes." Screw it. I'm standing my ground.

"Jesus Christ," was all he said.

"Holy fuck ... really, Samantha?" was what Connor said.

"Really? It was your idea." Seriously. It was his idea. What the hell is wrong with these two?

"Yeah, but I didn't think you would go for it. I was thinking you'd give up on the whole thing between you two after you figured out I'd be a dick and never let this go, and after you thought about how awful of an idea it actually was ... *But a date it is then*. What's your sister look like, Prince Charming?"

Connor didn't know when to just stop.

"You have got to be fucking kidding me. If she even agrees to go, you better not even so much as look at her the wrong way." Liam didn't know when to let it go either.

"I just can't even go there with this dude," Connor said to me while pointing his thumb and shaking his head at Liam.

"Let me know what you guys decide, I'm going back up front. I can't take any more of this shit." With that Connor left. He fucking left after detonating my day into a thousand pieces.

"I am so sorry Liam. I honestly don't know what to say."

"Me either. Truthfully, a part of me wants to thank Connor because you actually agreed to go out with me … but really, Red? I just don't fucking know. What the hell just happened?" Liam just shook his head.

"I have to get back to work. Just know, this conversation is nowhere near being over. We really need to talk about it. I'm going to call you as soon as I get home today. Holy. Shit. This was not at all what I was expecting when I came here today. So much for going over the basics, huh? There was absolutely *nothing* basic about today. Jesus, I'll just talk to you later. Bye, Samantha."

With that being said, he grabbed up his things and headed towards the door.

The door he just walked out of.

I followed his exit like always, but he didn't turn around and wink at me. Why not? Was he angry at what just happened? Was he upset with me? Disgusted? Royally pissed off at Connor *and* me? He would have every right to be, though he did kind of agree with Connor first. If anyone should be pissed off in this scenario it should rightfully be me.

I kept watching him, seeing that he was coming down the sidewalk in front of where we had been sitting. I was looking at him, but he was looking at the ground. I was completely disappointed, but then he stopped right in front of me on the other side of the window. It was like he knew exactly when to stop and that I would still be sitting there watching, waiting. He looked at me, his eyes catching mine, and then he smiled at me, right before he *winked*. I felt the smile take over my face before he turned away to keep on walking.

"Did he just seriously fucking wink at you?"

Connor.

I felt my shoulders slump.

Of course he came back to where I was sitting once Liam left the shop.

I refused to acknowledge him but that didn't stop him from coming closer, or from speaking to me again.

"I'm sorry Sam, okay? I'm just trying to look out for you. I tried to be fine with the guy … but *holy fuck*, he's Ryan's friend? Ryan? The stuff that guys done … the things I've seen and heard. Shit, Sam. I needed a way to make sure that Liam's not like him, and I don't know what happened – those words just came out of my mouth about his sister and the date, and everything. I know you're old enough to make your own decisions, I know I said I would stay out of it and let you handle things … but when I heard about Ryan … I don't know Sam, I just lost it."

I didn't know what to think about any of this.

Connor put way too many thoughts in my head.

He now has me wondering about Liam's friend Ryan and what Ryan has done. Even worse, Connor has me now thinking if Liam is anything like his friend – a friend that Connor has a major problem with.

Did I seriously just think a few minutes ago that there was no way a date would *ever* include Connor?

"*What the fuck did you just do Connor?*"

"Christ, Sam. I really don't fucking know."

Chapter 10

Fucking Connor! As if I didn't have enough things to worry about with Liam before, Connor just had to add to the ever-growing list by introducing new thoughts into my head – like Liam's vast wealth of experience with the opposite sex. I knew that Liam was a twenty-five year old man, who looked like every girl's version of the ultimate sexy bad-boy with his tattoos and muscles and his unbelievable smirk and dimples, and also every girl's version of a smooth talking millionaire with his tailored suits and expensive ties, not to mention his position at one of the best marketing firms in the country, so I subconsciously knew that he had to have had a lot of experience beforehand.

I mean, I was even thinking about him with other women when we had the whole conversation about breakfast in bed.

I just didn't equate his experience to that of Ryan's. The things I know about Ryan and what he's done – it's all too much. I don't think Connor meant to say some of the things Ryan had done in front of me that one night we were out. We had been out drinking with a group of our friends, and he was bullshitting with the guys, telling them stories about some people he knew … one of which was Ryan. If he had known that I was paying attention to him and not the girls we were with, I know for a fact he wouldn't have said half of what he did. I kind of wish now that I didn't hear anything that he *did* say.

I, more than anyone, should know that you shouldn't judge a person by the friends that they keep. At times Allie could definitely be a bit of a party-girl, and I was anything but that, and look at the whole thing with Aiden and me. I couldn't have picked two friends who were my complete opposite more than Allie and Aiden. Even knowing all that, I just couldn't help but wonder: exactly how close was Liam's character to that of the disgusting character of his good friend Ryan? I was completely obsessed with that question from the moment that Liam left the shop, until right now.

I don't know why I was getting myself so worked up over something I would never have an answer to, because it's not like I could come out and ask Liam when I finally talked to him. I was supposed to only be his friend. Even if I wanted to be more than his friend it's not like I had any right to question him about what he did before me. Right? I can't imagine asking him to discuss everything he's done with women before he met me. I don't think I would want to know *all* of it anyway even if he wanted to talk about it. I think it would drive me bat-shit crazy to know every little thing. Couples don't really divulge shit like that to one another, do they?

For hours I couldn't turn my brain away from this topic.

I still can't.

I just keep thinking about Ryan's dirty deeds, and what possible dirty deeds are hidden in Liam's past. Holy hell. *Fucking Connor!*

This is all his goddamn fault.

****

As the hours ticked by it got worse – *I got worse.*

At about 6:45 I started staring at my phone, just waiting for it to ring. I knew that Liam didn't live far from work, so I knew that he should be calling any minute. He seemed as eager to finish our conversation from lunch as I did, he told me as much before he left the café. When I heard the dings letting me know I had a text message, I snatched the phone off of the coffee table to see if it was Liam.

Thank God it was.

I couldn't take much more of this waiting around bullshit.

Liam: Hey, Red. I got stuck with a last minute project, so I'm still at work. I had to sneak away from the boardroom so I could send you this text. I don't know when I'll be home ... I know I said I'd call you when I got home ... but I have no idea when that'll be.

This had to be a freaking joke. I waited hours to talk to him and he's stuck at work? I needed to talk to him and see how he felt about everything that had gone on during lunch. I needed to know how he felt about the "date," and if he still wanted to even bother. I had so *many* things to discuss with him, and now this? Screw it, I don't care how late he gets home, we need to talk.

Me: Thanks for letting me know ... But I still want to talk to you. Best guess on when you'll be home?

I'd wait all night if I had to. I needed to know that everything was okay – that we were okay. I don't know when I became this needy woman who needed reassurances, but in this moment I am and I do.

Liam: I don't know. My father wants me to lead one of his new projects, so I'm here going over all the info with him and a few others. I'm trying to figure out who I want on my team. It's a very important project, so I need to get caught up on everything and hit the ground running. I wish I could tell you when I'd be home, to see if it would be alright to call you, because I really want to talk to you, Red ... I just don't know.

When I heard the beeps of his responding text, I knew it didn't matter what it was going to say. I knew if he said four in the morning I'd still want him to call me. So responding was quick and simple enough.

Me: It doesn't matter. Call me anyway.

Liam: You sure?

Me: Positive. Doesn't matter what time.

Liam: Alright, then. I'm happy that you said that, Red. I can't wait to hear your voice. I have to get back now. Talk to you later.

I didn't say anything back. Truth is, I couldn't wait to hear his voice either, but I wasn't ready to say things like that to him yet. Things like that are completely new to me.

I wonder how easy it is for him to be saying things like that to *me*.

Did he say things like that to women all the time? How many other voices has he wanted to hear?

Is it only my voice right now? He said there wasn't anyone else – that he wasn't *involved* with anyone else.

How involved has he been with others before me though?

Can I ask him that?

That was probably a question I could ask him at some point. There was nothing sexual about that.

It's not like I would be asking him how many women he's slept with, or if he's slept with more than one at the same time. It's not like I would be asking if he had multiple relationships at once, and if he slept with each partner at the same time as well. It's not like I would be asking him where he's done it, or how's he done it – nothing like that.

Jesus, and now I'm back to comparing him to Ryan and what I've heard.

I knew it was going to be an extremely long wait for him to finally get home and call me.

****

It was after midnight when I heard my cell phone ringing. It was on the nightstand next to my bed, so I put my book down and picked it up. I knew he would be calling, but hearing his ringtone made me smile anyway. It was hard turning off the thoughts in my head before, but with a good book I was able to forget about things for a little while. Now it looked like I was back in the world of reality.

I answered my phone.

"Hey, Liam. Finally home?" I'd hate to think that he was still at work, calling me only to tell me that he's sorry and can't talk to me like he'd said he would.

"Yeah, Red. I'm finally home. I didn't wake you did I?"

I could hear him doing something on the other end of the line. I imagined him taking off his suit jacket, his tie, maybe unbuttoning his shirt and taking it off. *Jesus.*

With the image of him in my head removing his clothes, I responded a little too breathily. "No you didn't wake me up. I was actually reading a really good book."

God, could I sound any more depressing? I'm a twenty-three year old college student who couldn't find anything better to do late at night than read a book? Why couldn't I have lied and come up with something better – something more interesting.

Shit. I'm not worrying about any of that right now. Liam told me he liked to read too. He didn't seem to have a problem with me not having an active social life. Why should I have a problem with it all of a sudden, and besides, it's a weekday after midnight. What should I be doing? What would he have been doing right now if he didn't just get home from work?

"Reading, huh? Well I'm glad I didn't wake you up. Though I must say, I wouldn't have minded hearing what your sexy sleepy voice sounds like."

"How do you even know my sleepy voice would sound sexy?" I just had to ask.

"Red, haven't you figured it out by now? I find everything about you sexy. There is no doubt in my mind your sleep voice would be sexy too. I thought we went over all of this before? Remember? Everything about you gets to me. Why do you think that is?"

When I didn't say anything Liam said, "I'll tell you, Red. It's because I think you're pretty freaking perfect."

Holy shit, he can't be serious.

"Liam, not to burst your bubble or anything, but you don't know that much about me to say you think I'm perfect. Trust me, I am anything but that."

I am so far from perfect.

Liam hasn't known me long enough to understand just how unbelievably imperfect I actually am.

"You know, Red, you may be right ..."

Um, what now? Even though it's not true that I'm perfect, you can't take something like that back!

"You do have an annoying ass brother ... and he's obviously a part of the Samantha package ... so you may be right. You *definitely* aren't perfect."

I just shook my head at what he said, even though I knew he couldn't see me.

See, I've been saying it all my life – *Fucking Connor*.

Liam started to laugh. I wanted to laugh too, but I couldn't. Liam was right. Connor was very much a part of me and he always would be, regardless of how much I completely hated it sometimes – *most of the times*. Liam stopped laughing, but he didn't stay silent. Instead I heard him breathe in, and then out, deeply.

I knew this was it.

"Seriously though Red, we need to talk about your brother and everything that happened today."

"I know," I said quietly.

"First, I think we need to clear up a few things. You said that I don't know you, and it's true that I don't know every little thing about you, but I do know some things. I got to know quite a bit about you during lunch I think. I found out some of your likes and dislikes. I found out a lot of your favorite things. I think I'm also beginning to be quite adept at figuring out your moods just by looking at your facial expressions, or a few of the gestures that you make. I think I know you more than any other woman I've known, for a very long time. I know more about you than most of the women I have been with, and I haven't even touched you yet."

He stopped talking. I wasn't sure if it was because he was done saying what he wanted to say, or because he realized what he had just said.

Other women?

He hasn't touched me … yet?

I knew that I should really say something back to him instead of letting there be an awkward silence, but what does one say when a guy they are starting to become interested in as way more than friends, starts talking about themselves with other women? Not to mention he's talking about touching me …what the hell do I say to that?

"With you not saying anything, I'm gonna take a wild guess and say that you don't like hearing about me with other women."

I knew this time I had to speak up, and not stay silent during a difficult conversation, like I did before when Connor was making plans to go on a date with us and ruin my life.

"No, I don't. But ever since lunch, and what Connor said about Ryan … Jesus Liam, I had already heard a few things about Ryan from my brother. Then when I found out you knew him – but not only that, that he's your *best-friend* – I can't help but wonder how much you two are alike … and now you're talking about yourself with other women … it's a little too much. So, *no*, Liam, I don't like it. I especially don't like that I haven't been able to think of anything but that, since this afternoon."

Yes, I blurted out the fact that I didn't like hearing about him with other women, and that I've been wondering how much he and Ryan are alike for hours now.

So much for my thoughts before on never being able to ask him these types of questions, or being able to talk about certain things.

In all fairness *he* was the one who brought up this topic and headed down this path. For better or worse, I needed to prepare myself, because it looked like we would indeed be talking about stuff like this. At least now anyway.

"Shit … I knew we were going to have to talk about this. I could see all the questions you had for me, plain as day, on your face before Samantha. I told you, in the span of a few short days I'm becoming quite proficient at reading what you're feeling. I guess it would be best to start with Ryan, yeah?"

He asked me like I had a choice over what he was going to say. I don't think anywhere he started with this conversation would be to my liking, but since Ryan had been plaguing my thoughts non-stop, I'm not going to argue if he had something to say about him and his lifestyle and whether or not it reflected his own.

"Yeah."

"Okay, then. First, Ryan and I have been friends since middle school. I've always lived here, but Ryan moved from California with his dad when his mom passed away. We both had that in common, plus we both played sports, so eventually we really hit it off. It was tough for him making friends, being the new kid and all, and being so vastly different with the way he looked and acted. I mean he surfed, had long hair, dressed differently, spoke differently … But we made it work. We've been friends ever since. We both went to the same high school, then the same college – we even live in the same apartment building now.

"Connor wasn't exactly wrong, though. I wouldn't want my sister, or you, anywhere near him if he was interested. He has the ability to charm the pants off of anyone, even the most sane and steadfast person. But he's not a bad guy. He's up front with all of the women he meets, and he normally gravitates towards the women who think the same way he does. I'm not saying that I've agreed one hundred percent with everything he's done, or how he treats all of the women he's with, but I haven't seen or heard anything that suggests that any of the women were displeased with anything that went on. I'm not going to say that he's not into crazy shit, because he is. And to be honest, I'm not comfortable with knowing some of the shit he does or has done, and I'm especially not comfortable talking about it with you. I can only imagine what you've heard from Connor, and most of its probably true, but please trust me when I say that's not all there is to Ryan. For the most part he is misunderstood, and he actually kind of likes it that way. He doesn't let too many people get close to him, so most people don't see the real deal when it comes to who he actually is. Especially not when it comes to his relationships with women."

Liam, took a break from what he was saying to exhale another deep breath, but he continued on, not giving me a chance to say anything in between.

"I also need you to trust me when I say that I am nothing like him. I've had one-night stands in the past, especially when I was in high school and my early years of college, but I haven't been that way in a while. Even when I was that way, I was never with a girl who didn't know that it would be a one-time thing, and I made sure that they were okay with it. Over the past few years, I've had a few women who I've been intimate with, but I knew them for a while first. I don't want to sound like a dick, especially not with you, because I think we might be going somewhere here – *I really fucking hope we are going somewhere* – but I need to be honest with you.

"Like I said, I've been intimate with women in the past few years, but I don't think that I've been in a relationship with any of them. I knew them, yes. But not enough for me to say I was in a relationship, or that I was committed. Even with that being the case though, I never cheated on them. If I was seeing someone casually I would never hook-up with anyone else until I let the other person know we were through."

Liam stopped for a moment before he continued on speaking, not really giving me enough time to process everything he was saying. I really felt like I needed time to process everything.

I didn't get that time though because what he said next really grabbed my attention.

"Lately, there hasn't been anyone at all. Not for months actually. And then I saw you. *I saw you, Red*. And all I want now is a relationship. I told you before, I haven't even held your hand or touched you in any way, and yet all I want to do is claim you and make you realize that we need to be so much more than friends. I don't know what it fucking is. *I sure as fuck don't understand any of it*, but you are so very different Samantha. *In the best possible way*. Every single thing about you, and what I want with you, is different. I knew it that first day, and I know it now ... and I really hope you don't disappear on me because of what I just told you, because I don't think I could willingly let you disappear from my life. I can't believe I'm saying this shit to you – I've probably fucking scared you with all of this. Believe me, normally I would've never brought up all the things I've said during this conversation ... we would've never talked about any of this, unless you brought it up and wanted to talk about it ... but like I said, I knew some things needed to be discussed after what happened before with Connor ... And ... *Jesus* ... *Holy fuck!* I seriously can't believe I just talked about all of that, and said all of that."

"Did I just blow it? Seriously ... Did I just blow it, Red? You need to talk to me now."

"Um, Liam?"

I heard a really loud inhale, then another long exhale. Then, "Yeah, Red?"

"I really don't want to talk about Ryan or your past experiences anymore."

Truthfully, compared to what I had envisioned about his past sexual experiences in my head, his experiences didn't appear to be as varied as I'd imagined. Sure, I know he didn't tell me every little detail, but I believed him when he said he wasn't like Ryan, and that the things in his past weren't as bad as what I'd been thinking.

I'm not naïve though. I knew he had been around the block a time or two, or twenty. Just as long as he hasn't been around the block hundreds of times exploring each and every single sight along the way, I was okay with it.

I was especially okay with what he said about me. A few days ago I would have been upset by what he said. I probably *would* have been running in the other direction because of how he was making me feel. After learning how much I get to him, and now knowing that he wants a relationship with me, *and* how I am different for him in a very good way … *all of that* mixed in with the way *he* makes *me* feel … I think I flew way past friendship and landed into falling hard.

I know I should be scared.

I should be *absolutely* scared.

I have no idea what I'm doing. I told myself over and over I didn't want any part of this. On so many levels I know that this whole thing could blow up in my face and leave me more devastated than I have ever been. I should be worried about our differences. I should be worried about all of the things I haven't told him about my own past yet, and about finding out all of the other things I don't know about him – and yet I'm not. Like I said, this whole thing could blow up in my face and leave me fucking shattered, and right now I don't give a shit. He said he wanted me, and he wants me in such a way that he hasn't wanted anyone else before.

I know I should be shouting friends, friends, friends, to myself, but I want to see where this goes with Liam. Just like he wants to see where this goes with me. I still want to be his friend. I want that foundation to be present in our relationship. But I also want so much more than that.

I want everything.

"You really don't want to talk about it anymore?" he asked. I could hear the worry in his voice. He must have really thought he said something that was pushing me away. He couldn't be more wrong.

"No, I really don't."

There was another pause. This pause was more significant than the others. This pause felt weighted. It felt like a moment in time that stops, right before you encounter something of importance.

"Is that a good thing, or a bad thing, that you don't want to talk about it anymore, Red?"

"It's a good thing, Liam. A *really, really*, good thing." I knew there was no way he could miss the smile that was reflected in my voice.

Once again, I heard another very loud and long exhale. I also could have sworn I heard a 'Thank fucking God' in there, but I couldn't be sure.

Whatever.

Thank fucking God indeed.

****

"So now that we're done with that, how did everything go at work? Did you get everything done?" I asked Liam.

"You really, completely, want to move on? You don't want to talk about Connor and the date?"

"I know we have to talk about that, I was just curious about how your night went, and I wanted to ask you about it first. So, anyway, does that happen to you a lot? Working late, heading up new projects? Sneaking away to send out texts?" I really shouldn't have added that last part in there, but I did anyway.

I never expected him to answer that part of the question. I was wrong.

"Let's see … First, I don't ever sneak away to send out texts. I've never particularly had a reason to. Nothing, and nobody, has ever been important enough to have me sneaking around like a criminal texting in secrecy. Seriously Red, if it was anyone else I wouldn't have bothered to let them know I'd be late. It sounds dickish I know, but it's the truth. I would've waited until it was convenient for me to make a call. Like I said though, you're different. To answer the other questions you had … no the working late thing doesn't normally happen a lot, or at least it didn't. These next few weeks though, it'll probably be crazy. I guess since I plan on spending quite a bit of time with you, and I plan on talking to you all the time, I should warn you that I'll be working some weird and annoyingly long hours. Hopefully that's okay with you. I'm normally never in this position. This is the first time my father is trusting me enough to take the lead on this type of a project.

"I told you before, he's letting me select my own team, and come up with my own ideas – *basically* he's giving me free rein. It really is a big opportunity for me, especially because I am so new to the company and don't have much experience, not to mention my father owns the company and I feel like I have a lot to prove to so many people. I can handle it though, it's just going to take a lot of hard work and a lot of long hours. I can't wait to tell my sister though. Riley is going to flip when I tell her that Dad gave me this account. Speaking of Riley, Red, I talked to her before …"

"That's pretty sweet that your dad's trusting you with a major project of your own. I'm sure you will kill it. Fair warning back … I plan on spending time with you too … and talking and texting, but I don't need you getting in trouble or hiding away to talk to me. I don't want to take you away from anything you need to be doing …"

"See, you're not understanding me here, Red. I need to be talking to you. I told you that you're important. I mean it. I don't care what I have going on, I will make time for you, even if it means sending out a text just to say hello. Got that?"

"Okay, Liam. Got it." What else could I possibly say to that? He's telling me I'm important and that he needs to talk to me.

"So anyway, I appreciate your vote of confidence in believing that I will kill it on my project, and I love that you agreed that you plan on spending all various types of time with me as well, but don't think I didn't notice how you cut me off when I brought up Riley."

Shit. Here it comes.

"So, I told her about the date ..."

I cut him off again.

"Wait! I need to ask ... How mad are you that Connor basically forced you into agreeing with him?"

"Shouldn't I be asking you that, Red? How mad are you? I know why I said yes, but I'm not really sure why you did. I know you said it was to get Connor off of our backs, but it seemed like more. Also, while you're at it, how mad are you about the way I was acting with Connor?"

"Seriously? Connor deserved everything you said to him, and more. He's an asshole at times, and he takes things too far, but in this instance he does have his reasons. I wouldn't say I am angry over the way Connor forced us into this though. I don't like it, and I can't believe we both agreed to it, but I actually understand it. I wish I could say I have no idea why Connor did it, but I do ... at least I think I do.

It was my turn to pause and take a deep breath before continuing.

"There's a situation in my past where Connor was wrong about someone. It's something I blamed him for, and something he blamed himself for, for a really long time. It doesn't matter if he thinks a person is

139

good or bad, he doesn't seem to fully trust his instincts when it comes to me and anyone else in my life, so he takes every situation overboard. As much as I hate it –and him sometimes when he does the things that he does, especially when he embarrasses me beyond reason – I know why he does it."

Once again I found myself inhaling and exhaling deeply, like Liam was before when he was telling me things about his past.

"I'm sure you want to ask me about it, but I can't get into it right now. I'm still not ready yet. I meant what I said to you the other day though … I do plan on telling you these things … but not right now. Just know that as much as you might hate the way Connor forced you into this, he did it for a reason."

"Okay, Samantha. I also meant it when I said that I wouldn't pressure you or force you into telling me anything until you're ready, but I'm thinking maybe you might want to consider that telling me sooner, rather than later, might be the best thing for both of us."

"I've been doing a whole lot of thinking about that lately, Liam. I'm working on it," I told him honestly.

"Well then, that's good enough for me. By the way, Riley said she would go. After I told her about the whole situation, she said she'd make sure she made the time to go out with us. She said she couldn't wait to meet Connor, 'the guy who pulled one over on me, or his sister, the girl who must be special enough that I'm putting up with all this shit for.' Her words, not mine. I think I would put up with anything for you. Even Connor, obviously."

"Oh, God. This is really going to be a disaster, huh?"

"Maybe not so much. There is a silver-lining that I am thoroughly looking forward to. I can't wait until Connor sees – and actually *meets* – Riley. He won't know what fucking hit him. That alone right there might be reason enough to go along peacefully with this whole group date thing. Actually … just thinking about those two … it might end up being a pretty fucking *awesome* idea."

"Seriously? Somehow I don't think that would be a good enough reason to still want to go on this date, Liam."

"You haven't met Riley yet, Red. Trust me, it's a great reason."

I heard some rustling around on his end again. Before when I heard that noise I pictured him undressing and getting comfortable after a long day of work. It felt like hours ago, but in reality it was less than a half hour. A lot had happened in a half hour. A lot had changed. Especially for me.

I was getting ready to speak again when he said nothing for a long time, but he beat me to it.

"Seriously Samantha, I meant what I said before I left *The Brew*. I don't like that we have to do it this way, but I am happy that you agreed to go on a date with me at all. I'll take a date with you any way I can get it."

"Yeah … when I first met you, I never thought I would ever agree to go on a date with you, and definitely not a date that includes my brother and your sister …" I let that comment linger for a while, hoping that he was as smart as I thought he was and that he would get the hint.

He *was* as smart as I thought he was.

"And now? What do you think now?" He asked me, in a voice that sounded so sensual I knew my cheeks were about to flood with the color he appreciated so much.

"Ask me."

"Samantha … Will you go on a date with me?"

"I'd love to." I meant every word of it. I would love to go out with him. "When?"

"I'd say right fucking now if I thought you would agree to it, and if there were any decent places still open."

I started to laugh. I couldn't help it. I just might have agreed if he asked me to go right now, and I wouldn't have cared in the least bit if we went to a decent place or not.

"How about Saturday, Red? Do you work on Saturday?"

"Nope. I have the day off. Saturday's perfect. What did you have in mind?"

Now that we set a date, I couldn't wait to go.

"I'm not sure yet. I want to think about it for a bit, if that's okay?"

"That's fine."

"I'm glad we had this talk Samantha. I'm really glad that we cleared up a lot of things, and I am *fucking thrilled* that you are going out with me, without Connor and Riley."

"Yeah, me too."

"I wish I could stay up all night and talk to you, but I think I need to go grab some food, jump in the shower, and get to sleep. Tomorrow is going to be an extremely long day for me. Do you work tomorrow?"

"Yes I do. Same hours as today … well, yesterday now."

"Yesterday … right. So, *today* is going to be a long day for me then. I don't know if I'll get the chance to see you later, but no matter what I'll text you or call you. No sneaking around though, I promise."

I had to laugh again.

"Okay."

"Well … Good-night Samantha. Sweet dreams."

"Good-night, Liam."

Once I hung up my phone, I knew that I would definitely be having sweet dreams.

How could I not? Liam put some of my worst fears at ease regarding his past experiences with women. He told me I was important to him and that he wants me in ways I can't even fathom yet. He asked me out on a real, actual, date. He's also not backing out of Connor's forced date because he knows what it means to me to have him keep it, even if he has to deal with Connor by doing so.

Seriously ... how could I not have sweet dreams?

Even dealing with all of these new feelings doesn't scare me. I'm loving them.

I would definitely be having sweet dreams.

I hope he did too.

Chapter 11

Liam wasn't kidding when he said he would be working crazy hours, and that he didn't know if he would be able to see me before Saturday. I didn't see him at all Wednesday after we made plans in the early morning hours to go on our first official date, and I didn't see him on Thursday either. He also wasn't kidding when he said he would make it a point to at least call or text me. He did both a few times a day, especially at night when he came home from work when we would sit and talk with each other for what seemed like hours.

What was funny was that I was so adamant that he wouldn't be sneaking around to text me while he was at work, and yet it turned out that it was actually *me* who ended up sneaking around instead. Each time my phone signaled that I had a new text, I had to make sure Connor wasn't anywhere near me before I looked to see what Liam had said.

I really couldn't wait for Connor to go back to the Firehouse. He was constantly asking me about the date with Liam and Riley. I didn't tell him that I knew Riley would go, because I didn't want to get into a conversation about how much I had been talking to Liam.

I think Connor was secretly pleased that Liam didn't come into the shop since Tuesday – he probably thought his plan to trap us into an awkward date had scared Liam off. Connor couldn't have been more wrong.

If he only knew what Liam and I had planned for Saturday.

I couldn't talk to him about any of it though. I knew that there would never be a simple conversation with Connor about Liam, at least until Connor got to know Liam enough to trust him. Even then, he would probably still give me a whole bunch of shit and would only trust Liam as far as he could throw him.

Over the course of each conversation that I had with Liam, I got to know him a little better. Each time I found out a little more about him, his family, his friends, and also more about his job.

What constantly surprised me about him is how completely wrong I was when I first initially saw him and talked to him. I learned that appearances could definitely be deceiving. He did have all the qualities that I'd assumed he possessed the first time I met him: he was playful, and cocky, smooth, and definitely *all* man. He was also very polished and intelligent, powerful and authoritative, as well as caring and intuitive. What was surprising though was how much he revealed to me about his feelings. I didn't think by his outward appearance, with all his muscles and his tattoos, and especially his smug smirk, that he would have told me that I get to him, that he can't see anyone else because he is too busy seeing only me and is interested in only me, or that he would tell me he hasn't been with a woman in months and that he wants to have something more with me than he's had with anyone else. Those words and feelings that come from inside Liam do not match up to what is on the exterior of him.

The whole package of him is truly amazing, and confusing, and so much more than I had imagined.

I am still trying to figure him out.

Something tells me I will always be trying to figure him out.

Each day I am thankful that he didn't give up on me, and that I didn't miss out on the chance to get to know someone like him when I tried to ignore him, or when I acted snotty and dismissive, or especially when I freaked out on him a few times. I tried to ignore him because of the tattoos and the muscles and the smirk, because I thought that there would be nothing of substance underneath. I also thought he would be too much like Aiden. How completely and utterly wrong I had been on both accounts.

Each time I talked to him, I actually enjoyed finding out all of the little things I was wrong about. I just wished I had more time with him to do so. I realized in the past few days how completely lucky I was that I didn't talk myself out of getting to know him. For as much as I tried to get rid of him, I also tried to stay away. If I had succeeded in staying away, all of what I'm beginning to enjoy and look forward to would have been non-existent, and that's something that's just too unbelievably sad to think about.

Even with all of the time we were missing out on, at least I had our date to look forward to. I still didn't know where we were going, but Liam assured me that he had everything planned and under control. I must have asked him about it twenty times in the past few days, but he wouldn't budge and give me even the tiniest clue. All I knew was that it was casual, and that I should be ready by 6:30. Those two things didn't help me much. For as much as I was excited to go out with him, not knowing anything about such an important night was making me a bit nervous. Not seeing him the past few days and only having limited contact with him was also playing into the fact that I was increasingly becoming a bundle of nerves.

Working at the shop was only keeping my thoughts in check when I was actually busy helping customers, but when I wasn't busy the chaotic mess in my mind was front and center.

I can't believe that in such a short period of time not only did my attitude change about wanting to only be his friend, but I let something such as a date consume my life. Ever since I started to realize that my feelings for Liam were growing deeper I wanted to spend more time with him, not less. It just looked like for the foreseeable future that wouldn't be happening, so I had to look forward to what I was able to get from him each day. Today sucked though. I haven't heard from him at all which is unusual.

Apparently he must've been really busy, and didn't get the chance to sneak away to let me know … *even though I completely didn't want him to have to do that type of thing, and made him promise not to.*

Jesus!

When, how, and why did I turn into someone who acts like this?

****

The when, of when I turned into the type of person who needs the guy they may or may not be seeing to call them, would probably be the first time I saw Liam if I'm being honest. I don't know that exactly, but I do know that Liam is changing everything for me that I thought I knew about myself. The how, I have no idea, other than to say it must be because of some inhuman super-secret power that Liam has. He must have some weird hold over me that makes me want to do nothing but talk to him and see him, and act like I am a fifteen year old girl who is obsessed over some guy. It has to be him, because I swear I don't think I had anything willingly to do with any of this teenage-girl garbage.

The *why*, of why I am acting like this all of a sudden ... *is currently standing right in front of me!*

I didn't expect to see him.

I was just upset that he hadn't called me yet today, and I was just going over in my mind the fact that I was acting like a whiny schoolgirl about it – completely surprising myself that I would *ever* be acting in such a way – and now here he is.

And now I know why I'm acting the way that I am.

How could I not?

"Hey there, Red," he said, smiling at me in such a way that I knew he was happy to see me. It wasn't a cocky smile, or one of his grins or smirks. It was a smile that told me he was just as happy as I was that he was here.

I couldn't do anything other than smile back and say, "Hi, Liam." I thought he would stop smiling after we got the 'hellos' out of the way but he didn't stop smiling, and because of that I didn't either.

"I was wondering when I would be talking to you today." It was more like I had been obsessing over why he hadn't texted or called yet, and more like worrying about how much of a hypocrite I was becoming, but he didn't need to know any of that. "I'm really happy that I get the chance to talk to you in person," I said instead.

"I know, me too. We're just as busy today at work as the last few days, but I needed to get out of there for a few minutes. I really wanted a decent cup of coffee, so I decided to come here. Seeing you is a bonus though." I don't doubt for a minute that he wanted the coffee, but I could tell by his smile before, and the teasing grin that he has on his face now, that I was the reason he came here and the exceptional coffee was the bonus. We both knew the truth.

"So, about this date tomorrow ..." I just couldn't resist asking. *Again.*

"Red, I'm not gonna tell you. Just wear something casual, and be ready at 6:30."

I looked around to make sure Connor wasn't lurking around anywhere. I really didn't feel like dealing with him finding out about our date. Maybe I shouldn't be asking Liam about the date when Connor could pop up at any second. He definitely has a problem with popping up when he's not wanted.

"So, you want your usual? Or do you want something to eat as well?" I asked, because the line was starting to build up, and because I didn't know how long he would be able to stay.

"Yeah, I would really love that coffee, Red. I also wanted to know if you could take a break and sit down with me for a minute."

God, I wanted to do that more than anything, but I just couldn't.

"Liam ... I would like nothing more than to take a break and be able to talk with you some more, but I just got back from my break a little while ago, and Allie's on lunch now. Shit, this sucks –" I couldn't even finish speaking. I was so disappointed with how this ended up turning out.

I was extremely happy to see him not even five minutes before, especially after being upset I hadn't heard from him, and now to know that he wanted to spend some time with me but I couldn't ... the word disappointed doesn't seem to fucking cover it.

"It's okay Red, I get it. I should've called before to see if you wanted to meet up for a few minutes, but I had no idea that I would even be coming here. Like I said, I really needed to get out of there, and the only place I wanted to go was here so I could see you. And I've seen you. Anything more than that is the bonus."

I really don't think I'll ever get used to this man saying things like that.

Words like that – statements like that – expressed feelings like that – they didn't fit with Liam's image, but I was realizing more and more, it was definitely him. Image or not, those words were definitely *all* Liam. From the way he said it I knew he meant it, but it wasn't only that. I knew he wasn't the least bit embarrassed by what he said, because he was more than comfortable with his own feelings. He was as comfortable with his feelings as he was with the tattoos displayed on his body, or with the designer suits that he wore. It was just him.

"So, I'll take that coffee to go then. I guess we can discuss our date that we are going on tomorrow later on when we –"

I immediately cut him off. "What do you mean we can discuss our date that we're going on tomorrow, later?" He had to be fucking kidding me. "You said you weren't going to tell me anything. Literally, you told me a minute ago that you weren't telling me anything, *again.* You haven't told me anything about it any time that I've asked … and I've been asking for days. And now when I can't sit down and talk to you, *that's* what you wanted to talk about? You're joking right? You're joking. You only said something like that because you knew I couldn't sit down with you … you had no intention of talking about the date … you just wanted to drive me crazy, right?" He better have just wanted to drive me crazy, because the alternative is just freaking cruel.

"*No* … I actually did want to talk about a few things regarding our date tomorrow. I definitely didn't plan on revealing where we are going, or what we are doing, but I did have a few things I wanted to ask …" he trailed off. Maybe he decided to stop speaking when he saw the fire shooting out of my eyes that was directed solely at him. How could he do this to me? It really was fucking cruel.

"It wasn't that big of a deal Samantha. We'll still talk about it before tomorrow. What we need to discuss are things I need to know, so I'll make it a point to talk to you about them later, regardless what time I get home. Okay?"

I couldn't help being flippant when I said, "I guess it's gonna have to be, now isn't it? We'll just have to wait and see if I actually answer your questions the same way you've answered mine the past few days, right?"

He must have enjoyed my snippiness because he actually laughed.

"Feisty, Red. I love it."

I guess his verbal response confirmed what I thought. I ignored his comment and turned around to get him his usual coffee. When I turned back around he had his money ready, but I waved him off again.

"I seriously don't want your money for coffee Liam. Anyway, I have to get to my other customers, and I guess you need to be getting back to work. I'll just talk to you later."

"Later, Red." With that simple good-bye he turned around to go. He sauntered away like there wasn't a care in the world, and as if he didn't just completely screw with my afternoon.

The person who was next in line didn't even wait for me to ask them what they would like. She got to the counter and started giving me a list of things including a Caramel Frappuccino, a blueberry muffin, a plain bagel with cream cheese, and so on and so on. She would have to just repeat her order because there was no way I was listening to her drone on and on when I had better things to do.

Seriously ... I needed to focus on Liam walking to the door so I could see his special good-bye.

That 'Later, Red' wasn't going to be cutting it for me. As he got to the door he did turn back, and then he winked.

When he winked at me it was about the same time as the woman in front of me asked, "Did you hear a word I said?" and when the door closed behind him it was the same time in which I replied, "No." The lady got all huffy, but she repeated her order.

I honestly wouldn't have cared if she got so upset that she decided to turn around and leave, taking everyone else in the store along with her. I was in no mood to deal with anyone else today. I just wanted to be done with my shift so I could go home and wait for Liam to call.

I really was starting to be that bad when it came to him.

****

Liam did call once again after midnight. I waited all day to find out what he wanted to discuss about our date, and dealt with the endless loop of various questions that ran through my head. For as much as I was mad that he wanted to finally talk about it before with me when I couldn't, I was also extremely excited to find out what he wanted to talk about. When I found out what he wanted to ask me about, I was back to being disappointed. He only wanted to know my address so he could pick me up, which is something he realized we never talked about, and he wanted to make sure there weren't any types of foods that I didn't like. That was it. I knew nothing more about our date than I did days ago. When I complained about that fact, Liam did nothing but laugh. No matter how sexy his laugh was, in that moment, it truly annoyed me.

But all of that happened hours ago.

I was completely over being upset about not knowing anything about the date, because I was firmly planted in the realm of 'freaking the fuck out' about the date.

It was my first official date – not just with Liam – it was my first official date, *ever*.

I went out with Aiden back in high school, and went out with groups of friends in college, but it was just friends going out. I didn't go on actual dates because I didn't want any guy to get the wrong idea.

It was different with Liam though.

I knew I said "just friends" with Liam, but we both knew that was bullshit, even if neither of us has said it.

This was definitely a date with Liam, and as excited as I'd been the last few days, I was entirely a mess now. It was no longer where are we going, but what should I wear, how should I wear my hair, how much makeup should I put on, what shoes, what would we talk about, will we hold hands, would he want to kiss me when we got home, what would it mean if he didn't – did I even want him to? Of *course*, but I didn't need to be worrying about it the whole night, wondering what it would mean if he did or didn't, and if it would be good or bad. It *was* Liam though so I'm sure it'd be freaking phenomenal. I hadn't even told him that I wanted to be more than friends yet, but we've established he is anything but stupid, so he must know that's where my mind is now.

I wasn't lying when I said I was a mess. I tried on skinny jeans of various colors, I tried on skirts and sundresses, tank-tops and flowy shirts, I tried on flip-flops and sandals, flat shoes and even high-heels. I put my hair up in a ponytail, then a messy bun, I had it in a braid and then tried a headband when I couldn't stand the way my hair looked. I put on a ton of makeup and then scrubbed it off and went for a more natural look, all before I decided that "natural" looked like I wasn't trying enough and I had to start all over.

After about an hour my bedroom looked like a tornado hit it, I went through every single article of clothing I owned, I realized that nothing worked, and I had absolutely no clue why I ever agreed to go out on a date in the first place.

Because Liam asked you to, that's why.

It was 6:15, and I still had no idea what to wear. After mixing and matching a whole bunch of different things I still didn't know what was appropriate for a first date. I was no good at any of this.

It honestly wouldn't have surprised me if I went insane because of an outfit at this point.

I honestly think I was already there.

But then I remembered.

Liam said I'm beautiful no matter what I wear.

I didn't really believe he meant it when he said it, and I still didn't believe it. However, just thinking about how he said it and the way he looked at me when he did, it gave me enough confidence to get my shit together and pick something.

It was a struggle, but I was ready when I heard the buzzer announcing that Liam was downstairs. I buzzed him in, and then checked myself one last time in the mirror. Dark skinny jeans, navy blue and white flowy top with spaghetti straps, and some flats, was just going to have to do.

I honestly don't know how people get ready for dates all the time. They deserve a goddamn medal. Maybe it gets easier the longer you go out with someone. I briefly wondered if it would ever get easier choosing an outfit if I continued to go on dates with Liam. I really hoped so.

I had just touched up my lip gloss in the hall mirror when I heard a knock on my door. I went to it and inhaled deeply before I opened it.

I wasn't able to exhale because the air had lodged in my throat.

Liam was someone who knew how to dress to impress on a first date.

His "casual" was my undoing.

It seemed like every time I saw him dressed differently than what I considered his "norm," I was left breathless. Liam was dressed in dark blue jeans, and a tight black Polo shirt that exposed not only his muscles, but also the tattoos that were on his arms. His face was clean-shaven and his hair had a bit of gel in it at the front making him look completely sexy, and his eyes seemed to glow while he was staring at me so that made it even worse.

Before I could say anything stupid about how he looked, he extended his arm towards me and gave me what was in his hand. I was so focused on the way he looked, I didn't fully register that he had something in his hands.

"These are for you, Red," he said, holding out a bouquet of flowers that I reached out and took from him. It was such a sweet gesture. He was constantly surprising me with everything he did.

I finally exhaled, and took another breath before saying, "Wow, Liam. These are absolutely beautiful. Daisies are my favorite. I'm surprised that you remembered. Thank you."

"I told you I remember everything, Red. But they are in no way as beautiful as you. You look amazing."

And there it is.

He said I looked beautiful, and amazing.

I don't know about *beautiful* or *amazing*, but if the look in his eyes is any indication to what he's thinking, I know I must've done a *decent* job finally settling on an outfit. At least I can breathe easy about that. Now I only had to worry about all of the other things that were on my list that I started to freak out about in the hours leading up to right now.

"Your hair is absolutely gorgeous by the way. I've never seen it down before," Liam said, cutting into my thoughts.

Really? He never saw me with my hair down? I tried thinking back to all the times I've seen him, and he's right. I looked at him and he *did* seem fascinated by my hair which was a little shocking. Before I could say anything to him, he continued by saying, "Just when I thought you couldn't get any more beautiful, you go and leave your hair down, Red. Absolutely stunning." He then reached out his hand and touched my hair with his fingers. It was a light touch, but it was enough to get my body to shudder.

I stood there completely mute, breathing heavily. He let go of my hair and took a step back, closing his eyes for a second. I didn't know what to say or do. I really needed to learn how to act and communicate better when he said or did things like that. He was constantly catching me off guard.

When he opened his eyes and looked at me again, I said, "You don't look too bad yourself," completely brushing off the past few moments. I needed to get away from him and his compelling eyes, and words, and touches for a few minutes so I followed that up with, "Let me go put these in water so we can get out of here."

As I turned to go into the kitchen to put the flowers in water and give myself a few moments to get myself together, I told Liam to make himself at home. It was barely a second before he was heading towards my fireplace mantle that held all of my family photos. I could already hear the questions he would have for me when he looked at certain ones. I didn't even make it into the kitchen when I heard, "Holy shit, Red! Is this you and Connor at his college graduation? What the hell happened to him?"

As I walked into the kitchen to get a very colorful pitcher to put the flowers in, I couldn't help but laugh at Liam's question. I could ask him the same thing in return. What happened to him to make him want to alter his own body in such a way? I wanted to know why he had all of his tattoos, a topic we hadn't had the chance to cover yet, but I knew it wasn't something I would be getting into right now. We had a date to get to.

Without answering his question, I arranged the flowers in my pitcher and took them out to where Liam was still standing. I moved around him and placed the pitcher in the now open spot, thanks to him holding the picture that was normally in that location. I heard him inhale kind of loudly, and I began to wonder what was wrong. He had only been looking at a picture of our family this past Christmas, so there was no reason for him to be as affected as he was. I looked at him but he wasn't staring at the picture, he was staring at the flowers.

"My mom used to do the same thing, Red. We had crystal vases, and other really expensive shit to put flowers in, but every time she got flowers she always put them in pitchers. I can still picture her arranging them and the smile on her face as she was doing it. Her favorite was a really weird looking blue one that looked about a thousand years old. It didn't matter if the flowers were picked out of the garden or the most expensive and exotic you could buy, she would put them in the blue pitcher and leave them out where everyone could see it. Her favorite color was blue. I often wonder if that's why I love the color so much, because she did ..." He stopped for a second, then said, "I remember after she died, my father didn't handle it very well ..." He stopped again and then he looked at me, looking away from the flowers.

"All of the things that reminded him the most about our mom he wanted to box away. I remember the staff boxing away her blue pitcher, and out of everything, *that* was the one thing that bothered me the most to see being put in a box to be packed away like she never existed. A fucking pitcher is what it took for me to be angry at him, to be angry at *everything*." This time he stopped talking for more than just a few breaths. I don't think he meant to say what he did. I don't think he meant to reveal so much about his mother, and because of the topic I didn't know how to respond to what he had told me.

He turned to look at the flowers again, and when he started speaking he surprised me. "I have her pitcher. He made the staff take all of the boxes to a room nobody ever used, so it was easy enough to get to. I went in there, and I took the pitcher and I hid it in my room. It was one of her favorite things, it made her happy, and he had no fucking right to pack it away like that –" He stopped again suddenly. He turned and looked at me again.

He shook his head, and his eyes cleared before he said, "I didn't mean to say all of that. Just seeing you using a pitcher, Red … it really reminded me of my mom. I didn't mean to start off our date this way. Come on, let's get out of here."

I grabbed the picture he held out towards me, and put it elsewhere on the mantle. I couldn't get over what he had said, how affected he was by it still, and I really couldn't get over my lack of anything to say in that moment when he revealed something as deeply as he did.

Since I was at a loss for words I did the only thing I could think of to do to offer him some comfort. I turned away from the mantle, I moved towards him, and then I hugged him.

I tucked my arms below his, wrapped my arms around his back, placed my head against his chest, and I just held him. It took only a moment for him to realize what was happening, but when he did, he lifted his arms around me and he hugged me back. His arms wrapped so tightly around me I thought he would break me. It was as if he never wanted to let me go, and in that moment, I was okay with that happening.

I heard him inhale loudly again, but I didn't want to examine too closely what this times inhale meant. I just wanted him to be okay.

We stayed like that for a few minutes, neither of us saying a word. Neither of us had to. When he was ready to let go, he pulled back and looked at me.

"Thank you, Samantha … for the hug, and also for the memories. I need you to know that the pitcher isn't a bad thing, but a good thing. I know I must have looked sad or upset, but honestly, it's a really great thing for me to have seen that. I'm not really sad or upset, Sam. I'm actually happy to be reminded of my mom in this specific instance, especially because … because, she would have *loved* you. This reminder of her, specifically of a connection to one of her favorite things, *one of my favorite things now* … it's perfect. It's perfect, Sam."

When he was done speaking, he came a little closer and kissed my forehead.

I never knew that a kiss on the forehead could be as sexy as that kiss to my forehead was. I know that many people would think a forehead kiss was chaste or something along those lines but that type of kiss in that moment, was anything but. It was my turn to inhale loudly.

I looked up at him when he moved back, and I felt like we were having another one of our special conversations with our eyes. Nothing was being said, and yet *everything* was being said.

Before I could think too deeply and get myself tangled into even more of the feelings and thoughts I had fluttering and floating around inside of my body, he grabbed my hand and started pulling me towards the door.

"How about we get going? I don't think I can handle any more deep revelations right this minute – or any more of this touching. You said friends remember, and I'm trying really fucking hard here ..."

When we got to the door he opened it for me. I grabbed my purse, locked the door, and then he grabbed my hand while we headed down and out of my building. He continued to hold my hand the whole way to where we were going.

He must have lied when said he couldn't take any more of our touching.

He lied ... the same way I did when I said I only wanted to be his friend.

****

I don't know why I didn't think of somewhere in the Inner Harbor, but that's where we were. During all of my imaginary dates with Liam, the Harbor – the place we both admitted to loving and going to, the place near where we both conveniently worked and lived – was not one of my date settings. It wasn't because I didn't like the idea of having a date at the Harbor, it's because I didn't picture him wanting to have dinner somewhere with so many people and distractions.

"Are you sure this is okay, because you seemed kind of surprised when we got here ... and I don't know if it's a good surprise or a bad one. I remember you saying that you like to come here and watch the tourists and feel all of the energy, but now I'm thinking maybe it wasn't such a good idea. I thought about going somewhere more private, but you talked about us being just friends, and even though I fully believe we're heading towards more, I didn't want you to think I'm pressuring you, so I figured with all of the people and the entertainment, and being by the water …"

With him rambling on, thinking I was displeased with his choice of location, I knew I needed to cut him off.

"Liam, its fine. Honestly, I'll admit that I didn't think about the Harbor when we set this date, but it's not a bad thing. Truthfully, I think it's better like this, and not just because of the whole '*friends*' thing. It's less formal, and I don't feel as pressured to act a certain way."

Liam gave me a funny look. It almost seemed as if he was displeased with something.

"Why would you think you have to act a certain way, Red? I just want you to act like you normally do. I want you to be yourself. If you haven't already figured it out by now, I'm pretty partial to how you are."

I don't know what had me saying what I did, but the truth came out.

Maybe it was because of how he said what he did, or maybe it was because he still seemed to think I wasn't telling the truth to being completely okay with having come to the Harbor where it was crowed and loud, and where we had people walking by looking at us because we were sitting at an outside table.

I don't know exactly what it was, I just knew I needed to tell him why I was okay with his choice, and why even though I imagined something different, it didn't mean that what I'd imagined would've been better.

"It's my first date."

Yes, I went there. I never thought I would've admitted it to him, but then here we are and I said it.

"What?" He definitely sounded strange.

"Yeah, I mean, I went out with a guy in high school, but he never actually *asked* me out. It was more just hanging out, doing a few things – you know, teenage stuff. Then, when I started college we went out as groups to football games and parties, and then when we were old enough to drink we went out to bars. Even now when we go out it's still the same thing ..."

"And I fucking brought you *here*?" Liam cut my rambling off, and *praise Jesus* for that, but he sounded mad and not at ease with his selection, which is what I was actually going for by telling him the truth. What the hell did I just do? I admitted something out loud I never wanted to, and now he's mad because of it? Perfect.

Just fucking perfect.

"I like here, Liam. I feel comfortable here. I feel like myself. That's why I told you what I just did. I was worried that if you took me somewhere fancy, or somewhere overly private or quiet I would feel awkward or different. It was making me nervous thinking about those places. I've never done this before – not like this – and I'm *happy* you chose this place. I don't feel weird here ... though I must say, with you looking at me like you are, and for acting like you did finding out this is my first date, I really am starting to feel uncomfortable and awkward ... and I know it's mainly my fault for blurting out the truth about the date thing but ... *Jesus Christ*, where is the waiter? I need a fucking drink."

Anyone who really knew me would have known in that very moment exactly how I was feeling. Though I had the mouth of a trucker, that mouth normally stayed in my head. I've been known to say bad words here and there, but mainly in a light way, however this time I definitely meant exactly what I said the way in which I said it. I needed that fucking drink.

Maybe Liam really did know me as much as I thought he was beginning to, because he was very quick to respond to what I had said.

"I'm sorry, Samantha. I didn't mean to make you feel awkward and uncomfortable. Just finding out it's your first actual date ... I wish I would have known. That's all. I would have done things a little differently."

"*Exactly*. You would have done things differently. I wanted to have *this* date. I didn't want something you went over the top for because you found out it was my first official date and you needed it to be something huge or special ..." I decided to admit a little bit more, so I went on to say, "It was going to be huge and special regardless of where we went, or what we did, because my first date is with you. I didn't need fancy, or private, or something *more* because you knew it was a first for me. It was special from the moment you asked me out and I said yes. It was going to be special because it was *you. Okay?*"

I can't believe I admitted that to him, but I did. He always admits things to me, I guess it was my turn.

"Wow, Samantha. Wow. Okay. *Okay*. I just need you to know one thing though. You being here with me ... you saying yes ... you spending your first date with me – you *wanting* to spend your first date with me – it's special and huge to me too. Truth is, I find not just this date but *you* so special that if I knew you wanted to eat at a fucking drive-through wearing sweatpants and a sweatshirt I would have. Just having you want to be with me is huge and special to me. Don't doubt that."

"I don't doubt it, Liam. Not for a second." And I didn't doubt it, because I could hear the sincerity in his voice and see it in his eyes.

How is this even my life right now?

Just then the waiter finally came over and asked us what we would like to order. Though I knew our date technically started from the moment I opened my door and he handed me the daisies, it seemed like right now it was truly beginning. I would never forget Liam opening up about his mother and sharing some of the memories he has of her with me, or the way that I hugged him and the way he held me, or my hand, or the way he kissed me on the forehead, but I was looking forward to what was going to be beginning *now*. It was my first date, and I intended on enjoying every moment of it.

$$****$$

Dinner was absolutely perfect. I honestly don't think I've had a more enjoyable night, and yet when I think about it, it was just dinner mixed with what Liam and I had been doing for days now … talking. We drank some wine, we talked through dinner, we got to know a few new things about one another, but you could just tell that it was more. There was a *feel* about it. When we left the restaurant he grabbed my hand again, and he interlaced his fingers with mine. He had touched my hand a few times during dinner but nothing lingering, and definitely not like this.

I didn't know what destination he had in mind, but I couldn't help but feel happy when I saw what direction we were heading in, and what was directly in front of me.

"Where are we going, Liam?"

"You really have a thing with that question, Red."

I completely turned my head to the side and looked up at him narrowing my eyes. My response earned me one of his really awesome grins.

"Where?" I asked once again.

"Where do you want to be going, Red?"

'Home with you,' definitely would have been too forward, though I almost wish I could say it just to see him falter a little. My luck, he would counter with his own witty comeback and I would be the one left faltering, or just my luck, stumbling and falling on my face in front of him. It's best if I don't go in that direction, even if my mind – *and oh, my God ... my heart* – wants me to.

When did I start thinking my heart was involved in any of this?

"Red?" I heard Liam ask, breaking into my thoughts.

I didn't even realize that we had stopped walking, that's how deep into my head I had been.

"What?" I responded.

There was nothing else I could say because I didn't know if he asked a question that I'd completely missed. How could I know if there was a question, when I didn't even know that we had stopped walking?

My heart?

What the hell?

He looked at me for a while. He was doing his searching thing, trying to figure out what was going on inside of my mind by staring at my face.

If he only knew.

Actually, I wonder what he would think if he knew *exactly* what was going on inside of my head. *And my heart?*

"Come on, Red. Let's go." He tugged on my hand a bit and led me directly to where I was hoping we would go. We crossed the little bridge pathway that led directly to one of my favorite places in the Harbor.

I couldn't do anything but smile as he tugged me towards the stairs that led to the bookstore.

"I couldn't help it, Red. Nothing about this night has really been a traditional first date type of thing, so why not make it even more so? I know you love books. Let's go buy you some books." He was definitely speaking my language, but once again without meaning to, his words put my insecurity of not having a stellar social life in the forefront. I was happy only seconds ago knowing that we were indeed going to the place I wanted to go, but now I was wondering how he felt about me being a homebody who liked to read in my spare time more than anything else.

Why was I even thinking this now? He likes me as I am. He said so numerous times.

I needed to stop all of the nonsense going on in my head. It was making me crazy again.

"What?" I asked once again. I needed to get my shit together.

"Let's go buy you some books," he repeated, gesturing with his free hand towards the bookstore. I heard him the first time, but I wasn't sure why he wanted to come here, or why he wanted to get me some books.

"Why?" I needed to know.

"Because, Red. I want whenever you read the books that we get, or whenever you see them after you're done with them and they're lying around somewhere, I want you to think about me and our date. I want you to think of when you got them, who got them, and I want you to remember *all* of this, and how happy you made me today with this first date, and for just being here with me. I'm being pretty fucking selfish, and maybe pretty fucking stupid, but I'm using the books we get to symbolize something pretty fucking special. So can we please just go get some books now?"

The smile that blossomed on my face could only have been rivaled by the flush that was overtaking my whole body.

Every emotion I am feeling in this moment must be written all over my face.

They probably are, and I don't care. I would never need books to remind me of the unexpected awesomeness and the beauty of this day – of *him* – but he wanted to go into the bookstore and get books for that reason, so we would go and get books.

I turned to walk up the stairs so we could go into the store, but I didn't get very far when he tugged on my hand pulling me back and around towards him. I looked up at him then, realizing we were only inches apart.

He let go of my hand, but he grabbed both of my cheeks instead, gently, cradling my face.

Once he did that, I felt my face get even warmer, and I could hear my breaths start to leave my body in wild spurts. I licked my lips, because I *knew* what was about to happen.

Liam made a noise in his throat, and he moved even closer to me, something that I didn't think would have been at all possible because there didn't seem to be enough room left.

"I can't fucking take it anymore, Sam," Liam said, right before he bent his head and kissed me.

I've been kissed a few times in my life, but it was nothing like Liam's kiss. With one press of his lips I felt like he had kissed my whole body instead of just my mouth. The warmth that I felt against my lips travelled throughout my body. I grabbed his shoulders to hold on and I leaned up on my tiptoes so I could deepen the kiss, but he removed his hands from my cheeks, broke the kiss, and stepped back before I could really participate.

Only a few hours ago I was wondering if he would or wouldn't kiss me – I was nervous about each scenario – and now all I was wondering was: *why did he stop?*

Just like him, I couldn't take any of this anymore. We needed to clarify a few things and get some stuff out in the open.

With a shaky voice I said, "You know we're just friends right?"

I was completely teasing, but I needed to know what he was thinking without revealing too much myself.

"I know, Red. Just friends."

He said what, now?

I stared at him because he said what he did in a very serious tone, and maybe it was my now muddled mind, but I had no idea if he was serious or not, or if he was teasing too.

Then he winked at me.

And he flashed me his grin with the finger-dipping-worthy dimples.

I couldn't help but to grin back, because I loved his wink, I loved his dimples, but most of all I loved how he was teasing me and we were both on the same page wanting more of each other.

I couldn't resist it.

I needed more.

It was my turn now.

I moved towards him, and I grabbed his cheeks in my hands this time. I don't know if I caught him off guard but he came willingly when I pulled him down to my level. I kissed him like I wanted him to kiss me before. I couldn't believe that I was the aggressor, but I swiped my tongue across his lips waiting for the invitation, and when he granted it I took the opportunity that he presented.

I wasn't the aggressor for long.

Once our tongues touched, Liam took swift control over the kiss, and I can honestly say our kiss was the best feeling I have ever had in my life.

The tingles.

The butterflies.

The weightlessness.

The *magic*.

When we finally parted, I don't know how I was able to think coherently but I was … at least I was enough that I was able to say, "Yes, Liam … *definitely* just friends."

I went around him, and up the steps, grinning the whole way into the bookstore.

I knew eventually he would catch up.

Chapter 12

I didn't need a book to remember anything about our date, but flipping through the pages of one of the ones Liam bought me before bed, I couldn't help but to think about the remainder of our date after we left the bookstore, or what happened the day after. Liam definitely caught up to me after I left him on the walkway after experiencing one of the best kisses of my life. I say *one* of the best, because it didn't compare to the one we shared when he finally left me at my door at the end of the night. That kiss was incomparable.

After he kissed me, he asked if I had any plans for the next day. I had work, but only until noon, so we set another date. Once again he wouldn't tell me where we would be going, he just said he would be picking me up at the shop, and to once again dress completely casual. With that he kissed me on my forehead and left. That forehead kiss of his was definitely something special too.

The next day I quickly learned that trying to find an outfit for a second date wasn't any easier than choosing an outfit for the first, but I didn't make myself as crazy as the first time. He'd said completely casual again, so completely casual it would be.

When Liam walked into the café to pick me up I couldn't contain my excitement. I felt the smile bloom on my face, and my heart do a little flutter at his smile in return. I hurriedly grabbed my things and went out the door with him. I had no idea where we were going but he grabbed my hand and said we would be walking a few blocks, and he hoped that would be okay.

Of course it was okay – he was walking right next to me holding my hand.

While we were walking he made a comment about how much he loved seeing me in shorts, and how for such a tiny thing I sure did have legs that went on for days. I guess the madness of picking out jean shorts and a simple white tank top paid off.

He wasn't so bad to look at either. He had on a pair of tan cargo shorts with a white t-shirt that fit his broad chest perfectly, and that showed off his tattoos to perfection. I was amazed at myself that I didn't blurt out how awesome he looked to *me*.

It was bad enough already that I was so lost in thought about how he looked, the events from the day before, the upcoming week and the unlikelihood of seeing him because of his crazy work schedule that we were practically at our destination before I realized where we were going. I should've known sooner where we were headed especially with the streets packed with people all wearing the same thing, and all acting in a boisterous manner, but I had been lost in my own thoughts.

Once I knew where we were going though, I was extremely touched once again by his thoughtfulness and his remembrance of things that I had mentioned to him only briefly.

We were going to a baseball game.

He was taking me to another place that I loved.

I stopped him by tugging on his hand once we reached a crosswalk. When I pulled and he stopped, he looked down at me, and when he did I told him that a baseball game was absolutely perfect.

And it was.

We sat on the third-base line which was my favorite spot to be, we grabbed hot dogs and pretzels, and beer and crackerjack, and we had the best time. Not only did we get food and beer, but after I told Liam that Connor and I had matching jerseys from our younger years that we wore to every single game that we went to together as a part of our tradition, Liam insisted on buying our own set so that we could wear them when we came to games too.

He said it could be *our* tradition.

After he had spent tons of money on the game, and all of the food and the beer, I should've tried to talk him out of buying us matching jerseys too, but when he said why he wanted us to have them, I couldn't say *no* to that. I *wanted* us to have a tradition. I *wanted* us to keep going to games in the future – a future that I was beginning to see that I desperately wanted to have with him. From the way he was talking, it seemed like he wanted that as well.

When the game was over, and with both of us wearing our brand new matching game jerseys, Liam walked me back to my apartment. I asked him if he wanted to come inside, but he declined. We stood outside of my door for a few minutes discussing the upcoming week. He didn't know when he would get the chance to see me again, which I had already figured would be the case on the walk to the stadium. I was upset, as was he, but if we didn't get to see each other during the week, there would always be next weekend to make up for all of the lost time.

Then we both remembered that the date with Connor and Riley was next weekend.

Fuck.

Talk about a mood-killer.

We both realized that Connor still didn't know the date was happening on Saturday, and that he would have to be told. I was definitely not looking forward to that.

Liam kissed me before he left, quickly on the lips and then the forehead, not lingering kisses like he had planted on me during the game or during the date yesterday, which I attributed to Connor's being brought into the conversation.

Fucking Connor!

****

Monday mornings always suck at the coffee shop, and this Monday morning is no different. Allie isn't here to help out, the new girl Beth is horrible with the customers so I have to constantly step in and do her job, Connor's not at the Firehouse so he's here hovering, and Joanna left Adam to close by himself last night – which is something we are never supposed to do alone – so either Connor or I need to talk to her because my parents left us in charge while they are visiting our aunt for a month. I'm not volunteering myself to talk to Joanna, so Connor needs to do it. He's been avoiding her like crazy but he needs to man-up. She gets one more chance then she's gone, but until then, one of us is going to have to work shifts with her.

This Monday just keeps getting better and better.

Before I could get into the various ways in which we could tell Joanna that she's fired once she messes up again, or before I could go in the back and tell Connor that he needed to have a talk with her and explain the new changes in our shifts, my cell phone beeped.

Liam: Our clients cancelled our lunch meeting today. Want to grab lunch with me? We can stay at The Brew if you want.

When I talked to Liam yesterday, it didn't look promising that he would be seeing me at all before Saturday's date. Finding out that he would be able to meet with me today, even with Connor here, I knew it wasn't something I would be passing up. It was just going to be tricky not letting our feelings show with Connor lurking about. A lot has developed between us in the past few days. I really didn't need Connor on my ass ... or Liam's.

Me: I'd love to have lunch with you. Here sounds perfect ... Allie isn't on today, and we have a new girl who isn't working out too great ... so I'd prefer to stay here in case she needs my help. Connor's here too just so you know.

Liam: That's fine. Why wouldn't Connor just help the new girl if she has trouble?

Me: He could, but I think it's best if I help her. He tried training someone once, and it didn't go so well ...

Liam: Okay then ... Got it. So I'll be by around 12-12:30.

Me: That's perfect. By the way ... I know I told you Connor's here ... he obviously doesn't know anything about us going out this past weekend ...

Liam: I know, Red. I won't grope you in public or anything like that!

I could feel my cheeks start to heat up. Besides kissing me and holding my hand, and hugging me back when I hugged him, Liam hasn't done any groping. I didn't know how to respond to what he said. I guess he figured as much because I heard some more beeps signaling the rapid incoming of multiple texts from him.

Liam: Unless you ask me to.

Liam: I wouldn't be against public groping you know.

Liam: So, all you have to do is ask, Red. Just let me know.

Liam: It's definitely a two-way street too … you can definitely grope me if you want! You never need my permission for that, just so you know …

God, what was I supposed to say to any of that? In the past few days, after experiencing his amazing kisses, of course I thought about *more* with him. I just never thought we would talk about more in a text conversation, or that we'd really talk about it at all. It was too weird for me.

I heard another beep.

Liam: I bet you're that beautiful shade I like to call, 'red as a fire engine' … I wish that I could see it, Red! That color is quickly becoming one of my favorites. It really is right up there with blue!

He is such an asshole!

I'm actually really happy he isn't here right now to see me, because I would never hear the end of it. I'm sure that I probably far surpassed that particular shade of red.

Liam: Alright, alright … I'll stop now, Red. You know I was just teasing. Seriously, though … I actually do love that particular color. It's your color, Red. But just so you know, I promise to be on my best behavior today, especially in front of your brother … no worries. See you soon.

I don't know how I was going to make it through lunch sitting across from Liam, especially with Connor around. I guess lunch was going to be a trial run for Saturday night. I made such a big deal about Liam behaving, but it wasn't only Liam I was worried about.

I needed to get my emotions under control, otherwise Connor would see right through everything.

****

It would figure that at exactly noon Connor would come up front, having finished doing some inventory in the back. It didn't help that about ten minutes later he was still up front when Liam walked through the door. It also didn't help that as soon as I saw Liam, my face started to heat up again. I tried to put his texts out of my mind, but it didn't work. I remembered what he said as soon as I saw him and my face warmed instantly. I knew that he saw my blush because he had a shit-eating grin on his face. It wasn't a normal smile letting me know that he was happy to see me, though I knew he was. It was a grin letting me know he knew *exactly* what I was thinking … *and he loved it.*

"So he didn't give up, huh?" Connor said when he saw Liam too.

"No, he didn't," was all I said.

Once again I'm thanking the sweet baby Jesus for Liam not giving up on me, and also for his clients cancelling. The sight of Liam in a suit the color of smoke is something that I would have never wanted to miss out on. I don't care how shallow it sounds, it's the honest truth – Liam knew how to wear a suit and missing him wearing *this one* would have been a fucking travesty. Liam is definitely drool-worthy, and if I don't start talking to Connor and try to work some magic to get rid of him, I may just actually embarrass myself and turn into a big pile of drool, and then Connor would surely know that there's more to Liam and me than he actually knows.

"We're having lunch here again. Can you cover for me Connor?"

"Fuck no. I'm having lunch now too."

What the fuck does he mean by that? There is no way he's eating with us. He definitely didn't mean for it to sound like that – even though it would be a total Connor thing to do.

Fuck!

"Where are you having lunch? And with who?" I knew I sounded worried, but I didn't give a shit. Connor could *not* be ruining my plans again – he just couldn't.

He just looked at me before answering. He didn't say anything about my tone, he just said, "I'm meeting someone at the pizzeria down the street for lunch. I'm gonna be gone a little longer than I should, but I don't think it should be a problem."

Thank God he wasn't staying. All those worries for nothing. His going out was definitely not a problem.

"No, it shouldn't be a problem. We're going to be here, so I'll be around if Beth has a problem. No need to worry about it …"

Connor cut me off by saying, "Yeah, I didn't think you would have a problem with it. Don't think I don't see how okay with it you are, now that you know I'm taking lunch at the same time but I'm going out to eat and not staying here. You don't fool me, Sam. You want to spend time with Prince Charming alone. You know what? That's fine. You're here after all. What kind of shit can you get into here? I just need to talk to him first before I go," he said before heading towards the back.

"Why do you need to talk to him?" I hurried up to ask before he disappeared through the back door. It didn't matter though. I knew he heard me, he just chose not to respond.

Great.

I could only imagine what he wanted to talk about.

Actually … I knew *exactly* what he wanted to talk about, and that's not such a bad thing. He probably wants to find out about his master plan of a date. He probably thinks that it'll never happen. Just because Liam and I agreed to it, it doesn't mean that Riley did, or that we'd all be going out. Riley did agree though, and for better or worse it was happening.

"Hey, Red. I'm a little disappointed that you aren't 'fire engine red' anymore, but I must say you are still a really pretty shade of pink."

A really pretty shade of pink … *seriously*?

I slid my gaze away from the back door and gave my full attention to Liam.

"Hello, Liam. My brother wants to talk to you for some unknown reason … though I think we both can accurately guess why. He should be back up front in a minute …"

I glanced towards the back door again but saw no sign of Connor just yet.

"What can I get you for lunch?"

"You know that turkey club I had last time was pretty good, so I think I'll have that again, and the iced tea too."

"Alright, I will just get it this time and bring it to you. Beth is still new to all of this, so I don't want her to have to bring us our stuff too, plus she's the only one here besides Connor and I, and we are both taking lunch at the same time … So, yeah. I'll bring us our stuff."

I knew I was rambling, but he threw me off for the millionth time with his mentioning my awesome pink color, and I was also a little anxious waiting for Connor to return. I was all over the place.

I wondered if I would ever be able to have one encounter with Liam without any rambling, mumbling, misunderstandings, blushes, awkwardness, or anything else that made me seem completely immature and socially inept.

Thank God he didn't seem to mind all of my flaws. He actually kind of liked them.

Like I said before … perfect package.

"How about I just wait for it here then, and we can take our food to the table together?"

I couldn't help but smile at the idea. I liked the sound of that. He wanted to be a gentleman and carry our things.

"Okay, that's fine."

I hurried up to the back to get him what he wanted for lunch. Connor was on his cell phone talking to someone, which explained why he was taking so long. I placed our order with our guy in the back, and waited for it to be done while trying not to eavesdrop on Connor's conversation. I hated it when he did that to me, besides I had more important things to think about than who he was talking to, or what he was saying.

The food was done and on the tray at the same time that Connor was finally done talking on the phone.

I grabbed the tray and headed back up front with Connor quickly following. Liam was right on the other side of the counter waiting, and when he saw me he immediately grabbed the tray from my hands and greeted Connor.

"Hey, Connor."

"Liam."

Wow, this wasn't going to be awkward at all. This whole thing felt very high school, especially with Liam carrying our lunch tray to the table as if we high school sweethearts. Connor must be loving this shit. As we sat down at the table, Connor wasted no time getting to the point of what he wanted to say.

"So, is Riley gonna go out with me?"

I whipped my head towards Connor, not believing he asked about the date quite like that. I should've expected something like that though. It *is* Connor after all. He just loves to rattle cages, and he now knows that he can rattle Liam's cage by bringing up his sister. I turned my head to look at Liam to see how he was feeling about what Connor had said, and I could tell by his clenched jaw, that this situation was not good.

Then I was shocked at what I saw happen next.

Liam's clenched jaw turned into that same shit-eating grin he had on his face when he first came into the shop a little while ago.

This was definitely not going to be good. I forgot that Connor and Liam were too much alike. They could both give as much as they could take.

"I talked to Riley the other day and told her all about you. I told her how eager you were to meet her, seeing as how your Samantha's brother and all. Don't worry though … I told her you're into guys so that way she doesn't feel weird, or set up, and so there wouldn't be any expectations. She's completely cool with it – you being into dudes and all. Her best friend is gay so she asked a lot of questions … I actually think she wants to hook you up with her friend, so you might want to be prepared for that shit. I don't know man … You sure you still want to go out with us? I mean Riley said she's in, but you know …"

I was equal parts horrified and impressed by what Liam said to Connor. I knew what he discussed with his sister, and it wasn't that, but I couldn't blame Liam for wanting to have a little fun at Connor's expense. Unfortunately, Connor didn't fall for it. It really would have been so much better if he did.

Connor started laughing so loud, a few of our customers actually turned around to look at us. He started talking while still laughing. "You … You know what? I wouldn't even be mad if you told her something like that, but you didn't. You know how I know? Because you like Sam too much, so you wouldn't lie about me like that. You probably told her I was an asshole, and a prick, or whatever … but not me being into other men. That was some funny shit though. Well played, Liam. Well fucking played." Connor actually did look a bit impressed.

"Yeah, I thought so. I really wanted to tell her something like that, but you're right. I wouldn't do that to Samantha, and I wouldn't lie to my sister. I'm already asking a lot of her by wanting her to come out with us, and be a part of this weird fucked up situation, so there was no way I wasn't giving her the full truth. I did tell her you were a complete asshole though, by the way. So she is definitely prepared for you. She comes home this weekend. She said Saturday is fine, if that's okay with you?"

Liam stopped talking and just stared at Connor waiting for what he had to say. I looked at Connor too, and I was shocked to see what I think was surprise on his face. He didn't think Riley would say yes, just like he didn't think Liam would agree when he came up with this stupid ass idea.

He should have known better not to underestimate these two siblings.

"Saturday? I can do Saturday. This is going to be *fucking fantastic!* Where are we going?"

"*Molly's*," Liam told Connor.

"Like I said, fucking fantastic! I love that goddamn place. I can't wait to meet Riley, Prince Charming. I can't fucking wait!"

I saw Liam clench his jaw again, but before he could say anything, Connor turned around and headed for the door. He just left. I guess he would get all of the details from me, just as soon as I actually got them from Liam. If I didn't completely dread this date on Saturday, I fully dreaded it now. Connor was not going to make this date easy. I knew the date wouldn't be easy before, but seeing Connor's reaction now, I knew it was going to be even worse than I had imagined. Liam really needed to be prepared.

****

I tried to warn Liam.

When Connor left on Monday to go to the pizzeria, I tried to make Liam understand that Connor would not relent on his teasing about Riley, because he knew how much it riled him up. Liam insisted it didn't bother him, but it clearly did. During lunch we talked more about the date on Saturday, a little more about Riley, and about how his job was going. His job really did suck, because after Monday I didn't see him the rest of the week. We went back to playing text-tag during the day, but at least I talked to him every night.

And before I knew it, it was Saturday. A part of me wanted the week to fly by so that I would finally be able to see Liam, however once it was Saturday I felt like the entire week flew by bringing us to the date with Connor and Riley. I seriously was in the mode of pray for the best, but prepare for the worst.

I really didn't know how bad it was going to be until Liam and Riley walked through the door to *Molly's*. Up until that moment Connor and I were just bullshitting about the situation with Joanna, how his conversation with her had gone, how annoying our new shifts were, and what our parents had to say about the whole situation when he told them.

What I found funny and odd was how Connor didn't bring up Riley or Liam all that much while we were waiting. It almost seemed like he was trying to avoid the whole reason of why we were actually having dinner together, as if it wasn't his idea to be doing all of this in the first place. If I didn't know any better I would actually think that Connor was nervous, *but I do know better*, and Connor doesn't *do* nervous. We grabbed a few drinks at the bar, headed to our table, and were just waiting for Liam and Riley so we could order and get this whole thing over with.

Then they were there, and Connor decided to turn into a freaking chatterbox.

"That's his sister? What the fuck is she wearing? It's hot outside and she has a jacket on … and a fucking beanie on her head? Is something *wrong* with her? You didn't tell me there's something wrong with her, Sam."

"Seriously, Connor? Why do you even care? It's not like she's your actual date. Calm down." Did I seriously have to remind him that this isn't a real date for him? I was worried about something like this. Liam probably was too, which is why he probably acted the way he did when Connor made his smartass comments.

I know what Riley actually looks like because I saw her picture pop up on Liam's phone. I knew what was under that jacket and beanie, but Connor didn't. I really wish that he would feel the same way as he does now when he sees the actual Riley, but I know Connor too well. He won't have the same reaction.

"You know, not for nothing Sam … I'm not into dudes, but I expected more from her seeing as how Prince Charming is her brother …"

I needed to cut him off right now. "Would you stop it? They are almost over here. Don't fucking embarrass me Connor … or yourself."

"Fuck that! No wonder why Liam was okay with this whole date shit. He knew he had nothing to fucking worry about …"

"Shut up! This isn't even a date for *you*. They really are almost here. Please be nice Connor. Don't ruin this."

I cannot wait until Connor sees how gorgeous Riley really is. I'll think of his reaction as payment for having to listen to all the fucked up shit he just said, and for roping all of us into this situation to begin with. As Liam and Riley finally got to the table I saw what Connor didn't see. I saw how Riley's tight jeans fit her long legs perfectly, I saw her unbelievably flawless skin, her sparkling blue eyes that were identical to Liam's, and I also saw her smirk. *Liam's smirk.* A smirk that might even be more potent than his.

In that moment I just knew she was messing around with my brother. She must have seen his reaction to her and she couldn't wait to knock him on his ass. Isn't that what Liam had said about her? I knew in that moment that Connor had just met his match.

I thought Liam was going to give Connor fits. Liam had nothing on his sister.

His sister was pure trouble, and she had set her eyes on my brother. *This shit will not end well ...*

"Hello, Samantha. Connor. I'd like you to meet my sister, Riley. Riley ... this is Samantha, and her brother Connor."

Riley extended her hand to each of us, and with one of the prettiest voices I had ever heard in my life she said it was very nice to meet us both. Once the introductions were done Liam asked her if she wanted him to take her coat.

"Yes, please." She turned to Connor and me and said, "I don't want you guys to think I'm weird or anything by wearing this jacket. My dad likes the house to be freezing during the summer, so I normally wear warm clothes when I'm home, but this was all I could find because most of my things are at school. It just so happened that I was wearing this over my clothes when Liam showed up and started honking the horn like a crazy person instead of being a gentleman and coming inside to get me ..." she looked back to Liam with an amused smile, "so I ran out to the car like this and of course Liam had the air conditioner set to freezing, so I just kept it on ... *and now here we are*." Riley explained why she was wearing what she was, but honestly to me it didn't matter.

I was secretly pleased that she was so bundled up because I *needed* the reaction that I was fully expecting from Connor in my life.

And that reaction was about to happen.

I couldn't help but to catch Liam's eye and grin at him before I turned to stare at Connor. Connor looked at me for a brief second probably wondering what my problem was, grinning at him like a fool, but then he turned back to look at what was going on with Liam and Riley.

Then I heard it; Connor gasped.

I knew in that moment that whatever Riley looked like, it far surpassed the photograph that Liam had programmed of her in his phone. I also saw Connor's jaw drop open a little bit.

Oh, my. I wasn't expecting all of that now.

I couldn't take it anymore. I knew she was gorgeous, but I'm sure Connor sees gorgeous women all the time. I needed to see what had him so captivated, and not acting like himself.

When I looked at her, I completely understood Connor's reaction.

She really was a sight to see, especially with her mountain of fantastic hair, mixed in with those eyes, and the smirk, and that face and body.

"Holy shit. Holy shit. Wow," I think I heard Connor say quietly.

I looked at Connor again, and I realized that he was absolutely stunned. *Stunned.* I had never seen my brother like this. Only seconds before I was in absolute glee knowing Connor would be eating his words about Riley, but now I don't feel so good for him.

I am okay with my feelings *now*, but I know exactly how he's feeling at the moment because I felt the same thing once before too, so I took pity on him and decided to help him out.

"Connor ... that's how I felt when I first saw Liam. If you don't want her to know, you need to close your mouth before they really start paying attention to us, you need to not say or do anything stupid ... and like I said before, please don't ruin *any of this*."

I was concerned at first that Connor didn't hear me, because I had to whisper so that Riley and Liam wouldn't hear, but when Connor's jaw snapped shut and he sat up a little straighter I knew that he heard me.

He also gave a nod of his head.

With that, I knew he wouldn't intentionally do anything to ruin tonight.

Instead of feeling extremely happy that I all but had a verbal confirmation that he would act his best and not deliberately ruin anything, I didn't feel that way, because I wasn't sure that Connor was doing it for the reasons I wanted him to be doing it.

I honestly didn't know if he was going to be good for me, or for himself.

Liam is so not going to like this.

"Oh ... My ... God ... Sam ... *What the fuck* ..." Connor started mumbling again. Mumbling. After he basically nodded that everything would be fine.

This is not good. This is not good. *This is so not fucking good.*

****

It really wasn't good because I could tell Connor was really into Riley. What's worse is that I knew that Liam could tell too. I didn't really know Riley, but she seemed to be into Connor right back. This whole situation couldn't have worked out any better for Connor. He pulled a completely dick maneuver and yet he was reaping the rewards left and right. He sure seemed to pull himself together fast after his first initial reaction to Riley. He was asking questions, getting answers, flirting, ordering drinks and appetizers, suggesting we all play pool. This was supposed to be mine and Liam's first date and he hijacked it. It didn't matter whether or not Liam and I went out a few times already, Connor had no business taking over like he did. So much for Connor being a mumbling fool who was stunned into silence. He bounced right out of that shit and planted himself firmly in Riley's orbit like he was the fucking sun, and the moon, and everything else in between.

I needed to put an end to this shit. I liked Riley, but Connor was going way too far.

"So, Riley, when do you go back to school?" I made sure I asked her the question and then looked over at Connor. I knew he knew that she was taking summer courses, but I didn't know if he comprehended that he couldn't get attached to her because she would be leaving.

What was I thinking? Connor doesn't get attached to women. Even if he did get attached to one, there is no way that it would be to Liam's sister. I still needed to get my point across though.

"I go back tomorrow. I'll be back for another visit soon though." She answered my question but I could have sworn that it was not at all directed towards me but to Connor. Liam must have noticed that too, because he clearly decided that he needed to be more of an active participant in the conversation.

"So, Riley … how's Brian doing?"

Whoa. Who's Brian?

"Liam! *Really*? You're going to bring him up *now*?" She narrowed her eyes at Liam, and I think if she could kill with her eyes, he'd be dead.

I felt Connor stiffen beside me. I turned to look at him and saw that his focus was solely on Riley. "Who's Brian?" he asked.

"Brian's just a friend of mine at school," she replied to Connor.

Connor blew out a really long breath before he said, "Yeah, I know all about guys who are supposed to be just friends at school. Don't you have one of those Sam?"

"Connor!" Now it was my turn to be pissed off. I knew he was thinking and speaking about Aaron. I'm sure Riley's connection to Brian is nothing like my situation with Aaron.

As if he read my mind Liam chimed in and said, "Brian's nothing like Aaron. I've met him."

"Who's Aaron?" Riley wanted to know.

"A fucking dead man if I ever see him harassing Samantha again. I swear if that kid knows what's good for him he will never come back into the shop. Samantha said you had to chase him out after he said some stuff, Liam. I can't believe the shit he said to her. Did you hear him when he said that filthy fucking trash to her? I can't believe him. He's lucky I wasn't there. He actually thinks he has a chance … over my dead body …"

"Wow." It was one word but it held a wealth of meaning. I looked over at Riley when she said it, and I think in that moment, she was feeling what I felt when Liam said something to Aaron. She now knew about

Connor, what I had learned about Liam that day. He said exactly what he meant, and he ultimately planned on acting upon it.

Moments like these really do something to a person.

Obviously it had done something to Riley. We all knew it.

Connor planned to capitalize on it.

"Riley, you want to play a game of pool with me? Give Prince Charming and Samantha a little alone time?"

Riley started to laugh at what Connor had said, but Liam didn't find it funny in the least.

"No fucking way," Liam said to both Connor and Riley.

I knew how he was feeling, but I wasn't expecting him to say something like that.

"Seriously, Prince Charming? You don't want to spend some time alone with Sam?" I don't think I have ever seen Connor look so smug in my life, and I have seen a shit ton of smugness coming from him in the past twenty years. I couldn't even look at him in all his smug glory. I was actually afraid that I would punch him in the throat for doing what he was doing.

He knew the position he put Liam in. Liam could either choose to spend the time talking to me leaving Riley to spend time alone with Connor, or he could insist that Riley stay here or we all go and play pool, which would pretty much mean that he and I would not be alone the whole night.

I looked at Liam. He did not look happy. I would've understood if he said he wanted to play pool too, or if he said he wanted to spend time with Riley because he hasn't seen her in a while, because Liam and I have secretly spent hours together. I tried to convey with my eyes that it was okay for him to do whatever he wanted, even though I thought he may be going a little overboard with how he was reacting

190

to Connor. He didn't like it when Connor did the same shit to us. The similarities of the two situations is killing me.

Liam looked at me some more, then he looked at his sister. I really wished that I knew what he was thinking, especially when he looked down and uttered the word, "fuck."

When he looked back up at me I could see confusion, determination, and *desire* in his eyes. I knew what the confusion was over, and I definitely knew what the desire was about, but the determination I wasn't so sure.

But then with one action, I completely understood.

Liam leaned over the table and grabbed my hand. It was the first outward display of affection he had shown towards me in front of my brother. This whole time he didn't grin at me, he didn't smirk at me, he didn't wink, he didn't flirt, he didn't allude that he knew more about me than he should, he was completely gentlemanly unlike Connor and his flagrant flirting, but now he looked at me and touched me as if he accepted Connor's unspoken challenge and won.

He was quiet for a few seconds, but then he finally spoke.

"Go ahead and go play pool. I'm going to stay here. This is exactly where I want to be."

Game. Set. Match.

Just like Liam, I didn't care anymore either. I didn't care that Connor was still sitting next to me and that he could clearly see not only my hand in Liam's, but what was also plainly written all over our faces. I didn't care that Riley was still at the table staring between her brother, and me, and Connor, all the while grinning at what had just taken place and what she could see as well. All I cared about was Liam sitting across from me.

Liam, who I could now stare openly at and appreciate. It was the first time tonight that I could really study him at length without caring about getting caught – and what perfection he is. His hair is spiked in front with gel giving him a look that said 'I just rolled out of bed' even though I know he put effort into his look, he has a black shirt on that matches the darkness of his tattoos, and he is sporting some scruff on his face which makes him look sexy, and mysterious, and broody … and his *eyes* – well his eyes are what always do me in along with his dimples, and right now they are currently glowing with desire. Staring at him now, I knew that it was a miracle that I had lasted this long without reaching out and touching him, or embarrassing myself over him in front of everyone, but I did it.

Not anymore though.

There is no way I am ever *not* touching him again because I'm nervous or worried about what people will think. Liam took a big step forward, and there was no way that I was going back.

This fucking game that we were playing before is over.

I thought Connor had been the ultimate winner before, maneuvering each of us where he wanted, but I was wrong.

I was wrong.

Liam was the ultimate winner in this situation, and by extension I was a winner too.

I don't think Connor knew what to say to what he was seeing. He just kept sitting there in silence staring at us. I think Riley took pity on him not knowing what to do or say because she got up from the table.

"I thought you were going to play pool with me?" she reminded him. He had to get up and play pool with her now, otherwise he would look like a total douche. We all knew he wanted to play pool alone with her before, and that he didn't only say what he did to get a rise out of Liam.

After a few seconds Connor got up, but he looked at Liam's hand in mine, not at either of us, before he turned and walked away to the other side of the bar to the pool tables. I could tell by his stride that he was not at all happy with the developments of the past few minutes. I knew the drive home with him was going to be pure fucking torture. After the last few minutes though, I'm pretty sure that I could handle anything that he threw at me.

I continued to watch Connor walk away, but only until I heard Liam say, "Motherfucker."

I whipped my head around to him. I knew Connor was a jerk, but he was still my brother and he really wasn't a bad guy. I really don't think he has any bad intentions when it comes to Liam's sister.

"Liam ..." I didn't get the chance to finish before he said, "I know, Red ... I'm going to leave it alone because I honestly don't know what the fuck to say. I honestly thought she wouldn't give him the time of day because of how he acts. But I guess he only acts that way towards me because he fucking charmed her in the span of five minutes. He calls *me* Prince Charming? What a fucking joke. But you know what? I'm not even going to get into that right now. I have so many things I want to say to you, and ask you ... and Connor and Riley is not *why* I said 'motherfucker' ... at least not completely. I said that because of the spot he put me in, and what it now means for you. I know you didn't want him to know that we've been going out and spending time together ... you wanted him to think we were only going to be friends, or at least friends for now, and I completely ruined that by doing what I did just now. He had to have seen what I was feeling ... I couldn't hide it anymore, Red. I *can't* hide it anymore. He has to know that there has been – that there *is* more. I just needed to hold on to you for a second before I completely lost it, but when I grabbed ahold of you … I couldn't let go … and I meant what I said – I am exactly where I want to be … with you …"

"Liam it's okay. I am *completely* fine with it. I'll deal with Connor later. I am exactly where I want to be too … even if it's with Connor and Riley here witnessing everything … I am with you, and I am more than okay with it. So … I think you said what you wanted to say, so ask me what you wanted to ask me. You said you had something to ask," I said before he could say anything more. I wasn't sure what to say about Connor and Riley any more than he did, and after what he said about me and him I really didn't want to talk about them anymore right now anyway.

"Last night when we hung up I started thinking about what I would like to do on our next date. I hate not being able to see you because of work and only having to settle for lunch here and there, and even that was only once this past week. So, like I said, I was thinking … what would you think if I asked you to come to my place Friday night and I'll cook you dinner? I mean, that way we are away from crowds, and bars, and other diners, and your brother and my sister … I know it's a lot different than what we've been doing, and I know you may not be comfortable with it, but I promise you Red – I promise that it's only dinner. I only want to spend uninterrupted time with you and only you, and –"

"Liam, stop. It sounds perfect."

And it did.

For a second I couldn't believe that I agreed to be alone with him at his place, but ever since he grabbed my hand in front of Connor and his sister, I knew that we had expressed that we were *more* to everyone, and not just to ourselves, or to each other. Going to his place felt okay. It felt like something I needed and wanted to do. It was out of my comfort zone for sure, but everything so far with Liam felt out of my comfort zone, and in the end everything always ended up being *magical*.

I wanted this.

It felt right.

"Really? You sure? Like I said it's just dinner, I have absolutely no expectations other than to feed you and talk with you, I just don't want you to feel uncomfortable ... so if you're afraid to say no because you think I'll be upset, or hurt, or let down, don't think that ..."

Once again I needed to cut him off so I started to talk right over him, not caring one bit about what he was saying, because it seemed like he was trying to talk me out of going over to his place for some God awful reason. He wanted to reassure me that I could honestly take my yes back and say no, and he wouldn't be upset. It was sweet that he was worried about these things now, but I didn't want to take my yes back. If anything, seeing him trying to backpedal because he was worried about my comfort, it only made me want to say *yes* even more.

"Liam I wasn't joking. I didn't say no because I thought you would be mad or upset or anything like that, but rather I said *yes* because it made *me* feel good when you asked me to have dinner with you and when you told me why you wanted to spend time with me. I actually said yes for me, more than I said it for you."

IIe just stared at me for a while. Then he gripped my hand even tighter, and squeezed.

"You know Red, you really are fucking perfect."

No, you are Liam.

I knew we had the rest of this date to get through, as well as the rest of this upcoming week, but I couldn't wait until Friday. I didn't know whether or not I would see Liam any more before then and neither did he, which made me wish that Friday was actually tomorrow. I can't believe he actually had me wishing days away.

Apparently when it comes to Liam … *wishes* are definitely my thing.

Chapter 13

Connor didn't speak to me the whole way home, and I didn't know what to make of it. I'd been prepared for questions, lecturing, yelling, but not the complete silence. I think his silence was more powerful than any of the words I was expecting him to say.

I don't know if the silence had more to do with me and Liam, or him and Riley.

It was definitely awkward for all of us when Connor and Riley came back to the table. After another round of drinks and some stilted conversation we decided to call it a night. I don't know what went wrong, but something sure did.

After saying goodbye to Liam and Riley I waited for the shit to hit the fan with Connor … but it didn't. Connor dropped me off at my apartment without saying a word, except a curt 'good-night,' and I haven't talked to him since.

That was three days ago.

I haven't seen Connor, or talked to him, so I still have no idea what his problem is.

When Liam called me that night after he got home I asked him if Riley had said anything about what happened when she and Connor were playing pool, but she didn't say anything. I guess we are both in a weird predicament with our siblings.

I knew Connor's idea of a group date was a bad idea and would bite everyone in the ass.

Though if I am being totally honest, going out on Saturday wasn't such a bad thing for Liam and me, considering it definitely moved us further along in our relationship, and now we are out in the open with everyone. After that date I can't wait to see what's going to happen next.

"Hi, Samantha."

I was so absorbed in my thoughts of Liam, Connor, and Riley, that I didn't notice Aaron until he was right in front of me.

"What are you doing back here Aaron?" I asked him. I didn't like that he was here, but there was nothing I could do about it now, other than to ask him to leave. I almost forgot about him because I was so consumed with Liam, which was a mistake.

"I wanted to apologize Samantha. Last time I was here I think you misunderstood what I was saying, and then that guy was all over me … I didn't get to explain," Aaron replied trying to sound innocent, but I could tell that he was lying. I could see the anger in his eyes.

I knew I needed to get him out of the store as quickly as possible which is why I told him that it was okay, and then I asked him if he would like anything to eat or drink. He ordered, said he would see me around, and then he left. There was nothing awkward about the run-in with Aaron this time, but it still made my skin crawl. Something about it just didn't feel right.

I sent text messages to both Liam and Connor about Aaron because it felt like the right thing to do. After I sent the texts I felt a bit like a tattletale, but it was better to be safe than sorry.

Both of their responses were almost immediate, but Connor's text came through first.

Connor: Are you fucking kidding me? I'm on my way. Keep an eye out for him. Make sure he doesn't come back.

I didn't need Connor to come running down here. That's not why I told him. Aaron had already left, and there was nothing that Connor could do. However, after thinking a little more about the skin-crawling, I decided that maybe it wouldn't be so bad to have some company after all.

I heard another few beeps and saw that the next text was from Liam.

Liam: Are you okay? Are you sure he left? I wish I could come down there to make sure everything is okay but I have a team meeting in ten minutes and I can't delay it or cancel. Jesus, Red … are you sure everything's fine?

Once again, how could I forget Connor and Liam's similarities? They want to rush in and protect, even though there is nothing to protect here. The threat is gone, and Aaron wasn't exactly threat-worthy today. I could tell he was lying when he apologized, and he did make my skin crawl, but he didn't say or do anything wrong.

Me: I'm fine … Everything's fine. I'm sure that he's gone, but don't worry … I told Connor what went on and he's heading here right now. He told me to keep my eyes open to make sure Aaron doesn't come back. I don't know what he expects to find, or what he plans on doing once he gets here … but I'm not going to argue with him. You know Connor …

Liam: Yeah, I do … Which is why I'm happy that he's going there and that he'll be with you in case that asshole comes back. I can't believe he had the fucking balls to come back or that he stood there and gave that bullshit apology. Fuck, Red, I wish that I could be there with you instead.

Me: Don't be silly Mr. Big Shot Team Leader … I know you can't leave at a moment's notice! Speaking of which … it's almost time for that meeting of yours. I guess I'll talk to you later.

Liam: Yeah, it is.

Liam: You know, Red … I really miss seeing your face. I can't wait to see you Friday.

Me: Liam … the things you say … I miss your face too. I can't wait to see you on Friday either.

Oh, my, wow!

I sent my text to him, but I didn't get one back. It was just as well because I really didn't know how much more of his comments, such as 'I miss seeing your face' I could take.

When I was done texting I put my phone away so I wasn't distracted. I didn't need what happened with Aaron to happen again.

Since I was staring at the door I didn't miss Connor entering. He made a beeline towards me and started hammering me with questions about Aaron, as if I didn't tell him everything that went on already.

"I really don't like this, Sam. Something doesn't seem right about that guy coming in here like that. You talked to him and set him straight, I did, and Liam did too. I even think Allie's said a few things to him."

Hearing both Liam and Connor voice the same things once again didn't make me feel any better.

"I'm gonna have to tell Mom and Dad about this, Sam. I glossed over the incident last time Aaron was here and bothered you because I didn't want them to worry while they're at Aunt Maggie's … but something just doesn't feel right about this. I have a weird feeling and I don't fucking like it. I'm trained to trust my instincts, and my instincts are telling me this dude is fucking wired wrong." He stopped talking but he kept moving, pacing back and forth behind me.

"Stupid fucking Joanna. If it weren't for her I would've been with you today and could've handled this shit once and for all. Maybe we should go back to our original shifts and just fire her ass already. Or maybe we could put her with Allie instead. Allie can handle her and make sure she doesn't do things she's not supposed to –"

"No. We can't do that. Joanna and Allie don't get along, and with Joanna acting the way she's been, I can imagine her starting with Allie and Allie really doesn't need that garbage from her. Allie's going through a lot right now, she really needs this job, and I don't want to make things worse for her when she comes here – like sticking her with that trash-starting bitch –"

"*Fuck. Fuck!* I know, I know. This just fucking sucks, Sam."

Yeah, you could definitely say that again. Connor didn't say anything else, probably because he was too busy thinking up different scenarios about how he could be here all the time.

I figured I would just leave him to his silence, but he didn't stay that way for long.

"So about Saturday ..." Connor said.

Fuck. He wanted to get into that now? *Now?* Nothing like a complete change in topics. "How long have you and Liam been together, Samantha?" *Jesus!* My eyes flashed up to his and I could tell this wasn't good.

"We went out on a few dates," I told him.

I was staring at him when I said it so I could see the emotions flash in his eyes, and across his face. It really wasn't looking good.

"Why didn't you say anything?" he asked. Was he kidding me with that question?

"Are you kidding me Connor? You forced us into going out as a group *with his sister*, you basically told Liam and I you didn't want him anywhere near me, *you wanted my first real date with anyone to include you* ... why *would* I tell you that I was seeing him? So you could ruin that too?" I knew I was getting louder the longer I talked, but I just didn't care. Was he fucking serious right now?

I didn't know if he was serious or not because he didn't say anything.

He just stared at me.

I couldn't take the emotions running through me anymore.

"I like him Connor. I mean, I *really* like him." I can't believe I said what I just did to Connor. I can't believe that I admitted that out loud, and to *him*. If he was Allie, sure. But him? These last few days must've really done a number on me to have me blurting out things like that to him, especially since I've been hiding my feelings and actions for weeks.

I was looking down now, but I heard him loudly exhale.

"I know, Sam. I know." *Wait ... what?* I looked back up, meeting his eyes.

"It's why I didn't say anything to you on Saturday after we left. For weeks I knew it was more. I knew that you both had feelings for each other. I knew even before I saw it written all over your faces when he grabbed your hand. I just didn't know what to say to you ... and I still don't. I felt like a dick for treating you both the way I've been, because it's more than obvious now that he is head over fucking heels for you ... but at the same time you are so fucking new to all of this Sam, and dick or not, *all* I want to do is drag you away so nothing bad happens to you. I just don't fucking know how to handle all of this. In the beginning I didn't like him because I could see myself in him ... and I didn't like it because I thought all he wanted was something quick and easy ... but like I said, I saw the way he looked at you these past few weeks and especially at *Molly's* and it's just different now ... for both of you. *Fuck*! I really don't know how to handle this fucking shit … I've never really had to with you before. The one time I thought I did have to handle it, I really fucking screwed things up. I don't know what to do with all of this, Samantha. I don't know what the fuck to do."

Wow. Just wow. I never expected any of this from Connor. I wasn't sure how to handle *any* of this either.

What he said next shocked me even more.

"I also don't know what to do because I really think I like his fucking sister. She gave me her number when we were playing pool and I decided to call her. At first I didn't know what to think about her giving me her number – it threw me for a bit. But shit. *I fucking like her.* And if you tell him any of that, I will make your life a living fucking hell. If you tell *anyone* I just said that shit like I'm some fucking girl talking about a secret crush, I swear to fucking God …" Connor just shook his head and walked to the back room where he barricaded himself inside until I was done for the day.

I have absolutely no idea what he did back there, but it wouldn't surprise me if he spent as much time thinking about a certain person's sister, as I did thinking about that sister's brother.

****

Liam and I were supposed to have lunch on Wednesday at a restaurant near his office, but he had to cancel on me at the last minute. It was a spur of the moment invitation so I was really excited about it because I hadn't planned on seeing him until Friday, but he had to back out on me because one of his group members was having a problem with a certain task and they needed to fix it.

To say I was disappointed was an understatement.

I had the day off with nothing to do, so I put some of the time to good use by going out and buying myself a new outfit for our date on Friday night. I knew that I could probably go casual again, but this date felt special for some reason, so I wanted to purchase something new and special too.

I was telling Allie about it the next night when I heard Liam's voice right in front of me. I wasn't supposed to be working that night, and with his busy schedule, it never even crossed my mind that he'd be coming in for coffee or that I would be seeing him. *Or that Karen would be with him and I would see her too*. She stayed outside the shop doing something on her phone but she glanced up and looked at Liam a few times, so I knew that they were together once again.

"What are you doing here at night, Red? I thought you were leaving here early?" Liam asked me in such a way that I didn't know whether he was happy to see me or not. There was no smile, no twinkling eyes, there were no pronounced dimples. There did seem to be something in his eyes that looked like concern though. Why? Was he concerned that I was giving evil death ray eyes to his busty blonde co-worker with the hope that she would explode?

"I wasn't meant to be working the closing shift. Connor was going to do it, but he was asked to fill in for someone at the Firehouse. It all happened so fast and I didn't talk to you today, so I didn't fill you in." I finished my response to him and wondered if now would be the appropriate time to ask him what he was doing with *her* after closing hours at his job?

"Oh. Yeah, I wanted to call you, or at least text you before, but it's been really busy. That's why we're making a coffee run now. We have a few hours left and we all need to refuel." Liam stopped talking, but all I could do was shake my head. I was still hung up on the 'we' part. *We?*

I think I lost all mental function because I just kept shaking my head over and over. Allie came to my rescue and asked what she could get him. I heard him order his usual black coffee with no sugar, but I also heard him order a medium iced coffee with hazelnut. I knew that had to be *Karen's* order. *Just fucking lovely.*

"I'll get it Allie. You don't have to worry about it." I think I said that more than anything so I would be able to turn around and get myself together and not have to face Liam acting more like a complete fool.

He must've known what I was thinking and why I was acting the way I was, because his voice cut into what I was doing.

"She's working on the project too you know."

Nothing like telling me this *now*, Liam.

I didn't even pretend to not know who or what he was talking about. I just said, "Oh."

"*Oh?* That's it? That's all you're going to say?" Liam said exasperated. How dare he be the one who gets exasperated – I wasn't the one who blindsided him again with *her*.

"What do you want me to say, Liam? No, I *didn't* know she was working on your project too, but thanks for telling me *now*," I said with a clearly bitchy voice.

"Really? That's all you wanted to say?"

"Like I said before … what do you want me to say?"

"What you're thinking."

Liam must be out of his fucking mind asking for an answer to something like that, especially in this instance.

"Trust me Liam, you don't want to know what I'm thinking." Truer words might possibly have never been spoken by me.

I heard him sigh before saying, "Red, we've talked about her. She works with me. Technically, she works *for* me …"

I still had my back turned to him so I couldn't look into his eyes to try and decipher what he was thinking, or see the truthfulness in his words.

"Samantha … it is absolutely nothing, and will never, *ever*, be anything more than that. I told you before … and I will tell you every day if you need me to … it's *you* … and *only* you."

This time I heard Allie's deep sigh.

I also felt my heart do a little flutter.

"Look at me, Sam," he said to my back that was *still* turned.

I knew I needed to turn around and give him his drinks, but I wasn't ready to let go of the fact that he was here with Karen again, even after he said something that moved me in such a way I literally felt my heart skip around a little. I had to do and say something though, so I turned around to face him.

"Okay," I said while placing his drinks onto the counter in front of him.

"Okay? That's it?" Liam asked in return to my simple response to his statement, with even more puzzlement in his voice than he had before.

"Yup. That's it. That will be $5.50, please." I was looking directly at him so I saw his confusion at first, and then his complete bafflement.

"*Are you serious*?" he asked still completely baffled.

"Yes, I'm completely serious. Give me the money for your coffee." Liam looked at me like he couldn't believe what I'd just said, and I couldn't blame him. I never take his money when he's in here. This isn't just his stuff though. It's *hers* too. And she's not getting a fucking thing from me. Liam just shook his head while he dug into his pants pocket.

Liam smiled at me as he handed over the twenty dollar bill he'd pulled out. I snatched it out of his hand, rung up his order, put the money in the till and slammed it shut.

"Aren't you going to give me my change, Red?" Liam asked with a definite smile in his voice.

"No," I growled back.

With my simple and curt response Liam burst out laughing. He moved towards me by leaning over the counter a little, then he grabbed my face in his hands bringing me half over the counter, meeting him right in the middle. His eyes roamed all over my face. Then he said, "Most girls don't look good when they're jealous Red, but goddamn, I *love* the way you look when you're jealous, even when you have absolutely no reason to be."

Jealous ... I wasn't exactly jealous ... was I?

"Instead of jealous, you might want to be worried, Red. You might want to be worried because I'm finding more and more things that I love about you, and you need to prepare yourself if you aren't already prepared for all of *this* and how much I'm feeling – because it's not going away. All of this is only getting bigger and deeper ..."

When he said what he did I gasped so quickly my mouth opened, and he took full advantage right there in front of the whole coffee shop by fusing his mouth to mine and kissing me like there would be no tomorrow, and like he was trying to convey everything he was feeling with that one earth shattering kiss.

It wasn't appropriate for where we were, but for him, *for both of us*, I think it was necessary.

I really don't remember much of what happened after he stopped kissing me and left. I don't remember much because all I kept thinking about was the kiss and the word *love*.

****

By the time Liam called me when he finally got home it was after one in the morning, so I didn't talk to him for long. I really didn't like that he was working with Karen until all hours of the night, and I think I had good reason to be upset about it. I trusted Liam when he said that there was nothing going on with them and that he wasn't interested, but I saw the way that she looked at him and I *knew* that she was definitely interested and wanted something to be going on. Maybe I was more than a little jealous of all the time she got to spend with him. Maybe I was also more than a little jealous about how stacked she was and how blonde, and blue-eyed, and tall, and just fucking perfect.

I really, really didn't like this whole jealousy thing. Unlike some of the many things I was introduced to because of Liam, I could definitely live without the introduction of jealousy. It really wasn't me. No matter what Liam said, I knew it really wasn't pretty on me. It was making me insane.

Liam was interested in me though, so I guess that made up for certain things.

With his cancelling on me the other day and with my thoughts of Karen, I found myself texting him a few times the next day to make sure we were still on for dinner at his place and that he wasn't running late. He assured me that everything was fine, and that our date was definitely still happening.

To get out of my head and away from all of the thoughts running through it, I decided to get ready for the date a little early. I put on the brand new light pink and blue printed maxi dress with a slit up the back that I bought for the occasion, as well as the new matching pink strapless bra and thong. I knew Liam wouldn't be seeing what was underneath my dress, but knowing what I had on made me feel sexy and confident, and after the last few days I needed sexy and confident. I added makeup to my face and a few dangling bracelets to my wrists, brushed my hair out again, and just waited.

All I had to do was wait. And think. And wonder. And worry.

All of those things weren't good before I had dinner alone with him at his apartment. I did it anyway though. I waited, thought, wondered, and worried. I thought about Liam's words to me, and I really don't know if I'm ready for any of what Liam's feeling or for what *I'm* feeling, because I really do think I'm falling for him.

Falling for him hard.

And I don't know what to do about it.

I've never felt like this before.

Before I could scare myself even more, I heard my phone beeping. There was no way he would cancel on me now. No fucking way. Thinking those things didn't keep the sick feeling out of my stomach though. I needed to look at my text.

Liam: I left work early. I know we said 7:00, but if you want to come earlier I'm here, and I can't wait to see you.

He wasn't cancelling on me thank God. As I re-read his text I knew there was no way I was going to pretend like I wasn't ready and not go over now. No way in hell. I couldn't wait to see him either.

Me: I'm on my way.

I grabbed my small wallet clutch, put on my new sandals, and headed out the door. I didn't know what the proper etiquette was when showing up to a man's apartment for dinner, but I decided to stop at the liquor store on the way and get a really expensive bottle of red wine.

It all felt really adult and new, but it also felt right.

Maybe it was because Liam was a little older and definitely more mature than some of the guys I've been around, maybe it was because he had wealth and a confidence about him, maybe it was because he was so put together and he knew exactly who he was and what he wanted, that this seemed very domestic, very advanced, and so much *more*.

I was in no way complaining about going to his place and doing any of this however, because even at my age doing something like this felt a little more comfortable than going out drinking or dancing.

Before I knew it though, and before I could get tangled up even more in my mind, I was standing outside of Liam's building waiting to be let in. I smoothed my hair with my free hand, clutched the neck of the wine bottle with the other and prayed to God that I wouldn't make a complete ass out of myself. I heard the buzzer and the release of the door, and then I was met by a guard who was seated at the front desk. All of the security screamed wealth and made me a little nervous. The guard asked me who I was there to see, told me the floor as if I didn't know, and led me to the elevators. As soon as I was on the elevator I prayed once again, pressed the button, and then I was there.

The top floor.

Of course it would be the top floor, why would it be anything but?

I went to Liam's door and knocked and it was barely ten seconds before the door swung open.

Liam stood there in his suit pants and a light blue dress shirt with the top few buttons unbuttoned and no tie, his shirt still tucked into his pants. He looked sinful.

"You look amazing, Red. I absolutely love that dress. I'm glad I didn't have a chance to change yet, because I think I would've felt sorely lacking in comparison to you. Come in, please." He opened the door even wider for me and moved to the side so I could enter. I only made it a few steps before I froze. The word apartment seems like an inappropriate word to be using when describing Liam's place. It is enormous, and the view of the city that is showcased by the floor to ceiling windows is absolutely magnificent. I had no idea how I would be staying away from the windows and focusing on dinner and Liam all night.

"I'm guessing you like my place?" Liam asked, moving around me because I was still rooted to my spot.

Along with the view, I was struck by how beautiful his home looked with the blue walls and blue accents.

"It's gorgeous, Liam. I guess you weren't joking about blue being your favorite color, huh? And the view! It's amazing."

He was looking directly at me when he said, "Yes, it is."

We both knew what he meant. I could feel my cheeks heating up. They heated up even more when he came towards me, and when he put his hands on them and lightly brushed my lips with his.

"I'm so happy you're here, Samantha. Please look around and make yourself at home. I didn't have much time to get things started, I hope that's okay. I'm just going to head to the kitchen and start prepping some things. Steak is okay right?"

"Steak's fine," I said before remembering that I still held the bottle of wine in my hand. "I forgot to give this to you. I hope this is alright. I've never done this before, so I wasn't sure what to bring …"

And there I went again admitting to all of these firsts with him. By his smile I could tell that he didn't mind that I haven't done this before in the least. He took the bottle from my hand and looked at the label.

"Wow, Red. This is a really expensive bottle of wine. I think we should have this with dinner and celebrate you having dinner at a man's house for the first time …" He couldn't keep a straight face while saying it.

"You're really pleased with yourself aren't you, that you were my first actual date, and now getting me to come here and have dinner with you …"

"You have no idea, Red. Let me go open this up and let it breathe for a while … go take a look around if you want, then come to the kitchen. I want to talk to you …" he said before turning around and heading towards the kitchen.

With the open layout of the apartment I was able to see what he was doing, and he was able to see me if he'd wanted, but I didn't let that stop me from searching around his home. I liked seeing his things all over the place. It gave me more insight into who he really was other than what he had told me so far, or what I'd already figured out on my own. He had tons of books all over which I appreciated as someone who loved books as well, though his collection leaned towards books focusing on architecture, art, business, marketing, biographies, a few mysteries, and sports. He also had a few pictures on his mantle like I did. I stopped to look at them and I was completely struck by how beautiful his mother was. There were a few of her with the whole family, and more of he and Riley and a few of Liam with his friends, but the one of his mother by herself really captured my attention. I still didn't know what had happened to her, but I knew it must have been devastating. By the bits and pieces I had gleaned from Liam, it was something that completely changed the dynamic of the family.

When I was done looking at the pictures I started looking at the paintings on the walls, because I had never seen such beautiful artwork before.

What I noticed about the paintings absolutely shocked me.

"Liam ... you painted this?" I turned around to look at him on the other side of the apartment. He was in the process of getting things out of the refrigerator but he stopped what he was doing to turn around and look at me.

"It's unbelievable," I continued by saying, because it absolutely was. He has an amazing talent.

"Yeah, Red. I painted all of the artwork hanging in here," he told me, but when he said it he didn't sound proud like one would expect of someone who painted with such brilliance, but rather in a way that said 'please don't make a big deal out of it.' Something clicked in my head and I remembered a conversation we had a while ago where he talked about his love of drawing and how he didn't do it as much as he liked to anymore because of his father and the career path that he chose. I didn't know he painted, but remembering the passion in his eyes when he was talking about drawing and art, it didn't surprise me that he painted as well.

I also remembered that he said he was working on something new, and the look he had in his eyes when he talked about it.

"Where's the piece you're working on?" I asked all of a sudden, full of curiosity and determination to see what he was creating.

"What?" he asked.

"A while ago we were talking about your drawings, and you mentioned that you were working on something. Did you finish it, or are you still working on it?"

I could tell by his face that he didn't want to answer my question for some reason. He seemed different all of a sudden – possibly nervous, or worried even.

"Liam?"

He left the kitchen and started walking towards me. As he neared me he started to speak. He said, "Don't freak out, okay?"

Why do people think that they can say that sentence, and that the person they say it to won't freak out?

Why would I freak out?

"Okay ..."

He grabbed ahold of my hand once he reached me and started walking me towards the kitchen, then past it, and towards one of the closed doors off of the kitchen and dining area.

He stopped in front of the door, inhaled and exhaled for a few moments, but then he grabbed the handle and opened the door. He turned on the lights, pulled me into the room behind him, and started walking into the center of the room where a big easel was set up with a cloth over it.

He grasped the cloth and pulled it down ... and I gasped.

I couldn't believe what I was seeing.

"Liam ... it's ... it's ... *me*."

He was painting me.

Me.

But it couldn't have been me, because the woman on the canvas was absolutely breathtaking. She was stunning. He couldn't possibly see me like that.

Jesus.

"I don't know what to say ..." and I really didn't. How could I say that she was beautiful when the she is supposed to be me, and I don't exactly see myself like that? I could tell he wasn't done creating yet, but what he had was unbelievably mesmerizing.

"You don't have to say anything, Red. You asked what I was working on, and now you know. Come on, let's go back out and get dinner going." He grabbed my hand again and started to lead me out, but I stopped him because I couldn't leave the room without saying *something.*

This was important. I knew it was important. *This was a moment.*

I looked up at him, into his eyes, and just asked, "Why?"

He let go of my hand, and he put his hands on the sides of my neck tangling his fingers in my long hair. He looked just as deeply into my eyes as I was looking into his.

For a minute I was afraid he wasn't going to say anything, but then he did.

"I had to. I needed to paint the most beautiful thing I have ever seen. When I first saw you, I knew that you were it. After that time in the shop when you told me to leave, I wasn't sure if I would ever see you again, or if you would let me near you, so I started drawing you and then painting you. I needed to get your face down before I forgot even the littlest of details because I knew I never wanted to forget anything about you – even the tiniest things. But when I saw you again, and I knew that things would be okay, I still kept on painting you ... but at a slower pace, because I didn't want to finish it ... I don't *ever* want to finish it. Every time I see you I learn something new, or I see something new – a new facial expression, a different light in your eyes, a little quirk of your brow or your nose that only you have, a freckle here or a beauty mark just there" he said while tapping at the very faint one right below my right eye. "I don't want it to ever be finished or for me to think it's perfect because then that means that there's nothing else for me to discover that's new … and every day I want to know you more and more … I want to see the different shades of a blush that you have, I want to see all the various emotions that blaze in your eyes, all the ways your feelings move your lips or cheeks or crinkle your forehead or light up your face – I want to see *everything*, Red. I don't *ever* want to be done with you …"

"Liam …" *Holy shit.*

Liam didn't say anything else. He just leaned down and kissed me on my forehead, then quickly on the lips before he grabbed ahold of my hand again and led me out of the room. I willingly went with him on shaky legs because I didn't know what else to do.

In that moment I would have went willingly with him anywhere, because I knew without a doubt that in that room my life had changed forever.

I wasn't falling anymore.

I didn't have to worry about that.

I didn't have to worry because I was already there.

I was in love with Liam.

Chapter 14

While sitting on a stool at the center island in Liam's kitchen, watching him get all the things together to make dinner, I couldn't help but to keep thinking about what I had just discovered. I was in *love* with him. And I wasn't exceptionally scared about it. Looking back now, I think that in the beginning I wanted nothing to do with Liam because I knew deep down inside that I'd end up feeling what I am right now, and with that feeling would come the knowledge that he had the power to shatter me if he didn't return my feelings, or if he did and then one day he didn't anymore. Sitting here now I do have that knowledge, and I realize that I should be terrified, but for some unknown reason I'm not. I'm actually more terrified by what I almost let slip by.

Just then he picked his head up and caught me studying him. He flashed me his wide dimpled smile and said, "What?" to which I replied "Nothing." I could tell that he didn't believe that for a second.

If only he knew what I was thinking.

"Would you like me to pour you some wine before I get started with my masterclass on cooking?" he asked. His smile definitely turned into a smirk.

"Yes, please. What would you like me to do to help?"

I offered to help, because I couldn't just sit here and stare at him. If I kept staring at him the way I've been, I'm sure that he'd be able to tell that I'm in love with him, and that's not something I'm ready to reveal yet.

This feeling, while I'm not against it, it's all so new and so *real*. I want to keep it to myself for a while.

"It would be a big help if you could go by that wall over there," he said while pointing in the direction he wanted me to go "and turn on the CD that I have in there, so we can have a little music with our wine while I get dinner made."

I went over to the wall and discovered that not only did he have the stereo system, but he also had a beautiful old record player and a wall full of albums. I can't believe I missed all of it on my first glance at the apartment, though I was distracted by his paintings.

"This is quite a selection of vinyl's you have here, Liam. I didn't know you collected. I know you said you loved music, but I didn't know anything about all of this."

"Most of them are my mom's old records she kept in our attic. I took them after I got this place. I started adding to the collection only recently. It's another way for me to keep a part of her near me now, you know?"

"That's a beautiful thing to do, Liam. I saw the picture of her on your mantle. She was absolutely beautiful. Riley looks a lot like her."

"She really was one of the most beautiful women I have ever known, both inside and out, Red. I said it to you before, but I'll say it again … she would have loved you."

I turned away from the albums to look at him, and I saw that he was looking at me. "Come on, put the CD on and come back here. I actually do have something else I need you to do," he said with a happy smile.

Okay, then.

It took me a few seconds to get the CD playing, and when I heard who it was I was absolutely pleased that he remembered yet another thing about me – my strange love of Otis Redding.

How could I not have fallen in love with him?

It was all of these little things that he did. It wasn't the big things, or the way he looked, or what he did for a living – it was the small things that got me. It was Otis Redding, the bookstore, the daisies, lunch at the café, baseball games, his love for his sister and his mom, his loyalty to his friends, grabbing my hand and claiming me as his in front of my brother without saying anything, his wanting to make me dinner in private so he could have me all to himself.

I never stood a chance.

"Red?" he called out when I stood frozen once again lost in my thoughts.

I snapped out of it quickly and walked back to the kitchen island. He handed me a glass of wine and told me to sit. According to him, that was all I was supposed to do that night.

Sit.

Enjoy.

Eat.

Talk.

And talking is what he wanted to do. He rolled up the sleeves of his dress shirt revealing the tattoos that captured my attention from the very first time that I met him, and started chopping up the vegetables that he was going to grill with the steak.

"I hope you don't mind if I grill up the steaks in here – I have one of those flat grills that go over the burners … but I thought since it is such a gorgeous night we could eat on the balcony. What do you think? I already set up the table out there when I got home, but I can always set up in here it's no problem …"

"Outside is fine. It really is a lovely night, and your view is amazing. I don't mind at all," I said, and then took a sip of wine.

I found my gaze drifting back to his arms as he was chopping and I couldn't take it anymore. I needed to ask the questions I was dying to know. The longer I looked at his tattoos the more I needed to know about them. Every time I saw them I wanted to trace them with my fingertips, I wanted to explore every inch of them and him, and I wanted to know more than anything what they meant.

"So Liam …" He looked up when I started to speak. I guess he could tell from my tone that I wanted to ask him something important, and that I wasn't just making idle conversation to fill the silence.

"Yes, Red …" he returned in the same sing-song like voice that I used to start my inquisition.

"When you were telling me about your drawings, you also mentioned that you designed all of your tattoos … so that got me thinking … Each of them must mean something right? You created them all … but why tattoos exactly? Why put something permanent on your body – what do they mean to you?"

"Red … after all this time, are you trying to tell me you don't like my tattoos?" He tried to look serious while he was saying it, but his grin won out and he completely blew the effect he was going for.

"Do I even need to respond to that?" I asked, feeling my cheeks heat up a bit.

"No, you really don't. I know you *love* my tattoos. I see you stare at them all the time when I have something on that doesn't keep them hidden. I've been waiting for you to ask me about them actually," he said to me.

Cocky bastard.

I felt my cheeks really start to flame now.

I narrowed my eyes at him but all he did was laugh.

"I started getting them once I turned eighteen. At first, I'll be honest, I did it because my dad fucking hated it, and for the longest time after my mom died I hated him, so inking up my skin was the perfect way to rebel against him, and his rules, and his dislikes. I already told you some of that. He hated the tattoos, but I loved them because the earliest ones were all a reminder of my mom and my family. You can see they all interconnect and they're all things that mean something most to me." He started pointing to specific pieces of his tattoos, explaining a lot of them in the next few minutes.

I thought that looking at Liam's home would give me the most insight to the man inside, more than I had already learned, but what was most insightful was his body. Not his beautiful face, or his toned muscles, but the creations that were flowing up and down his arms.

"You should see what I have all over the rest of me, Red. You want me to take my clothes off for you so you can see and ask me about the rest?" He raised his eyebrows and moved his hands to the front of his shirt like he would start unbuttoning it even more if I gave him the go-ahead.

I knew my jaw fell open. How could it not? I knew that he had more tattoos on his upper arms, ones that I couldn't completely see, but that he explained. What else did he have and *where*?

When I didn't say anything he just smiled and shook his head. "Some other time, maybe?" He just left it at that, which was the best thing he could've done for me at the moment.

He went back to cutting up the veggies and then moved them to the side of the cutting board. I went back to drinking my wine thinking about all the things I still didn't know about him. He told me that he never wanted to fully feel like he knew me because he wanted to constantly be surprised and get to know me more and more every single day. I felt the same exact way. For as much as I wanted to know right now, there was something special in knowing and hoping that I didn't know quite enough yet – that I had the opportunity to get to know more.

I just continued to stare at him.

I knew that what was happening between us, and especially inside me, was special. I found myself asking once again, how could I be so lucky?

About ten seconds later, I didn't feel so lucky anymore.

I heard Liam sigh, so I looked up and met his eyes. He held my stare while he started talking to me.

"It's been a while now, Red. Are you ever going to tell me what's been holding you back?" He must've sensed my discomfort when I only continued to stare without answering, because he changed his voice to a slight tease when he continued on and said, "I mean … I know there must've been a guy in your past who broke your heart or something like that – there *has* to be – otherwise you would be in love with me already, and you're not there yet Samantha. I would know."

He would know?

Really?

Because I discovered about a half hour ago that I was in fact in love with him and he didn't see that brand new emotion in my eyes. I guess he did still have things to discover about me after all, since he couldn't detect my love for him. I guess I should be happy that he knew none of this, that he was so completely wrong. To have him mention something I actually do feel for him and have it still be so fresh and new, and then to bring up someone breaking my heart in the

past in the same sentence – I don't know whether to feel amused,
confused, anxious, hurt, let down, sad.

I didn't want to bring any thoughts of Aiden into this.

But it looked like I had to.

So much for magical luck.

I wanted so much to be amused, and I would've been, if I knew I
didn't have to talk about Aiden to Liam. I would've been amused at
Liam's comment about how I would've been in love with him already –
as if it was a foregone conclusion – *especially because I was*. I just
couldn't be amused. I couldn't even crack a smile at his teasing voice, at
his beautiful grin with the pronounced dimples that were just begging for
my touch.

Because I didn't smile back, because I didn't have a witty comeback
to his cocky remark, because I knew I must've been staring at him
blankly, he lost his grin and stood up a little straighter. He knew that
something was wrong.

I knew I had to get it over with. I was in love with him and he
deserved the truth.

"Do you really want to know?" I asked in a quiet voice full of the
trepidation I was feeling coursing through me. I really didn't want to have
all of the awesome feelings I was feeling not even five minutes ago
minimized right now, but thinking about what I needed to say was
impeding on my happiness. I finally realized I am in *love* with Liam. I
realized that nothing was holding me back any more like he thought.

I didn't want bad memories with Aiden, or of Aiden, to taint any of
tonight, but he probably did need to know what held me back before. He
needed to know all of it.

Without hesitation Liam said, "Yes. Of course. Absolutely."

What else could I do? "Okay, I need a few minutes though. How about I tell you all about it while we eat?"

"Okay. Let me get everything on the grill then," he replied.

"Perfect."

It was so not perfect.

****

Apparently all Liam needed was a little promise of answers that he'd been seeking for a while now as motivation to get his ass in gear and have dinner prepared in no time. Once I knew what awaited me during dinner, I could only think of one thing to do – I filled up my wine glass and I drank.

Nothing like some liquid courage to get me through what's to come.

When Liam was done grilling, he placed the food on big platters and started taking them outside. When he was on the balcony I seized the opportunity to once again refill my wine glass. Though I could already feel a buzz, it didn't stop me from drinking.

When Liam came back in to get me and the last remaining items, he noticed the empty bottle and my now full glass.

"Um, Red … are you okay?" He didn't sound like he was going to like my answer.

I completely lied when I said, "I'm fine." *I was not fine.* In minutes I would have to choke down his wonderfully smelling dinner, while regurgitating my past experiences that I would rather leave buried. Whatever could be wrong with that?

"Okay then. I'll go grab another bottle of wine, you can go outside, and I'll meet you out there."

While on my way to balcony all I could think about was the conversation we were going to have. I just needed to choose my words wisely, reveal enough without revealing too much, and move it along. Simple as that.

When I stepped outside all thoughts of the conversation disappeared. *I was enchanted.*

I didn't notice before how beautiful the balcony was or how big. I also didn't notice the beautifully set table with a white tablecloth, fine china, a smattering of candles, or his mother's uniquely charming blue pitcher with the bushel of daisies in the center. There were lights everywhere outside, and though it wasn't dark yet, the candles that were lit made the outside where we were eating seem as if we were in a fairytale.

It was pure romance.

Once again, it was the details and the little things like this that had me falling in love with him way before I knew that I was even falling. Before I actually fell. I knew without a doubt that I was head over heels.

"Do you like it?" Liam asked from behind me. I didn't even know that he came out, that is how enchanted I was by the sight before me.

"I *love* it. I especially love your mom's pitcher in the center of the table. I'm happy that I get the chance to see it."

"Me too. Come on, let's sit. It's time to eat before it gets cold."

I started towards a chair, but before I could get it myself, Liam pulled it out and sat me at the table.

I really did feel like I was in a fairytale, and that he really was Prince Charming.

When I was settled, I placed my glass in front of me, but I picked it right back up and took a big gulp.

This was it.

Now or never.

"Samantha … you don't have to tell me anything if you don't want to. Ever since I brought up what's holding you back, something's changed. I don't see the sparkle in your eyes anymore, and you're drinking as if you hope to pass out before we get the chance to talk. I don't want that to happen, nor do I ever want you to feel uncomfortable talking to me. Ever. I don't need to know anything about the past okay? I only need to know about now and the future."

I wanted to take the "out" he was offering, but I couldn't.

I needed to talk about Aiden. I wanted to let Liam know what was holding me back in the beginning, but not anymore. I was in love with Liam now. I didn't need any interference, and definitely not from anything having to do with Aiden. If I didn't say anything now Liam would always wonder, even though he said he would forget it, and that's not fair to him or to our future.

I took another sip from my wine glass and began.

"There was a guy in high school. When I met him he was so far out of my league I don't know why he wanted anything to do with me, and I still don't. He made it a point to hang out with me, and to be my friend. He was my *best* friend. We went out. I told you about that before … we went here and there, but we weren't dating. We were friends. *Not like how you and I are friends … Jesus …* I'm making a mess of this …"

I grabbed my wine again and took a deep sip, and would've probably drained it if Liam didn't grab my free hand that was resting on the table and give it a squeeze.

"It's okay Samantha. You aren't messing up anything. You can stop if you want, or continue on. It's up to you," he reassured me.

I needed to get it all out of my system once and for all.

"We did a lot of things together even though we were complete opposites in every way you could think of. I went to his house a bit and hung out with him, but he never came by my parents place. My parents, nor Connor, would've ever understood. That's why I never told them about him. That was one of my greatest mistakes ..."

I looked up at Liam to try and detect what he was thinking or feeling, but I couldn't tell. I knew I needed to push on through and not worry about what he was thinking or feeling right now.

"One night in the shop, Connor was closing up with me. He normally never did that, but he was home from college so he was there. The guy ... he always walked me home if I closed up at night, he didn't like me being alone. He didn't know Connor was there, and I never thought to mention it to him. It should have been fine." I stopped for a few moments lost in the memory once again, of what had happened next. Liam squeezed my hand again as if knowing I was lost in thought, and that I needed a little encouragement. "It should have been fine," I said again. "It wasn't though. It was far from fine. He came into the shop and he was drunk. I'd never seen him drunk before – he shouldn't have been drinking – I don't know why he was. He came on to me ... *really* came on to me, and I tried to get him to stop. I knew Connor was in the back and that he would be coming up front at any moment, but he just *wouldn't stop –*"

"*Samantha!*" Liam's voice cut into my memories. I looked at him. "You're crying baby. You don't have to tell me any more. It's okay," he said, right before he removed his hand from mine, grabbed my face with both of his hands and wiped the tears that I didn't even know I was shedding from my face with his thumbs.

"I'm fine. I'm fine, Liam. I promise." I was almost done telling him what happened. I just needed to get through the last little bit, and I needed him to do it. I grabbed his hand that was holding mine before from my cheek, I wrapped my fingers in his again, and I brought our hands back to the table.

I needed the connection to him more than he knew.

"Connor came in as I was trying to push him off me. It looked far worse than it was, especially for Connor. You know how Connor is. Just imagine him five years younger thinking his sister was getting attacked. Connor beat the shit out of him. He hurt him really, *really* bad. It was awful and disgusting, and it *broke* me. They fought and when it was over Connor was yelling at me because I was defending the other guy, begging Connor to leave him alone, screaming and crying that he had no clue what was happening, but it just didn't matter. None of it mattered, Liam, because in the end the guy left. He left and he never came back. He left town, he never called, and he never wrote, he never answered my calls, I couldn't even get his family to tell me anything. He took every piece of himself away from me, and he fucking wrecked my heart."

And that was it.

I told him.

I told him that some man had the power over me to wreck me once. That at one point I was broken. That at one point I was stupid. I hate that he knows, as much as I'm relieved that he does.

I told him everything he needed to know.

Well, except the most important thing. I took a deep breath and looked him square in the eyes. I needed him to see that what I am going to be telling him now is the most important thing that he needed to hear. This time I squeezed *his* hand.

"I need you to know this though, more than anything else. He may have wrecked my heart, or I may have thought that for a good long while, but he didn't. I put myself back together, and I made peace with everything that had happened. I did love him, but not like you may be thinking, and not like I even thought I had once upon a time. But he *is* the reason why I never wanted anything to do with men, or why I closed myself off to so many people. I was afraid that I would get too close to someone, too attached, and I would get hurt again when they left me. Or when something happened. I put up a shield, and I was more than fine with that. I was content and perfect with it even. But then you came along. He is part of the reason why I tried to ignore you in the beginning, and then why I only wanted to be your friend. You didn't make it easy on me though. You kept coming back. You kept showing up and insisting that there be more. You made me like you Liam ... *so much more than I probably should* ... But I need you to know that I am *so fucking thankful you didn't give up on me*, and I need you to know that nothing's holding me back anymore." I told him the one thing I have been telling myself for a while now. I am so fucking lucky he didn't give up on me.

He just stared at me for a few moments. I didn't even mind that he was silent because I could tell by the look in his eyes that we were okay. That whatever I said was okay. *We would be okay.* I don't know why I was so scared to talk about Aiden with him. Maybe because Aiden was the last piece of myself that I was holding back from Liam, like Liam had said. Not any more though. I was one hundred percent honest with him. There was nothing holding me back anymore. It should've been scary, but like my loving Liam ... it wasn't scary at all.

"God Samantha ... I don't even know what to say. I'm so fucking sorry you were hurt, I am so fucking sorry for what happened to you, and *I am so fucking thankful that I didn't give up on you and that you gave me a fucking chance*. And I'm *so* very happy that nothing's holding you back anymore. I hate what you went through, and I don't know why you let *me* of all people in, but I'm grateful that you did – and I am going to show you and prove to you every day that you have absolutely no reason to regret that choice. I promise."

I normally hated promises, but something tells me that Liam's promises are different. I instinctively know that they mean something, and that I can count on them.

I squeezed his hand again and then grabbed my wine glass.

"Red ... how about we eat now?"

Just like that, with one suggestion, I felt like I was floating and free.

I couldn't help but laugh. I honestly felt at peace. I felt like we were back in our fairytale.

"Thank you, Red," Liam said.

"For what?"

"For telling me about it. For trusting me with it, and with everything. Just thank you for *everything*."

God ... didn't he get it?

"No, Liam. *Thank you.* For *everything*."

****

Liam really did know how to cook. Though it was a little cold by the time we actually ate, the meal was still exceptional. I don't know how we were able to move past the whole Aiden situation, but we were. Our mood went back to what it was before he said he wanted to know my last and final secret. Well, maybe not the *last* one. I still had a few left, but those weren't bad things. At least I didn't think they were. And they were definitely not things holding me back from Liam in any way.

"So, Liam, who taught you how to cook like this? It's absolutely amazing." I was genuinely curious how he learned to cook. Once again I learned something new about him that surprised me.

He took a sip of his wine before he started telling me about his mother, and learning how to cook. I was riveted to his stories about his mom. I especially loved how he said they had a staff on hand growing up that could prepare their meals, but their mom wanted to do it. She didn't grow up in wealth and privilege, and she didn't want her children taking everything for granted – she wanted them to know how to do things for themselves, hence the cooking.

He spoke about his parent's differences, but also their common love. He was speaking of his mom with such love, and also such longing, that my heart broke for not only the man sitting in front of me, but for the young boy who didn't have his mom nearly long enough.

"Liam, what happened to your mom?" I found myself asking before I could stop myself. He looked at me with a sad smile, but he didn't seem upset by my question.

"She died of breast cancer when I was in middle school. It was devastating to me and Riley, and especially to my dad. It's still hard. I just miss her so much you know? Especially now. Especially when I've found *you* and she can't meet you ... or you her ... it hurts. I know I've said it a lot, Red, but she would have loved you."

"I'm sure if she was anything like you, I would've loved her too."

No.

No. No. No.

It came out right, but at the same time it came out *so, so* wrong.

I was looking at him when I said it so I saw the way his eyes flared, but he didn't say anything about what I had just said.

Or let slip.

It wasn't as if I declared my love for him or anything. I didn't exactly *say* that. Kind of like he didn't say he loved me the other day either, just that he loved *things* about me. That's the same as that, right?

Right?

"How about we move this inside, Red? I'll open another bottle of wine if you'd like, I'll turn the fireplace on, we can listen to some music – I think it would be a perfect end to the evening. What do you think?"

I'll take the reprieve any way I can get it, thanks. "That would be great, Liam."

As we both started to rise, I reached out for the wine and my plate.

"Leave the plate, I'll bring the stuff inside after I get the fire going."

"Liam, you really don't have to do everything by yourself. Let me help."

"Red, I just want you to enjoy tonight," he said grabbing ahold of my empty hand. "Let's get you inside." We started to head towards the door leading inside but I stopped. I let go of his hand and then I turned around, because there was one thing I wanted to take inside myself. I went back to the table and grabbed the pitcher of flowers off of the table.

Liam just stared at me as I walked back to him. "I want to take this inside."

I don't think he knew what to say to that. I don't even know why I had the urge to take his mom's pitcher inside, but I did. I knew it wasn't mine, but I felt an attachment to it for some reason. Just like I felt an attachment to its owner.

I went inside ahead of him and placed the flowers on the table in front of the sofa. As I sat, Liam went to the fireplace, lit it, and then turned on the stereo before going outside to clean up.

Leaving me alone, Liam gave me ample time to mull over what had happened so far that night.

Regardless of everything that had happened, and everything that was said, there was only one thing that I kept coming back around to in my mind.

I fell in love with Liam. I am in love. I love him. I want him to be mine. I want to be his.

Forever?

As I was sitting on the sofa thinking, watching the fireplace dance, and listening to the music softly play, I was sipping my wine and becoming lulled into a blissful state of pure happiness. I knew for a fact that I had never, ever, felt like this. Everything was just perfect.

Liam came over and sat next to me when he was finished cleaning up. I was so happy that I couldn't even feel bad for not helping him out. He filled up his glass a little more, asked me if I would like more as well, and though I knew it was probably a bad idea, I decided to go for it anyway. I was having such a wonderful time that I really didn't think anything at all about having to get home, or getting sick – nothing sensible like that. I was only thinking of the mood, my feelings, and the weightlessness I was feeling once again.

He poured me some wine, and then we started talking some more. I still couldn't believe how easy it is to talk to him.

"So, out of curiosity …" he started to grin. Uh-oh. What did he want to know?

"How are you able to live where you do?" Liam asked me.

I wasn't expecting that question, even though I'm surprised we've never talked about it before now. I normally keep my financials to myself, but it makes sense that he's curious about how I'm able to afford such things, especially at my age and while working at a coffee shop and being a college student.

When I didn't answer him right away, he continued on a little differently.

"I hope that didn't come out the wrong way … it's just your apartment is beautiful, you live in an expensive part of the city, you have a very nice car, but you still go to college, and you only work at the café sometimes …" He stopped speaking as if he realized what he was saying now wasn't any better than what he said before.

I decided to go with a little teasing in the hopes of relieving the awkwardness.

"Sort of like you? You have a beautiful apartment that is far nicer than mine and in an even better location obviously, you have an incredibly expensive car that I would love to drive by the way, you dress in designer suits all the time, and all of that other stuff? Really?" I knew how he was able to afford everything, but he had no clue about me. I actually did find it shocking that after weeks we've never discussed it. My wealth is not something I broadcast or ever get asked about, but like I said before, I guess it makes sense that he would be curious.

"*Samantha* …" Liam said with a teasing glint in his eyes, and a smirk on his face. He just shook his head at me.

"Alright, alright. My grandparents left Connor and me a trust fund. We were able to access it once we turned twenty-one. My parents own *The Brew*, as you know, and it does very well, but my grandparents owned a chain of coffee houses throughout the country. Needless to say they did unbelievably better than 'very well.'" I snuck a peek to see what he thought about that. He was just shaking his head again with an incredulous look.

"So if you were thinking that I want to shack up with you because of your money you're completely wrong ..." I couldn't help but to say it, and then I cracked up laughing. It was definitely the wine getting to me. I've never joked about money and the privileges I knew I was lucky to have because of it. It was just something about this night, and talking with him, and the way I was feeling, that was making me looser, freer, and more open.

"Really, Red? Then *why do you* want to shack up with me?" Liam teased me right back.

I shook my head at him this time.

I had nothing good to say to him.

Because I love you was not the appropriate response at a time like this, and as an answer to a question like that.

He seemed to understand that I didn't know how to, or that I didn't particularly want to respond to his question, so he left it at that. He also left the money situation alone too.

We were sitting on the sofa facing each other now with our knees practically touching, with neither of us saying anything, and it just seemed so right. It felt like we had done this a thousand times before.

"Dance with me?"

Did Liam just ask me to dance with him? Seriously? I looked at him questioningly.

"Seriously. Dance with me, Samantha," he said again before he put his wine glass on the table, rose from the sofa, and extended his hand towards me.

My favorite song had just started playing so it seemed like fate that he asked me to dance at that precise moment. As I stood I realized that I really didn't know how I was going to be able to dance with him. The wine made my legs feel like jelly … or I guess it could be Liam and the way he's looking at me.

I leaned over and put my own glass of wine on the table before I grasped his hand. He led me on shaky legs to a spot next to the fireplace where there was enough room for both of us to sway to the music. His arms came to rest around my lower back, and I placed my outstretched arms on his shoulders. When I came in before I took my sandals off and put them next to the couch, so now dancing with him so close I was able to truly see just how much taller he was than me. How much bigger all around he was. In his arms I felt tiny, but secure. I felt beautiful, I felt sheltered … I felt wanted and loved. As we moved back and forth so close together I started to get sleepy by the motion. All I wanted to do was rest my head on his chest, snuggle in and stay there forever. I couldn't believe how quickly all of these feelings had washed over me and wrapped themselves around me.

As I bent my head to snuggle into his chest he leaned back a little. I lifted my head up to see what was wrong, and I quickly discovered that nothing was.

Everything was perfectly alright.

He dipped his head to mine and I became even more lost in him than I was before. The kiss started out slow and sweet, but it turned into fast, rough, wanting, wicked.

And most of that was because of me.

His tongue danced with mine, and we were both giving as well as taking. My hands moved from his shoulders to behind his neck, and then they moved up to grasp at his hair bringing me even closer into his body. His hands were roaming all over my back and then lower to cup my ass. I gasped into his mouth when I felt him grab me and lift me a little, brushing and rocking me against the hardness that was now in his pants, and that seemed to get his attention more than my hands pulling at his hair, my tongue darting in and out of his mouth, or my teeth biting and tugging at his bottom lip. He quickly broke the kiss and pulled away from me.

That was not what I had been expecting.

"Why'd you stop?" I asked him, concerned that I did something wrong. I definitely didn't have that much experience doing any of this, so I was a little embarrassed that maybe I had done something he didn't like.

"Because you've been drinking Sam – I've been drinking – and I don't want to start something like this when you aren't ready – when I'm not even sure what you want this to be. I didn't ask you here for this. I made you a promise. I think it's time I got you home." He moved even further away from me, as if being near me was a bad thing. I didn't like it.

"I didn't want you to stop Liam," I said, as I started to move towards him. I really didn't want him to stop. I didn't have much experience, and I didn't know if I was fully ready for what I knew this was leading to, but I knew that I loved him and trusted him, and I was especially enjoying the way he was making me feel and I didn't want it to end.

"You say that now. I haven't seen you like this before though, Red. I don't want you to do anything you aren't comfortable doing, and I don't want to do anything to ruin what we're starting to have –"

"You won't be ruining anything, Liam. I was actively participating in what was happening" I cut him off to let him know that I wanted what was happening. What didn't he get?

"Sam …" he said before he rubbed his forehead, looked down, and then muttered the word "*fuck.*"

"*Fuck!*" he said again, a little louder this time.

"I don't think I can drive you home, and there is no way in hell that I am putting you in a cab by yourself, or having you walk home even with me with you."

He stopped speaking, but I could tell that he had something more to say, so I just waited.

"How about you stay over …" I looked at him and I could feel my eyes widen a bit at what he said. Was he actually giving in to me, and was I still okay with it?

"I'll sleep in one of the spare bedrooms. You can have my room."

I guess it didn't matter if I was ready or not, or what I still wanted, because he wasn't giving in to me. He was just concerned for our safety and driving.

"Spare bedroom?" I asked.

"Yes, Samantha … the spare bedroom. As much as I would love to sleep with you … *only* sleep … I don't think it's a good idea."

"Why not?" I asked with complete false innocence.

"Are you fucking kidding me? After what just happened when we were dancing? It was only supposed to be a dance. That was it. It took about one second for it to turn into more than that."

"Please?" I asked with more of that sugary innocence that I completely didn't feel. I wanted to fall asleep wrapped up in him. I wanted to know what it felt like to sleep with a man. But not just any man … *him*.

"Are you serious, Sam? You want me to sleep with you? *Only* sleep right?" He asked in a way that I knew he was considering it after all, and I knew all I had to do was say yes to get my way.

"Yes. I'll stay here the night if you sleep with me. How about that?"

He didn't say anything for a while. I was so sure that he would agree to it once I said yes, but now he had me worried because he was taking too long in saying anything.

Then he came towards me, grabbed my hands in his and said, "Okay."

Okay.

Liam went to the fireplace to extinguish the fire, he started turning off lights, then he turned off the radio and came back to me before he grabbed my hand and led me to his bedroom.

I knew that we would only be sleeping, but I felt nervous all of a sudden. This was another first for me, and though I trusted Liam with every part of me, I couldn't help but feel those little butterflies start fluttering away in my stomach. I walked into the room and all I could focus on was the massive bed. I didn't even care about the spectacular view that his room had. It was the bed that was the centerpiece. The room was done in a beautiful blue color, with black and white framed photos on the walls, a black dresser and armoire, a black chair for sitting with a table as well, but it was the bed that held me captivated. It was black as well, but with a deep blue bedspread that I just wanted to dive into like it was the ocean.

"Nobody else has slept in here but me," Liam spoke quietly into the silence.

What? What was he saying?

"What?" I asked. I wasn't sure I was understanding what he was saying. Did he mean that he had never had another woman here? Because if that's what he meant that is *more* than fine with me.

"I shouldn't have said that. I'm sorry, Red."

Fuck that. What did he mean?

"What did you mean, 'nobody else has slept in here but me,' Liam?" I was not letting this go. He better answer the freaking question.

He sighed loudly before he started speaking.

"It's just … I know you are new to a lot of this. I mean, you said you had never been to a man's place for dinner before … I just didn't want you to think this was something I did all the time. Not since I've lived here have I brought a woman back to my place. I don't know why I brought it up, it just felt important to point that out."

I guess I could've been upset about the talk of other women and what he's done and not done, but knowing what he's just told me, I'm happy he mentioned what he did. I turned towards him and moved into him before I stood on my tiptoes, placed my hands on his chest, and lightly kissed him.

"Thank you for telling me. It means something that you told me that."

"Okay then. *Okay*. Let's find you something to wear."

Just then I felt my cheeks warm up. The thought of removing my clothes sent my body into a boil.

"Jesus, Red … I was beginning to wonder if I had lost my effect on you. You haven't blushed as much as I thought you would tonight. It's good to know I still have it … *and so do you*." Liam started to laugh, and so did I. I knew he was laughing at me, but I ended up just laughing at the whole situation.

Liam went over to a set of drawers and took out a black undershirt. Because of our height and weight difference I knew that the shirt would be more than fine for me.

He came over to me and handed me the shirt. "Is this okay, Red? I don't think I have anything else that would work for you."

"Do you have any shorts I could use? I could always roll them at the waist a few times so they can fit …"

He stared at me and I could feel my blush deepen. What was he thinking? It's not like I was going commando. *Oh my God! Is that what he was thinking?* Because I asked for shorts too? I know I shouldn't be embarrassed, especially considering what I had been about to do with him before, but I was, and that was that.

"I have boxer shorts that might work. Would those do?"

"That's perfect!" I nearly shouted. Just give them to me already so I can change and climb into bed and forget about the last two minutes. *Holy fuck.*

He went back to the dresser, grabbed a pair of really expensive looking black boxers, and handed them to me. He pointed to a door in his bedroom and told me that it was a bathroom and I could change in there if I wanted. He said it with a smirk, almost daring me to change right there in front of him. A little more wine, I might have done it just to see what he would've said and done then, but I was definitely too chicken to do something like that right this moment. I turned and went quickly into his connecting bathroom.

When I was done changing I went back into the bedroom. Liam had turned off the lights, put on some very soft music, and was already in bed. It wasn't completely dark because he left the drapes open, so I was able to see him somewhat clearly.

And oh, wow!

Seeing him how he was, it was then that I realized I was a little apprehensive after all, getting into bed with him.

I stood frozen to the floor just outside of the bathroom, feeling like a fairy who was dwarfed in his shirt. I felt really young and out of place all of a sudden. I knew he was looking at me and could see me as clearly as I did him, but I couldn't tell what he was feeling.

"Come here," he said in a raspy voice; a raspy voice that was somehow connected to my heart and other parts of me. *My God!*

I did the only thing I could do when Liam said 'come here,' in that specific voice … I went.

He lifted the comforter for me and I got in right next to him. I laid on the mattress on my back, unmoving, because I didn't know what to do. My head was at least on a pillow, and I had the comforter to keep me warm since Liam really did like his temperature set to freezing like his sister mentioned, so I should have been just fine.

I wasn't though.

I felt awkward.

I knew he was almost touching me, but he wasn't.

"It's only sleep Samantha. I can feel how tense you are. Just go to sleep. It's fine. We're fine."

But I wasn't fine.

Now that I'm in his bed I wanted him to hold me.

Now that I'm in his bed I had the same urge to snuggle into him as I did before when we were dancing.

Unlike last time, this time I was going to. I rolled over on to my side to face him. I scooted closer, and when I did, he instinctively moved his arm so I could place my own arm on his chest. His completely bare chest.

I looked at him, and with the light filtering in from the window, I could see that he did have more tattoos on his torso. I started to trace them with my fingertips before he grabbed my hand and held it still.

"Maybe this isn't such a good idea after all …" he started to say with a voice that was now all gravelly, and even sexier than before.

I couldn't let him think that and go away so I cut him off quickly by saying, "I'll stop."

He continued to hold my hand steady on his chest. I moved even closer into him and I heard him groan. I tucked my head under his chin and placed the side of my face on top of his chest. Then to make myself even more comfortable, and apparently him even more miserable if his hiss was any indication, I moved my thigh up and draped it over his leg.

I was only semi-sorry for my action. I was a little sorrier when I then rocked my body a bit to get myself in an even comfier position and I heard him groan again, even deeper this time. I think he was afraid of me rocking again because his free hand came down and wrapped around me. His hand rested right on my hip bracketing me to him, making sure I didn't go anywhere else. As if I wanted to go anywhere else … *except maybe on top of him* … but I knew that that would be way too much.

When I was finally comfortable, I thought about my actions over the last few minutes and I couldn't believe how flagrantly I plastered myself to him. *Jesus.* What the hell had come over me? What was I thinking? What was *he* thinking? Was he mad? He let me do it, so probably not. And I felt wonderful after all.

So there was that.

There really was no feeling like it in the world. At least that I knew of.

I really was starting to get sleepy in the cocoon of Liam's arms, while being surrounded by his amazing scent and body. His heartbeat and his breathing were lulling me into a state of peacefulness.

Before I fell totally asleep I mumbled, "Good-night" to Liam.

He mumbled back in his deep, sexy, husky voice, "Good-night, Red."

I don't know what came over me, but I kissed his chest before I let out a sigh, burrowed in a little deeper and closed my eyes.

I felt his grip on me tighten a little after I kissed him and burrowed in, but I didn't mind in the least.

I loved being held tight by him.

It was a little while before I felt his grip relax, right before I plunged into dreams that I hoped one day would become reality.

Chapter 15

I knew I overslept. I could just tell by the way I felt and how bright it was outside already. "Allie is going to *kill* me for being late," I said to myself as I closed my eyes again. She told me to be early because she wanted to know every little detail about my date with Liam.

My date ... with Liam.

Liam.

Oh. My. God.

I never left.

I slept with him.

I remembered everything.

I blinked my eyes open so fast after I remembered where I was, and everything that had happened the night before, worrying about so many things including what I would say, do, how I would act, and my morning breath, my *freaking* morning breath, that I practically gave myself a heart attack right then and there in the span of seconds. I sat up in bed looking for him but he was nowhere to be found. I remembered falling asleep wrapped in his arms, but I was all alone right now.

I didn't know how to feel about that.

Is it a good thing or a bad thing that he wasn't in bed with me anymore? Did he not want to sleep with me? Did he leave because my breath was awful and I was breathing on him? Did he leave because I snore in my sleep and he couldn't take it anymore? Did I toss and turn too much? Did I try to grope him in my sleep? Did I drool all over him? Did I say things when I was knocked out that I wasn't supposed to? Oh, God, did I tell him I *love* him?

"I honestly don't think I've ever seen you look more beautiful, Red." Liam's voice shocked me out of my horrible thoughts. I looked up to where I heard his voice, and saw him standing by the door holding a tray in his hands. He thought I looked beautiful? He should see how *he* looked. He was still shirtless and I couldn't get enough of seeing his naked chest. I was finally able to see all of the designs I was only able to get brief glimpses of last night.

He was a work of art.

His hair was all messed up, he had stubble all over his jaw, his sleep pants were hanging dangerously low, and just like he said to me – I had never seen him look more beautiful. But then he smiled and he took beautiful to the next level.

"What's wrong, Red? When I came in here you looked like you were either ready to bolt, throw up, cry, or bury yourself back in the blankets. Are you feeling okay?"

Really? And he thought all of *that* looked beautiful? Jesus. Surprisingly though I felt fine this morning after drinking a shit ton last night. That's not what my problem was. *Fuck.*

"You know, I can't even pretend Liam ... I have no idea what to do."

I was over being embarrassed and awkward. Maybe it was being in love with him that I felt I had nothing to worry about if I said these things. I knew he wouldn't make fun of me. I just needed him to help me get through this, because I didn't want anything to go wrong. After last night, I needed this morning to be okay too.

"You really kill me, you know that, Red? Here maybe this will help," he said walking to where I was still sitting up in bed. As he got closer, I was finally able to see what was on the tray he was carrying.

"I know you said you aren't a breakfast person, and that you've never had breakfast in bed, but I was hoping you would make an exception for me this time. I can be your first breakfast in bed … and you can be mine, too. How about that?"

"What? You talked to me about this. You've done the whole breakfast in bed thing already –"

"No I haven't," Liam cut me off. "I never said I had breakfast in bed with anyone. I was just teasing you that day. I brought up the whole mess of breakfast in bed to get a rise out of you, and to see your absolutely gorgeous blush, and it worked. *You* are the only one. I knew as soon as you said you've never done it, that we'd end up doing it together at some point. And here we are. Have breakfast in bed with me, Samantha?"

What a cocky bastard. And I absolutely loved it.

He looked at me and with a husky voice said, "I promise if we make a mess I'll clean it all up."

Holy, oh my God.

I wonder what he would say about me not having done other things, and if he would want to participate and help me with those things too. I'm sure if I gave him a list of things I haven't done he would make it his personal mission to check them all off. I'm thinking he would like to start with something major that I was eventually going to have to talk to him about.

But not right now. We had breakfast to eat now.

Like he had done for me last night, I scooted over in bed and held the comforter open for him so he could get in next to me, leaving the comforter draped back so we were sitting on the sheets. He placed the tray on the bed, and we got to eating. He made scrambled eggs, bacon, toast, he had cut up some fruit, and he put together mimosas and coffee. How had I slept through all of that?

Who the hell *is* this guy?

We had been eating for a while, making small talk and commenting here and there, but then we found ourselves in silence; not an awkward silence, but an appreciative one. Breakfast in bed really wasn't a bad thing, as I had thought.

"You know, I love seeing you in my bed in the morning, Sam, and I especially love you wearing my clothes." I felt the warmth of his comment heat up not only my cheeks and neck, but my whole body. There was that word again: *love*.

"You know, Liam, I loved waking up here in the morning even though it took me a little while to wrap my head around all of it, and I loved waking up in your clothes, in your bed, surrounded by your scent after having fallen asleep in your arms – " I stopped and cut my own self off this time. What was I saying to him? The truth obviously, but I didn't know if it was all too much for right now. I was only starting to get used to *him* saying things like this, and revealing things to me. I didn't know how I felt yet about revealing this much to him. It had to be the love thing – my feeling it, and his throwing the word around all the time.

"You really do slay me, Sam," Liam said before he leaned over and brushed my cheek gently with his fingers, before he kissed me softly on the lips.

"What are we doing?" he asked, once he pulled back from my lips.

I was searching for the right thing to say when I heard my cell phone start ringing. I didn't even know that I had brought it in the bedroom with me last night. It must be something important for it to be ringing this early instead of beeping with the signal of incoming texts. I glanced to where the sound was coming from, and noticed my phone on the nightstand that Liam was currently closest to.

"I'm sorry about that. Can you please hand me my phone? Normally nobody calls me this early in the morning, so it must be important." He grabbed my phone, and handed it to me, but not before looking down and saying *"Perfect."*

I knew even before I grabbed the phone out of his hand who it would be. Connor. *Fucking Connor.*

"What, Connor!" I said answering the phone. I wasn't in the mood to hear from him. I didn't like him interrupting my morning with Liam.

"Where the fuck are you, Sam? It's eleven. You were supposed to be here at the shop hours ago," he was speaking quickly into the phone. I could hear voices and loud noises in the background. He wasn't supposed to be at the shop today. *Shit!* Then it hit me. *Eleven o'clock.*

"It's *eleven?*" I asked Connor, but I was really looking at Liam with my eyes widening as I realized I not only overslept, but I completely fucked up by being really late to work, and now my brother was definitely going to know something was up. I never did stuff like this.

"Seriously, Sam. Where the fuck *are* you?" Connor asked again. He was significantly louder this time.

"Give me about ... *shit –*" I needed to go home and take a shower and change before I headed into work. "Give me about an hour Connor ... I'll be there." Then I hung up on him, without giving him the chance to say anything else.

My phone immediately started ringing again, but I ignored it.

This was not good. This was *so* not fucking good.

"It's eleven o'clock, Liam? *Eleven?* I was supposed to be at work more than two hours ago. My brother is going to *kill* me." Liam just grinned at me the whole time. He got up and moved the tray off of the bed, putting it on the table at the far side of the room. He came back and sat down facing me.

"I guess that means you're leaving, Red?" he asked me with that grin of his still on his face, teasing me over being completely freaked out.

I really couldn't take it anymore, and after what went on last night and this morning, I felt like I deserved a little something. So, I was taking the opportunity to do what I'd wanted to do for an incredibly long time.

I reached out towards his face with both hands, grasped his cheeks, and put both tips of my thumbs into the grooves of his dimples. I was able to do it for maybe five seconds before he grabbed my hands to stop me from moving my fingers back and forth.

"Red …" he groaned.

"I've wanted to do that for a really long time," I said looking up at him and away from my thumbs on his dimples. I could see that his eyes had turned into mini-blue flames. I had about one second to register what was happening before I found myself flat on my back with Liam over me, kissing me in such a way that I feared I might spontaneously combust.

His kisses were just *that* explosive.

I felt them everywhere.

I could literally feel *him* everywhere.

His tongue was in my mouth, his hands were roaming up my sides and stopped really close to my breasts, his bottom half was melded to mine with my legs spread open giving him all the room he wanted to rock against me while we kissed. I have never felt anything like it before. My senses were on overload. One minute I had been feeling his dimples, but the next I was exploring his mouth, his bare back, and down lower. Liam was kissing me deeper and deeper but then he stopped. He lifted his head and looked at me, his eyes an even more fiery blue than they were before. He was breathing roughly on top of me, but that didn't stop him from doing some more exploring of his own. He leaned down and he kissed my forehead, then my nose, my mouth, my chin, and he kept on going lower. I turned my head to give him better access to my neck and he took full advantage by sucking and then nipping, causing me to moan out loud. I thought for a second I should be embarrassed by the sounds I was making, but why should I be, when I heard him moaning before too.

Liam kept nibbling at my neck, but then he grabbed my hands that had fallen to my sides, grasped them both, and raised them over my head. He held my hands above my head in one of his own, while the other started to make its way under my shirt – under *his* shirt. I could feel the goose bumps rising on my flesh from the touch of his hand moving over me, but at the same time I could feel the tingly warmth that he was creating within me spread all throughout my body. I knew where he was heading, and I instinctively lifted myself towards him, inviting him to touch me. As his hand got closer to where I wanted him, Liam stopped torturing my neck and he looked up at me. I could tell that he saw what I wanted in my eyes because the next thing I knew his mouth was back on mine and his hand finally got to where I wanted it. The feeling of his hand on my breast, his thumb grazing my nipple, had me arching even more into his body, moaning.

"Samantha," I heard Liam groan at my mouth. He let go of my hands, and I was so thankful because I needed to be able to touch him too. I wanted him to take my shirt off so we could be skin to skin. I was getting impatient, especially since I could feel his other hand slipping up my body, and I knew what would be happening next. I started to rock myself into him like he had been doing, creating a sweet friction that had me a second away from begging him for more. Before he was able to take my other breast in his hand to give it the same attention as the other, possibly, *hopefully* even more than that, my phone started blaring out of nowhere again.

I moaned, but for an entirely different reason than I had been for the past few minutes. Liam's head slammed down, hard, on the mattress next to mine, while his hands and body froze.

I think I heard the words, "You've got to be fucking kidding me," mumbled into the mattress. If I heard him correctly, there were no truer words.

The phone kept ringing and ringing. It was Liam's turn to groan at the ringing. He pulled his hands out of my shirt, rolled himself out from between my legs and went to the side of the bed where my phone was once again.

"I really hate your fucking brother, Samantha. I have never hated anyone more in my entire *fucking* life."

Me either.

"Liam … I think I have to go now," I said to his back, because he was still facing away from me. I actually felt really awkward *now*. Now I really didn't have any idea of what to do.

"I know, Red. I'll take our breakfast out to the kitchen so you can get dressed," he said, and then he finally looked over his shoulder at me. He gave me a small smile, but it didn't reach his eyes. It almost seemed like something was wrong. Was it because of Connor's interruption or something else?

"Liam –" I started to say, because I needed to ask him what was wrong. He didn't let me though.

"Get dressed, Red. I'll see you in the kitchen." With that he turned around, grabbed the tray, and went out the door, closing it behind him.

What the hell had just happened?

Something was definitely fucking wrong.

****

I wasted no time changing out of Liam's shirt and boxer shorts.

I was apprehensive about going to the kitchen, especially after Liam's mood had changed so drastically, but I needed to know what had happened and the sooner the better. When I was done in the bathroom I took his clothes and placed them on his bed.

I really did love his bed. I wish I had more time in it. Unfortunately, I had other places to be.

When I made my way out of the bedroom I immediately saw Liam standing behind the kitchen island. It almost seemed like he was there on purpose, putting distance between us. I didn't like it.

At all.

"What's wrong, Liam?" I decided to take a page out of his book and get right to the point. Like I said, I think I lost some of my embarrassment around him the night before, and definitely after what had just happened in the bedroom. I needed to know what was wrong so we could fix it, because I wanted whatever we had going on right after breakfast to keep going on.

"Nothing, Red," he said with a sigh.

"I don't believe you, Liam. Everything was wonderful last night, and then this morning with breakfast, and then just right now in your bed, but then Connor called again, and you completely changed on me. It doesn't seem wonderful anymore …" I took a deep breath because even though I said I wasn't embarrassed, I *was* a little afraid to find out the specific answer to my next question, but I needed to know, so I continued on by asking, "Did I do something wrong?"

I lowered my eyes to the floor worried he would say yes.

I hurriedly looked up though when I heard him moving around the counter, coming towards me. I saw him approach, and watched him reach out to grasp both of my cheeks in his hands. He bent at the knees a little to be on my level, so he could look deeply into my eyes.

"You did absolutely nothing wrong, Samantha. I did. I told you that what happened in there" he tilted his head towards the bedroom, "wouldn't happen. I didn't ask you here for that. I didn't have you sleep over, or make you breakfast in bed so I could do that with you in the morning. As much as I hated the fucking interruption, I'm thankful for it, and I'm just fucking pissed at myself. As much as I wanted something to happen, I'm glad it didn't. Our first time shouldn't be rushed. It shouldn't be something that *I* rush you into. The timing of all of this isn't right. I want it to be right for you – for us. Though it would have meant everything to me, *you* deserve more than what that would've been. I honestly don't know if you're ready for any of this Samantha, or if you were just caught up in the moment. I seriously don't fucking know. I *know* what I feel about you though, Sam. I know I want *everything* with you, but it's not happening like this. There is *nothing* fucking wrong with you. I've told you before … you're fucking *perfect*. This time, it was all completely me." He didn't lean down and kiss me, or hug me, or squeeze me like I thought he would. He just stared at me. It took me a while to realize he was waiting for me to say something.

I needed to tell him how I felt. Yesterday and just before I was a little concerned with revealing too much, but I knew that this was probably the moment where I should let him know exactly how I feel.

I had waited too long though, because my phone started up again, ruining another moment.

"He's not gonna give up, Red. He knows something's up." I just shook my head in the affirmative because I knew he was right. "You need to go." I still kept shaking my head because he was still right. "Is it okay if I stop in later? What time are you working until?"

"I was only supposed to be on until twelve, but obviously I won't be going in until that time. Now I have no idea what time I'll be working until. How about I text you when I know more?"

"That's fine."

"Okay, then."

"Okay, then," he said back.

"Liam … thank you for dinner last night, and breakfast this morning, and for everything else." Everything such as the painting, telling me about your mother, dancing with me, taking care of me, showing me that I really am in love with you, and that it's okay to be, because I really think you may love me too.

"You're welcome, Red." He leaned down and kissed me, before we headed towards the door where he kissed me again. He didn't close the door until I was on the elevator.

It wasn't until I was out of the elevator and walking past the same security guard that I realized I was doing a 'walk of shame,' wearing last night's clothes and looking thoroughly rumpled. The guard looked at me with a knowing smile on his face, but he didn't know anything. It didn't even matter what he thought though … nothing would ruin the way I was feeling.

****

"Where the fuck have you been, Samantha?" Connor said as I walked through the door. I didn't even make it five steps inside before he was upon me. *He would not ruin my good mood.*

"I overslept," I told him honestly.

At least I wasn't lying.

"Want to try that again?" Connor said.

"What?" I asked, completely pissed that he didn't believe me. I really *did* oversleep.

"Allie let it slip that you had a date with Liam last night, and then you don't show up for work this morning – something you never do – and you didn't bother to call and say you'd be late ... So you want to fucking try that again?" Connor was definitely angry.

I was angry too.

I shot my eyes over to where Allie was standing behind the counter. She looked worried when I narrowed my eyes at her and she mouthed the words, "I'm sorry."

Traitorous bitch!

Wait until I get ahold of her later.

Right now, I had to think of what to say.

"I really did oversleep Connor. I wasn't lying."

Maybe that wasn't the best thing to say to my already angry brother?

"Are you fucking *kidding* me?" *Yeah*, definitely wasn't the best thing to say.

"You fucking slept with him, didn't you?"

Whoa. Whoa. Whoa. Whoa. He did *not* have the right to ask me shit like that.

"That's none of your goddamn business, Connor." I couldn't believe we were having this conversation in the café with customers staring at us as if we were nuts.

"I don't ask you who you sleep with, because you are an adult, Connor. Same as me. I'm a twenty-three year old college student, who has her own place, her own car, who works, and pays her own bills. I don't need to answer to you," I reminded him as if he needed a reminder that he wasn't entitled to know any of what goes on with Liam and me.

He seemed to deflate a little, which was what I was hoping for.

He rubbed the back of his neck and said, "I know, Sam. I know. Jesus fucking Christ, I told you I didn't know how to handle this shit. It's just … you *slept* with him? *Really?* You barely know the guy."

Once again how was this any of his business – and *seriously* – let's not pretend he didn't do the one-night shit thing all the time, and he wants to talk about barely knowing a person?

From my facial expression he must have understood what I was thinking because he said, "It's not the same."

Are you kidding me? He wants to pull that shit? The double-fucking-standard?

I couldn't take it anymore. I went around him and headed to the back to put my stuff away. I was done talking to Connor about all of this. Unfortunately he wasn't done talking to me. As he followed me through the back door he started talking again.

"Look okay, I freaked out. You just … you don't do this shit. And then to not call? We didn't know where you were. Adam called out, which is why I'm here with Allie, and then to find out why I'm here, and you weren't … holy shit, Sam! I know I told you I think Liam is definitely into you … but already, Samantha? You're sleeping over and blowing off work … what's next?"

"Stop it, Connor! I don't owe you *any* explanations, but I'm tired of you running your mouth about shit you don't know. I *did* have plans with Liam last night at his place. He cooked me dinner – and before you act like even more of a *dick* – he was a perfect gentleman. He cooked an awesome dinner, I got to see his place, and we talked about *Aiden*, Connor. I actually told him everything … but I drank a lot to get me through all of it. We had both been drinking, he knew we couldn't drive, so he made me stay the night. Nothing happened. Even if it did, it's none of your business. I'm a big girl. I will admit, I messed up by oversleeping. I *really* did. And you're right, I don't do things like this. I'm sorry if you were worried, but you need to cut me some slack okay?"

Connor seemed to be thinking about what I just said.

"Fine, but I still don't like it, Sam. I just don't feel right thinking all of this shit, and knowing all of this shit. You're my baby sister."

"Connor, that's just it. I'm not a baby. You need to stop," I told him.

"I don't know if I can." *And once again*, truer words probably never existed.

"Just try, okay. For me."

"*Fuck* … I'll try," he assured me. I knew that this conversation was probably not over, but I needed to get back out to the front and help Allie.

"So you told him about Aiden? How did he take it?" Connor stopped me in my tracks by asking me about my conversation with Liam, before I had the chance to make my way out front. I turned around to look at him and said, "He seemed to take it just fine. It was me who didn't handle it well at first, but after I told him, everything was fine."

Connor looked at me like he was confused. "He really took it fine?"

Now it was my turn to be confused. "Yeah, why wouldn't he?"

"No reason. Just wondering," Connor said, before he headed out the door first. Why did Connor make it seem like it wasn't fine? Liam had no problem with what I said. We were fine after we talked about it. *More than fine*. Why was Connor always stirring up shit in my head? Jesus Christ. If it wasn't one thing with him it was another.

****

Liam came into the shop just after four o'clock. He texted to see if it was okay to come in, and seeing as how Connor seemed to be good now, I told him it would be fine. Maybe I overestimated Connor.

"You know, I'm thinking about driving down next weekend to see your sister. You think she'd let me spend the night with her so I don't have to drive home?" Connor said by way of greeting, once Liam got to the counter.

I narrowed my eyes at Connor. I knew exactly what he was doing.

So did Liam.

"Probably not, because she's not gonna be there. I talked to her a little while ago, and she said she's coming home next weekend." Liam didn't seem the least bit bothered by what Connor had to say.

"Really? She didn't mention it when I talked to her yesterday. I guess I'll have to give her a call again, and ask her if she wants to go out when she's here."

That definitely got Liam's attention.

"What are you talking about?" Liam asked Connor, no longer going along with Connor's shit.

"Sam didn't tell you?" Connor asked looking at me. *Fucking shit stirrer.* "Yeah, your sister gave me her number when we went to *Molly's*. I've been talking to her since then."

I looked at Liam, who didn't look happy with me all of a sudden. *Shit.*

"I have to make a call. I'll be right back," Liam said before turning around, and heading out the door.

I waited exactly one second after the door closed before rounding on Connor. "What the fuck, Connor?"

"What? What'd I do? I was the one who said not to tell him I was talking to his sister. I never said I wouldn't tell him though. Did you see his face? That shit was fucking *priceless.* Anyway, it shouldn't be a big deal that I talk to her. We're friends. She's smart, and funny, and like I told you before, I like her. I actually hope I get the chance to hang out with her next weekend. I really do have to give her a call."

"Seriously, Connor? After all that shit you gave me about me and him a few hours ago, you're going to go and take out his sister? Really? And let's not forget all the shit you gave me about Liam and me just being friends."

"What? *It's not like I am going to sleep with her*," Connor said. At least that was a relief. *I think.* The longer I stared at him I couldn't tell if he was telling the truth or not. *Fuck!*

Connor and I didn't say anything else to one another. We just ignored each other until Liam came back in. He was out there for quite a few minutes talking animatedly with whoever was on the other end of the line. I kind of had a feeling who it was, and I didn't know what to make of it.

I loved my brother, but I loved Liam now too. I was definitely in a hard place right now when it came to both of them and their tug-of-war over Riley.

Liam came over and wiggled his cell phone that was still in his hand.

"Yeah, I just got off the phone with Riley. She's definitely coming up next weekend. Saturday she has plans all day with some people, and then my dad is taking her out to dinner. She has to go back really early Sunday, so the only day she has free is Friday." He looked pointedly at Connor then. "Don't worry about calling her to make plans. It seems that she wanted the chance to hang out with Samantha some more so I told her we'd love to go out with her on Friday. What do you think about that, Red? Want to go out to *Molly's* again Friday night?"

So much for not being in a hard place with these two.

"You did that fucking shit on purpose!" Connor said to Liam.

"*As if you didn't?* Dropping that fucking bomb about talking to my sister like she's just any fucking girl? Don't even get me started on you driving down there to spend the fucking night …"

"What? Like the fucking bomb I got dropped on me this morning, finding out about your cozy situation with *my sister* last night?"

"ENOUGH!" I yelled at both of them. I yelled it so loudly that customers swiveled their heads around to get a look at what was going on, and Allie came storming through the back doors intent on finding out what was up.

"God Connor, I thought we were past this already. And Liam … I'm sorry. I should have told you about Connor talking to your sister, but when he told me I didn't think it was that big of a deal, and he didn't say anything else since, so I didn't bring it up. But honestly, none of it matters to me right now. I just can't take this from either of you anymore," I said to both of them, before I walked out from behind the counter and went to sit at a table.

It wasn't long before Liam joined me. To my surprise, it wasn't only him.

Connor was the first one to speak. "I'm sorry, Samantha. About all of it." He then looked at Liam before he said something I totally wasn't expecting. "I'm sorry too, man. It was a shitty thing to do, bringing up your sister like that. I just wanted to give you back a little of what I felt this morning."

Liam nodded his head when Connor was done speaking. It didn't escape my notice that he didn't verbally accept the apology, or offer one in return.

"Seriously though, how about you just let me ask Riley to go out that Friday, and you can plan another time with her?" Connor said.

"*Did you really just fucking say that?*" Liam asked exactly what I was thinking.

"Yeah, okay. I didn't think so, but it was worth a shot," Connor said with a smirk. "I guess I'll just have to tag along to *Molly's* with you Friday."

Neither Liam nor I said anything to Connor's last statement.

"I'll give you a call later Samantha, so we can go over some things. I'm out of here. I have to work later on." With that Connor bent down and kissed the top of my head. For as much as he was a pain in my ass, I still loved him. "Be safe," I said before he left.

When he was out of the shop I really got down to the whole business with Liam.

"I really *am* sorry for not telling you about Connor and Riley."

"Don't worry about it. I'll admit I'm concerned, but what can I do?"

"Make Connor and Riley's life a living hell, like Connor is making mine and yours?" I asked Liam while smiling.

"Yeah, I guess I could, but I'm not going to. Riley doesn't deserve that."

"You do know that Connor's going to find a way to go out with us on Friday night, right?" I asked him.

Liam sighed. "Yeah, I know, Red. I'm not going to worry about that now though. I'd much rather concentrate on us," he said. I definitely loved the sound of that.

"So about next Friday night? You sure you don't mind going out with Riley? I was going to ask you to go out again, but when I called her to see what she had planned, she mentioned going out."

"It's fine. I like your sister. I wouldn't mind spending more time with her."

"Okay, then. So if we're doing something with my sister, and probably your brother if he has anything to say about it on Friday, how about we get together tomorrow night? Want to grab dinner before the hellishness of my workweek starts again? I most likely won't get the chance to see you until Friday night otherwise, unless it's in passing here at the shop."

"Going out tomorrow's perfect. I work until 2:30 so I could do dinner," I told him, feeling all types of happy inside.

"Okay then. I'm going to get out of here and let you get back to work. Call me when you get home, Red. I'll be looking forward to hearing your voice," he said before standing.

He leaned down towards me caging me in with his palm on the table and his other hand on my chair, as he kissed me on my lips. It wasn't a deep kiss, or a long lingering kiss, but a kiss that turned me on faster than both, because after he kissed me he bit at my bottom lip with his teeth and tugged on it, before swiping his tongue across it, and kissing me again.

And quickly, once again.

I tried to hurry up and grab the sides of his face to hold him in place to get him to kiss me again and deeper, but he was too quick for me. He pulled away, said "Later, Red," and headed towards the door.

I was definitely in a daze watching him walk away, but my mind wasn't clouded enough that I didn't fully appreciate his wink when he turned around to look at me before he headed out the door.

God, I was so helplessly in love with that man.

****

The next day, I opened the door to find Liam on the other side holding a pizza box in one hand, and a six pack in the other. We were supposed to go out to dinner, but Adam called out once again, leaving me to cover the shop until six. Liam didn't mind when I called to tell him what was going on and asked if we could stay in at my place instead. Liam said he'd pick up a pizza and come over, which was more than fine with me. It was one of my favorites after all, and I was more than happy we didn't have to cancel.

We decided to hang on the couch and watch the baseball game, which was nice. After a really long weekend it was good to kick back and not have to worry about what to wear, where we were going, or anything like that. It just felt comfortable. It felt *right*. Neither of us minded eating on paper plates, wiping our hands on paper towels, or yelling at the television. It was a very different experience than when I went over to Liam's just a few nights before – with his fancy china, home-cooked meal, music, twinkling lights, dancing, and expensive wine – but both of the dates felt exactly like *us*.

Probably because it was us.

We were fine with fancier, and completely fine with what I considered normal. It was another thing I loved about us.

We didn't talk much while we were eating or watching the game. We made a few comments about how our days went, the calls that were made during the game that we didn't agree with, our upcoming week, and the group date that was set for Friday night. It was all very basic, and I loved it.

"So, Red, what do you want to do now?" Liam asked me when the game was finally over.

I don't know why it didn't hit me before then.

For some reason having Liam here felt like something that had happened a thousand times before, and because of that feeling I didn't think about he and I being alone in my apartment – *not like that anyway*. Not until now. I didn't think about what had happened just yesterday morning, and what it could mean for us tonight. I remembered what he said yesterday about not rushing me, and it not being the right time, and all of that. I thought about it a lot yesterday, and I realized that I *was* ready. It wasn't an 'in the moment' thing. I was in love with him and I wanted to be with him in every way that I could. I wouldn't have regretted a thing if we made love yesterday, even if it was rushed and unplanned.

Did he want that now, though?

I didn't have enough time to shower when I got home, I still had my work clothes on, my hair was a little crazy, and now I felt a little gross from eating all of that pizza – *shit* how does this even *fucking* work?

"Jesus, Red. That must be a serious conversation you have going on in your head," Liam said, cutting into those very thoughts I was having. I looked up at him and he was smiling from ear to freaking ear.

He brought his fingertips up to the side of my face and he brushed his fingers up and down one of my cheeks.

"I don't think I've ever seen this particular shade on you before," he said, right before he let loose his stunning grin. When I jerked my head away from his touch he started to laugh.

I really needed to stop thinking his laugh and smile were so damn sexy, especially when they appeared on his face at my expense.

"Want to tell me what you're thinking, Red?" he asked me when he finally stopped laughing.

We were sitting right next to each other on the couch. I was turned into him a little, while he had one arm on the back of the couch behind me and the other now on the armrest and away from my flaming cheeks. He looked a little too comfortable and smug for my liking.

I don't know where it came from – maybe it was the way he looked right then from laughing, or maybe it was the way he seemed right at home in my place, it could've been the way he teased me, or maybe because I wanted to be the smug one for once, and it just may have been because I just fucking *wanted* too, and I didn't care about the clothes, or my hair, or not having taken a shower, or feeling a little too full – but I looked him dead in the eyes and said, "I don't want to tell you, Liam, I'd much rather show you."

I saw the way his eyes widened a second before I leaned towards him and planted my mouth against his. I leaned over even more and placed my hands on both of his shoulders before I turned my head to the side and deepened the kiss.

The kiss that I had control over for about five seconds before all bets were off.

I briefly wondered if I would *ever* be in control when it came to things like this with Liam, but once his tongue started moving with mine, I really didn't give a shit who controlled what. All I knew was one second I was leaning over him kissing him, then the next I was on him kissing him, while straddling his lap. I tangled my hands in his hair, while he moved his hands under the back of my shirt, and I just went with it. I told him I knew what I wanted, and this was only the tip of the iceberg. I knew I wanted to feel what I felt yesterday, and I wanted to hear what I heard too – his skin under my hands and his moaning in my ear. I didn't know if I was going about it the right way, but I was taking what I wanted and doing what I wanted, regardless.

I leaned back a little and started pulling up his shirt. When I couldn't get it all the way off without his help, I said the word "please," but it definitely sounded way more like a whimper than I had intended. He hesitated a moment before he helped me remove his shirt, and I wondered what the hell was up with that. Only for a moment did I give it a thought though because his shirt was gone and my hands could finally roam all over his well-defined chest and arms.

One thing I regretted about yesterday was not being skin to skin, and though I knew I wasn't exactly looking my best, I truly didn't care. I *needed* this. So without any help from him, or encouragement, I took of my shirt.

I heard his gasp and then his words. "Holy fucking Christ, Red. You're so fucking beautiful."

Those words came at the exact right time.

Nobody had ever seen me like this, and once my shirt was over my head I felt a brief tinge of fear, embarrassment, worry … but I should've known better than to feel those things with him. This time it was Liam who grabbed me and started kissing. I leaned closer to his body so I could rub my chest against his, and I couldn't contain the moan from bubbling out of my mouth. The zings of pleasure that shot through my body at the contact of his chest against mine had me rocking against him seeking an end to the torture his touches created. When I started rolling my body into him, he started rocking up to meet me. Our kisses got deeper and more frenzied, our hands got rougher and our breaths more shallow. I *needed* something *more*.

"Liam … please …" I didn't know exactly what I was asking – what I was *begging* – for. I just knew he was the one that had to give me whatever it was.

"Red …" he said right before his hands moved up my back to the clasp of my bra. He unsnapped the flimsy material and then moved away from me a little so he could watch himself move the straps down my arms and take it completely off. It may have been awkward to some being bare that first time, but the way he was looking at me, and the way I was feeling, it wasn't anything in the realm of awkward. It was in the realm of not-fucking-enough. Not nearly enough.

"My God …" he said right before he lifted one hand to my breast, and bent his head down to latch onto the other.

Right then it was me who was speaking to God and not the other way around.

His mouth on my breast sucking, while the other hand was caressing and then tugging, was driving me fucking insane. I couldn't stop my hips from grinding down on him, any more than I could catch my breath.

"You taste fucking sweet," he said before he switched his mouth to my other breast. I was expecting his hand to cup the breast his mouth was no longer attached to, but he moved it around to grab ahold of my ass, guiding me in the rhythm he wanted me to be moving in against his hardness.

I may not have the experience he has, but I knew what was happening inside of me. Much more of this and I knew I would explode – but in the *very best way possible*. I knew it couldn't be like this though. Not *this* way.

I needed more of him.

I started to move my hands further down his torso, feeling his body jump a little once I reached the muscles of his abs. I started to tuck my hands under the waistband of his jeans, fully intent on unbuttoning them, when I felt him freeze underneath me, and stop what he was doing.

Every part of his body froze.

This could *not* be fucking happening *again!*

"Liam … why'd you stop?" I rasped at him. How *could* he fucking stop?

His forehead dipped to mine before he said, "We can't do this now like this."

Is he fucking kidding me with this shit? Again? Why was he the one always stopping it? I know he wants this. I can feel how much he wants it. I can see how much he fucking wants it. I can hear it, and fucking taste it. What the fuck is wrong with him?

Though his forehead was touching mine, I was looking down asking myself all these questions in my head when I felt him shake me gently to get my attention back on him. I looked him right in the eyes so he must have seen my complete and utter confusion.

"I need you to be one hundred percent sure, Red. Once we go all the way there is no turning back. You *will* be *mine*." He made it sound like a threat and a promise all rolled into one.

I don't think he ever sounded sexier.

I made sure I kept my eyes trained on his when I spoke to him. I didn't want him to misunderstand a word I said. I wanted no confusion.

"I am sure, Liam. I've never been more sure of anything in my life. I know once we go there we can never go back. I won't want to go back – I promise. I *will* be yours, and I am more than okay with that."

I didn't know what I was expecting, but it sure as hell wasn't silence. Maybe a shit ton more kissing? Maybe a lot more touching? Maybe he would finally make love to me?

I wasn't expecting *nothing* though.

He just stared at me. For the longest fucking time.

Then his hands that were resting on my hips tightened to the point of pain.

"Jesus, Red … you just might be ready after all." His hands got even tighter before they loosened. "But our first time shouldn't be like *this* either."

Jesus Christ!

I thought I was the virgin and not him.

What was it with him and not wanting to rush things, or wanting to make things perfect? Saying things can't happen like 'this?' What the flying fuck? I don't understand. Shouldn't it be me worried about things like that?

I could honestly care less. I just want him inside me and that's it.

Holy fuck!

He seemed to be thinking about something. *Hopefully* he's thinking about how wrong he is in regards to what he just said, and he's thinking about a way to say he takes it back without sounding like a douche before he throws me down on the couch and has his wicked way with me.

No such luck though.

"How about Friday night, after we go out with Connor and Riley, you come over and plan on spending the night at my place, but for real this time? I'm talking about packing a bag, and plan on staying for a while. When we do this, I fully intend on taking my time with you Samantha. I want the whole night, *and* the morning, Red. Then, I want the afternoon too. That can't happen tonight, or tomorrow. I don't want either of us going *anywhere*. I want an *official* breakfast in bed with you. I want *Every. Fucking. Thing.*"

Breathless and Speechless. Wanting and Aching. That's how Liam has me.

Maybe timing was everything.

Hearing his words I am beginning to believe that.

Maybe there was a fantastic fucking reason not to rush things. Maybe he really knew what he was talking about after all. Who was I to doubt him?

With my body tingling even more than it was only moments ago just thinking about what was going to happen on Friday, it was no wonder that my cheeks flooded with even more color and my breath came out incredibly shaky when I said, "Okay."

Liam looked at me as if I had just given him all the secrets of the universe.

"Okay? Really? You'll come home with me Friday?"

"Yes," I confirmed again, right before his mouth captured mine for a few more minutes. When he finally pulled away he grabbed up both of our clothes, got us dressed, and headed towards the door to go home.

Did he think I had any choice in the matter? Did he think I'd say no?

I was *his*. He just had to finally claim me already.

Chapter 16

I shouldn't have been nervous, but I was. Tonight was what I'd wanted more than anything, what I had initiated the other day, but none of that mattered now. I would be spending the night over at Liam's. *Making love*, for the first time. And I was *nervous.*

Liam texted me a few minutes ago saying that he was double-parked outside of my building so I knew that it was now or never. It would've been so much easier if we just had sex the other night on the couch, or when we were at his place Saturday morning. Then it was spur of the moment and I didn't give it too much thought, but this – tonight's plans were all I could think about the whole week.

I had too much time to think.

The butterflies that were in constant motion all week turned into birds taking flight the moment I got his text letting me know he was here.

I was ready though, and had been for a while. I packed my overnight bag hours ago, took a shower, shaved all the pertinent places, blow dried my hair to perfection, applied my makeup like a beauty school master, and dressed casually on the outside but a little more provocatively underneath with lace and bows; I was ready outwardly, it was the inside that I was having a problem with.

All I had to do was grab my bag and my purse and go.

I don't know why I couldn't seem to get myself to go out the door. I loved Liam. I was ready for everything with him. I was just a little scared all of a sudden.

Almost as if he knew I needed a little push, my phone started beeping.

Liam: So, it's been a while now since you've known I'm here. I'm going to go with you are either stuck in the elevator … which is so NOT cool … or you are freaking the fuck out about tonight right now … which is COMPLETELY fine … all of its fine. Well except for the elevator thing … that would just suck. Ha-ha. Seriously though, Red, I need you to know that if all you want to do is just go out and have dinner and then I bring you home – it's fine. If you want to go to dinner and go to my place and just sleep over, and only sleep, that's more than fine too. I have NO problem with just holding you in my arms, Red. Don't be worried or scared about anything. I've got you, Red. Now come on … I miss seeing your beautiful face, and I'm dying to see it already … so hurry your gorgeous ass down here!

I don't know how he knows what to say to me, but that was definitely what I needed to hear. I was still nervous, and scared, but I knew he would make everything okay for me – for us. He found a way to calm me down and get me out of the door. I knew he'd find a way if I did end up 'freaking the fuck out' later.

As I was in the elevator I was hoping that he also found a magic way to get me through sitting and having drinks and dinner with my brother and his sister. I don't know how I was going to pull off acting like I had no clue what would be happening once we left *Molly's* in front of them. I was going to have to keep it together though. If I wasn't letting myself ruin tonight, there was no way I was letting

Connor get wind of what was happening between Liam and I and having him ruin it. He's ruined enough.

When I left my building I saw Liam by his car. If his words didn't make me feel a thousand times better about tonight, the way he was looking at me now would have. The nerves I had before turned into full-blown wanting. The scared feeling turned into full-blown lust. What the hell *had* I been thinking before? Maybe it was a week of not seeing him. Maybe it was a week of wondering how we would get back into the swing of things. Who knows? I should've known better. One look at him and everything was fine. Tonight was the night, and neither one of us was putting a stop to it.

****

After Liam grabbed my overnight bag, and kissed me on the mouth and asked me if everything was fine, I made it a point to let him know that everything was more than alright before I got into his car. I made sure he knew that I couldn't wait to spend the night with him later. That news made for a very interesting drive.

We got to *Molly's* before Connor and Riley which was a good, and not so good thing. Connor was picking up Riley from her dad's much to Liam's annoyance.

"I can't believe your brother's picking my sister up at my dad's house," Liam said once we sat at a table, after grabbing our first round of drinks at the bar.

"Well, I'm personally happy he's picking her up and taking her home. It makes it a lot easier for me to leave with you and spend the night."

Just talking about the night ahead with Liam makes me get warm all over.

"Red, I love your blushes. You know I do. I might love them more than most things in my life. In fact, I can't wait to see where else you blush – where else I can *make* you blush, Red – but you need to try and control them when your brother's around. Maybe you can *try* to not think about later?" he asked in a way that suggested it wouldn't be possible for either of us.

I blew out a breath. "How do you expect me not to blush when you say things like that to me? I'll try not to blush, if you try to stop saying things like that. I can't guarantee anything though. *And stop staring at me like that*, all smoldering and stuff. It's not fair. Tonight is all I've thought about for a while, and those looks of yours, and your words to me, it isn't helping. God, Liam … I can't wait for tonight." As I said that last part to him I felt my color deepen, I heard my voice get huskier, and I felt my body start to churn. The way he was looking at me should be banned. It's fucking *lethal.*

Maybe I should go back to being scared of tonight after all. The wickedness, and the promises of things to come in his eyes – it's really screwing with my heart, and my over-heated body.

"Sam … you can't say those things to me right now … Holy fucking shit …" he said before he drank deeply from his beer bottle. Just watching him drink was sensual. I didn't think I was going to be able to control any of my feelings. I was feeling too much right now. I wanted his mouth on me, his hands on me, his tongue on me, his body on me – in me.

Yeah, there was no way I was going to be able to control *any* of this.

"Liam –" I said in a throaty whisper.

"Shit, they're here. Seriously, Red ... I can't take much more ..." he practically pleaded with me.

I cleared my throat and sat up straighter. "I'm sorry, Liam ... I'm trying. I'll try and keep it together." *Please Lord let me keep it together!*

"Hey guys!" Liam's sister chirped out when she got to the table. She came around to me and gave me a semi-hug before going over to Liam's side and giving him a hug and a kiss. We decided to sit on opposite sides of the table, which I think is best. I don't know how I would've been able to keep my hands off of him if he had been sitting next to me.

And with that thought I felt myself flush all over again.

"You hot, Sam?" Connor asked coming up to the table. "It is fucking hot in here, isn't it?" he said, and thank God for small miracles. If Connor thought I was warm he might not question my constant rosy cheeks that I'm sure I would have regardless of my trying to control them.

Once we were all seated the waitress came over to take Connor and Riley's drink orders, she asked if Liam and I wanted refills, and she also asked us if we wanted anything to eat. Once we got everything ordered, we started in on talking. Tonight's conversations were not as one-sided as they were at our previous outing to *Molly's* which was great, but that meant that Liam and I were talking more this time. Every time I heard his deep voice, or his laugh, I couldn't help but to have thoughts of later on that night. I wanted to hear just how deep that voice of his could go. I wanted to experience all his different sounds. I felt him brush the side of my calf with his foot. I looked up at him, and I knew I must have been broadcasting my thoughts all over my face. I tried to clear my face but it wasn't working, especially with him touching me under the table and looking at me like he was.

Thankfully the waitress came back with our orders so Riley and Connor were distracted while I tried to get myself under control. This night couldn't be going any slower. I wasn't going to make it another hour or two. Maybe if I pretended that I wasn't feeling well we could get out of here early. Why the *hell* didn't I think of that before?

I was completely in my own world thinking of the best way I could get out of this date and into Liam's bed without drawing too much attention or suspicion from Connor, when I heard Connor inhale quickly and loudly.

He pulled me out of my own thoughts swiftly.

I wasn't prepared for the bite in his voice when he barked out, "You've got to be fucking kidding me. *After all this fucking time?* I don't want to deal with this shit, Samantha."

I stared at him wide-eyed. We all did. We all must've been shocked at his tone and intensity, and what he had said. What was he talking about? Whatever it was it was a complete mood-changer. What didn't he want to deal with? And what did he mean 'after all this time?' I didn't know what it was, but Connor's demeanor seemed icy and tense all of a sudden. Whatever it was I knew it wasn't good. I didn't want to ask, but I needed to know what was wrong.

"What shit don't you feel like dealing with, Connor?" I asked quietly. I don't know why I asked quietly, but it just felt like something I should be doing.

Connor just turned his head to look at me. He looked at me in such a way that I felt like my world should be shattering. He looked at me, but then he looked away from me and past me. What I saw in his eyes after he looked past me was confusion, anger, and *worry?*

He then looked back at me, then at Liam. I didn't understand that look he gave Liam. What was it? Why was he looking at me like my world's going to shatter and at Liam who I can tell is tense now, too?

He turned back to look at me again, focusing *only* on me – on my eyes.

He spoke to me slowly. And my world *did* shatter some.

"Aiden's back."

Chapter 17

No. No. No. No. No.

I had to have heard Connor wrong. I couldn't have heard him right.

"What did you just say?" I *needed* him to repeat himself before I started freaking the fuck out. He couldn't have said what he did. There is *no* way.

"Aiden's back, Samantha." He said it again. I didn't hear him wrong. Now I know why he looked at me the way that he did. How he was *still* looking at me. I could feel his eyes boring into mine, like I could feel Liam's eyes boring into the side of my face. There was so much tension at the table you could cut through it with a knife. I didn't know whose feelings were radiating the most tension: mine, Connor's, or Liam's.

I whipped my head towards the door where Connor had been looking past me earlier. I had turned so quickly my hair fanned out around me. *How could this be happening now? After years of not seeing him? After years, and when I'm finally happy with a man who I also happen to be in love with? I was just thinking of excuses to leave and go home with Liam – to make love with him. I was thinking of all the things we would be doing together tonight, and now this?*

What the fuck is happening?

I couldn't miss him by the door. He's older now, as we all are, but he's still the Aiden I remember. He still has the same broad build, but he definitely filled out a little more. He added to his tattoo collection, still had a few piercings, still had the 'I don't give a fuck' attitude written all over his face and body. He still had the same chocolate brown eyes of my best-friend.

I couldn't help but to lock onto those eyes. I saw them widen right before he started to swagger his way over to our table, as if he were meeting us – as if he *belonged* with us. He never did lack confidence.

Connor took the time to point out the obvious by saying, "He's coming over here." We could all see that he was coming to our table, and that he was determined. His eyes had been locked on mine since he started coming our way. With the way he's looking at me as he walks, I get the eerie flashback to a time not too long ago when another man looked at me the same way, with complete determination and focus, me being his sole intent. A man who looks similar with his toned body, his tattoos, and his attitude. A man who I finally look at, who I can tell is not at all happy anymore.

Oh, Liam.

Liam's looking at me in such a way I've never seen him look at me before. I didn't like it. It sent chills all throughout my body, but not in a good way … not in *his* way. It was scary. What happened to the Liam who was making me blush, think dirty things, count down the minutes until I could go home with him? Liam stopped looking at me, instead he looked towards the side of the table. I knew Aiden must have reached our table because if it was at all possible, the tension in our little area got even worse.

I looked to where Liam was looking – where Aiden was standing – and I saw that Aiden was looking at me and only me. What he did next did shatter me a bit. And probably Liam too.

He spoke.

"Hi, Princess," he said.

When he said it he released a smile, and his eyes lit up, and I could almost pretend we were eighteen again. I could almost pretend that he didn't break me, that he never left, that he was still my best friend, and that nothing had happened.

Almost.

I heard Liam's quick intake of air, but I didn't look over at him; I heard Riley's sigh, which I knew wasn't good; I heard Connor's quiet "fuck," so I knew this was only going to get worse really quickly if I didn't say anything.

"Hi, Aiden," I said back to him.

"Can we talk?" he asked, "In private?"

"You've got to be fucking kidding me," Connor chimed in louder this time, as if he had any say in the matter.

"Please, Princess," Aiden steamrolled right over him. "I need to talk to you."

I *knew* I should say no, I *knew* I should look away, tell him to leave, but I *couldn't*. Even feeling the heat from two very pissed off sets of eyes on me, I couldn't look away. I knew what I should say but I couldn't, because it was different from what I wanted to say – what I *had* to say. I knew Connor and Liam wouldn't like it, but they didn't know what was going on in my head right now. They would eventually understand when I explained it to them, but I couldn't get into it now in front of everyone. I needed to talk to Aiden.

"Sure. Okay. I'll meet you out back. Just give me a minute, okay?" I told him, continuing to hold his gaze and only his.

He nodded his head, smiled at me again, ignored everyone else at the table including Liam and my brother, before he turned and went out the back door.

The door wasn't even closed before Connor started in on me.

"What the fuck was that, Sam?" he roared so loudly that people at other tables turned to look at us. As if the tension wasn't a killer before, Connor had to go and raise it to catastrophic.

I was having *none* of it.

"Shut the fuck up, Connor!" I roared right back.

I could tell that everyone was a little taken aback by my outburst and rude language. I didn't normally say things like that, or yell like that, but he didn't know what was going on, and it wasn't any of his fucking business. I didn't expect him to keep his mouth shut, but I didn't need any shit from him right now. I felt like my world was turning upside down and I didn't need to deal with his shit too. It wasn't fucking fair.

"No seriously, Samantha, Connor's right. What the fuck?" Liam started in now, too. "So that was him. The guy who hurt you? The guy from high school? The guy you can't wait to blow me off for after you haven't seen him for years? He comes back and asks you to talk, and you jump right on in? You're just going to blow me off … blow off what we had planned for tonight, for *him*?" Now it's Liam's turn to roar, except he wasn't yelling. No, he was speaking quietly but what he was saying and how he was saying it was so much deadlier – it was so much more than a roar.

"What the fuck did you two have planned later?" Connor broke in, but I paid him no attention. Of course he would pick up on that one detail and run with it.

"I'm not blowing you off, Liam! Don't think that. It's not like that. I just need to talk to him for a minute. After everything I told you, you should understand that," I pleaded with him.

"I don't understand, Sam," he countered, "You *need* to talk to him? No you don't. He's the one who hurt you – I know it was him.

Why are you okay with talking to him now? Years, Sam. It's been fucking years."

"You really don't understand, then, if you have to ask me that. I'll explain it to you later. I just need to do this now," I said to him again.

I can't believe how this night – which was so full of anticipation and excitement, and wanting and love – turned into such a fucking nightmare. Everyone was mad at me. Connor, Liam and even Riley, who now had her eyes narrowed at me. Why wasn't Liam understanding that I needed to do this?

"You're right. I don't fucking understand. I've asked you about him, and you apparently only told me what you wanted, but obviously there is so much more. I thought you told me *everything* at my place the other night, I believed you told me everything, but I was fucking *wrong*. He called you 'Princess' and you practically fucking melted for him. You do remember what happened when I called you 'Princess,' right? He's the one who made you closed-off and shielded, right? *Him?* You know what, Samantha? Forget it. There's a lot I don't understand. Like the fact that when you were mentioning a guy in high school who broke your heart, you skipped over the part that he's still a pretty big fucking deal. You said you put yourself together and everything was fine now, that you would be holding nothing back, but that's a fucking joke. He's holding you back right now and you're letting him! He's obviously a pretty important person if you're willing to go against what Connor and I think you should do … if you have no problem fucking *hurting* me – *us* – in the process. One look … one look from him, and *everything* comes crumbling down. One fucking look, one fucking question, one fucking decision. For *weeks* I have tried to get you to see how awesome we could be together … how right … how fucking *perfect*. For weeks I have tried building an *'us'* with you … but you know what? Forget it. Seriously fucking forget it,

Princess. I was a goddamn fool for believing you moved on and were whole. That you could be mine and only mine. That I could have every fucking piece of you. Fuck it. I'm out of here."

And he left.

He got up, he went right out of the front door and he never looked back.

And I let him leave.

I sat there frozen and watched him walk out on 'us.'

I watched him go.

****

"You just let him walk out of here, Sam? You really didn't go after him?" Connor broke the silence. I watched the door for a while, waiting for Liam to come back in. Waiting and waiting. Waiting for *something.*

He wasn't coming back.

"Oh my God, Connor. What did I do?" I whispered. I felt like if I talked any louder, I just might break apart.

Did I make the wrong decision in wanting to talk to Aiden? Liam didn't have to leave. I wanted him here. I was going to talk to Aiden, then come back to Liam. We were going to go to his place. We were going to make love. I was going to tell him that I loved him. We were going to continue to build on our future together.

He wasn't supposed to walk out on me.

He wasn't supposed to say those things that he did to me. He wasn't supposed to act like I've never seen him act before. He wasn't supposed to hurt me with his words.

And Aiden was never supposed to fucking return.

I made peace with that a while ago. Why the fuck was he here now. *Now?* And where the fuck had he been?

I realized that I had kept him waiting too long, that he might disappear, then all of this would have been for *nothing.* I was not about to let that happen.

"I need to go talk to Aiden, Connor. You, even more so than Liam, should understand that."

Connor just looked at me. He didn't say anything, but Riley did. "I don't understand though, Samantha. Who is Aiden? And why did my brother storm out of here like that after saying such things? What was all of that?"

I looked at her, and then at Connor. I really needed to get outside.

"Connor, can tell you. I'll explain more when I get back."

Connor looked at me like he wanted to argue, but he must have thought better of it because he said, "Go do what you have to do. We'll be here."

I just nodded my head and went.

****

I took a deep breath in and out before I pushed open the back door and came face to face with Aiden.

I was not holding anything back with him. He shattered my world years ago, and he may have just contributed to what could possibly be my shattered future. He was not getting off easy. That happened once already.

"Where the fuck have you been, Aiden?" I yelled at him.

"Well somebody sure did grow up," he returned in a lazy drawl. How I didn't haul off and slap his face, kick him in the nuts, punch him in the throat, or ground him into dust with the bottom of my shoe I didn't know. I honestly had no fucking clue how I reined myself in.

"Don't start with me Aiden. I'm warning you. I'm not the same girl you left heartbroken and shattered who wandered all around for days like a lost puppy looking for you. I grew up, I moved on. It took me a long time, and I am fucking happy now. I *was* fucking happy. For years I wondered what I did wrong. For years I wondered where you were, why you wouldn't return my calls, or texts, or emails. I wondered why your aunt and uncle wouldn't tell me a thing. I wondered how it was so easy for you to walk away and not look back. I wondered what the *fuck* you were thinking that night. You were my only fucking friend, and then you were *nothing*. You made *me* nothing, too. I had *nothing* and *no one* when you left. I struggled, but I *survived*. I put you in a box and left you there. For a good long while I wanted you out of that box so I could have my answers, so I could ask my questions, so I could see you weren't really worth it after all. Now I wish that you never came out of that fucking box. So I'll ask you again, Aiden … where the fuck have you been, and why the *fuck* are you back *now*?"

I was looking directly at him while I said everything I needed to say, so I could see what my words were doing to him. I wanted to feel bad. I wanted to feel bad for the boy who was my best friend once, but I remembered that that boy broke me to pieces. I remembered that his silence, that his disappearance from my life was way harsher than any words that I just spewed at him. He could take this shit and so much more. He's the one who ruined everything. He can't look at me like that, expecting me to feel sorry.

"Princess –" he started speaking, but I put a stop to that.

"Don't. I'm not your Princess. I'm not even your friend anymore, Aiden. I just need to know *why?* After all these years, I deserve that much."

It really was all about me, and not him. I needed these answers. I needed the closure once and for all. Maybe Liam was partly right after all. I was holding back, but not to him – to myself. I thought I'd moved on but if I had, why did I still need closure? Why did I still need answers?

"Samantha. I'm so fucking sorry. More sorry than you could ever possibly know. That night, the night I left … I found out that my mom died …"

What?

I could literally feel all of the angry flush draining from my face.

"She died a few days earlier, and my piece of shit father didn't even bother to let us know about it because he was in jail for killing her. He had been drinking and driving, and of course she was the one who paid the price. She *always* paid the fucking price. There's a little more to it Sam, but needless to say I didn't handle it well. You saw how well I handled it. I didn't know what I was doing that night. I don't know what I was *trying* to do. We weren't even like that. I loved you as a friend. But I just don't know what the fuck I was thinking. I didn't want to lose you too, but then I did anyway. When I left … even before then, I knew it would be the last time I was seeing you. I knew I needed to go back home. I had a sister to take care of."

What? He never told me he had a sister? How could he be my best friend, and I didn't know that?

"Yeah, I never talked about her. I missed her so much when my dad kicked me out of the house. I think that's why I latched on to you right away. You reminded me of her, and you looked like you needed a friend, and all I wanted to do was protect you – something I couldn't do for her –" he kept on speaking.

At least that explained the why, of why he chose me to be his friend when we were nothing alike. I was a substitute for his sister. I wanted to be upset by that, but I couldn't get there. God, what had he gone through?

"You really were my best friend though. I really needed you. You made every day happy and normal for me. It wasn't easy leaving you. I hated that. You think I left you broken and shattered? Well, so was I. I missed you all of the time. I missed your sense of humor, your laugh, your smile, your love of everything, your caring nature … I missed your easy acceptance. I missed how you just made everything okay all of the time. I *hated* remembering that look on your face when I left. I hated remembering the way you were crying. I hated remembering that I *did* that to you. I had to leave you though. I needed to take care of my sister. And I can't regret that. *I will never regret going home to be with her.* I will regret not getting in touch with you though, for losing you. Hearing you say those things to me about how you were after I left … I will probably regret that forever. But I *thought* it was for the best. Not for you – and I'm sorry for that … but for me. I didn't want to leave the only true friend I ever had but I needed to break myself away from you. I didn't want to lose you, but I knew I had to. I'm so fucking sorry, Princess. So fucking sorry. I know I shouldn't be here asking you for forgiveness … but I am. Please, Sam. Please don't fucking hate me anymore. Don't think that I wasn't worth it."

Oh, God.

I knew right away that I didn't hate him. I also didn't think that he wasn't worth it. He may have broken a part of me when we were younger by his careless actions, but he wasn't the man then that I see standing before me now. He was young then too, just like me. I will never agree with his not letting me know why he left all of those years ago, but I needed to let it go. He had his reasons – pretty important ones – more important that I could probably imagine. I didn't know how his life was then, what it was like in the years in between, I didn't know what it was like now ... I just knew what my life was, is, and what I want it to be.

The clarity I had now was life-altering.

Oh, God!

How did I not see this until now?

How did I not understand all of this?

Why is this only making sense in this moment?

Deep breath in; Deep breath out. It's okay now.

"I don't hate you Aiden. I also don't need to forgive you. You *hurt* me by walking away from me, by leaving me with so many questions ... but if you didn't leave, I don't know where or who I would be right now. Or who I would be with. And I love where I am at right now, and *who* I am. I may not have my future planned out exactly as I want it, but I'm in love Aiden. I'm in love, and I don't know if I would be with him if it actually weren't for you and the decisions you made and the decisions I made after ..."

And I didn't think about that until you came back into my life, answered my questions, and set all of this free for me.

"How fucked up is that? If you didn't walk out and you stayed ... where would I be? If I didn't stay away from all men because I thought they would all leave me like you –"

At his strangled sound, I knew I had to amend what I was saying.

"I didn't exactly mean it like that, Aiden. It's just for so long I blamed you for everything ... but part of it was me too. I never delved into your past. If I had, maybe I would've known where you were going, or what was going on. I didn't know anything about your parents, or that you even had a sister. I knew there had to be more to the story, before, and after you left, of *why* you left, but I was so busy being hurt, and angry, that I couldn't think clearly. We both made mistakes. Maybe something good came out of all of this though. Your actions set up my game-plan in life that put me directly in the path of Liam. It sounds crazy, but I think it's true. Who knows … maybe after all this time I should thank you."

"God, Samantha," Aiden said while rubbing the back of his neck. "So … Liam is the guy in there?" he asked. He probably wasn't sure what else to say after what I'd just said to him.

"He *was*. He left when I said I wanted to talk to you. I just recently told him about you, and I thought he understood everything, but I think he misunderstands some stuff. We got in an argument … I don't know what's going on … I need to set things straight."

"Well, I hope you get things settled with him, Sam. I'm happy for you, Princess. Really happy. It looks like you found your one." And he did look happy for me. *And I did find my 'one.'* He also seemed sad as well though. Why?

"What about you?" I asked. "Have you found your one?" I then narrowed my eyes and asked once again, "And why are you here?"

"No I didn't find my *one* yet … and I'm here because I live here now. I just moved back with my sister last week. My aunt and uncle moved to Florida a few months ago, so we moved into their place. Living at my parent's house – it never felt like home to me. Too much went on there. Too many bad fucking things. The only place that ever felt like *home* was here. So when I found out they were selling the house, I knew what I had to do. I needed to come home."

"You're staying?" I asked him. I didn't know how I felt about that. Just a few minutes ago I was wishing he never came back. I wished that he could've stayed away forever. Now knowing what I know, and realizing that maybe everything happened exactly how it was supposed to – that maybe I was supposed to hurt for all of them years so I could meet up with Liam at the exact time that I did – it had me reconsidering the years of hurt and anger. I didn't dismiss it, but I didn't want to dwell on it any longer.

"Yes. And I'd really like to make things right with you, Sam. I didn't expect to see you here tonight. It was always my intention to seek you out though, and explain. I'm glad I got the chance now, but I am sorry that I ruined your night."

"It's okay," I told him, even though it wasn't exactly okay. It happened and there was no changing that now.

"I know it's a lot to ask, but do you think we can work our way towards being friends again? After all these years I still miss you, and I'd really like to get to know you again, and have you meet my sister. Maybe I could patch things up with your brother, after I officially meet him that is. Meet your boyfriend ..." Aiden asked me, sounding hopeful.

I really didn't know how all of this was going to work, and if it was even a good idea.

One thing that I knew, that truly surprised me, after everything that had happened ... I was happy that he was finally home. I was happy that he finally *found* his "home."

"Maybe Aiden ... maybe. That's all I can say for right now."

He shook his head and rubbed the back of his neck again. "Okay Sam, I'll take it. Your parents still have the shop?"

"Yeah. I still work there sometimes. Maybe I'll see you around? I need to get back inside now though. I have some fixing to do ..."

"Okay, yeah … sorry. Sorry for taking up so much of your time … and well, I'm just so fucking sorry for *everything*," he said once again.

"Me too, Aiden. Me too. I'm sorry about your mom, and for you having to leave to go take care of your sister. I'm sorry that you felt you had to leave everything including me behind … but I *am* happy you're back now. Bring your sister by the shop one of these days. I'd love to meet her."

I just stared at him for a moment. I really couldn't believe he was standing in front of me and that he wasn't leaving again to go somewhere that I didn't know. A huge chunk of my life had revolved around this man before me – both good and bad. I knew that the bad finally got some closure.

Because of the good that was still there, I went towards him and gave him a tight hug. He wasted no time hugging me back.

It wasn't a hug like I'd experienced with Liam. It didn't leave me breathless and fluttery. It wasn't even a hug like I experienced rarely with Connor that left me feeling protected and safe. Aiden's hug felt like *peace*.

****

I left Aiden outside, after he told me he was heading home from there, and I went back to my brother and Riley's table. Though I hadn't been outside more than a handful of minutes talking to Aiden, it felt like forever. It also felt like so much had changed while I had been away from them.

Connor looked at me as I sat down and asked, "Are you okay?"

"I will be once I talk to Liam. I need to clear everything up with him. Aiden and I are fine. There's so much that happened to him Connor ... so many *awful* things ... I can't get into it now though. I need to find Liam and talk to him. Can we leave now? Can you give me a ride home?" I asked both Connor and Riley. Riley just nodded and grabbed her purse. She didn't seem as mad at me or the situation anymore, so I know Connor must have filled her in.

When we got to Connor's car I wasted no time calling Liam.

He didn't pick up, it just kept ringing and ringing. I tried over and over again, leaving voicemail after voicemail, not caring that my brother and his sister were hearing every word. I was beyond that right now. I sent text messages too, and nothing. He wouldn't let me explain. He wouldn't let me in.

I kept going over and over his final words to me, and I kept seeing how angry he was, and how he walked out the door. His final actions were scaring me.

I didn't know that I was crying until Connor pulled up in front of my building. I didn't even realize that we had stopped, or that he was waiting for me to get out. He started speaking to me, but I couldn't focus on anything he was saying. I guess he must have understood that I was in no shape to go anywhere, because instead of pushing me out of the car to actually get me to move, he headed into my building's parking garage. After he pulled into my spare spot, he opened my door after Riley's and helped me out.

"He wouldn't answer, Connor," I said to him with tears running down my cheeks, as if he could have missed all my pathetic attempts to get ahold of Liam.

"I know, Sam. Let's get you upstairs," he said to me like I was a child.

When we were finally in the apartment, I really started to cry. I finally got the closure I needed on my past with Aiden, but at what cost? What did I do?

I was finally able to see everything clearly now, but my insides were so fucking cloudy it overshadowed all the rest. Everything was breaking apart inside of me.

I needed to call him again.

I dialed his number and it rang and rang, again. Riley came to sit next to me, putting her arm around my shoulders. When she did I just sobbed. I had turned into that teenage girl I hated. I was an adult woman who was acting like a sixteen year old, crying because her boyfriend wouldn't talk to her after a fight. What the *hell* has happened to me?

When I got control over myself, I tried calling again.

"He's not answering, Riley …" I said to her, when he didn't pick up, *again.*

I didn't want to look weak in front of either of them, but I needed someone right now. She hugged me to her a little tighter and I was so grateful that she didn't hate me for making her brother this angry at me.

"It's his voicemail again," I said before I started to leave another message. "Liam … please …" I started in a wobbly voice before the phone was snatched out of my hand by Connor. He clicked the end button, and threw the phone next to me on the couch.

"Stop it Sam. You need to stop it. He doesn't want to talk to you right now, and I can't even fucking blame him. I know you said Aiden had his reasons for doing what he did and you magically fucking forgive him, and you had your own reasons for wanting to talk to him

– all well and good, Sam – but for you. It was all well and good, *for you*. I think you need to leave Liam alone for a while."

It felt like Connor had punched me in the stomach. Why was he saying that? He's supposed to be on my side and supporting me.

I shook my head as tears leaked out of my eyes even more.

Did I really make a huge mistake?

My heart really fucking hurts.

It hurts so badly. Worse than it's ever felt.

I needed to make this right!

"I don't agree Connor," Riley said, completely shocking me. She let go of my shoulders and took my hands in hers. "I know my brother, and I know he needs you. I know he needs you, and you need him. I'm not going to pretend I understand everything that happened tonight, Sam. But I'm a woman, and I can see it in your eyes … you love my brother. You need to go to him, you need to tell him, and you need to fix this. You need to fix this because I am pretty sure he loves you too, and I don't want him hurt. And I know he's hurting. I have never seen him like that before, other than when we were younger and our mom died. Nobody could make it right for him then. Only *you* can make this right for him *now*." She got up and went to her purse that she left by the door, and grabbed her keys and wallet out of it. She removed one of the keys from her keychain, and then dug in her wallet and pulled out a card.

"It's for his apartment. You should go to him. He's not going to answer his phone, or answer your texts. He's too mad and stubborn right now. He's too hurt. But he needs you. He needs to see you, and he needs to hear you. Regardless of what his actions say, he wants you. He's probably regretting his decision over having left you, and he's probably as mad and angry at himself as he is with you. You both need to fix this."

She opened my hand and placed the key inside of it along with the swipe-card, before she closed my hand around them. She turned and looked at Connor, and said "I think it's time we go now, Connor."

Connor just shook his head and followed her to the door. Before he left, he turned around and said, "Be careful, Samantha. I don't want you hurt ever again. I love you too much for that shit."

God! Leave it to Connor.

"I love you too, Connor. I'll be careful."

And then I was alone.

I was all alone again.

Alone. Again.

Liam left me all alone. I needed him. And he left.

I needed him. I was hurting. He left me all alone.

But he was hurting too.

I hurt him. But I loved him.

So many things went through my head in seconds. His words, my words, his actions, my actions, my feelings, and his. I was hurt, and mad, and confused, and scared.

Most of all ... I was in love. With him.

And it was time that he knew it.

Chapter 18

I love him, I love him, I love him … *I am in love with him.* He hurt me, but I hurt him too. I hurt him *first.* He left me all alone, something I was terrified would happen if I let someone into my life again, but in a way I left him too. I needed to fix everything, and I *needed* him. I knew I couldn't do anything without him. I don't care how pathetic it sounded, I *know* it's pathetic, but I *needed* him.

That was what I told myself in the hours leading up to me going to Liam's. You would think I ran out the door once Connor and Riley left, so I could rush to Liam, but I didn't.

I sat paralyzed.

What if it really was over? What was it really, anyway? It had only been a few weeks of a few dates, some shared feelings, a few intimate caresses, and him … *completely changing my life around.*

I was afraid.

I was afraid that I had pushed him too far. That I hadn't given him enough of myself. That he didn't really know how much he meant to me – how much he *means* to me – that he honestly thought I would brush him aside for someone else. I wasn't experienced in any of this, so maybe how I had handled the situation sent him a completely different signal than I intended. What if he didn't answer my calls not only because he was mad and hurt, but because he really was done with me, and he wanted to move on? I couldn't wrap my head around no Liam in my life.

So, because of that I sat paralyzed.

It wasn't until I thought about all of the things I let slip through my fingers over the years because I was afraid, that I decided to move. I let so many things go, I didn't give things a chance – I almost let Liam pass me by at one point. What if I had? What if I never got the chance to know him? I would have *never* been better off without him. I knew that now. Just like I know that I'll never be the same if I don't go and fight for what I want. I couldn't let him shut me out and be okay with it. I couldn't let him think for one more second that I didn't love him. *That I wasn't his.* I couldn't let him think for one more second that there was anyone else out there for me that I thought was better, or that I wanted.

It was him.

And it would only ever be him.

When I thought about all of that, I wasn't paralyzed anymore. I got up and went to the bathroom to fix my face and my hair, I changed my shirt, and then I grabbed my phone and our keys and I went to him. And I was going to stay.

****

It didn't occur to me until I was outside of his door how easy it had all been. The drive, the opening of the door, going past security who didn't even glance my way because I had the card that allowed me access. It was easy getting into the elevator, pushing the button and walking to the door. It had all been so easy.

What wasn't easy was the choice of whether or not to knock, or use the key. If I knocked and he didn't answer, or told me to go away, it would kill me. If I went in and he didn't want me there and told me to leave, it would kill me. What I also didn't calculate was what if he was inside with someone else? What if he really did move on in a few short hours and he had some woman over? That would fucking destroy me. What happened if he wasn't home, because he was out with some other woman at *her* place? That would fucking destroy me too. Why didn't I think about these things before?

Because you didn't have to.

Because you don't have to.

Because he wouldn't do that to me. I knew better than that. Riley told me to come. She said that she thinks he loves me. He wouldn't move on so fast.

He better not have.

I was going in. My mind was made up. I could take whatever he had to throw at me. What I couldn't take was giving up and not fighting. Not again. Never again.

I put his key in the door and let myself in.

I didn't make it ten steps inside before I heard his voice.

"Riley, I really don't want to talk to you tonight. Just go home," he called out from behind his closed bedroom door.

"Seriously, I can't fucking deal with any of this tonight," he continued by saying. His voice didn't sound angry, just tired … but then again he wasn't mad at Riley, he was mad at me.

I didn't say anything to correct him, I just kept moving into his apartment. After I closed his door and locked it behind me, I knew I committed to whatever was going to happen when we came face to face.

If the sounds were any indication I would be finding out what's going to happen soon because I could hear him moving in his bedroom. I froze by the kitchen and waited. With the open layout of the apartment I could see everything. I saw the empty beer bottles on the coffee table, and the shattered one by the fireplace. I saw that the door next to his bedroom was open where my face was staring out at me uncovered. I don't know why he was in there, but I'm happy that the painting wasn't destroyed. I also saw his mother's pitcher on the dining room table and I sent up a silent prayer to her that she would give me some guidance and strength to make things right with her son, because I loved him and needed him.

I should have also prayed that he didn't throw me out.

When he opened the door and saw who it was I thought I would die.

The only thing he had on was a pair of really low hanging sleep pants, and a scowl.

He was not happy to see me. I could tell that from looking at his face. His normally beautiful face that was always so full of life, mischief, want, laughter, charm, and challenge, was now a mask of anger, hurt, and annoyance.

He never looked at me like that. He didn't need to say any words to hurt me. His face said it all for him.

He still spoke anyway though.

"What the fuck are you doing here, Samantha? How the fuck did you get in? You need to leave," he said to me in a very cold, hard, whip of a voice.

He couldn't be this way with me. That wasn't my Liam. He needed to stop.

"Liam … please listen to me, and let me explain. It's not what you think –"

"Really Samantha, you have no idea what I'm fucking thinking. You don't *want* to know what I'm thinking. Trust me. You want me to listen to your explanation? I've done that before ... and guess what? You sure as shit didn't tell me every fucking thing. Why should I believe any word you say now? Why –"

I had had enough. I never lied to him. I told him exactly what had happened between Aiden and me. I was not going around and around with this shit anymore. I was not standing here and listening to him call me a liar, questioning what I've told him. Who the fuck was he? I didn't care if I was in love with him or not. He doesn't get to say that shit. Not to me.

"What happened to 'I only need to know about now and the future,' Liam? What happened to 'I don't need to know anything about the past.' Remember when I came over for dinner? You said those *exact* words to me. Those exact *fucking* words. I didn't want to tell you everything, but I did. Because you deserved to know, and I needed to tell you so we could move on. I told you *everything*. I didn't fucking lie," I told him. I had more to say but I stopped because of the way he was looking at me all of a sudden.

He looked a little deflated, which had deflated me some too. I decided that it would be best for both of us, if I just gave him the truth of what happened tonight, and he could just believe what he wanted. I wanted to fight for him, but he needed to believe and want to fight for me too. He had to want us. *He had to want us as much as me.*

"Liam ... I think you believe that I still have feelings for Aiden, or that I want him in some way. You think that I chose him over you by wanting to talk to him, and it was so, so, not that ..."

"Really? Then what the fuck was it?" He cut me off by asking. I should've known better than to think just because he seemed deflated that he wasn't still upset, because it definitely didn't mean that. His words still rang out with hurt, anger, and disbelief.

"Liam, I told you before, he was my best friend. Aiden and I hung out, and we did a lot of things together. We were so different, but we just fit, you know?" I looked at him before continuing on saying, "Then one day Connor and Aiden got in a fight. It was a complete misunderstanding – I told you about it. Aiden's the one that Connor made the mistake with – it's why Connor was so hard on you ... but that's beside the point. *Shit! I am making a complete mess of this.*"

Just breathe, Sam. Holy Christ.

"After the fight Aiden left. He left and he never came back ... and *Jesus*, you know that too. You also know that's the first time I've seen him in over four years. Four *years*. When he left I was broken, or at least I thought I was for a while. I just didn't understand. He left me with nothing – no answers, no friendship, and for a long while, no happiness. I already mentioned that he is why I didn't want to get too attached to any guy again ... *especially* you. At first, you reminded me so much of him and I *hated* it. I put him in a box and I moved on ... or at least I thought I did ... but then you showed up and brought all the memories back. But they weren't memories followed by longing or wanting, okay?" I asked him.

Liam just took a deep breath, most likely processing everything, so I continued.

"When I saw him tonight and how I acted, when I said I wanted to talk to him, it wasn't my intention to hurt you. It was never that. It was about me needing to be free from everything once and for all. When I saw him in that moment walking towards me, I knew ... I knew he was *never* anything more than just a friend. He was *never* anything to me as much as *you* are. What I feel for you is epic, and it's so fucking scary, and you ..."

I looked him deep in the eyes to make sure he was understanding me and following me, because I wanted absolutely no misunderstandings, no confusion. I went closer to him because I needed to be closer for what I had to say. When he didn't move away, I took it as a good sign so I moved even closer.

"You not talking to me for a few hours practically *killed* me, when I survived without talking to Aiden for years. I wanted answers from him and I got them, but I really hope I didn't lose you because of it, because … *because* I could live without *ever* knowing those answers or seeing Aiden again … but Liam … I could never, *ever*, live without seeing you."

I heard him deeply inhale, before I took a step even closer to him. I needed to get it all out there. I needed him to understand and know. *He is it for me.*

It was my turn to inhale deeply. I looked in his eyes and I could feel my eyes start to tear up. I was so overwhelmed with emotion – so scared but so ready to be taking this chance.

When he saw the tears in my eyes he took his own step closer, worried. I needed to speak before he started talking.

"*I love you.* God, Liam … I am so in love with you, and I hate that you think that I have any feelings left over for Aiden. I have no feelings for *anyone* but you. I knew I was in love with you when I came over for dinner the other night and you showed me your painting of me. When you said you never wanted to figure me out – how you always wanted to be surprised, how you never wanted to be done with me … I knew right then that I was in love with you. Before then it was all the little things building together that had me falling, but it wasn't until you said those things about me that I undoubtedly knew. I didn't tell you before – not because I was scared or terrified or unsure – but because it was all so new and I didn't know exactly how you felt – and okay, *okay*, maybe I was a little scared after all – but seriously, Liam … I am *so fucking in love with you –*"

I didn't even see him move the rest of the way towards me. One second I was talking and the other I was wrapped up so tightly in his arms with his mouth devouring mine. His hands were everywhere and it took me a few seconds to catch up. When I did catch up, he threw me off balance once again. His hands grabbed my ass and he lifted me up in the air. I instinctively wrapped my legs around his waist and my hands around his neck. His hands stayed where they were rocking me into his body. All I could do was hold on for dear life, and try and kiss him back the way he was kissing me.

He started moving with me towards his bedroom, and I knew what it meant, but instead of feeling anxious or nervous, I couldn't fucking wait.

He lowered me onto the center of his bed with his arms bracketing me and my legs still wrapped firmly around him. He moved his hands but only so he could grab the hem of my shirt so he could pull it up over my head. He didn't take his time like the other night, instead he reached behind my back to unclasp my lacy bra and he threw it over the side of the bed and onto the floor. He wasted no time latching onto my breasts with both of his hands, his mouth and tongue … his teeth. *God his teeth.* I didn't know what to do other than to keep hold and explore the skin that was within my reach and roll my hips up and down to meet his thrusts.

He kept sucking and pulling at my nipples, and I couldn't take it anymore. I needed more than what he was doing. *I needed to feel everything.*

"Liam ... please ..." was all it took to get his attention. He looked up at me, and I knew there would be no more waiting for us – there would be no more right time, no more let's wait, no more not here or now. It was supposed to be tonight before, and it was going to be tonight now.

Liam moved further down my body kissing his way from my breasts to my belly button making my insides quiver even more than they were before. He licked inside my belly button and I swear I jerked my body so hard I thought I might push him off the bed. I could tell he enjoyed my reaction because I could feel his lips tilt up into a smile against my skin. He just kept kissing lower and lower until he got to the button of my jeans.

He looked up at me again and held my eyes while he unbuttoned my button and then slid down my zipper. He kissed more of the skin that was revealed to him before he got to his knees so he could remove my pants from my body. He made very quick work of that action, leaving me only in my lacy panties that were currently soaking wet. I had the briefest thought that I should be embarrassed by how wet they were, but that thought was quickly erased from my mind when Liam moved back up my body to hook his thumbs into the sides of my thong so he could remove it too. The way his eyes kept darting between my eyes and my body, showing me their molten color, I knew I didn't have a thing to worry about. He was enjoying everything he was seeing and feeling, which left me wanting so much more.

And then my panties were no longer there – Liam and his magical hands were.

I started to close my legs, feeling extremely exposed, but Liam was having none of that. His large hands grasped my upper thighs spreading my legs even wider than they were before. Before he came back over me he looked his fill, and then he finally touched me where no man has touched me before.

If I thought I was wet before it was nothing compared to what I was now. The first time his fingers touched me I jumped at the contact, which had his eyes immediately seeking and searching mine. The sensation of that light touch had electric sparks shooting throughout my body. The feelings he was creating inside me with his fingers were too much. When he moved one of his fingers inside of me, it was my complete undoing … and *his*.

"Fuck, Sam … you're so tight," he said groaning. He kept his finger where it was for a few seconds, before he started pumping it in and out of me. I couldn't help but move my body in the rhythm he was setting, instinctively seeking more. It became worse when he moved his thumb to the top of my sex and started to rub, and when his mouth glued itself to my breast. The overload of sensations became too much, too soon.

I felt his movements inside of me, I heard my moans and pants, I heard his whispered words and groans, and I could feel myself getting closer and closer to something I've never experienced with someone else.

"Liam!" I cried out desperately. I started clutching his hair trying to bring him up my body, because everything that he was doing was bringing me to the edge, and I didn't want to go over alone.

It was all so much and yet not nearly enough.

He seemed to understand what I wanted, because he stopped what he was doing. He removed his fingers which was a damn shame, and he let go of my nipple by popping it out of his mouth … but he was far from finished.

"Red …" he said to me, with a raspy voice made only more potent because of the situation we were in.

I was completely naked, wet, open. *And waiting.*

He half turned his body away from mine, stretching his arm out towards his nightstand. I didn't know what he was doing at first until I saw him grab a condom out of the drawer.

I don't know how I was able to come up with a coherent thought, but my mind flashed back to the other night and Liam saying he'd never had a woman here before.

So why would he have condoms in his nightstand next to his bed?

He must have felt my body freeze under him because when he turned to look at me I could see the questions in his eyes.

"What's wrong, Red?" he asked me.

"Why do you have condoms in your nightstand drawer, right next to your *bed*, if you don't bring women here?" I asked him.

And just like that his face cleared and he smiled.

Why the fuck was he smiling?

"God, you had me worried. I thought you were going to ask me to stop. *Holy fuck, Sam.* I knew you were supposed to be sleeping over tonight, before everything happened, and even though I would have been cool with it if you wanted nothing to happen tonight, I moved condoms to the drawer just in case. And I'm really fucking happy that I did."

God, I was happy too.

I couldn't help but to return his smile. I knew what was going to be happening next, and I couldn't wait, but there was still something I didn't tell him – something we never talked about. My smile started to falter trying to think of what to say to him.

I really didn't think it would matter, but he should still know.

I got lost for a second though when he started kissing me. I got even more lost when he started touching my nipples, and when he started teasing me again. He kept rubbing and rubbing and I could feel my climax fast approaching once again. Before I went over the edge by myself, he moved away, and took off his sweats, and *oh my god* –

He ripped open the condom wrapper with his teeth and then smoothly and quickly put on the condom. I didn't get the chance to really study him or explore him the way he did me, because before I knew it he was back in between my legs, spreading me wide, lifting my hips so I could wrap my legs around his waist where he and I both apparently wanted them. I could feel his hardness against the opening of my body, and I froze.

He was never, ever going to fit.

I needed to let him know he would never fit, that this was wrong. *Holy Christ!*

I was absolutely still. I tensed up. I didn't move. I was scared after all.

The only thing I was able to do was clutch at his shoulders, and dig my nails in.

He had to have known something was wrong because his eyes flashed to mine.

"What's wrong, Sam?" he asked me with a pained and pleading voice, as if he thought that this was the time I was going to stop him.

He might just be right.

I didn't know how to tell him. Maybe I shouldn't have waited until right now. No, I *know* I shouldn't have waited until right now. Fuck! I can't believe that the moment we are about to have sex, I have to have a conversation with him. We could be making love right now, if he was actually able to get himself inside of me, but I don't think that's physically possible ... so we need to talk. Way to fucking ruin it, Sam.

Here goes nothing.

"Remember when I didn't tell you about our first date being *my* first date because I just wanted it to be normal, and not be over the top, and for it to just be something that happened ..." I asked him, while he just stared at me looking confused.

Yeah, I didn't expect to be having a conversation at a time like this either, Liam.

I had to keep on going otherwise everything really would be fucking ruined.

"Well I wanted this to be the same way ... so I didn't mention it ... but now I think I *have* to ... and well I haven't done this before either ..." I knew I was rambling.

Oh God kill me now. NO! Not right now. I think I still want to make love to Liam first ... maybe after ...

He still looked at me a little confused, but then I saw understanding start to filter into his eyes.

"What?" he croaked out.

"I've never done this ... have sex ... I –" I didn't get the chance to finish.

He pushed up on his hands creating some space between us so he could see me better. I could tell from his eyes he definitely understood me now.

"What do you mean, you've never? How is that even possible? How are you only telling me this *now*?" he asked in a voice I wasn't expecting. Was he mad? Was that what I was detecting in his voice? No fucking way!

That sent me over the edge.

"Well, what were you actually expecting, Liam? I told you that you were my first date, I told you I'd never slept in a man's bed before … that I've kept men away … what the fuck did you expect?"

"So what? Nowadays that doesn't mean shit …"

Oh, *hell no!* I dropped my legs from around his waist and removed my hands from his shoulders.

"Thanks a lot Liam …" I said a little hurt.

"I didn't mean it like that … *Jesus*, I thought you messed around in high school or at least in college … just because you didn't "officially" go out with anyone doesn't mean you didn't fool around. I thought everyone screws around then … you don't need dates or anyone special for that –" he said, but then cut himself off.

Did he just fucking say that? Nothing like a fucking mood-killer. Before I could say anything to him, he started in again.

"You know … when we were talking about my experiences that day, after you found out about Ryan being my friend, and you were worried about the things I'd done, *why*, *why* Samantha, *why* wouldn't you *maybe* mention something then about something like this … or *I don't know*, any fucking day after?" he started questioning me like I did something fucking wrong again.

"Are you seriously fucking mad at me about this? You're mad at me because I'm a virgin and I haven't slept with anyone else? I can't believe this. I can't fucking believe this! Would you have been happier if I didn't say anything and just let it happen? Would you've been happier if I fucked someone else and then we wouldn't have to have this conversation –" I didn't get any further with what I was saying because he yelled over me and said "NO!" before he swooped down and kissed me. I was so mad that he seemed pissed off that I didn't tell him about my lack of sexual experience. I was mad enough that he had me speaking like a trucker and had me thinking mean things that I shouldn't be, but those feelings dissolved when he smashed his mouth to mine.

He kept on kissing me deeper and deeper. His body crushed back into mine, and once again my legs instinctively wrapped around his waist bringing me into stark contact with his hardness. As the kiss went on I found myself rocking against him over and over.

He started to move against me too, and it wasn't long before we got the right angle and the right thrust, causing him to enter me a little. We both froze, and I moaned while he groaned. He broke the kiss and looked deeply into my eyes.

"Please tell me we are done arguing about this Liam. I just thought you should know. I didn't mean to tell you now, I planned on telling you before, but I just didn't ... and seriously ... I want my first to be you. I've only ever wanted you –" He started kissing me again. He grabbed the sides of my face with his hands, moved himself back a little, lifted himself onto his knees, and just kissed me.

"I wish you would've told me before," Liam said when he broke the kiss again, "I can't even tell you what it does to me that I'm your first ... and to think of you fucking anyone else like you said – holy fucking shit, I want to kill that imaginary prick. I really never thought that I'd be lucky enough to have this – something this special – I just wish that I'd known so that way I could've prepared, that this could've been different –"

I cut him off this time by grabbing his cheeks in *my* hands and lifting my upper half to kiss him. There was no fucking way he was pulling this shit again, talking about timing and rushing, and doing things different. No fucking way.

I broke our kiss and laid back against the mattress, looking up into his eyes. "I don't care about the timing ... I don't care about how this started

… and I don't *want* anything different, Liam. I just want *you*. I *love* you. Don't you get that? The timing is right, because *you* are right. *We are right*. Please, *please*, don't stop." I pleaded.

He leaned down over me again slowly, covering my whole body with his.

"Are you sure?" he asked me in the deepest voice I've ever heard come out of his mouth.

"I'm sure, don't stop," I whispered back, before kissing him lightly on the lips.

And he didn't stop.

He started deeply kissing me again, touching me again, and exploring me again.

I did the same.

I was back to my original position before everything went sideways for a few minutes, with my legs wrapped firmly around him, my hands grasping his shoulders, with him poised at my entrance.

He looked me deeply in the eyes, and I knew this was it.

He started to enter me and for a moment I couldn't catch my breath. The feeling of him moving inside of me is something I would have never been able to dream about, because I don't think you can ever dream this feeling.

It was beautiful, consuming, and enjoyable … until it started to burn.

I felt myself tense up at the pain. I knew it would hurt the first time, but I still wasn't prepared for it to feel like it did.

Liam must have felt me tense up, because he tensed up too.

He grabbed my hands off of his shoulders and placed them on the mattress next to my head. He laced our fingers together and he gave them a squeeze before he leaned down and quickly kissed me on my lips.

"Sam, I've got to ..." he started, when he broke away from the kiss.

"I know ..." I didn't let him finish. I knew what he had to do.

He leaned on me again and started kissing me with tongue and teeth. When he was kissing me like that I forgot about the burning, I forgot about what had to happen, I forgot everything but Liam and his tongue and his hands grasping mine. I felt his tongue flick at my bottom lip before his teeth bit down hard and pulled. The stinging of my lip where he bit and pulled was a delicious ache, whereas the stinging of a certain area that Liam simultaneously pushed through while I was wrapped up in his kisses and his biting, was not.

My body was immediately back to being tense and I couldn't help but to release the cry that came from deep within my body, or the two tears from falling out of my eyes and down my face at the searing feeling within me.

Liam was frozen over me, looking deeply into my eyes.

"Red ..." he said while he untangled our hands so he could swipe his thumbs across my face, wiping away my tears.

He leaned down to kiss me some more, softly and gradually this time, until the hurt feeling inside of me went away. The pain went away rather quickly, and with his kisses, and his body on me, and the fullness of him *in* me, I needed *more*. Liam still didn't move though, but I needed him to.

I broke away from the kiss and turned my head to the side intent on telling him to move.

He must not have known what I intended to say because he grabbed my chin in his hand and turned me towards him. I could see from the look in his eyes he was worried about me.

"Are you okay, Red? I'll stop this right now. I'm so fucking sorry I hurt you ..." he said, and then he started to pull out. The motion of him pulling out set me on fire again, shooting little zings throughout my core. I couldn't let him go. I pulled my legs even tighter around him forcing him to stop, while my body rocked against him causing him to slip the few inches back in that he had given up in his attempt to stop hurting me by pulling out. That action caused us both to moan, and it had me saying, "Don't leave, don't stop, I'm fine … we *are* doing this."

"Are you sure?" he asked. I shook my head up and down. That was all he needed to know.

He pulled out some more than he had before, but then he plunged right back in. I had never done this before, but somehow my body knew what to do because it took only seconds for my body to catch and match the rhythm he was setting for us.

Liam started out slow, probably making sure I was telling the truth and that I was okay, but then as it became more and more overwhelming for me and as I became more and more vocal, his pace picked up. His hands were roaming everywhere, as was his mouth. He was kissing me, then he had his mouth on my breast and his finger went back to my clit rubbing while he was moving inside me.

I couldn't take much more of the sensory overload, and from the way he was speaking and moaning too, I don't think he was able to take much more either.

I grasped at Liam's hair and he immediately looked at me. He came back to eye level, obviously knowing I was close, and he never took his eyes off me.

"Liam … I don't … I can't … *Please –"* I begged. He knew exactly what I wanted and what I needed.

"You can … *you will.* Let yourself go, Sam. I've got you," he said. His hips thrust even quicker, he moved even deeper inside of me, his finger started rubbing even faster, and then I was gone ... floating ... shuddering ... exploding ... *shattering.*

I heard myself scream his name, but it sounded as if it came from a distance.

I could feel him going quicker still, and then I felt him jerk inside of me, whispering out my name reverently during his release.

I was still quaking, and I still felt shattered, but at the same time I was never more full, more whole, more together, or more *complete.*

Liam and I had both stopped moving, and we were both breathing deeply just staring at one another. After everything we had just done, I had never felt more exposed until now, just staring into his eyes. I had honestly never felt better or more overwhelmed in my life than I did in this moment.

Until he spoke.

"I really fucking love you too, Samantha. *I am so fucking in love with you too,*" he said right before he kissed me, long, slow, and deep.

When he stopped he said, "You may have said it first, but I knew I was in love with you long before you knew you were in love with me. So just remember, Red ... I loved you first." He said what he did with the wickedest grin I had ever seen on his face. I never loved his grin more than I did in this moment.

He leaned down and started kissing me again, caressing my body with his hands. Some people might feel awkward after their first time, but I felt nothing but pure and utter bliss.

"Hey, you know what this means right?" Liam asked, when he finally let both of us get some air.

"What?" I asked him.

"It means that we get to have an official breakfast in bed tomorrow morning," he said with another devilish smile on his face.

I couldn't help but to laugh at his words. After everything that had happened tonight – *everything that had happened* – it was the breakfast in bed comment that really did me in. He finally told me that he was in love with me, I had finally made love with him, and yet it was his comment on breakfast that made me fall in love with him even more.

It was the little things.

He kissed me some more after that, and I knew by the way both of our bodies were responding that I would get my chance very, very soon, to show him just how much more in love with him I really was.

Chapter 19

It had been a little over a week since the night Aiden came back, and Liam and I had made love for the first time. I still can't believe how unbelievably happy I am. How unbelievably *in love* I am. After Liam and I made love the first time, we made love again and then talked about all the things we needed to talk about. We also had our first "official" breakfast in bed the next morning, then we made love *again*, and I finally learned the true meaning of the 'mess' part of that whole breakfast in bed thing, but Liam was right of course … I didn't mind in the least – *it really was the best part*.

During the last week there were various different 'firsts' for me, and I loved and enjoyed each and every one of them. I was beginning to expect and anticipate that there would be more, and I knew I would love them all too.

Though Liam got home late because of work, he made it a point to stop by my place every night for a few hours. Things were still chaotic at his job, but I was told that everything would be getting better the following week. He and his team were in the final stages of their project, so everything would slow down and return to normal. I was excited and anxious to get Liam all to myself for a while, especially with our relationship so new, and with me going back to school in a few months. I knew that school was something we would need to talk about more, but I was content for now to leave that until later.

I also saw Aiden this past week, and got to meet his sister who is an absolute beauty, *and* a charmer. Liam and I talked about Aiden quite a bit since that night, and though he still doesn't like Aiden because he hurt me all those years ago, he said it was up to me whether or not I wanted to let him back into my life. I told Liam the same thing I told Aiden – I believed all of it, every little thing, had happened for a reason. I believed that everything had to happen the way it did in order for me to meet up with Liam like I had. I don't know if he believed in all of that, but I did, and that's what matters. It was because of that I decided to give Aiden another chance, even though I knew we'd never have what we once did.

As I got ready for work I found myself counting down the hours. I couldn't wait until I got to see Liam again later on. I knew that there were only three more days until his big meeting and then he would be *all* mine. He was meeting me at the shop because I worked the closing shift, and then we were going home where we would more than likely end up doing some more "exploring" of one another.

I was so excited about his meeting me later, that I didn't even mind that I had to work with Joanna. I was letting nothing put a damper on my day, especially someone like her. Nothing at all.

****

I should've known better than to think that nothing could dampen my day, or screw with my night. I was able to ignore Joanna's bitchiness all day because I knew what was waiting for me at night. I just had to focus on that to get me through. I just had to focus on spending the night with Liam, and the fact that my parents were coming home next week after extending their vacation so they could deal with Joanna themselves when they got back. I just had to make it a few more days.

But I should have known better.

It was the end of shift and Joanna and I were cleaning the shop. Everyone had gone, so it was just me and her. I was surprised that Liam wasn't here yet, especially since he assured me he would be meeting me no later than ten, and it was now after eleven and I haven't heard a word from him. I couldn't expect Joanna to wait around much longer, especially because she was getting huffier the longer I took cleaning up the counters trying to bide my time.

"Seriously, Samantha. The counter is clean, everything is clean, it's late and I have plans. I know you don't have a social life, but some of us have more important things to do than this shit," she said to me, with her complete bitch voice, and narrowed eyes.

I wasn't stooping to her level so I just breathed in and breathed out. She didn't have to be an insulting bitch even if she was partly right; there was better shit to be doing than scrubbing a counter for the fifth time.

"Give me a minute," I told her, before I grabbed my phone and texted Liam to ask where he was.

It was close to a minute before he responded.

Liam: Shit, I'm sorry, Red. There was a small problem. I had to fix it … I'm walking out right now. Give me no more than ten minutes. See you soon. Love you.

I should've been annoyed that he didn't let me know he'd be late before now, but I found myself smiling at his text instead. I don't think I'll ever get used to his saying 'I love you' to me. Even reading it in a text, it melts me.

Joanna definitely must not have liked my smile though, or my sending and answering texts, especially when she was in a complete rush to leave.

"Seriously? We shouldn't even be here, we're fucking done, and you're drooling over a fucking text, wasting more of *my* time? You are so fucking pathetic. I'm so out of here," she said before she turned around and headed towards the door.

She got on my last nerve. Who the *fuck* did she think she is?

"You can't leave. And you also can't talk to me like that. You leave and that's it! You'll be fired. You had one more chance ... but that's it!" I warned her. I didn't need my parents. This bitch pushed me too far.

"Fuck you, bitch! I don't need this job anyway," she yelled before slamming through the door. She didn't even turn around when she said it. As much as I would've loved to follow her outside, pull her bleached hair out and bitch slapped her a few times, I couldn't be bothered. Sure it pissed me off what she said, and it pissed me off that we were going to now have to fill her spots along with all of Beth's because we had yet to find someone to replace her, but – *Holy Shit!* – the bitch was finally gone. I didn't care that I was going to have to explain this to my parents. Hallelujah, was all I was thinking as I went into the back to grab my things, so I could be ready when Liam finally got here. Screw being mad; I was going home with Liam, Joanna was gone from all our lives, I'd fucking deal with the fallout.

As I got to my locker I heard the front door open.

Liam must've really hauled ass to get here. It hadn't been ten minutes yet, it probably hadn't even been five.

I grabbed up my things, and was putting my phone into my purse, smiling because he really must have rushed over, when I headed back

out front. I looked around for Liam but didn't see him. What the hell? I
went around the counter, and it wasn't until I did a search of the tables
that I saw him. I was looking for Liam to be standing, so I didn't register
the sitting person at first.

He got up from the table, and I knew it wasn't good. None of this was
good.

"What are you doing here, Aaron?" I asked in a very small voice. I
guess my subconscious knew that all of this was wrong. I could barely get
my words out.

It *definitely* must have known something was wrong because my
hands got clammy at the same time that goose-bumps started to rise up all
over my flesh and little tingles of fear and panic went up and down my
spine.

I was scared.

My whole body knew it.

And Aaron did too.

He started walking towards me, while I instinctively started backing
up.

I just didn't back up fast enough.

Aaron grabbed ahold of me, keeping me from moving anywhere else.

"I told you I wanted you Samantha. I've been watching you. Waiting.
I saw your car on the side tonight, so I knew you were here late. Imagine
my luck when I saw that stupid slut co-worker of yours come storming
out of here a few minutes ago. She left you all alone didn't she? She
shouldn't have done that, should she? But she did. And like I said … just
my luck …" he said, right before he pulled me into him so hard I
immediately felt the bruises bloom on my arms. I tried to push him away,
but he was too strong. I never imagined how strong he could be. He didn't

look like he could be this overpowering, and that was my mistake. I made so many when it came to him.

I tried pulling away, I tried pushing him, I tried getting my knee up between his legs but nothing worked. He forced his face onto mine, cutting my lip as he mashed his mouth onto my own. I tried biting him but it didn't work, and I only ended up hurting myself more. I was struggling with everything I had. I almost pulled away from him, but he started pulling me towards him again, shaking me like I was nothing more than a ragdoll. He shook me so hard my teeth rattled together and my neck snapped back and forth.

During the struggle – I don't know how I was able to do it – but I got one hand free and was able to rake my nails down the side of his face. He yelled out in pain, and I had a brief second of elation that I hurt him, and a brief second where I thought I had the upper hand and I would get free, when he smacked me so hard across the face I toppled over onto one of the tables before I slammed onto the floor and saw stars.

And then he was on top me.

I knew it *really* wasn't good then.

I knew that the floor at my back, with him on top of me, is the last place I wanted to be. I knew what he was going to try and do. I knew I wasn't strong enough. I couldn't even get loose of him when I was standing up, so I knew that I wouldn't be able to get him off of me when he was on top.

He was on top of me, and I continued to struggle against him with everything that I had. I would *not* let him rape me. I just had to fight him. I had to either get away, or last long enough for Liam to get here. *Oh, God, Liam.*

Where is he?

I was struggling and screaming, praying that someone would hear me, but nobody did. Aaron put his hand over my mouth while he tried pulling at my shirt. He made a huge error because I was able to bite his hand, and bite I did. I bit him so hard I drew blood, and he reared back just enough for me to get my knee up in between his legs. He was stunned for a moment, in absolute pain I was sure, but I had no time to be happy about that. I pushed him off of me and scrambled to my feet, trying to run away. My legs were definitely shaky from fear and panic so I didn't go as quickly as I was supposed to.

I don't know how Aaron recovered as quickly as he did, but he did.

I was so close to being out the door.

I was so close to getting away.

But then Aaron grabbed me by my hair and he pulled me as hard as he could back towards him.

It hurt so bad.

He pulled me into him and then turned me around to face him. The look on his face was pure evil. The look on his face told me everything I needed to know.

He was going to hurt me, he was going to enjoy it, and there was nothing I could do about it.

The last thought I had was of Liam walking in the door and seeing me hurt, bloodied, and broken, just lying on the floor.

It was the last thought I had because Aaron punched me so hard in the face that my head snapped back, my body fell backwards, and my head cracked with a sickening thud against the floor.

After that, I didn't remember anything else.

Chapter 20

The first thing that hit me was the smell. Quickly after was the constant throbbing in my head. Following right behind that was the sounds of beeping and hushed voices. The last thing I paid attention to before I opened my eyes, was the sensation of being watched.

I blinked my eyes open and quickly shut them. The brightness of the room hurt my eyes, and made my head throb even more. From the quick look and the awful smell I knew that I was in a hospital. I had no idea why I would be in a hospital though. I opened my eyes because I couldn't shake the sensation of being stared at, and I didn't like it. I needed to know what was going on, even more than I needed my head to stop hurting.

I opened my eyes again, and looked around the room. I tried not to turn my head too much because when I did, I felt like someone was stabbing me in it. I finally saw who was staring at me, and I caught my breath. *Who was he? And better yet, why was he staring at me that way? I needed to figure out why I was here, why I felt like this, and I had to know who he was.*

He definitely wasn't a doctor, or anyone I would associate with, but maybe he could help me.

Before I could say anything, he stood up straighter and said, "Red?"

What's red? Is my face red? Do I have blood on me, like he has on him? What's he talking about? Is that why I can't remember anything? I was hurt? Something bad happened? It had to, otherwise I wouldn't be here. I knew I was in a hospital, but where exactly was I, and where's my family?

"Where am I?"

Silence.

"What happened?"

More Silence.

"Who are you?"

A look of confusion.

"Who *are* you?"

A look of horror.

I started out asking the questions quietly, but found myself getting louder and louder when the man standing next to me stayed silent. A man who was overwhelmingly gorgeous despite the bruises, the cuts, and the ripped and bloody clothing.

What the hell happened to him? And who the hell is he? And why is he not answering my questions? Why is he staring at me like that?

"Don't you remember?" he asked me. "Anything?" he pleaded.

I stared at him trying to remember, but I remembered nothing. What were those emotions running through his eyes? Why was he emotional? Who the hell is he, and why don't I remember anything? Why doesn't he just give me the answers I'm looking for?

After my own prolonged silence and my lack of response he slowly says, "I'm Liam," as if that's supposed to be the key that unlocks all the answers I am seeking. As if that one revelation is supposed to be important to me.

It doesn't, and it's not.

'Liam' means nothing. This man means nothing. His emotions mean nothing.

He then added, "I'm pretty sure I'm your boyfriend."

Okay.

What? What does that even mean? How does he not know if he is my boyfriend or not?

That doesn't help me. It doesn't unlock anything. It doesn't reveal anything.

It … *he* … still means *nothing*.

And then it hit me. He said he was my boyfriend. I didn't have a boyfriend. I kept myself away from men. Especially men who look like him.

"What do you mean you *think* you're my boyfriend? Seriously, what does that even mean? I don't have a boyfriend," I half questioned, half told him.

Before he could answer me, the door swung open revealing a very familiar face. A face that I haven't seen in forever, one that I should be extremely mad at, but I needed to know what was going on, so I would take whatever I could get. I noticed Liam looking towards the door as well. He seemed to know him too, which made no sense to me. Maybe they were friends? But he said he was my boyfriend – *I was so confused.* They both nodded to each other, but wearily. Not friends then. I turned to look solely at the one face in the room I recognized.

"Hey, Princess."

"Hey, Aiden," I said. I hadn't seen him in years, but it felt like it was only yesterday.

Why did it feel like only yesterday? And why didn't I feel mad at him like I expected to be? Why do I feel like we cleared things up? What am I missing?

My brain flashed to me seeing him at the shop and us talking with a girl. *His sister*. But that made no sense. That couldn't have happened. I was really missing something. There was something wrong with me – with this whole situation.

Where is my family?

I had so many things to talk to him about, but more than anything I needed to know what the fuck was going on, *now*. Before I could ask him anything, the stranger spoke up.

"*You've got to be fucking kidding me!* You remember *him?*"

He looks like someone just *shattered* his world.

I didn't understand why he looked like that, or why he was speaking to me the way he was, but I felt sorry for him. Nobody should look like he did. I also didn't understand why my heart was beating fast all of a sudden for him. I didn't like seeing him hurt and upset for some reason. I didn't understand one bit of what was happening.

I looked back at Aiden because Liam's face was making me feel all types of uncomfortable. Aiden was looking at Liam, but then he looked at me, and then he looked at Liam again before he finally spoke.

"What do you mean, remember me?" Aiden asked him.

"She doesn't remember who I am," Liam said back.

I was looking back and forth between them, and saw Aiden's head go down before I heard his mumbled, "Holy shit." He picked his head back up and looked at me.

"Princess ... you don't remember Liam? I'm pretty sure that he's your boyfriend ..."

"Why did you both say it just like that?" I cut Aiden off. I looked over at Liam and asked, "Are you, or are you not, my boyfriend?"

Liam took a deep breath, and came closer to my bed. He seemed unsure of what to say, or what to do with his hands. It almost looked like he wanted to reach out and touch me, but he stopped himself.

"God, Red ... *Samantha* ... *Fuck!* Look, we have a thing, you and me ... we said in the beginning we were only going to be friends ... we started out that way, and we *are* friends ... but we are so much more than that. We fell in love. I love you ... you love me, too ..." he kept on speaking, but I only heard buzzing in my ears after he said that we were in love. There was no way. *No fucking way.* He was lying. I had to stop him.

"So I call you my boyfriend?" I asked, speaking right over what he was saying.

He hesitated before he said, "No."

See, I knew it.

"Then you're not my boyfriend," I told him matter-of-factly.

He just shook his head, and Aiden didn't say anything.

The stranger was breathtakingly handsome even bloodied and bruised, and with torn clothing and busted hands. He appeared to have had a suit on, but he had lost the tie and jacket at some point. I could see the tattoos on his arms, because of his rolled up sleeves, and I could definitely tell that he was more than in shape, but he wasn't my type – I stayed away from men who looked like him, because of the other man in the room with us.

I didn't need any of this confusing shit right now. I needed answers. I needed my family. Where were they?

"Where are my parents? Where's Connor?" I asked Aiden.

"Connor's outside talking to your parents. When you were brought here, and Connor found out, he got on the phone with your parents immediately. They were still at your Aunt Maggie's, but they packed up and headed for home right away. They won't be here for another few hours though, but Connor wanted to check in with them. We'll let him know you're awake. He'll want to see you. He was a fucking mess when I got here —" Aiden said.

"Why *are* you here? Why am I even here? What happened? Was I in an accident?" I asked Aiden.

"You really don't remember what happened to you, Red?" Liam said.

"No I don't," I replied to the guy who he thinks he's my boyfriend, before curiosity got the best of me and I asked, "Why do you keep calling me 'Red?'"

He didn't respond to my question, instead he just looked at me with hurt and sadness in his eyes before he dropped his head and stared at the floor for a few moments. I saw his body heaving up and down, and I heard him breathing deeply in and out.

When he looked back up and into my eyes, I felt like my heart was breaking and I didn't know why, and I really didn't like the feeling. The cracking in my heart rivaled the throbbing in my head. I didn't know which was worse.

"I'm gonna go out and tell Connor that you're awake," he said, before he disappeared out the door.

I don't know why I felt like something more than him had disappeared out of the room when he left, but it did. Once again, none of my feelings were making sense.

I looked away from the door and toward Aiden who came even closer to my side.

"You really don't remember him?" he asked me. I shook my head and said, "No."

"What about me? Do you remember me coming back last week, and us talking and settling everything between us over the last few days? Do you remember meeting my sister Lizzy?" Aiden asked hopefully. I didn't know what to tell him. I had a brief flash of seeing him and a girl who I knew was his sister, and I didn't feel *mad, upset,* or *hurt* seeing him, so I knew that what he told me must be the truth, but I just didn't remember all of it.

But if I was so willing to believe him, how come I didn't believe Liam? How come I had no memories of him?

"I had a flash of you, and a girl. I don't clearly remember it though. I know when I saw you I thought I *should* be mad, or hurt, or pissed, or something ... but I wasn't. So I guess we did patch things up, but I just don't remember. Aiden ... was that guy ... Liam ... *was* he telling me the truth? He's really my boyfriend and I actually *love* him?"

"I can only say what you told me, Princess. That night when I first came back you told me you loved him. That you were happy with him. You told me that everything had to happen the way that it did for you to meet up with him when you did. I don't know about all that ... but you sure seemed to believe it ... and since you were willing to put things behind us because of that thought, I sure as shit believed in it for you. From what I've heard from you these past few days, he's your boyfriend and he loves you, and you love him –" Aiden kept on saying.

"But he doesn't seem like someone I would give the time of day to. And we're together? I just don't understand any of this. If I loved him ... if I was in love with him ... why wouldn't I *remember* him?" I asked more to myself than to Aiden.

Neither of us got the chance to really ponder that question because we both heard yelling out in the hall, and I knew the voice belonged to my brother.

"Where the *FUCK* were you?" Connor yelled.

I didn't hear any response through the door, but I heard Connor continue to yell.

"I texted my sister because I knew she was closing and I was fucking worried about her with that scumbag still out there, and her being there at night with that stupid worthless bitch, and she told me not to worry. She said that *YOU* would be there to pick her up. *WHERE WERE YOU?!*" Connor was really screaming now. I didn't like the sound of it. I knew he had a bad temper, and I knew he got loud easily, but I had only ever heard him like this once. That time changed my life forever, and for some reason this felt the same way. I was really worried.

"Aiden, please go see what's going on."

Aiden went to the door and when he opened it I was able to see my brother and Liam almost chest to chest. They both looked towards the door when Aiden opened it, and Liam's gaze immediately found mine before the door closed.

When his eyes locked with mine this time, I had the briefest recollection of his eyes glowing heatedly before he kissed me, but that flash was gone in an instant. It couldn't have been a memory, more like a projection of being caught in his eyes and fantasizing what I had no business fantasizing about, especially in the condition that I was in. He wasn't my boyfriend … none of that had happened.

The voices quieted down, and after a few minutes Aiden returned to my room, quickly followed by Connor. Liam didn't follow behind them and I suffered a pang of disappointment, which I swiftly dismissed. There was no reason to feel disappointed.

"Are you alright, Sam? Jesus Christ, when I found out what happened …" Connor broke off and just shook his head. "I'm sorry about what you just heard, Sam. I know that I should be thankful that Liam got to you in time, that he beat the shit out of Aaron – that he made sure Aaron couldn't hurt you worse than he already did … but Aaron would've *never* got the fucking chance if Liam would've been there. Where the fuck was he? There's no excuse for leaving you there alone, especially knowing that bitch was with you –"

He broke off when I gasped.

"What? What's wrong?" he asked worriedly.

I remembered what had happened. *Oh, God ...*

"Joanna. She was bitchy because I was taking forever … I don't know why – but she had such an attitude … and then she said she was leaving and I told her if she left that was it, and she left anyway. And then Aaron was there … He … He … *Oh, my, God, Connor*. He was hitting me and on top of me, and he wouldn't get off. He was trying … he was pulling at … Did he … Connor, did he –" I couldn't even finish. I could hear the terror in my voice recounting what had happened. I was going to be sick.

"*NO!* No, Samantha. No. Liam got there in time. He found you. Aaron was trying – but Liam got there. Nothing like that happened. I am so sorry that any of this happened to you. I am so fucking sorry that you got hurt. I am so fucking *pissed* that Liam got to beat Aaron within an inch of his life –" Connor cut himself off looking towards Aiden.

"Aaron will *never be bothering you again*. Don't even worry about him," Connor said in a deadly voice. "If Liam had just been there when he said he would –"

"Connor," Aiden said shaking his head, and my brother finally stopped talking.

"What?" Connor asked. I still couldn't believe these two were in the same room. Did they clear the air between them too? Why was Aiden even here? I still didn't understand any of this.

"She doesn't remember," Aiden said to Connor.

"She just told us about Aaron and what happened, so she remembers it," Connor said back.

"Not that. She doesn't remember Liam."

"What do you mean?" Connor said looking at me now. "You don't remember Liam?" When I just shook my head, he looked stunned.

"He's your boyfriend, Sam. You really don't remember him? The doctors didn't say you wouldn't remember things. They said you may be fuzzy on what happened in the store, but not that you'd forget other shit. No wonder he looked like he did and didn't say anything back to me. I thought he was just upset over what happened – *as he fucking should be* … but *holy shit*. You don't remember him … *at all?*"

I just shook my head, because what else could I do?

"Sam … nothing? You don't remember meeting him in the coffee shop, or us going out to dinner with his sister? You don't remember what happened at *Molly's* when *this* guy showed up?" he asked pointing towards Aiden. "You don't remember Riley giving you the keys to his place and telling you to go make it right, which you obviously *must* have because you've been walking on cloud-fucking-nine since then." He broke off and just shook his head when I continued to only shake mine.

Connor started to rub the back of his neck, so I knew this situation wasn't good. I knew it wasn't good before, but now Connor was worried too, which had me *really* freaked out.

"Holy motherfucker. Holy fucking shit. Sam … its Liam. For as pissed as I am that he wasn't there to protect you from the beginning of what happened, I know he'd move Heaven and fucking Earth for you. That guy … Sam, I've never seen a guy look at a woman the way Liam looks at you. I've never seen a dude more in love with someone. It's actually kind of sad and embarrassing. You really don't remember him?"

"No. No, I don't remember him Connor. What's wrong with me?" I said as I started to cry. I didn't remember Liam, but I knew Connor wouldn't lie to me. That guy who was here, the guy who I thought was all wrong for me, *was* my guy. He loved me, and I was supposed to love him back. I just didn't remember him.

"I think we need to find the doctor. Something's really not right here Sam. We need to know what's wrong with you." Connor said finally.

I couldn't agree with him more. Something was definitely wrong with me.

****

The doctors didn't know *what* was wrong. They assured me that I should be able to remember Liam, and that nothing was wrong with my head, even though it hurt like a bitch and I clearly didn't remember some very important things.

Connor tried to help me, but it didn't work. He told me more stories about Liam and me, but the stories didn't help me remember him. Some of the things Connor had said made me laugh, but it also made me sad because I didn't remember any of it. The more and more I learned, the more and more I wondered: *how could I forget?*

Liam wasn't the only one I forgot though. I forgot things that had happened with Aiden too. I remembered everything about our shared past, but the present – besides those few flashes – was completely lost. Aiden tried to fill me in on what I was missing, but like with Liam, it didn't help.

Nothing helped.

Aiden didn't stay too long though trying to make me remember. He actually left not long after Liam, and just like Liam he never came back the rest of the day. At least I knew where Aiden went when he left though, unlike Liam. Aiden went back to the Police Department to finish his shift and deal with some things having to do with Aaron.

Apparently Aiden was a detective in Baltimore, something that completely blew my mind, but it did answer my questions of how he knew I was in the hospital, and more importantly *why* he had stopped by. It really was a surprise that Aiden ended up being in law enforcement. I don't know if he had mentioned it to me this past week, but now that I know, I am amazed as well as shocked.

Another shock to my system occurred when my parents finally arrived. They went completely overboard with their hovering, their questions, their hugs, and their comments about what happened.

Of course they had questions about what had happened, how it happened, and most importantly who Liam was. I wish I could've told them about Liam, but unfortunately I had the same goddamn questions about him that they had.

I had about an hour of peace and quiet when my family finally left to go eat, but when my mom came back it started again.

Connor must have filled my parents in even more about Liam when they went to the cafeteria, because she had plenty to say about a man she'd never met before.

"That boy must really be special Samantha. Your brother was really worked up about how Liam was late coming to get you, and how everything had happened, but he also had a lot to say about him otherwise. Your brother seems to approve of him, and you know that means a lot. As much as I love your brother – he's difficult. He's always been difficult, even as a boy. So, your Liam … he must be a fine man. I want to meet him. Me and your father both. We want to meet him, and see if we approve too. I did see him in the store once. I remembered that day after your brother mentioned it. I didn't like the look of him then, and the way he was looking at you. I thought he was up to no good. But from what your brother has said … We want him over for dinner, Samantha. When everything gets worked out, Sunday dinner." She spoke in such a way that said she would get what she wanted, but there was a problem – how could I bring him to dinner, when I didn't even remember who he was to me. *My Liam?* God. Didn't they get it? They talked and talked about him – my parents who didn't even know him, and Connor even more so – as if all they had to do was talk about him and I would eventually remember. That I would be okay again.

But I wasn't okay.

I wasn't fucking okay. Maybe if I saw him again. Maybe if I saw him and I put his face together with mine, and imagined all the things I've heard about us – maybe if I did that it would all come back to me.

But he didn't come back though.

And neither did my memories.

****

339

The next day I woke up still in the hospital, but I was surrounded by flowers, balloons and stuffed animals. You would think I had just given birth, not been knocked on the head and roughed up a bit. I was told that I only had to endure one more day in the hospital and then I would be able to go home. My parents argued that I should go home with them, but I needed to go to *my* home. Though I still had no recollection of Liam and all the things we had done, or most of the memories of this past week with Aiden, I was fine otherwise. There was no reason for me to not go home.

When I finally rolled over I was taken aback by the beautiful new arrangement of daisies sitting on the table next to me. The stormy blue pitcher the daisies were in was absolutely beautiful.

I've never seen anything like it.

I don't think.

Something about it seemed familiar. Looking at it, it caused a deep ache in my chest.

Why?

Why does it feel like I've seen all these beautiful flowers of every single color imaginable before, along with the vase? Why do I feel like this arrangement is more special than the others? Why?

Why is it *familiar*?

My heart started to speed up, and I was just about to reach out for the flowers, when my door opened.

I looked away from the flowers and towards the door to see another flower arrangement enter right before the body of a very beautiful woman. I rolled back over and sat up in bed, and just stared at the woman. I have no idea who she is, but something about her eyes seems familiar.

The pale blue of her eyes seems so inviting and warm even though the color of them screams icy and cold.

For someone who looks as gorgeous as she does, she seems a little uncomfortable. I didn't like her looking like that for some reason, so I decided I needed to be the one to talk first.

"Hi," I said to her.

It was a little awkward, with her still holding the huge flower bouquet, but she said, "Hi," back.

"I brought you flowers," she said, holding them up a little with a small smile. The dimples that flashed in her cheeks when she gave the small smile, caused another familiar pang to shoot right through me.

"They're beautiful. We can put them on the table over here if you want," I told her, while pointing next to the daisies in the pitcher that I was mesmerized with before she got here.

She looked to where I was pointing and said, "Oh. My. God."

"I know. I felt the same way. That vase is unbelievable isn't it? And the flowers? They are definitely beautiful, but together with the vase, they're spectacular. I don't know who they're from, they were here when I got up this morning – right before you got here actually…"

I was talking to her while gazing at the flowers, and the pretty blue pitcher.

"You don't know who they're from?" she asked me in an incredulous voice. I whipped my head towards her because I could tell from her tone that she knew who the flowers were from.

"No."

"So you still don't remember Liam, then?" she asked me, sounding disappointed.

Him again! How did this gorgeous woman know him? Did I even want to know?

"No. Why?" I asked her cautiously.

"He's my brother. I'm Riley," she said pointedly.

I knew the name because I had heard the stories. I didn't remember her though, either. However, it now made sense, the familiarity with the eyes and the smile. Liam did have those exact same eyes.

"You don't remember me either, obviously. You know, I was really hoping you would remember Liam by now Samantha. This is killing him," she informed me.

Well, Riley, it's killing me too.

"I haven't seen him since I woke up yesterday. He and my brother got in an argument, Liam left, and he never came back," I told her.

"Yes, I know *all* about that argument," she said sounding pissed off all of a sudden, her eyes flashing to a blue fury before they cleared again, and she continued, "but he's definitely been back here. Those flowers in the pitcher are from him," she said.

He'd been back? In my room while I was asleep? Why didn't he wake me? Would it have mattered if he did?

"How do you know those are from him?" I asked her.

She just looked at me and then at the flowers. She took a while to respond and I felt like she was looking for the right words to say before she said them. I was expecting a good reason of why she was so sure, but she just said, "I just know. They are most definitely from him." And that was that.

Riley stayed a little longer talking to me, but it was all completely awkward and uncomfortable. I had no recollection of her and her brother, and she seemed put off because of it. I couldn't blame her, but she didn't need to look at me like she blamed me. It wasn't my fault.

Before she got up to go, she said, "Please, Samantha … I know you don't remember him … but those *are* his flowers. No matter what

... *please* don't leave them and the vase here, okay? I know you don't understand ... but ... just take them with you. It's important that you do." She looked at me a little teary-eyed, and that hurt more than her eyes that had implored me all throughout her visit to just remember him and her.

When she left I rolled back over and just stared at the flowers Liam had brought me. It had to have meant something. It obviously meant something to her. She *knew* he brought that specific arrangement, there wasn't a doubt in her mind. I didn't understand it, but I would do what she asked. I had planned on taking them anyway. There was no way that I would leave something that beautiful behind.

Throughout the rest of the day I had plenty of visitors. Allie and Aiden stopped by to check up on me, Connor came by and dropped off a new cell phone since mine was destroyed during Aaron's attack, my parents visited and stayed for a few hours, and even some of the people from work filtered on through ... but no Liam. I know I shouldn't be hurt by not seeing him, especially seeing as how I didn't even remember him, but I did feel hurt. I felt hurt, and sad, and incomplete, and even broken. I knew my body was battered, I knew my head was cracked, I knew I had every right to feel hurt, but it wasn't the hurts on the outside that were killing me.

It was the hurt on the inside that was making me feel broken, and battered, and sad.

Chapter 21

I was finally home. My parents, along with Connor, reluctantly brought me home from the hospital, and I couldn't be more thrilled to be out of that place. When we got to my apartment we brought all of my flowers inside, including the ones from Liam, that I would not let go of the whole way out of the hospital and the whole way here. I put his flowers on the mantle as soon as I got home, next to a picture of him and me in baseball jerseys, taken at a baseball game that I don't remember. The picture was kind of grainy, almost as if we took it with one of our phones, but even with the picture distorted I could tell that I had never looked happier. The smile on my face and the happiness that was pouring out of my eyes – and *his* – was hard to miss.

There was no mistaking our feelings for each other in that picture.

How could I not remember any of this? Or him?

Connor cleared his throat behind me, reminding me of his presence. He let my parents drive ahead home without him, deciding to stay with me a while before he headed into the shop. There were a few things I needed to ask him that he needed to give me answers to. He told me about Liam, he told me about a few of our dates, he didn't need to tell me about Aaron because I remembered, but I needed to know why he was angry at Liam that day besides the obvious that he had been late. Why, even though I know he brought me flowers, Liam hadn't come around to actually see me.

"Connor, what really happened that night? I know what happened with Aaron, but why were you *that* mad at Liam?" I asked him.

The look I must've given him must have conveyed my need for no more bullshit, because he sighed, looked away and then back, before he started.

"He was supposed to meet you at the shop at around ten. He was supposed to just hang out there until closing so he could take you home. We tried to keep you off of the closing shift until we got shit straight with Aaron, or at least until mom and dad got home and one of them could be there with you, but that day it was unavoidable. He was supposed to be there for you, but he got caught up by one of his co-workers who had a problem."

Connor said that last part with complete disdain in his voice. I didn't know why, but I couldn't get into it right then because he started talking some more. "He forgot to text you to tell you he was going to be late. *He fucking forgot, Sam*," Connor stopped talking and just looked at me. He seemed to catch what he was saying, and decided to collect himself before he continued.

"You texted him a little after closing asking him where he was. He realized then that he was really late, so he said he would be right there, and he left. He said it was just bullshit anyway what he was taking care of – he said it really wasn't even a problem, he didn't understand why it turned into something so big – *I don't fucking know*, Sam. Anyway, he said it didn't take him more than ten minutes to get to *The Brew* because he left right away. But when he got there –" Connor broke off, and I didn't really need to know any more. I could only imagine what Liam saw.

Connor went on anyway though.

"He said he saw Aaron on top of you, trying to tear at your clothes. He said he saw blood on your face, and Aaron's, he saw the shop completely messed up, and he also saw you laying there and not fighting back. I know you tried fighting back … you told us that already … and I'm so fucking happy you did, Sam. If you didn't hold him off until Liam got there – *I can't even fucking think about it!* That stupid fucking prick didn't even hear Liam come in that's how intent he was on hurting you. Liam said he just grabbed him off of you and kept on punching him until he wasn't moving anymore. After that he went to you, but you weren't moving either. He knew you were breathing, but you weren't moving. You wouldn't answer him, open your eyes, or move. Nothing. He called for help and just waited, trying to get you to respond. It wasn't until he was in the ambulance on the way to the hospital that he called his sister so he could get my number to call me. When I got the call about you – I … I … *fuck*, Sam. Just fuck. I went right over from the Firehouse. I said a few words to the Chief and I left. I had to.

"When I got to the hospital it was fucking awful. Liam was a mess. His knuckles were all fucked up, he had some bruises and cuts, some nurse was trying to work on him, but all I saw was the blood on his clothes. Aaron's, his, *your* blood. He was crying Sam. When I saw him, he had tears coming out of his fucking eyes, and I thought you were gone or that something really, really, bad fucking happened to you. I thought we lost you, because how he looked … it just wasn't right."

Connor stopped talking for a minute and he had a faraway look on his face.

I didn't realize that I was crying until I felt the tears drip off of my cheeks and onto my hands.

As I was wiping off my face, Connor started to speak once again.

"When Liam finally noticed that I was there, he looked at me with such tortured fucking eyes Sam, and he said, 'she's being checked over by the doctors now, but she never woke up. She never woke up.'"

Connor blew out a stuttering breath.

"And to him Samantha … *you still haven't woken up*, because you don't remember him. For him, it really is like you're gone. And for as pissed off at him as I was – I can't be anything but sorry for him and sad … and fucking worried about him – *for* him. And, Christ, that's a fucking kick in the ass let me tell you that."

Connor just looked at me. At my tears.

"You still don't remember him? Anything?" Connor asked me.

It was what everyone asked me.

"No."

I didn't tell him that a few things seemed familiar at times. Or that I would get a brief flash of something, but then it would go away. I couldn't talk about that because then it might give everyone hope, and there really was nothing to feel hopeful about because I really wasn't remembering anything substantial.

I didn't know how I felt about remembering Liam. He didn't seem like someone I would love, but I saw the picture, I heard the stories, I saw the flowers, and met his sister, I saw it in his eyes when I first woke up … they all knew something I didn't. I wasn't sure how I would feel remembering, but I know that I needed to. I *had* to. And the sooner the better.

****

Three days. It had been three days since I had been back to work, well over a week since Aaron had attacked me, and I still didn't remember Liam even though he stopped by every day for coffee while I was at work. The first day I saw him it was the middle of the day and he was looking impeccable, and incredible, in a charcoal gray suit. When I saw him walking towards me I had one of those flashes again, of him walking in the door making a beeline towards me, but it was gone in an instant. He looked at me, begging me with his eyes to remember, but I didn't.

"Hey, Red," he said, before quickly saying, "Samantha." When he said my name his shoulders seemed to slump a little, and his eyes looked even sadder than they were only moments before.

"Hi," I said back, not knowing what else to say.

"My usual is a large coffee, black, with no sugar," he told me. I didn't get any flashes when he said it though. I turned around to make him his coffee and I could feel his eyes boring into my back. When I was done I handed him his coffee and waited for him to give me his money. He sighed, dug into his pocket and handed me a twenty dollar bill. I took the money from his hand, but unlike when he said his order, this time I did have another flash of snatching a twenty dollar bill out of his hand at some other time. I froze for a few seconds, willing the whole scene to play out in my head. I didn't want the memory to flash and go, but it did, like all the other times.

"Red, what's wrong?" Liam asked, not correcting himself this time. I looked up at him, and I could tell he was hoping that I remembered something. But I really didn't. Not exactly.

"Nothing. I'll get your change," I told him.

"Don't worry about it. Keep it," he said, before he turned around and headed towards the door. I couldn't take my eyes off of him. Me keeping the money seemed important for some reason, I just didn't know why.

What also seemed important was me keeping my eyes on him, so I tracked him all the way to the door. Once he got there, he turned around and locked eyes with me, and he seemed very pleased that I was still looking at him. I tilted my head to the side, searching my brain for a certain memory because it felt like I was missing something very significant. We stared intently at one another, but then his face transformed right in front of me. He smiled so big his dimples winked at me, and then his eye did.

I felt butterflies dance in my belly when I saw his dimples and his wink.

Butterflies.

Dimples.

And that sexy as sin wink.

How could I have forgotten that?

The next day it was the same, as was the day after that. Each time he asked for his usual, he handed over a twenty dollar bill and told me to keep the change, he walked to the door, where he winked at me and then he left. Each day he seemed disappointed that I still didn't remember something, anything, *everything*, but he came anyway. What was it with that fucking money and that wink? It meant something. I *know* it did. I just couldn't figure it out.

I was lost in my thoughts when I heard a throat clear in front of me. I looked up to see a very voluptuous blonde woman in a tight skirt, skyscraper heels, and a silk blouse. Her hair was styled to perfection, her eyes were bright and bold, and her face was absolutely flawless. The smile though, that was smug and superior.

"Hello, Samantha. I'll have a large coffee with some hazelnut," she said in a voice that dripped with fake enthusiasm.

I didn't know who she was, but I knew I didn't like her. Just like with Liam and Riley, I felt a certain familiarity, but not a recollection. It registered with me that she said my name, so I had to know her somehow. She talked to me as if she knew me.

"Do I know you?" I asked her.

"Not exactly. I'm a friend of Liam's. I work with him and stuff. He and I have stopped by a time or two, but you and I have never been properly introduced. I'm Karen," she said, fake smile in place. What the hell did the 'and stuff' part mean?

That name of hers sounded familiar. I couldn't place her before the night Aaron attacked me, so it must have been something more recent. What was it? I think I heard Connor mention her name to my parents, but I just couldn't remember what was said.

Shit!

I smiled my own fake smile in return, and then turned around to make Karen her drink. Just like with Liam, I could tell she was staring at me up and down while my back was turned. Where Liam's stares gave me nothing but butterflies and warmth, hers gave me the creeps. Who the fuck was she, and why did I feel such an intense hate for her?

When I handed over her coffee she asked, "Would you like me to tell Liam you said 'hello?' I'll be with him later on after all." *Wait ... what?*

"Um, no, thanks. I saw him a little while ago," I said to her rather shortly. I don't know why I said what I did, but she just put me on edge and it felt like something I had to say to her in just that way.

"Really? He still comes here?" she asked me, with a whole bunch of disbelief in her voice, as if I wasn't telling the truth.

"Yes. He's been by to see me the last few days," I told her, to which her eyes immediately narrowed.

"Hmm, I thought you didn't remember him," she said. She sure knew a lot of my business. She must be a very important co-worker to know all of the things she apparently does.

"I don't," I told her in a very specific tone. *But he sure remembers me*, I didn't add, but wanted to. I think she knew what I wanted to add on though, because she narrowed her eyes even more.

"Okay then. Well I have to get back to Liam. Bye, now," she said after she handed me over the money for the drink and left. What the fuck did she mean by 'she had to get back to Liam?' And why the fuck did she look so pleased that I didn't remember him? And why the fuck was I acting like a jealous girlfriend?

Shit.

Maybe because I was.

Maybe I had a reason to be.

I know I didn't remember him, but that didn't make it okay for that bitch to act like he was hers. What the fuck. I really was going off the rails if I was acting like this about some woman with a guy I didn't remember.

Shit, he was my guy though!

My Liam.

I needed to remember who she is. Maybe she was the key to remembering Liam.

I know what I need to do.

I need to get ahold of Connor. He needed to clue me in on a few things. I know he mentioned something about that *woman*, but I just don't remember what he said. One more hour until I was off shift and then I was figuring this all out.

****

Me: Who's Karen?

I didn't even wait one minute after I got home to text Connor. It seemed like the longest hour of my life to get out of the shop.

Connor: I'm at a stop light. Give me about a half hour to get home. I'll get back to you.

What the fuck? He couldn't just answer my question? It would have taken no more than ten goddamn seconds. *Fucking Connor!*

I guess it wasn't a bad thing though. I could use the time to take a shower and clear my head. I don't know why Karen got under my skin, but she did. In the worst possible way.

After my shower, I blow dried my hair, put some clothes and makeup on and just waited for Connor to get back to me. Half hour my ass. I couldn't take it anymore.

Me: Who is she Connor?

Connor: Why are you asking?

Why wouldn't he just fucking tell me? I *knew* he was home and avoiding getting back to me. Why? I could feel my heart start to beat faster. I didn't like where this was going.

Me: Because she came into The Brew today and she acted all smug. Like I was missing something. She acted really possessive over Liam, saying she was a co-worker and a friend and 'stuff,' and she seemed really fucking happy that I didn't remember him, and also really fucking pissed that he's been by to see me the last few days. She made some snide comments to me. Things I didn't like. Really catty. Something was off. I could feel it.

Connor: You're not wrong, Sam. She does work with him though. According to you, and Allie, she wants him. As in she wants him to be hers. You got pissed off a few times when she came into the shop with him. Like really fucking pissed off ...

I knew there was more. I knew there was something he wasn't telling me. I remember him saying something about her. I remember hearing her name come out of his mouth recently.

Me: What am I missing Connor? That was all before I was attacked. I remember you talking about her after that. I remember her name, but not what you said. What is it?

He didn't text me back, because he was calling me instead. My phone was ringing in my hand and I knew it mustn't be good if he was calling me.

"What Connor!" I said into the phone. As soon as the words were out of my mouth I had another flash of me in bed answering the phone almost the same exact way. I wasn't in *my bed* though, and I *wasn't* alone. *Holy ...*

What the hell was that?

"Look, Sam ... I'm sure it's nothing ... But ... She's the reason he was late," he said.

"What?" I asked him a little distracted from trying to hold on to the memory that was trying to break through. I think I knew what he meant but I had to be sure in case I missed something.

"She's the reason he was late getting to the shop to pick you up that night. He was helping her with something. She came to him when they were all ready to leave and she said she had some issue. He let everyone else go, and he stayed to help her out. It was something stupid and small and they were done in no time, but she kept talking and talking ... they were there at work until you texted him. You know the rest."

It was her.

She kept him late.

He wasn't with me because of her. I was attacked by a fucking psychopath who could have raped and killed me … I lost all of my memories of Liam … *and it was all because of her.*

And she fucking knew it.

That's why she was so smug. That's why she seemed victorious. *What a fucking whore.*

I guess I had every fucking right to feel jealous and the intense hatred that I felt towards her.

"Sam," my brother's voice called out from the other end of the line.

"What Connor?" I said to him again.

"Are you okay?" he asked me.

"No, I'm not okay. She made a play for him. She had to have. Maybe he didn't see it, but she did. Aaron hurt me, but she did too. And she practically fucking gloated about it today. In a way, she's worse than Aaron. He obviously had a screw loose, but her … she's just a fucking whore who went after someone who would *never* be hers –"

"Sam, you don't know that that's what happened" Connor started to say, but I did. *I knew.* I was a woman, and we fucking knew these things about other women. Especially ones like her. You could see it written all over her face.

"No, Connor. Just don't, okay? I have to go. I'll talk to you later," I said to him before I hung up. I didn't know what to do. *Karen.* Karen and Liam. She knew what she was up to. She knew I didn't remember. Who knew what she was saying to him now. What she was plotting and doing.

What was *he* thinking?

I didn't remember him, and he had no idea if I would. Would he fall for all of her words and actions thinking there was no hope for us? And why did that practically break my heart into pieces?

I honestly felt like my heart was breaking into little tiny shards. Why couldn't I remember?

Oh God, oh God, oh God.

I felt the anger bubbling up inside of me. This anger was more intense than the anger I had inside of me after I'd remembered that Aaron attacked me, it was more than when I remembered what he had done, more than I had when I realized what I had lost.

I just couldn't contain myself anymore. I was so fucking angry at *everything*.

I didn't mean to do what I did, but I did it.

I whipped my cell phone so hard across the room towards the mantle that it hit into the pictures, some of which fell and shattered on the floor. My phone bounced off of the wall, and it hit into the blue pitcher that was still on the mantle. *Liam's gift.* When I saw my phone hit the pitcher, and the pitcher start to topple back and forth, all I could think was:

Oh, God, no ... not Liam's mom's pitcher. Not that. Anything but that!

I raced to the mantle to make sure it didn't fall, and as I placed my hands on it to hold it steady, it all came flooding back.

Everything.

His mom's pitcher, and Liam telling me about it before we went out on our first official date. The way he acted when he found out that it was my first official date. Liam taking me to get books, the way he kissed me, the way that I grabbed him and kissed him and left him speechless. His kisses on my forehead. The way he looked and acted the first time I saw him across the room at The Brew. The flashes I had of a future I didn't even want with him – of a house, and kids, and forever. Oh, God, I remembered why he calls me Red. The blushes that he loved ... he loved seeing me blush, and he loved seeing everywhere that he made me blush when I was wrapped up in his arms, and he was loving me. As I looked down to the smashed photos, I remembered the baseball game and our matching jerseys, watching baseball at my place while eating pizza, and eating at his apartment. I remembered the painting, oh God, the painting and what he said, and my realizing in that moment that I was in fact in love with him. I remembered slow dancing with him to my favorite song, and twinkling lights, expensive wine, excellent food, and sleeping in his clothes and his arms. I remembered the way he smelled, and the way he tasted, the way he felt. I remembered Molly's and the date Connor pushed on us, I remembered Riley, and Aiden coming back, and my hurting Liam. I remembered Liam taking my virginity after our stupid argument, and then making love with him again after, and then I remembered us having breakfast in bed. I remembered the heat in his eyes as we made love in the shower, the intensity in them as I rode him one night to completion in my bed. I remembered the way he looked in the morning when he woke up with my mouth on him, and when he showed me what to do and what he liked. I remembered everything he taught me, not only about making love, but being in love, giving love, and being loved in return. I remembered how I felt the first time I saw him in a suit, the first time I traced his tattoos with my fingers and then my tongue. I remembered trying to wrap my head around both sides of Liam – his outside and the inside. I remembered sticking my fingers into his dimples the first time, and the times after. I remembered those dimples attached to his wicked grin, and his sinful smile, and devilish smirk. I remembered telling him I love him, I remembered fighting for him and for us, and I remembered him telling me that he loved me too ... that he loved me first. God, he told me to remember that he loved me first. I remembered the fucking twenty dollar bill. I was so jealous of him with Karen that I made him pay for his drink and hers, and I refused to give him change. He loved that I was jealous. I remembered all of the times he came to the shop. I remembered every thought, every feeling, every time he said he loved something about me, and I remembered every freaking time he winked at me before leaving. I remembered only wanting to be his friend because I was scared, but wanting him so badly regardless of all of that. I remembered him not giving up on me.

Worst of all though, I remembered the way he looked at me when I didn't remember him. How he looked completely devastated at what happened to me, and then how shattered he looked when I didn't remember who he was. How he looked when I still didn't remember him for days and days. How lost, how sad, how crushed, how heart-broken, how hurt, and worried, and alone.

"Oh, God," I cried out. I doubled-over and cried out, "Oh, God," again, and again.

I cried, and cried, letting more memories wash over me.

"How could I forget?" I whimpered through the flashbacks.

"How could I forget him?"

I took a wobbly breath in. "I forgot him," I choked out. "How could I do this to *him?*"

My heart was breaking again, but not for me this time – not from just an imaginary feeling. This time I knew everything. Everything was completely real. This time it hurt so much worse. My heart was breaking for him.

My heart was breaking for us.

I needed to get to him. I needed to fix this. I needed to tell him that I was sorry.

I needed to tell him that I loved him, that I remembered, that he was my *world*.

I needed to get to him and tell him that I was his, and only his.

I needed to go to him and tell him that I remembered that he was mine, and only mine.

I needed to tell him that I remembered *everything*.

I remembered *us*.

Chapter 22

"I need to go to him," I said out loud to myself. "I need to go to him right now."

I ran into the bathroom, fixed up my face, ran a brush through my hair, grabbed my smashed cell phone, and ran out the door.

I knew it was still early in the day so I knew Liam wouldn't be home, so that left only one option … he would be at work – with *her*. I wouldn't think about that now though. In a few minutes she wouldn't matter anymore. None of her bullshit would matter. I guess in a weird way I should be thanking her. She was a part of the reason I forgot about Liam, but she was also the reason I remembered him.

I had never been to his downtown office, but somehow I don't think he'd mind me showing up uninvited today. And if anybody else had a problem with it – that was just too goddamn bad.

I had other things to be thinking about now that I had my memories back, and who would be bothered if I showered up at Liam's job was not one of them.

"How could he only *think* that he was my boyfriend?" I asked myself out loud, going back to the time in my hospital room. Why was he so unsure of himself? After everything we had been through, and *done*? We didn't actually classify what we were, but how could he not see that he *was* my boyfriend. He was – he *is* – my *everything*. *Holy shit!* I had a lot to make up for. Though I know it wasn't my fault that I couldn't remember him, that I shouldn't feel blame, it still hurt me knowing all the ways I ended up unintentionally hurting him.

When I finally made it to his building I couldn't wait to get to him. I told security that I was there for Sullivan Marketing and they pointed me in the right direction. As I went into the elevator and pressed the button for the floor, I smiled because I should've known they would be on the top floor.

I could feel my heartbeat start to race on the ride up, throbbing in anticipation and excitement. I couldn't wait to see his face when he learned that I had remembered. I just needed to make it through his reaction, and then I could turn into a complete mess. When the elevator dinged signaling I was at my floor, that's when I started to get nervous. For as excited and anxious as I was, I was still at his place of employment – a place where he was a team leader, a place where he worked with his father who owned the company, a place where he worked with Karen – and who knows who else. I felt a little out of my depth all of a sudden. For as much as I loved him, and him me, and for as much as we talked about his work and our future career paths, seeing this place – the vastness and what it all meant – it made me a little unsure how I fit in with everything. I knew this was only a *part* of Liam though. I knew I had my own wealth, but this seemed on a whole different scale. I knew I needed to leave all of that for later too. Now I needed to go get my man.

I went over to the receptionist who sat behind a mammoth desk. She looked me over in my jeans, and flip-flops, before she said, "Can I help you?" She said it in such a way that suggested I must be lost, and the only thing she would gladly help me with was leaving.

"I'm here to see Liam Sullivan." I was proud of myself for keeping my voice steady. I will not feel beneath this place. I was here for

Liam. I was in love with him. He was in love with me. We didn't care about this type of shit before. I would not care about this shit now.

"Who are you?" she asked me. She then looked to her right where an older, distinguished looking gentleman, came out of a set of doors the lead to Sullivan Marketing. He was dressed in a dark blue suit, he carried a briefcase, and held himself in such a way that I knew he was either an executive or the boss. When I had the thought of boss, I started to see the resemblance.

Holy shit, it was Liam's father.

The dragon behind the desk smiled brightly for him when he finally stopped in front of her. I don't know why he stopped, but he was staring at me. As if he *knew* me.

He smiled a little, and said to the dragon lady, "Who is this?" He then turned to look at me again.

"I don't know who she is, but she wants to see Liam." I swear I heard her sniff her nose at me before she started speaking.

Liam's father nodded his head. It was almost like he was expecting that answer.

"You're her." He nodded his head again, and then he started to smile. I had no idea what he meant by that, but his smile seemed warm and familiar, so I would wait to see what he meant.

"My son doesn't have women show up here asking for him. He also doesn't think that I pay attention to him, but I do. He's been different the past few weeks. Happy. Lighter. But then something changed this past week. He hasn't been himself. He's been worse than I have ever seen him. Worse, even, than when his mother died. He thinks that I didn't know or care what was going on then, or now. But I love my son. I might not have shown it how I should have, I've done many things wrong, but I do love him. I'm willing to bet all of this," he said opening his hands to indicate where we were, "that you are the reason for both changes in him. I don't know what happened young lady, but I am expecting you to fix it. He deserves the happiness, and the love."

It was my turn to nod and shake my head. I was not expecting that. From what Liam had said about his father, this was the furthest thing I could have envisioned him saying when I met him. I wish Liam knew how much his father cared.

"Mr. Sullivan ... I don't know what to say," which was the absolute truth. I *was* definitely the reason for the change in Liam this past week, and I could only hope I was the positive change in him the weeks before that. I prayed that I would be the reason for the best change in him from the moment I saw him again and onward.

"You don't have to say anything, you just need to go and get him. He's not here though. His team is out celebrating the close of a big deal. They're just down the street at *The Tap House*," he told me.

"Thank you, Mr. Sullivan."

"No need to thank me. What you need to do is convince my son to bring you to dinner one night. I would like to get to know you, *and him*, better."

And because I thought not only did his dad need it, but Liam did as well, I said to Mr. Sullivan, "I'll work on it." I then gave them both the brightest smile and headed towards the elevator.

Then I stopped, and turned around. "It was nice to meet you Mr. Sullivan."

"You too ..." he stopped, questioningly.

"Oh, God. It's Samantha. My name's Samantha," I said, as I felt my blush work itself up my neck and into my cheeks. *But your son calls me 'Red.'*

When the elevator dinged I got onto it, and turned to see Mr. Sullivan and the dragon lady staring at me with amused expressions.

I couldn't wait to tell Liam all of this. I don't know what he'd say about what his dad said, or about the dinner invitation, or the complete randomness of it all – but everything happens for a reason, right? I don't know what the reason is for running into Liam's dad – *maybe I'm supposed to be a bridge that can bring them back together?* – I don't know.

I can't sit and wonder about what the reasoning is now though, because I have more important things to do and say to him when I see him.

****

I have never been to *The Tap House*. When I walked in the door it had the feel of *Molly's* but it was definitely a little more upscale. It would figure that they would choose a spot like this to celebrate. I felt a little out of place like I did when I walked into Liam's office building. I was in jeans and flip-flops, and the clientele here was predominantly more suits and dresses. It took me no time to find the group I was looking for because it was hard to miss the knockout blonde. I had thought that they would be at a table, but they were at the bar instead.

I don't know what possessed me to not go up to him right away. I don't know why I stood a few feet away from him instead of planting myself firmly in his lap. It was all I had wanted to do since I reclaimed my memories of him, but something instinctively held me back. Maybe it was the way he looked relaxed instead of sad, sitting in his chair with his profile towards me, facing Karen. Maybe it was the way she was touching his shoulder in a familiar sort of way. Maybe it was the other men and the few other women who were surrounding them all lost in their conversations, as if they saw the two of them act like that all of the time, like nothing was out of the ordinary. It was all completely normal for all of them.

But not for me.

Instead of my heart beating fast for all the right reasons, it was beating fast for all of the wrong ones. My stomach didn't have butterflies at the sight of him as it normally did, it had lead and the sickening feeling of dread. My eyes weren't bright with happiness and love, but rather watery with tears, and hurt, and confusion. I knew something wasn't right by the way she was touching him and the way he was letting her.

My brain had taken too long to give me my memories back.

Now that I had all of them back, it made seeing what I was seeing that much worse.

How could all of this be happening?

I couldn't move when I saw her lean towards him. I stood paralyzed just watching. I didn't even breathe.

She leaned over and she kissed him. She grasped both of his shoulders in her hands, moved her body into his space, and she kissed him, with her long blond hair brushing his thighs.

I stood motionless waiting for him to push her back. I waited for him to get up from his chair, ask her what the fuck she was doing, and leave. I expected him to pull back, wipe his mouth off, and fire her. I willed my body to move so I could tear her off of him and punch her in the face.

None of it happened.

I stood there while the tears poured down my face.

He sat there ... while she kissed him.

She moved even closer tilting her head sideways, intent on deepening the kiss.

His other co-workers were just there, fucking oblivious.

Except one.

One turned his head and looked at me. He looked at me, and then what I was looking at. He pushed Liam on the back, kind of hard, because I saw both of their bodies jerk. What I witnessed could not have been more than ten seconds, I consciously knew that, but it was enough.

More than enough.

Liam turned to look at the man not even registering I was there, but Karen did. She saw me, and she looked at me like a cat who ate the canary.

I guess I was the fucking bird ... or was that Liam?

Why was I even fucking thinking things like this?

I couldn't stand there anymore looking like a complete fucking fool.

He kissed someone else. I saw him *kiss* someone else.

I hurt him, I knew that, but then he hurt me so much more. *What he did was so much worse.* I couldn't remember him, but he remembered me just fine. He remembered every touch, every kiss, every word, every promise, and yet he *kissed someone else.*

I needed to leave.

I was stuck in place.

I could only stand there motionless while I watched the man point to me. While I watched Liam turn.

I was still stuck in place when we locked eyes.

Mine were still full of tears, and his were widening and darkening in understanding.

I don't know how he could be as fucking beautiful as he is, in the very moment that I hate him the most.

Life was fucking unbelievable.

I didn't expect what I saw, but life was just full of unexpected shit. I didn't expect to meet him in the first place all those weeks ago. I didn't expect to like him. I didn't expect for us to become friends. I didn't expect that I would want him, or that I would need him. I didn't expect that I would fall in love with him, and him with me. I really didn't expect that I would lose my memories and that I would forget him. I definitely didn't expect to see him kissing another woman right in front of me.

I didn't expect any of that.

I didn't expect for him to see me crying my eyes out standing paralyzed in my own stupidity. I didn't expect for anyone to see that. I didn't expect him, after everything we had been through, to throw away everything and not fucking wait.

I breathed in deep, shaking my head back and forth as if I could shake the images of what had just happened from my mind.

I saw him start to rise.

I wanted him to rise before – *away from her* – but not now. I wanted him to stay where he was, and to stay the fuck away from me.

Liam rising was apparently what I needed to snap me out of my paralysis. I was able to finally move from my spot. I was able to turn around and make my way quickly out of the place.

I heard him calling out from behind me, but I didn't care.

If I didn't get away from him, *from what I saw*, I knew it wouldn't be pretty. All the times that I thought I was broken before, I now knew that I wasn't.

The feeling that I'm feeling now … this was what broken felt like.

This feeling ... this was me breaking.

****

I don't know how I was able to make it outside without slamming into people, or crumbling onto the floor sobbing and screaming, but I did. I was outside, heading towards home, when I heard Liam once again yelling my name from behind me.

"Red ... Samantha ... Sam!" I could hear him getting closer and closer to me. I didn't want to hear him, and I didn't want to see him. I didn't want to fucking *feel* like this.

I sped up a little, but it didn't matter. I felt his arm snake around my waist, I felt myself being pulled backwards until his chest slammed against my back, and with his strong hold I was lifted off of my feet and turned around to face him.

"Samantha –" he started to say when he put me down.

"DON'T FUCKING TOUCH ME!!!" I screamed at him, at the same time I put my hands on his chest to push him back away from me.

I don't know how it was possible but my hurt turned into full-blown anger pretty fucking quick.

Liam stumbled back onto the heels of his feet, but he didn't move anywhere.

He grabbed onto my cheeks and lifted my head forcing me to look into his eyes.

"Baby, it's not what you're thinking," he started to say. His hands were on my cheeks, his eyes were imploring me to listen to him, and all I could think was – *oh, the fucking irony.*

"You have no idea what the fuck I'm thinking," I yelled at him. I felt better with the anger consuming my body, not the hurt. I remembered a time like this where the positions were reversed, and how he reacted. What I did was *nothing* compared to what I'd just witnessed.

"Babe – what you just saw ... I have no idea what the fuck that was, Red. She just kissed me. Out of nowhere. I was fucking stunned –"

Yeah, well, not as fucking stunned as I was.

"It took me a second to realize what was even happening, and when I did, John clapped me on the back, and then I saw you standing there crying ... you were fucking *crying*, and my heart just about stopped."

"Red," he gripped my face even tighter in his hands, "I did *not* want her to fucking kiss me. The only one I want kissing me, who I *ever* want kissing me, is you. Seeing you crying and then storming out ... baby, you were crying as if your heart was breaking –" *great fucking assumption* "and I absolutely fucking hated seeing you like that – *like this* – but please, *please* tell me that this is because you remember ... that you remember us ..." he broke off and moved his hands behind my neck, bringing me in closer while bending down to get a better view of my eyes.

"*You were right, Liam.* I *was* crying because you broke my fucking heart," I said to him before I pushed him away again, and was actually able to break his hold this time. I turned around to walk away, when I was grabbed up from behind and whipped around, *again.*

"No. NO! You don't get to walk away again! You don't get to shut me out anymore, and pretend I don't exist. You don't get to leave me alone, all by myself. You don't get to pretend that I *wanted* what you just saw. You don't get to be angry at me for *that!* For days, I have waited for you to remember me. For days, I worried that you never fucking would. For days, I had to replay over and over again the way you looked at me when you woke up. Like I was *nothing.* For days, I have dreamed of you remembering me. Of you coming to me and telling me you remember – Every. Fucking. Thing. Of you saying you *love me.* I have had to live with knowing that I was the reason you couldn't remember me. If I wasn't late you would have been fine. I've called your brother every fucking day, numerous times a day, asking about you. Do you know what that's like? Calling your brother and begging him to let me know about you, when I know that we both blame me for what happened to you? You will not shut me out because of what you saw. I hate seeing you fucking cry, and I hate what you fucking saw, but those tears, they mean that what you saw fucking matters to you. You fucking hated it. You said I broke your fucking heart ... *Holy FUCK! I fucking love you!* Do you hear me, Samantha? I fucking love you, and only you. I want you, and only you. I need you, and only you. I will only ever *love, want, and need you. YOU!* You remember me. You remember *everything.* You might have been hurt by what you saw. I would have been hurt too. I would have been fucking crushed. But that had *nothing* to do with me. I would have *never* hurt you like that. Please, Red ... *Please.*"

I believed him.

There was not a doubt in my mind that he was telling me the truth. I knew he wanted me and only me. Just seeing him with her after everything that had happened was too much. All of it was too much. I feel like everything that had happened to us from the beginning was too much. We were constantly on a roller-coaster of emotions, and seeing that, that *kiss*, it just pushed me over the edge.

I believed him and that's what matters most, because I knew he didn't want that kiss. He just wanted me.

"Please, Red. Please tell me you remember. Say it."

"I remember, Liam. I remember you. I remember everything."

I was crushed into his body so fast.

He held on to me so tight while he buried his head into my shoulder. I think I heard him say, "Thank fucking God" but I can't be sure.

I felt him take his own shaky breath before he let me go.

"Let's go home, Red. Let's just go home," he said before he grabbed my hand and started pulling me along with him.

I didn't bother to tell him that I was already home. That by remembering, that by being back in his arms, surrounded by his love, his warmth, his smell, his strength, his hope, I was already there.

I knew that from now on, *home*, would be wherever he was, but I didn't mind going along with him wherever he wanted me to go.

****

Liam led me to his car which was parked around the block and he set me inside. We didn't speak the whole way to his apartment, and I think it was better that way. I knew we had a lot to discuss, a lot to get straight, and a lot of time to make up for, but I was perfectly content with us knowing what we knew, and us being where we were at right now. We had each other, we were back where we needed to be, and that's what mattered most.

By being silent it gave me the opportunity to think. I wanted to let it go, I really did, but I couldn't let it go fully. I was still processing that kiss, and seeing it for what it really was. I wanted the images out of my head, but I needed to know where I went wrong. I believed him one hundred percent, but I had to look at it with clear eyes, and decipher it for myself. And then it hit me. Thinking back, I remembered her with *her* hands grabbing him, *her* moving into *his* space, her moving *her* head – not to *deepen* the kiss but trying to get *him* to respond. I should have known without his words that he wanted none of it, but in the moment, with all of my heightened emotions, it made sense why I only saw what I did at the time.

I was grateful that I was paralyzed in that moment. That Liam saw me. That he came after me, and made me see. What would have happened if he didn't, and I got away? It hurts so much just thinking about that possibility.

Everything happens for a reason though. I was thinking of all those reasons as we drove to his place. It seemed to take no time at all, and yet it seemed to take forever.

We finally pulled into the garage of his apartment, and then before I knew it we were at the top floor, and Liam was closing the door behind me.

I didn't know what to expect. I hadn't been here in a while, we hadn't talked the whole way over, and I was actually a little scared all of a sudden.

There were so many things that I needed to say. So many things that I needed to say I was sorry for. So many things that I needed to make right.

"Liam –" I started, but didn't get the chance to finish.

His mouth was on mine, and my back was suddenly plastered against the back of the door. His palms were next to my head, his body was pressed solidly to mine and I could feel his hardness against me. I heard him groan at the meeting of our tongues and I could feel a single tear slipping down my cheek.

How could I have forgotten any of this?

How could I have thought that he would throw all of this away for some stupid girl? How could I have thought he would let all of this go by accepting a kiss?

He moved his palms to my cheeks and his hand came into contact with my tear. He pulled back and looked at me. He swiped his thumb across my cheek wiping the teardrop away.

"What's wrong, Sam?" he asked, the concern evident within his raspy voice.

"I'm so sorry, Liam. *I'm so sorry*. I'm sorry that I didn't remember you. *That I didn't remember us*. I am sorry that it took me so long to get it all back. I almost broke your mom's vase," at his look and his quick breath, I hurried on "but I didn't. I didn't. It's how I remembered. It's a long story, but it's how I remembered. I remembered everything, but I forgot you. I don't know how or why … but I did, and I am so fucking sorry I put you through all of that. I love you. *I am so in love with you it actually hurts*. When I remembered … I couldn't wait to get to you. I went to your job, and I saw your dad … *and that's another long story*, but he told me where you were – and I rushed right over. Then I saw you with her –"

"Red … I told you –" he cut in, intent on telling me once again what I already knew.

"I know, I know. Let me finish. When I saw you with her, it fucking *killed me*. I felt like what was happening, what I was seeing, was breaking my world apart. I honestly thought in that moment that that is what was happening. But thinking about it now, it's so much worse. Not the kiss … But what I thought because of it. I was thinking, what happened if you didn't see me? What would have happened if I just left, and left you behind? Then – at that moment in the bar – I was thinking … I knew what we were to each other, what we meant, but maybe I had hurt you too much, and you couldn't take it anymore and you wanted to forget … What if I left thinking that you had moved on and I never told you I remembered, and I never wanted to see you again because of what I thought had happened. What if –"

"Don't" he said. "Just fucking don't. I would have *never* given up on you. I love you. I don't care if it would have taken weeks, months, or years for you to get your memories back. I would have fought *you* for you *again* if you didn't remember me. I made you fall in love with me once when you were hell bent against it, I was prepared to do it again. And I would have fucking won. *Again*. You were mine before, you are mine now, and you *will* be mine forever. Same as me with you. I don't need your apologies, Red. I only need you. I will Only. Ever. Need. You."

And that was the last thing we said about that, for a long, long time.

His mouth fused itself back to mine, and neither of us wanted to break the hold.

He lifted me up in his arms and took me to the bedroom. He didn't place me gently on his bed. Not this time. We had waited too long for this. He threw me down in the center of the bed before he pulled me roughly to the edge. He wasted no time getting rid of my shirt and bra, and then unbuttoning and unzipping my jeans. He drew them down my legs at the same time as he removed my panties. He pulled me even further to the edge of the bed, where he raised my knees and planted my feet on the mattress, before he got to his own knees on the floor. I was looking at him looking at me, and I knew exactly what was coming. Then he lowered his head and thrust his tongue in between my thighs, proving me right. I reared off the bed, but I was held in place by his heavy arm that came down on my stomach.

"I've fucking missed this Red," he rasped against me. "I've missed your fucking taste, and fucking you like this" he said before he continued on licking and sucking and plunging.

God, I've missed him, and this, and his dirty fucking mouth and the way he makes me feel when he says the things that he does when we are doing things like this.

It didn't escape my mind that he was still in his suit, with his head buried between my legs while I was completely naked, barreling towards an orgasm.

"Why aren't you naked?" I asked him, gripping his hair trying to get his attention. He looked up at me with that devilish smirk that I loved and said, "Because if I was naked too, you'd want to touch me, and do what I'm doing to you, and then this would all be over way too soon, Red. I don't want this to be over that soon. Besides … *you fucking love me in my suit*," he winked at me before he swooped down and placed his tongue back on me. God, I love his fucking wink … and his fucking tongue.

I laughed on the inside at his comment. Believe me I did. What actually came out of my mouth though was a ragged moan because he finally put his long finger inside of me pumping along with the flick of his tongue on my clit. He licked my clit up and down while he pushed two fingers inside of me, curling them, and then I was done.

I cried out his name, but he didn't show me any mercy. He continued to rub, and lick, and suck, and pump, until I went over again … and then over, *again*.

I was completely boneless by the time he rose from his knees. I didn't think that I had any more to give.

Then he started to loosen his tie, and unbutton his shirt.

He took his shirt off, revealing his fabulous chest with his swirls of tattoos. He reached for the button on his pants, and then all too soon they were gone, and so were his boxer briefs. All that remained was his long, thick, hard length and I wanted it.

I definitely had *way* more to give after all.

I wanted him in me, and now, and any which way he wanted. I needed to feel the connectedness to him.

The beauty that made up Liam, both inside and out, amazed me. It was all so unexpected, but it was mine. *All mine.*

"Liam, please," I said as I reached out towards him.

"Move to the center of the bed, Samantha. We are going to need the room."

Oh. My. God.

His eyes were glittering as he stroked himself, staring at me with such overwhelming love and want, that I didn't know how I didn't orgasm just from his look.

There was no graceful way for me to get to the center of the bed, so I decided the easiest would be if I rolled over and crawled up. I didn't realize until it was too late how that would look to him.

I heard his growl as I felt the bed dip down, and then I felt the warmth of his body at my back.

"Do you have any fucking idea how amazing you look right now?" he growled again, this time into my ear. I was still on my hands and knees with him behind me, his erection poking into my asscheek.

I could hear myself practically panting in and out. I could feel him everywhere. Everywhere except where I wanted him to be the most. I moved my body back against him, letting him know exactly where I wanted him, and I heard him hiss, loudly.

Never one to be outdone, he leaned even further over me, moved my hair over the side of my neck and kissed the top of my spine. His actions made me shiver and whimper. He kissed me again a little lower, and then lower again. He kissed from the top of my spine to the base of my spine, and back again, and I have no idea how I was able to keep my weight on my shaky arms.

"Roll over Samantha," he whispered in my ear when he was done.

I wasn't expecting him to say that.

"I want to look at you while I love you."

Those words caused my arms to finally give out.

I felt my front hit the mattress, but it wasn't there for long because Liam rolled me over onto my back.

The look in his eyes this time while he grabbed for a condom, put it on and leaned over me, absolutely sizzled my blood.

His hands tangled in my hair, while his hips moved in between mine, creating a space for his large body. He looked me deeply in my eyes before he started to push himself inside of me.

I just held my breath and let myself feel.

When he was all the way in I let out my breath I'd been holding and just stared at him. I didn't reach for his face to get lost in a kiss, I didn't reach for his hands to anchor myself to him, I didn't do anything like that.

I just wanted to be still and feel it – him – for a minute.

I felt him pulsing inside of me, and it was the best feeling on earth.

He blinked his eyes closed for a moment, and then opened them again. His nostrils flared a second before he started moving.

I grabbed onto his shoulders while my legs wrapped around his waist. He kept his hands tangled in my hair and his eyes on mine, and

I was perfect with that. I wanted to see everything that moved in his eyes, and I wanted him to see everything that came and went in mine.

He went deeper and deeper inside of me, and it was almost as if he was trying to bury himself inside of me so he never had to leave.

I never wanted him to.

As we got closer and closer to spiraling over the edge we started becoming louder and louder. It was becoming too much, way too much, but we never once took our eyes off of each other.

When he put his forehead against mine bringing his eyes even closer, all but pulling me inside of him with such emotions in their depths, he sent me right over the edge, and I came while crying out his name.

He followed right behind doing the same.

I've always felt unbelievable while making love to Liam, but the way in which I felt now, looking into his eyes the whole time, it was nothing short of shattering. I always said he had the ability to shatter my world ... *and he did* ... in the best possible way.

Liam moved to lay next to me, pulling my body on top of his, tucking my head underneath his chin. His one hand was still tangled in my hair, and he pulled on it a little so I would look up at him, while his other was causing little sparks in my body from his fingertips making a trail up and down my spine.

"I've missed you, Red," he whispered to me. He brought his lips down to mine and gave me the sweetest peck on the lips.

"I was so worried ... I couldn't lose you ... I can't even begin to tell you what it was like – how it was when you didn't know me ..." he stopped speaking and moving his hand up and down my spine. He moved his hands to cup both sides of my face making sure I was looking directly into his eyes.

I could see the tears that were in them.

Tears.

"*I love you.*" I saw one of the tears fall, and it was my turn to cup *his* cheek and rub away the tear with my thumb.

For this man to show such deep emotion … I felt like my heart was going to burst.

I continued to cup his face while staring deeply into his eyes. The conversation we had without saying anything at all, is something I hope we never lose.

I don't know how I ever forgot him.

I don't know how I ever doubted that I loved him.

All I knew was *never, ever, again.*

"I love you so much Liam," I whispered to him as I felt my own eyes start to water.

"Always and forever, Liam. That's me and you. We are always and forever."

And I knew without a doubt that we were always and forever. If we had survived all of this, I knew we could, and would, survive anything. I knew that we would have differences, and that we would stumble, that we would have to endure the unexpected, but that was the beauty of being loved and loving back – you knew that you would overcome no matter what. You didn't sit and worry about the unexpected, and the obstacles, and the downs. You embraced them and moved on and knew that at the end you would be better because of them. When you knew that the other half of you feels the exact same way, and that they would do whatever it takes at all times, it didn't matter what you had to face in the future because you knew that you would always make it. Liam knew that we would make it. He knew that no matter what had happened I would find my way back to him and he would always be with me. He knew, and deep-down I realize that I had always known too.

Liam and I will always make it.

We're always and forever.

"Forever," he whispered back to me.

I don't know who moved first, all I know is that we kissed, and we loved.

__Epilogue__

Liam

There are many moments in my life that I will never forget. Waking up with Samantha still asleep in my arms with her hand resting on my heart, her warm soft body draped over me, and her head on my chest with her hair fanned out all around us after a night full of making love after she regained her memories of us, is currently at the top of my list.

I woke up a while ago and I couldn't do anything but watch her sleep. She was curled all around me, and I don't think I have ever seen her more beautiful or felt anything more peaceful. She fell asleep on me like this the first time she slept over my apartment after I invited her over and made her dinner, and like the morning after that time, I could do nothing but the same thing now. I watched her sleep, amazed that she was with me, and that she was mine.

Like then, I didn't want to wake her, but I knew we needed to start the day – we needed to start the rest of our lives.

"Red?" I spoke while rubbing my fingertips gently up and down her spine. She loved when I rubbed her this way, but I didn't get the response from her that I was expecting. She didn't stir.

"Babe," I murmured to her this time, while moving my hand even lower to cup her ass and shift her closer to where I wanted her. Still nothing.

"Samantha," I dipped my head down so I could kiss her forehead. She rocked her body against me this time, and then buried her face even more solidly into my chest before she let out a contented sigh.

God, I fucking love her.

I knew that this was definitely a moment.

This right here.

Her in my arms, back where she was meant to be.

Every moment with her, whether good or bad, is a moment that I will never forget. Some may be clearer and brighter than others, some may have more significance, but they all mean something.

I wrapped my arms around her, held on a little tighter as the memories started filtering through my head. I couldn't help but to think of all of them – little flashes of moments – some big, some small, but *all* important.

I will never forget the first time I went into *The Brew* and I saw her across the room. Her beautiful dark hair was up revealing her absolutely gorgeous face, her warm brown eyes were as mesmerizing as they were haunting, and that body of hers was an absolute stunner. I felt an instant jolt of lust and want, but it wasn't until I started talking to her that I *knew* that it was more than just her body I was interested in.

I know I acted like a dick with her that day. I was a complete cocky bastard, but underneath all the roadblocks she tried to throw my way, I could tell she wanted me. I could see it in her eyes, and the emotions that were written all over her face.

I could see it in the blush that fully engulfed her cheeks. She definitely wanted me, and there was no fucking doubt that I wanted her. Since that moment she became my 'Red.' I'll never forget the way she looked when I called her 'Red' that first time, and the way she blushed even more when she found out why. I wasn't thinking that name would stick, but it did. Her blush was absolutely adorable, and it really was 'fire engine red,' so I just went with it. Like I said, I was a dick that day, but *God* I couldn't help it.

I'll also never forget that day because it was the first time that I experienced a swift bout of jealousy. When a man came out of the back room and she seemed so happy to see him, I felt like I got kneed in the nuts. I didn't know what was happening, or why I felt like I did. To say that when I found out it was her brother I was thrilled, would be an understatement. Though I should've known better than to be happy that he was her brother. I really should have fucking known.

There are many more moments with her that I will never forget after that first initial meeting. I will never forget the day she saw me in a suit for the first time, or even the time after that, just like I will never forget how I felt the first time I saw her in something other than her work clothes. I would love her in anything she wore, but that first time, she seriously stole my fucking breath. I'll never forget the ways she tried to hide the fact that she was attracted to my tattoos or the way she was affected by my deliberate smirks and grins, just like I'll never forget the way I felt when I saw her with her hair down for the first time, or the first time I saw her bare legs, or her in a dress.

I will also never fucking forget the day I hurt her when I called her Princess, and she completely fell apart.

I didn't know what I did, but I knew that I hurt her. The way she acted, and the way that she asked me to leave – the way her voice sounded – is something I hope to one day forget, because I know that we are past that now. For now though, it is something that is firmly planted in my mind. As is the day when I finally saw her again after that happened, and Karen was with me and Sam completely misunderstood the situation. I will never forget that look that was in her eyes, and the way she turned away from me and left me calling after her. The hurt, the sadness, the anger, the confusion. I was confused too.

I will never forget starting on her drawing after the day I hurt her, not because of how I felt when I started it, but because of how I started to really feel while creating it. Even when she was just lines on a page, I knew that I was falling in love with her. I think I probably knew even before then. Hell, it might have been from the first minute we locked eyes in the café and I felt my whole world turn upside down.

I would always remember the day when she came to my apartment for the first time and saw the painting I had created off of the drawing. I could tell something had changed that night for us, but I didn't know the full extent of what it was until she told me days later that she had fallen in love with me that night. When I told her how I felt, and when we danced next to the fireplace and everything in between – when I knew she trusted me enough to tell me about her past hurts, when she slept with me, when I made her breakfast in bed, when she touched my dimples for the first time and I completely lost it with her – I thought the closeness between us is what had changed, *and it was the closeness*, but it was so much *more* … I will *never* forget those times.

Spending days with her, and talking to her, getting to know her … it just made my love for her more firm and more full. Day by day I was capturing every little piece of her, while giving her more and more pieces of me.

I will never forget our first ballgame and buying the jersey's I wanted us to have. When she told me about her traditions with her dad and with Connor, I wanted to have something like that with her too. I'll never forget her face when I told her I wanted to take a picture of us together at the game. I surprised myself with that one too, but then wanting to do things like that with her shouldn't have surprised me.

Another absolutely special moment in my life was mine and Sam's first official date – or her first official date, *ever*. I didn't know that specific detail beforehand otherwise I would have tried to do something spectacular, but she insisted everything was perfect. It truly did end up being perfect though. We shared our first kiss, and the way she kissed me outside of that bookstore – she fucking rocked my world and drop-kicked me on my ass. I knew she had that desire and aggression and sexiness in her – I knew she possessed *all of it* – but when she laid it on me like she did, I was fucking floored. And fucking destroyed.

I knew I met my match in every single fucking way.

With great moments come bad moments though.

I looked down at Sam still sleeping so peacefully, thinking about the bad moments that we've had to endure. I know that the bad moments were followed by the good, but I still started running my fingers through her hair gently, needing the connection to her, as I started thinking about some of those things.

Aiden. Aaron. Karen. Me.

When Aiden came back, it was initially a bad moment, and one I won't *ever* forget. I know I acted badly by talking to her the way that I did, and by accusing her of things I shouldn't have. I know I left her alone to deal with her past – one that I knew had hurt her. I know that I was a complete asshole who let jealousy get the best of him. The way she looked at him though when she first saw him again, it was as if I didn't exist. It hurt bone deep. It hurt *soul* deep.

So I left her. And she let me. And that seriously fucking hurt.

That hurt didn't last for long though.

She showed up after she talked to him, after she worked things out in her head, and she fought for me ... she didn't let me spin out of control and distance myself. She didn't let me keep thinking all of the dirty, nasty thoughts that were running through my head.

She made me see reason, and then she fucking made me see Heaven.

She told me she loved me.

Actually, she said a lot to me before she said that she was *fucking in love with me*, and then gave me her virginity.

I am still in shock over that.

I swear her first time felt like my first time because with her everything was new, different, and special, and just so unbelievably fucking *perfect*. I don't know what I did to deserve that gift she gave me, but *holy fuck* – complete douchebag thing to say or not – I am so fucking thankful that nobody had her before me.

Plain and fucking simple.

In another bad and completely awful moment, I know I almost completely ruined that time for her by arguing with her about still being a virgin and not telling me, but that's because I was just scared about fucking everything up never having been with a virgin before and wanting everything to be perfect for her.

She needed to have perfect, because she's perfect, and she deserves nothing but the fucking best. I think she knew where I was coming from, because *God* she took pity on me. She let me have her, and though there have been other nights, and days, and mornings for us that were even better than that time, even last night when we finally got back together, *nothing* compares to the specialness of that first time with her. That night, it was the first time she said she loved me, and it was the first time I said it to her too. I loved her, and I teased her, and I told her that I loved her first – I knew that I loved her before she knew she loved me, and I wanted her to know.

I told her to remember that. *Always.*

But always almost never happened.

I went back to wrapping my arms firmly around Sam as if she would disappear on me. I could hear my breaths going in and out of my body in loud inhales and exhales, and I knew that I would never be able to forget that one moment of time I'm currently thinking of.

Never.

I made the biggest mistake of my life that night. It's a moment that I will always remember with crystal clear clarity, a moment I will always regret with every fiber of my being, a moment that changed not only my life but hers, a moment that tops all other awful moments because it not only broke me, but it broke her too.

As I was recalling all of the moments in my life with her so far, I knew I would eventually get to this specific one. How could I not?

I was late to pick Sam up because Karen claimed she had an issue that needed to be fixed, and then she just kept on talking and talking, keeping me at work well after we were done. I didn't know how to fucking dismiss her and that's something I will regret for the rest of my life. It wasn't until I got Sam's text that I knew how late it really was. There was no indulging Karen, Sam needed me, and so I left not giving a shit anymore that I was the boss and how rude I'd been to just leave. As I was walking to the café I came to the conclusion that Sam was right, and that we probably did have a problem on our hands with Karen, but she was a damn fine worker so I needed to figure out how to handle it. My thoughts on the way to the café seem so trivial now. So *pathetic*. I was thinking about how to get rid of one woman, while the woman I was in love with was in the process of becoming lost to me.

It took less than ten minutes to get to the café, but that didn't matter.

It took too long.

When I got to the café I opened the door, and all I saw was chaos.

I could feel my heartbeat beating rapidly in my chest just thinking about it now.

Tables were flipped over, chairs were all over the place, and Samantha was laying on the floor covered in blood, not moving, with Aaron on top of her trying to pull her clothes off. She was bloodied, hurt, broken and all I could see was *red.* I flew through the store and Aaron didn't even fucking hear me until I pulled his body off of hers, because he was too busy with his plans of hurting her some more. She didn't make a fucking sound or even twitch when his weight was off of her. I had a second to register that before my fist was slamming into his face over and over again. I had him on the floor with one punch, but I kept punching and punching, until his blood was spraying everywhere, and he was no longer moving.

I felt no satisfaction over what I had done because I knew that Sam was hurt and I let it happen. Even now I still feel no satisfaction over breaking his bones, making him bloody, *giving him pain.*

What he handed out was so much worse than what I gave him back.

So much fucking worse.

I don't know how I was able to get off of him and not fucking kill him – to this day I have no clue, but I did. I went over to Sam but she still didn't move. I saw every cut, every bruise, every gash, every torn piece of clothing, and every pool of blood. Her head was cracked open, and I couldn't do a fucking thing. I called for help and just held her hand willing her to wake up. I wanted to grab her up in my arms, promise that she would be okay, but I was told not to move her and I honestly didn't know if *anything* would be okay ever again.

She didn't wake up.

I will never forget having to deal with the cops, the trip to the hospital, or the call I had to make to Connor. I will never forget breaking down in the waiting room when the doctors were working on her, when I had the chance to fully grasp what had just happened, what I had seen – what I had *done*. I should have trusted my gut when it came to Aaron. I knew it wasn't just jealousy the first time I saw them talking together. I *knew* it wasn't just jealousy when I heard his comments to her. I should have followed through and kicked his ass and let it be known that he should stay the fuck away from her the first time I saw him. I knew he was a problem when he kept coming back. I should have protected her. I should have protected what was mine!

I should have never left her alone.

I will never forget the look on Connor's face when I saw him at the hospital, when he got the news of what had happened and what was wrong with her, and the horrible fact that she still would not wake up. I will never forget the sight of his tears, or the sound of his voice when I heard him talking to his parents on the phone. When he had to break the news of what I had let happen to their daughter. I will never forget talking to Aiden when he showed up, and I will never, ever, forget the strings he pulled for me that night when it came to the things I had done to Aaron.

I will *never* forget how I felt watching Samantha for hours when all the questioning was done, willing her to wake up, willing her to be okay, willing her to just doing *something*.

I will *never* forget how I felt when she finally did wake up.

When she didn't remember me.

When she had no idea who I was.

She remembered everyone else, including *Aiden*, but not me. She looked at me like I was *nothing*. She looked right *through* me. It hurt, more than anything I had ever felt to that point, and I had endured a lot in my lifetime.

I won't forget Connor yelling at me when I finally left her bedside. He was yelling at me, wanting to know where I was.

What did it fucking matter?

I wasn't there, and she got hurt. She was beaten, almost raped, Aaron could have killed her if I hadn't gotten there in time to stop him, and it was all because of me – because I didn't show up when I should have. I had no excuse, I had no good answer. *It would never matter.* Even having her back with me now, even having her forgiveness for it all, I would never *ever* forgive *myself*. I almost lost *everything*.

After I realized she didn't remember me, I went home and I drank, and drank, and drank some more. I wanted to forget all of the blood, her not moving, the sight of her broken body, all of the thoughts of what could have happened. I wanted to forget the thoughts of that motherfucker on top of her, of his hands, his mouth, and his body on her, of what he planned on doing to her. I wanted to forget that look in her eyes when she didn't recognize me. So I drank until I forgot.

I didn't stay that way for long though.

She needed me whether she knew it or not, and I *had* to be there for her. Not being there for her is what had caused her to be hurt in the first place. I made a promise to myself that I would not fuck up again.

I needed her to get her memories back more than I had ever needed anything else. I knew that if she couldn't regain them herself, I needed to make her remember. I knew I had to find a way to make her remember me. To remember us.

And then I had it.

I knew it was the prefect thing to take to her – *to give her*. She knew – or at least one time she knew – how much it meant to me, how important it was. She meant so much to me too, so I knew that it was only right that she had it. *My mother's pitcher.*

It meant something. It meant *everything*.

She would see it, and she would know.

But it didn't fucking work.

I was in her hospital room no more than five minutes before a nurse chased me out. The whole time Sam didn't open her beautiful eyes to see that I was there. I couldn't bring myself to wake her. Part of me wanted to kiss her awake and see if she remembered me, but another part, a deeper part, was terrified that she would open her eyes and look at me with a vacant stare again.

So I left her.

I waited all day for the call telling me that she remembered, that everything was okay in my world again, that my mom's pitcher that offered me so much comfort after she died was the trigger that gave her all of her memories back.

That call never came.

I texted or called Connor every day to find out about her. I hated it, but I had to do it.

She didn't remember. And I couldn't fucking forget.

I had to go on with my everyday life, but I felt like a fucking zombie. I hated every fucking second that she didn't remember me. I hated every fucking second that I had to be without her. When she went back to work I made it a point to go in there every day. I *had* to see her, like I had to breathe. I had to see if she had a flicker of anything.

She didn't remember me.

It hurt so fucking bad I thought my heart would rip out of my chest.

Until she showed me a moment.

Until she gave me some hope.

There was *one* thing she got caught up on … the twenty dollar bill. I remembered the significance – another fucking thing that Karen had been involved with – so I made it a point to give her twenties every time I saw her. I knew she was trying to fight for a memory, and that's all I needed to know.

She wanted to remember me, not bury me.

I knew I would fight for her, every fucking second of every day. I would never give up, I had every intention of getting her back, making her mine again. I fought her once already to get her to love me, I would have done it again, and again, a million times over. I made her overcome her fears, and her doubts, and I was able to get past that wall that she had erected once, I had no doubt that I could tackle her lost memories and get her to love me again. I would have made new fucking memories with her if I had to, in order to win her over and get her to love me. I would have done whatever it fucking took. She was it for me, and I knew it from the first day that I saw. *She was it*. She just had to figure it out once again, too.

I saw little glimpses of want from her during those days when I went in the shop, blushes that I fell in love with ages ago and all over again, and though it wasn't nearly enough, it was a start.

And then fucking Karen.

Again.

Red said after the fact, that we should be thankful to her because she was the one who inadvertently made Samantha remember me, but I wasn't thankful in any regard to that stupid manipulative bitch. She single-handedly screwed with my life the most these past few weeks. If it weren't for her – *Fuck!*

I knew I should have been happy to celebrate the end of working on our major project. I knew I would have been fucking ecstatic about it if Sam remembered me. I was planning on asking her if she wanted to take a few days off and go away with me somewhere private – somewhere we would finally have time together without any interruptions – but then Karen had to go and keep me late, I had to be distracted, Aaron had attacked Sam, and I was just floating along without the love of my life.

I went though.

I had to.

That's apparently what a good team leader does.

I didn't want to be there though. I didn't want Karen anywhere near me. Ever since that night Sam got attacked I felt the vibe that Sam was talking about coming off of Karen in waves. I didn't like it. It was all completely wrong.

We were at the bar, talking, and she put her hand on my shoulder. I didn't understand why she was touching me, and I was just about to reach out to move her hand, when she fucking leaned over and kissed me. In that instant I knew Red was *more than* right ... she was spot fucking on. I didn't know if it was proper to push a woman back with as much force as

I wanted to use, but before I could determine if I could get away with pushing her without being labeled an abusive prick, I was slapped on the back so hard she got jolted off my mouth.

I had never been more thankful to be slammed that hard on the back in my entire fucking life.

Then my world came tumbling down even more than it had before, *and holy fucking Christ*, in the past few days before that it had come crumbling down a lot. My friend John said 'what the fuck,' before he pointed somewhere, and when I saw where he was pointing, I definitely echoed his sentiments.

I saw Samantha crying.

She was crying so badly, it was as if her heart was breaking, as if she would never, ever, be okay again, and though it fucking slayed me to see her cry like that, it hit me all at once. She was there for *me*, she remembered it *all*, but she had also just seen me kissing another woman. *A woman she fucking hated.* It didn't matter that I didn't want it, I knew it looked unbelievably fucking bad, but she fucking remembered and that's all that *mattered* to me. I started to go to her but I froze when she started shaking her head back and forth. It was pretty fucking clear that I definitely fucked up, and it was also pretty fucking clear that there were more important things that mattered to *her* than getting her memories back.

When Samantha turned around and ran, it felt like she was taking my heart with her *again*. For a second, knowing she remembered, I felt whole again and my heart felt intact, but when she ran I was back to feeling broken. I ran after her screaming her name but she wouldn't stop. I finally grabbed her when I caught up to her, and having her in my arms was a fucking relief even though she was spitting fire and pushing me away. I wanted none of that. I needed her to listen. I had to make her listen any way I could.

I had to tell her how I felt, what had happened, what I wanted. I needed her to understand and *fucking see.*

I made her listen. I made her see.

I got through to her.

Which is why we are here now laying in my bed like all of the other times that I had missed so much. I know I told her I would have done everything I fucking could to get her back, and I would have, but there's a part of me that knows I could have lost her for good too. She had to want me back like I wanted her – that's the only way it truly would have worked.

She told me last night that she did, that she wanted me the same way. *That me and her were always and forever.*

I believe her. She *is* my always and forever.

Samantha and I have been through so much already, and I'm sure we will face even more ups and downs – like the trial Aaron will be facing for hurting her – but I know without a doubt that no matter what excitements or what shit-storms come our way, we will fucking weather it. I don't plan on having too much bad shit to go through though … I plan to make it my fucking mission in life to make sure everything is perfect for her – *for us.*

I know that eventually we are going to have to talk more about her relationship with Aiden, everything that had happened to her with Aaron, and I know that I am going to either have to fire Karen or have her moved somewhere else because I don't want to ever fucking see her again – I just wanted her fucking gone, and I know we have to talk about her going back to school, and her hopefully moving in here with me and being with me for the rest of our lives, *and* we needed to deal with the terrifying fact that we had to make dinner plans with both of our parents which was a nice little bombshell she dropped on me last night ... but regardless of *all* of that that needed to be talked over, I knew whatever we decided to do about all of it, it would be okay. From here on out we would be doing all types of things together. Big things and little things.

Like now ... Having breakfast in bed.

I knew it was time for me to get up and start making breakfast. I know she's not a fan of breakfast, but I'm trying to get her to see the error of her ways. I think she's catching on though. She sure hasn't seemed to mind eating breakfast with me yet so far.

I knew that I was a lucky fucking bastard who got the opportunity to do this again. *To even have this in the first place.*

I also knew that today would be one of those days, one of those moments that I would be adding to my collection with her.

She didn't know it yet, but I fully intend on taking her on that trip I had wanted to go on with her when the project was over. I texted Connor last night to let him know what was up, and to see if he could cover her shifts. Even though he was cool with me taking Sam away for a few days, I knew I needed to patch things up with him, and the sooner the better. I fully intended on being around forever so he needed to get over his shit with me. I didn't need any more of his interfering.

I leaned down and instead of running my fingertips down her spine, grabbing her ass, tangling my hands in her hair, or squeezing the life out of her, I placed my mouth against hers and just started kissing.

I felt her start to stir. I felt her start to wake up. I felt her kiss me back.

I heard her moan, and then felt her rock.

"Liam …" I heard her breathily say.

I needed to get her up, I needed to get us fed, and then we needed to hit the road.

She rocked against me a little more and let out a whimper, causing me to groan and get immediately hard.

Maybe I could spare a few minutes before everything else.

Only a few though.

She and I had many, many, more memories to make from this day forward.

We had the memories that we would plan on making in advance, we'd have the ones that we would create spur of the moment, and we would most *definitely* have the ones that will come along unexpected, the ones that knock us on our asses but inevitably make us better.

We would have *all of it*.

And I couldn't fucking wait.

Author's Note

I am someone who absolutely loves to read, and there is nothing that I love to read more than standalone books that are also a part of a series. I like closure at the end of my books, but I also like to read about my favorite characters from time to time and see what they're up to ... which is why though I am done with Samantha and Liam's story, they will most definitely be hanging around. We have not seen the last of them.

When I started this journey it was always my intention on having at least three books in this series. I made a promise to myself that even if the reviews were mixed, even if my story wasn't that well received, and even if the readers were only family and close friends, I would still write Connor and Aiden's stories. I *had* to – I *have* to – write their stories. They deserve them, as do the awesome women who are meant to be with them.

It truly has been a dream of mine to write. I didn't know if I would love writing as much as I do reading – but I do. For those of you who know me, and know my absolute passion for reading books, you know that what I just said is extraordinary. For those of you who don't know me, *trust me* ... its extraordinary!

With that being said, I really hope that you enjoyed Samantha and Liam as much as I did – as much as I do! I also hope that you continue the journey with me and that you want to get to know Connor even more. No matter how much I loved writing Sam and Liam, I couldn't wait to get my hands on Connor. From the first scene I wrote with him in *Unexpected Beauty*, I knew I was in love with him. He made me laugh, smirk, cringe, he made me want to either slap him or maybe punch him in the throat, and so much more. He fought with me the whole time I was writing to give him more exposure. I can definitely tell you now, from what I am writing in *Chaotic Beauty*, he is definitely e*xposed*.

I hope you enjoy the **Sneak Peak of Book 2 in the series, told in duel POV:** *Chaotic Beauty*

Connor

What the *fuck* is she doing here? And with *him?* She's not even supposed to be in Baltimore. She's supposed to be hours away finishing up her last year of college. She should definitely not be *here* with *him.* Her brother would *fucking* flip if he saw them two together.

Why the fuck was she here, and with him?

Maybe I should text her brother and let him know. Or better yet, maybe I should take a picture of them two together and send it. He'd fucking *love* that.

Seriously though. *What the fuck!*

I pulled out my phone and sent a quick text. I'm not trying to be a girl and gossip, or be a fucking narc, but really? *Really?*

Me: Dude your sister just showed up at the shop, and Aiden's with her. What the fuck am I seeing right now? Isn't she supposed to be at school, and nowhere near here? Or him? Why the fuck is he here with her?

I stared at my phone expecting it to ring right back, like I'm some fucking teenage girl who texted her best friend a juicy story about their goddamn crush. Jesus, what the fuck is wrong with me?

Something pretty fucking big because I started rapidly typing on my phone again when he didn't answer me right back. Did this guy not care that his sister is with Aiden? I mean I know the guy helped Liam out of a jam when Liam practically killed the guy who was attacking my sister a few months ago – as he fucking *should have* – but still. What the fuck was he doing that he didn't jump all over this shit?

Me: What the fuck are you doing?

I heard the beeps. Fucking *finally*.

Liam: Your sister.

Holy Motherfuck! He better be fucking kidding. They didn't have sex. *Ever*.

There were just some things you never talked about. Like having sex with someone's sister, when the person you are talking to is their brother. *Holy fucking shit*.

I felt my phone vibrate in my hand, and all I could think was that asshole better be telling me that he was fucking joking.

Samantha: Liam told me what happened, and what he just said. What he said … that was NOT happening. Not now anyway. LOL. What's going on, Connor?

Fuck! Liam's seriously corrupted my sweet, innocent, baby sister. They are probably at their home laughing at this shit. It's not that fucking funny. I probably would've thought it was funny if I said it about *his* sister, but this? Too fucking far.

Shit, who am I kidding? I should've expected that shit from them. A lot has changed in the past few months for all of us, especially with me and Liam.

Six months ago my sister and I didn't even know who Liam was. Now my sister was in love with him, he was in love with her, they were living together, and all that other shit. When I saw him come into the café that first day and saw Sam's reaction to him, and his to her – not only that day but the few times after – I knew that something was going to happen between them. I just wasn't sure that whatever it was would be something good. I may have acted like a total prick when it came to them two in the beginning – *maybe just a little* – but everything worked out for them in the end. I knew that not everything for them was fucking rainbows and roses ... one thing in particular to be exact had turned their world upside down.

It fucking turned my world upside down too.

I thought I was starting to fall for someone.

I actually thought there might be a "one" after all.

What a fucking joke.

A few careless words, a few heated statements ... that's all it fucking took for her to hit the road.

I'm glad that she never knew how I felt. The only one who really knew how I felt was my sister. And there was no way she told her boyfriend, because if she did, I would never hear the end of it. He would be all over my fucking back the same way I was with him. It was his sister after all.

Talk about a fucking nightmare.

"Hi, Connor," her voice whipped out coolly. I looked up from my cell phone to see that she and Aiden made their way over to the counter. *Fucking perfect.* Instead of being a gossiping bitch and texting Liam, I should've gone into the back and did some fucking inventory and let someone else handle this shit.

Wait ... what?

Did I seriously just fucking say that I should've ducked and covered? That I should've hid out like a scared little girl?

What is this fucking woman *doing to me*?

The tone of her voice still rang in my head. Her voice didn't match how she looks. For a voice so cold, she sure did look all warm and soft, and absolutely fucking mouth-watering. I had firsthand knowledge that she was all warm and soft, and I knew she was absolutely breathtaking. Her long dark hair was silky, and she used to love when I ran my fingers through it. Her body was a fucking eleven, and the confidence that rolls off of her in waves is enough to bring any goddamn man to his knees. Her baby blues are a killer though. Those pale eyes of hers that make me think of hazy, hot, summer days are unbelievably expressive and captivating, but looking at them now they are like shards of ice.

Why the fuck is she the one who gets to act like this?

Fuck that. I'm Connor *fucking* Brennan. I got this.

"Hey, Riley," I said to her all polite and shit. Then I turned my head a bit to her left and said, "Aiden." I nodded my head up and down as a way of greeting.

No need to let her know that her being here with him was pissing me the fuck off. No need at all.

My simple un-dickish greeting made me proud of myself. It was simple and clear enough that if you read between the lines, it meant hurry up and order your shit and get the fuck out of my store, without me actually saying it and being a complete prick. I was definitely fucking proud of myself.

"Not working at the Firehouse today?" Riley asked with her unique voice that I hadn't heard in months. A voice that I had fantasized about since the first moment I heard her speak. A voice that was currently still cold and icy.

Apparently she didn't care to read between the lines.

There was only so much I could take. I tried to rein it in, I tried to play it cool … but *fuck that.*

"No why? Did you plan on avoiding me some more? Sorry to disappoint you, babe. I'm here today." Since I was looking at her closely I saw her eyes switch from cold steel to a wicked blue flame, all in the span of seconds. She definitely didn't like that I suggested she was avoiding me, and she really didn't like that I called her 'babe.' She used to like it.

She used to fucking love it.

She didn't say anything though. She just stared at me. I actually tried my best, but I couldn't fucking do it anymore. I smirked at her.

I saw the blush creep into her cheeks. I *knew* it. She was affected. Probably just as much as I was. Her eyes gave it away, as did her blush, and the tightening of her mouth. She might have avoided me, but she definitely wasn't done with me.

You should know better than to play this game with me sweetheart. I made up the fucking rules for this one.

"Hey man, can I get a large black coffee," Aiden interrupted.

What? Did he seriously just fucking speak? What the fuck was he even doing here with her? Did he not see that there was something going on here between me and Riley? Did he not hear what I just said to her? He needed to fucking disappear. Like now.

"Yeah me too. I'd like a small coffee." I would have taken some satisfaction in the way her voice sounded now, all small and not as confident as it normally is, but how the fuck can I feel satisfied with this asshole here with her? Just when I thought him and me patched things up for that one night all those years ago, he had to do something that planted him firmly back on my shit list. You know … I don't even care why he was here anymore, he just was. Fucking shit list.

Why the fuck did my sister have to go back to school? She should be here dealing with this shit. Then she could ask them why the fuck they were together. I didn't even know that they knew each other. I saw them together in the same room once, and they never said a word to each other.

What the fuck is this?

Holy fucking Christ.

I continued to stare at them. What the fuck was I doing? I must look like a complete idiot.

Well you know what? I felt like one right about now. And that pissed me off more.

But then it hit me.

I don't know where the thought came from, but I couldn't help smirking again. It was too fucking perfect.

I needed the ball back in my goddamn court.

"Hey Aiden ..." I said, making sure I had a good enough amount of questioning in just those two little words.

He looked at me wearily. Yeah, you should be worried.

"Yeah?" he finally said.

"You have a sister right?"

God, I was such an asshole. This was the same road I traveled with Liam all those months ago when I forced us all into a group date – Riley included.

Aiden just stared at me then glanced at Riley. I glanced at Riley too. From the way her eyes were shooting blue flames my way, and from the way her face seemed unnaturally pale all of a sudden, I knew that she knew what I was doing.

"Yes, I do. Lizzy." He told me what I already knew. I've talked to her a few times actually. Samantha introduced us when Elizabeth came in by herself without him. She was a sweet girl, but to me, she was nothing more than that. He didn't have to know any of that though. Neither did Riley. She sure as shit didn't need to know anything.

"Lizzy, huh? How old is she?" I asked, faking complete ignorance.

"Stop it Connor," Riley said quietly.

Aiden looked towards her, finally clueing into what I was doing.

I'm surprised he couldn't feel the tension before now.

He was a fucking detective?

"Seriously man, what's the deal?" Aiden asked me, looking between me and Riley again.

Riley spoke up and saved me from having to answer Aiden, which should've been a good thing because I really didn't have a fucking answer for him – I had no clue what the *fuck* I was doing – but it wasn't a good thing.

"You know what? Just forget it. We'll go somewhere else," she said before grabbing Aiden's hand and walking towards the door.

I stood there frozen.

She grabbed ahold of his hand. *They were fucking holding hands.*

He was fucking *touching* her.

What the fuck just happened? What did I just see? *What the fuck just happened!?!*

I don't give a shit what it made me look like, I grabbed up my phone and started dialing Liam's number.

Fuck that whole texting shit.

I needed to fucking talk to him.

Now.

Riley

I hate him. I absolutely *hate* him. I hate every goddamn thing about him. I hate his smug smirk, and cocky smile, I hate his annoyingly handsome face, I hate the liquid heat that I always see in his eyes, I hate his colorful tattoos, and I hate his goddamn fucking knowingness, his arrogance, his carefree fucking attitude, all his stupid fucking questions and dumbass ideas, and most especially his rock-hard fucking body. I definitely fucking hate that. *I hate him. All* of him.

No you don't.

You're a liar.

You want him.

You fucking love him.

That last part was definitely not true, but I was almost there once. How the hell did everything go sideways?

His sister got attacked by some psycho and he blamed your brother. He said awful, hurtful things, and you couldn't forgive him even though you should have, especially since Liam did.

The voice inside of my head was pissing me off. It was right. It seemed to always be right when it came to Connor. I knew I messed up by not forgiving him when he told me he was sorry for everything he had said. I knew he was just blowing off steam, and that he was angry, hurt, and worried. His sister was in the hospital for Christ's sake. She was beaten, nearly raped, she had lost a good chunk of her memories, so it was only fair that Connor was upset and angry, but it wasn't my brother's fault even if he had been late picking Samantha up. It was the sick bastard's fault who hurt her.

We all knew it. We all moved past it for the most part.

Well some of us.

I couldn't think about that right now though. Or him. I actually had more important things going on in my life than whether or not I was currently avoiding Connor – *which I'm not* – even though my inner voice is screaming at me that I am.

I couldn't deal with all of that right now, or try and make it right.

With the way Connor acted today, I'm not sure I wanted to.

"Riley," Aiden said tugging on my hand.

Oh, right … I still held his hand.

I let go of his hand quickly, and snatched my own hand back.

This was the more important part.

I needed to take care of this first.

"I'm sorry, Aiden," I said. "I didn't mean to drag you out of there like that, but I knew where that conversation was going, and where it was going was nowhere good. And it also wasn't about you, or your sister, it was about me … and you shouldn't be dragged into the pissing match between me and Connor."

He started to smile. "Pissing match?" he asked in such a way, like I completely caught him off guard with what I said, or something along those lines. Christ, I probably had.

"Jesus, sorry. You can blame all my horrible language on Liam. For as sophisticated as he looks in a suit – trust me – he's really not. I mean he can be when he wants to, but for the most part his mouth is just plain awful. Growing up he definitely didn't censor himself around me, so it rubbed off on me. Then there was Connor – *Jesus Christ* I am not getting into that … but I really am trying to work on my language, because I know it is not at all ladylike and proper. So, like I said, I blame Liam … hence all the pissing matches, the fuck words, the pricks and dicks and everything else coming out of my mouth –" and *oh, God,* did I just seriously say the *dicks coming out of my mouth?*

How the fuck did this topic even start anyway? When the fuck did I take a wrong turn?

I heard Aiden's deep throaty laugh, so yeah, I definitely said it the way it sounded. Holy shit. My face felt like it was on fire. I ramble when I'm nervous, and I cuss a lot when I am overwhelmed and annoyed, and in a lot of other situations, and *definitely* when I am around Connor because that seems to be how he communicates best. I wasn't lying, I *really* am trying to work on it. I know how that type of language sounds, and I know it isn't good. *What must Aiden think of me?*

"Okay then," was what he managed to wheeze out in response.

Just great. Wonderful first impression so far. I'm sure he's just eager to help me out now.

"Look, do you want to go somewhere else so we can talk?" I asked him.

"Sure," he said, all professional now. He must have sensed my change in attitude.

I know he must be curious as to why I called him. He didn't even know me before today, though he did see me once. I learned about Aiden a few months ago from Connor and Sam. I learned even more from Liam after that. I knew that Aiden was a detective with the Baltimore Police Department, and when I knew without a doubt I had a problem, I knew he was the only solution for me.

I couldn't tell Liam about my problem, because after what happened to Samantha I knew he would freak the fuck out. I couldn't tell Sam, because I am almost positive she would tell my brother. I couldn't tell my dad, because even though things are better between all of us now, I don't know how he would handle it, and there was also the possibility that he would tell my brother too. And I couldn't tell my friends because I wasn't sure if I could trust any of them.

The only person left who I might've considered telling was Connor, and I couldn't tell him because we aren't exactly on speaking terms, and telling him would be complicated. I didn't know who else to turn to … so here we are now.

I still can't believe how I got us here though. What a mess!

I got the phone number for the Police Department online, and I called and asked around until I finally found Aiden. I was transferred a few times, and hung up on even more, but it was understandable when I started off the conversation with 'Hi, are you Aiden, a detective who knows Samantha and Connor Brennan, and Liam Sullivan?'

It wasn't exactly the smoothest or smartest path getting to here, but like I said, here we are now.

A few streets away we came upon another coffee house. It wasn't as good as *The Brew* – I would know seeing as how I've been coming to this place the past few weeks instead of risking the chance of running into Connor over at his. *Okay, so I was avoiding him.*

I had a good reason for avoiding him though.

I don't know why if I was avoiding him I picked his shop as the place to meet Aiden, but I did.

Maybe because ironically I felt safe and protected there – who knows?

Aiden and I ordered our drinks and then sat down.

"So Riley, why did you call me out of the blue like that? You said on the phone that you have a problem, and that even though I don't know you, you think I'm the only one who can help you. I'll admit, you knowing Sam and Liam, and even Connor, is the biggest reason I said I'd meet you outside of the station as you requested, and I am intrigued to find out what the problem is especially seeing as how you used some pretty unorthodox methods to get in touch with me, but I'm not sure I can help you," he said sounding confused, worried, and also sincere.

"I'm pretty sure you can help me," I told him.

"Why do you think that?" he asked holding my gaze.

I blew out a deep breath and said, "Because you're a detective, and I need your kind of help."

He seemed to straighten up a little at my response, probably because he knew I was finally about to tell him what he wanted to know.

I told him before that I needed help when I introduced myself on the phone, but I told him I didn't want to get into the specifics until I met with him in person. He reluctantly agreed to meet me outside of work, and like he said, it was only because I name-dropped. I didn't blame him for his hesitation in regards to meeting me, seeing as how he has no clue who I really am, or what is going on. *Or what I may be getting him into.* I should be thankful that he agreed to meet me at all.

"Okay. So, Riley. Why do you need a detective?"

He asked me the question in a voice that sounded an awful lot like he was trying to put me at ease.

It didn't really help though.

Once I said it, it would all be real.

Too real.

Someone else besides me would know.

Would Aiden keep it to himself? Didn't he have to? Wasn't this confidential or something? Or was it not?

Shit.

Would he tell Sam? And then would she tell Liam? And then would it trickle down to Connor? That's what I didn't want to happen.

I didn't need them to worry. Or get involved.

Maybe I should've gone to another detective. Another police officer. Someone who didn't know me, or have connections to me.

But you didn't want to go to someone else, because you were worried that nobody else would believe you. That's why you contacted Aiden. Because people you know, and love, know him.

Maybe I shouldn't have said anything at all then. Maybe I should have kept this all to myself and tried to deal with it on my own. I knew better than that though. I couldn't deal with this on my own. This situation wouldn't get any better. It wouldn't go away. I *did* need help.

"Riley –" Aiden cut into my thoughts with a much sterner voice.

I took a deep breath.

All or nothing.

I needed help.

"I think I have a stalker."

Acknowledgments

First, I need to thank my husband. For the fifteen years we have been together you have dealt with, and have tried to understand, my endless love and passion for books. You don't mind when I disappear on you for hours because I want to read in my 'bubble.' You don't mind the hundreds and hundreds of books lying around everywhere, taking up every available space, or the obscene amounts of money we spend because I need books, books, and more books. You understand that when I say Nora, Abbi, Jamie, Diana, Colleen, Molly, Jay or Penelope, I'm not talking about random people, but my favorite authors. You've listened to me talk for years about my love of books and what I would do differently if I were writing – what I would say, what I would have happen, who I would pair up ... and you've always said 'write a book.' You didn't say it to stop the conversation, or to appease me, you said it because you believed I could do it. When I finally believed in myself and started on this journey, you encouraged me and supported me every step of the way. In all the years we've been together you probably thought you've seen everything from me ... but writing this book brought out some serious crazy, and you dealt with, and understood that, too. Seriously, Giovanni ... your support, encouragement, your ear, your shoulder, your words, but most of all your love (and your insanely brilliant computer skills) means the world to me! None of this would be possible without you by my side loving me, and letting me be exactly who I am. I know that I am lucky to have you, and your love. And I love you too.

I need to thank my parents Sharon and Mike. You both have given me nothing but endless love, support, and encouragement to follow my dreams. From day one to age thirty-one you have given me and taught me so many things. I think the most important thing you've taught me besides how to love, have faith, and to follow your dreams ... is to be yourself. After all these years, I've finally found "me." Mom, as I said before, you knew this would be my reality and that this is who I was meant to be before I did. I love you. I absolutely love you both.

Ashley – you were the first person I trusted reading this book from beginning to end. Your enthusiasm and encouragement and your love of Sam and Liam, and especially Connor, means more than you can ever possibly know. Your awesome words always seem to come at the times when I've needed them the most. There were times when I doubted my writing, when I doubted specific parts, when I thought I wasn't good enough, but you told me I would find my voice, that I had my story, and you enjoyed it! Coming from someone who reads and loves books as much as I do, those words were/are priceless. You championed Sam and Liam, but you also championed me too. The words 'thank you,' aren't nearly enough.

Last, but definitely not the least, I need to thank *you*, the readers. Thank you, thank you, thank you! Whether you enjoyed my book or not (though I really hope you did), you are amazing because you picked up the book and read it in the first place. You took a chance, and that's all any of us do when we open a new book, and start a new journey – we never know if the story will be good or bad, if we will love or hate the characters, we start the story because we love to read and want to get lost for a while. There is nothing like diving into a new book, or getting completely lost in an old one. At least for me. I hope it is the same way for you too. I really hope you enjoyed this one, and that you take a chance on me and my stories again!

About the Author

Tara Sosa grew up in New Jersey, went to a few of its colleges and earned her degree with honors, as well as her teaching credentials, along the way. Though she is technically a High School English teacher, she finds it much more enjoyable to read and write all day without restrictions, which is why she is literally without a classroom and students.

From a very early age she knew she was in love with books and always would be, and though she tries to get everyone to love them too, she is constantly disappointed to find out that not everyone does. She absolutely loves her family, including her husband and two babies – of the four-legged variety. One day soon she hopes to add a few of the two-legged kind to her total, where she hopes at least one of them has the good sense to love reading and writing as much as she does.

Tara would love to hear from her readers. You can follow her on Twitter (@TaraSosaAuthor), Facebook, or you can email her at TaraSosaAuthor@gmail.com. You can also visit her author page at tarasosa.com where you can read about her Beauty Series books, and find some sneak peeks of upcoming books & releases.

Credits

Front Cover Photograph © by NotarYES/Shutterstock

Back Cover Photograph © by Verbena/Shutterstock